WILD MEN
OF ALASKA

Four Alaska Novellas by

Tiffinie Helmer

This is a work of fiction. Names, characters, places, brands, media, and incidents are either the product of the author's imagination or are used fictitiously, and any resemblance to actual persons, living or dead, business establishments, events, or locales is entirely coincidental.

For more information, please direct your correspondence to:
The Story Vault
c/o Marketing Department
P.O. Box 11826
Charleston, WV 25339-1826

http://www.tiffiniehelmer.com
Cover by Kelli Ann Morgan
http://www.inspirecreativeservices.com

DEDICATION

For my amazing children: Mikelynn, Tayt, Montgomery, and Tess. Dare to dream and laugh in the face of anyone who tells you that you can't achieve your dreams.

ACKNOWLEDGEMENTS

There is a small village to thank for bringing this book to fruition.

First my agent, Christine Witthohn of Book Cents Literary Agency. She's been with me from the beginning and was bound and determined to get me published. Thank you so much for your undying belief in me and your amazing work ethic.

To my mother, Barb Blanc—for moving us to Alaska and giving me the chance to grow up in a place not heavy on civilized constraints. And you were worried.

Thank you to my fellow Musketeers—Porthos and Aramis, aka best selling authors Kerrigan Byrne and Cindy Stark. You are the best of swordswomen.

To the Writers of Imminent Death—Natalie Ainge, Mikki Kells, Heather Wallace, and Heidi Turner for the bleeding ink and killer laughs.

To Kerri LeRoy—for the friendship and mad editing skills.

To all my Barnes & Noble peeps—for being so supportive and a blast to work with.

To cover artist, Kelli Ann Morgan, of Inspire Creative Services thank you for putting up with me and rocking my covers.

To law enforcement supervisor Chris Johnson of the Kenai National Wildlife Refuge. Thank you for patiently answering all my questions regarding the duties and challenges of being an Alaska Wildlife Refuge Officer. Any mistakes in the book are mine and mine alone.

Finally to my husband and children—thank you for being understanding and putting up with the many nights of take out, semi-forced self-sufficiency, and taking it in stride when I argue with myself.

You all rock!

Contents

IMPACT

CHAPTER ONE

Damn, he looked good.

Why couldn't he show his age like the rest of them? Was it too much to hope for that he'd let himself go? Sported a beer belly? Lost his hair?

Five years had passed since Wren Terni's last encounter with Skip Ozhuwan. Five years since he'd arrested her.

Not her finest hour.

It was official. Whatever puny luck the gods had deemed to give her had run out.

The only thing going her way was that he hadn't seen her yet. Taking a couple of steps back, she stood off to the side behind a pillar in the small airport in King Salmon, Alaska. She wasn't hiding, really. She just needed a moment to prepare herself before walking up to him and pretending he didn't mean squat to her.

She'd known they were bound to see each other this weekend. It was his sister's wedding, after all. But what trick of fate had her sharing the same puddle jumper to Egegik with him?

This weekend needed to hurry up and be over with. The sooner she returned to her life the better for everyone. So far she'd done a pretty bang up job of not dealing with her past. She was the type who moved on.

Past was past.

She'd hoped she could've put off seeing Skip until the actual wedding. Her plan was to suffer through the reception and then dart out of there like a wily fox with no words exchanged between them.

There was nothing to say to the man she'd loved—the man who'd incarcerated her—other than cursing his manhood and future offspring.

She schooled her features to try and appear bored instead of revealing the panic and yearning bubbling to the surface. Skip looked better than she'd remembered, more mature, more muscular. His hair was blacker than the deep winter nights on the Bering Sea of Alaska. His mouth set in the same smile that used to infuriate and arouse her at the same time. Broad shoulders V'ed into a trim waist, and his thighs were roped with muscle. Muscle that was defined through his unzipped jacket, t-shirt and jeans. She'd never felt safer in any man's arms than when she'd been held by Skip Ozhuwan.

While he was only five ten, he seemed to tower over men much taller than him. His commanding presence left no question of who was in charge when he was in the room. She'd heard he now worked for the AWT, Alaska Wildlife Troopers and wondered what the small fishing village of Egegik thought about one of their own now working as a fish cop. How did he cope with that?

If she could have stayed away from the wedding, she would have. She'd given her best excuse, but when one is commanded—threatened—by her best friend since infancy and given the title of maid of honor, you go.

Fortunately, Skip hadn't seen her yet, giving her time to compose herself, though she'd spent too much time on that already. None of it seemed to have done any good. She was torn with whether she wanted to kiss him or kill him. He'd sent her up the river, but worse than that, he'd broken her heart. Had he even written her? No. Sent a Christmas card or a care package? Cigarettes for barter? No. Nothing in all those years.

Yeah, she pretty much hated him.

She'd done her time, gotten clean and had a pretty quiet existence since being sprung from the joint.

And still not one word from him.

He must have felt her stare from across the small terminal for he suddenly turned, and his piercing umber eyes met hers.

She gulped.

You hate him, remember?

Then why did her mouth suddenly feel like the cold, barren arctic desert of Anwar while that other place further south—the one she didn't want to acknowledge—feel just the opposite?

Skip started toward her, his stride sure and confident in his Timberline boots, eating up the distance between them. He obviously hadn't had to prepare to meet her like she had.

"Wren," he said.

She couldn't tell by his voice if he was happy to see her or not. Convinced, he probably looked on this as an obligatory chore, she wished she could run and find an alternate way to Egegik. But there was no other, expedient, way to the isolated village.

Their thirty minute flight was going to drag out like a winter squall. Hopefully the flight would cool down parts of her that had unexpectedly come to life. She was too young for hot flashes, wasn't she?

No way in hell did she still find him attractive.

"I've been waiting for you," he said, his voice a deep rumble that sent vibrations over her exposed skin, raising goose bumps.

His eyes traveled down her body in a slow inspection and then back up again.

Did he like what he saw? Why hadn't she checked her make up? She should've worn something more becoming than old jeans and a SeaHawks Sweatshirt. This was Alaska. It would have been insane to wear a skirt and heels. But then

11

why did she care? She wished she could read his mind to know what he was thinking.

He reached for her carryon. "Let me take that."

"I've got it." She tightened her grip when he tried to take it from her. A childish tug of war ensued until he finally let go.

"Suit yourself. This way." Was that a smile teasing the corners of his lips before he turned away? If he was laughing at her, well she'd...She'd what?

Get a grip, Wren. The man hasn't given you a thought in the last five years. Get over him already.

Besides, she didn't need to follow him. She knew the way. It wasn't like King Salmon was a huge airport. It was a dinky one-room building that saw most of its traffic in the summer months from fishermen passing through on their way to Bristol Bay. The richest salmon fishing grounds in the world was just thirty miles west of King Salmon. King Salmon also had the closest airport to freedom from Egegik. Thanks to the government who'd set up an Air Force base during World War II, because of the strategic position this area held to Russia and Japan.

Wren fell into step behind Skip and refused to admire his firm, muscular backside. She wiped the lie off her brow along with the fine sheen of sweat that had gathered there.

"Jim, she's here," Skip informed the tall man in Carhartt overalls. He was well over six feet with a buzz cut of salt and pepper hair and a closely cropped beard. How he folded himself into the cockpit of the small plane that would fly them across the miles of spongy tundra pock marked with lakes was beyond her?

"All right. Let's get this bird in the air," Jim said. He looked Wren up and down. "You're what, a hundred and thirty-five, hundred and forty pounds?"

Holy Mother of Pearl.

A fiery blush heated her face. She'd forgotten that when flying in small bush planes, pilots required actual weight in order to help distribute everything evenly in the plane. Having that number out there in front of Skip was one more indignity to add to the list.

"One-thirty-eight," she said through gritted teeth. How she wanted to lie and tell them both that she carried a trim one hundred and twenty pounds on her small five foot three inch frame. It was heading into winter and she'd need those few extra pounds as insulation. Sounded good in her head. Not so much in practice. So she was hippy and had generous breasts. Breasts like hers didn't happen naturally without a little bit of weight to fill them out.

"Skip?" Jim didn't bat an eye as he consulted his clipboard. "Need your weight."

"Two-ten."

And all of it muscle.

"Okay, let's load up." Jim turned and headed out the door to the tarmac. Skip grabbed his backpack and hitched it onto his shoulders—along with her carryon.

"I can get that," she sputtered, reaching for her stuff. The whole idea of Skip anywhere near her personal items wigged her out. She had a tough enough time dealing with him this close to her person.

"So can I," Skip said, walking out into the dreary afternoon.

Rain had started to spit. No surprise there. The only time it didn't rain in King Salmon was when it was snowing and blowing and you were thankful because if the weather was stagnant the mosquitoes ate you alive.

"I'll help Jim load the plane," Skip said. "You climb in."

Even though she wanted to ignore anything that Skip told her to do, there was no way to refute what had to be done. She had to get to Egegik. In order to do that, she needed to board the plane. Her luggage also had to reach the small village, and Skip and Jim were more apt at loading than she was. She'd only be in the way. Besides, she wanted to get as far away from Skip as she possibly could, as fast as she could. She buttoned up and climbed into the Cessna 206, taking the backseat, buckling in and praying that Skip wouldn't sit next to her.

The plane dipped with weight as first Jim and then Skip climbed in and buckled into the front seats of the tiny aircraft. Thank God she had the backseat to herself.

Maybe she'd survive this flight after all.

Skip tried not to stare when Wren climbed into the back of the plane. Damn, she still got his blood pumping. An ass like that was a piece of art. It was damn hard not to admire it, reach out and cup it in his hands, lift and press it against him.

There wasn't a woman alive who could make him madder or hornier.

Jim punched him in the arm. "Gawk later. Storm's coming in."

Skip lurched forward toward the plane. He knew seeing Wren again would be a strain and not just to the zipper on his pants. His heart beat fast enough that he had to practice some deep breathing exercises to settle it down. He climbed into the cockpit, turned, and without thinking asked, "You okay back there? Buckled in safely?"

She narrowed those big sooty eyes until they were mere slits. "Not my first plane ride."

At least she'd spoken a few words to him before staring out the small window, telling him loud and clear that she didn't want to have anything to do with him. Would the woman ever get over him arresting her? Talk about holding a grudge.

"All right, folks," Jim said. "Let's blow this popsicle stand before we're stuck here. There's a winter front coming in from Siberia, and I want to be held up somewhere warm when it hits." He started the engine, while securing his headphone and talking into the headset. Covering the microphone with his hand, he addressed Skip and Wren, "Survival kit in the tail, fire extinguisher under my seat and behind yours. Any questions?"

They both shook their heads, having heard it all before. Living out here on the edge of the world made traveling in small planes as common place as catching a bus for those who lived in the big cities.

Skip glanced back at Wren, wishing he could sit beside her. How would he get a moment to talk with her before they landed? He'd purposely planned flying to Egegik with her before the wedding. Once they landed, the village would swallow her up, and he wouldn't get within a few feet of her. He cursed himself for not thinking far enough ahead to how he would get her alone for any length of time.

She looked good. Strong and healthy.

He knew from the network of tabs he had in law enforcement that she'd completed her court appointed rehab and her drug tests had been clean for the last three years. She was thriving in Anchorage as a glass artist and had started seeing some contractor on a regular basis.

Had he waited too long? God, he hoped not.

It would be hard enough breaking through her crabby shell with another man in the picture. He'd given her time and space. No more.

Jim engaged the engine, and they taxied down the runway.

It took a special type of person to enjoy this part of the country. Skip understood the desire to escape it, either with drugs or planes. Both created distance. But to him it was stunning. He relaxed in his seat as the plane lifted off and focused on the wild, untouched beauty outside his window. The threatening storm gave the surrounding landscape a misty, magical feel. The spider web of creeks and rivers reflected the grayish-purple of the clouds, highlighting the golden-red of the tundra falling below them.

The plane bounced along with the wind as they gained altitude and banked southwest. The greenish-gray waters of Bristol Bay chopped with whitecaps and ate at thirty foot high banks.

Wren couldn't wait to leave this place. He wondered how she was feeling now that she'd returned. Did she find any joy in the wild openness below them? Or was she counting down the hours until she was back in the big city?

Away from him?

Wren's breath caught as the plane jerked again. She hated these damn flying coffins. She was the only one in the family who got carsick, plane sick, and seasick, but bush planes were a necessity of living in Alaska's Bush. Didn't mean she had to like it, though. Exhaling slowly, she focused on the horizon. The last thing she needed was to throw up.

Why hadn't she taken a Dramamine?

Deep breaths, concentrate. In out. In out. Shit. No way was she going to be sick in front of Skip. Bad enough the last time he'd seen her she'd been strung out on coke. She'd puked on his shoes when he'd cuffed her. What she wouldn't give to be anywhere but here right now. She could feel him glancing at her every few minutes.

Face forward, buddy. Nothing to see here.

So she wasn't the underweight druggie, he'd last seen. Now she was overweight and sober.

Hell.

The plane pitched and so did her stomach. Were the clouds outside her window getting darker? Meaner? Nearer?

She looked at Skip and then Jim to see if either had noticed. Skip's jaw seemed tighter, the skin stretched taut. It was harder to see the pilot, but his hands seemed busy as they pushed and pulled knobs.

The plane suddenly dropped fast, and the seatbelt clinched tight around her waist. A pathetic squeal escaped her, and her hands flew out to grab the cold wall and low ceiling of the plane. It banked right then left. There was some fast scrambling up front. Skip's hands were on the wheel thingy, and he seemed anxious.

What the hell was going on?

Jim's hands slumped lifeless at his sides, and his head lulled forward.

"Skip?" she yelled his name but knew he couldn't hear her over the roar of the engine and static of the wind. The plane leaped and fell, the tundra suddenly too close as the nose dipped. Over the noise and panic, she heard Skip swear followed by his shout, "Brace for impact!"

"What?" He didn't just say that. "Oh God, no." She reached out and grabbed Jim's shoulders and shook them. He slumped farther forward in his seat.

Skip didn't spare her a glance. One handed, he grabbed the headphones from Jim and slammed them onto his head. Next she heard, "Mayday, mayday, mayday!"

The plane seesawed back and forth with the wind, trying to find some sort of balance, or perch, but the wind seemed to laugh as it blew them down toward the rapidly rising ground. They touched—a brush really—then a slam that knocked the wind out of her, followed quickly by the nose digging into the tundra and the plane somersaulting.

Then nothing.

Chapter Two

Wren moaned and wiped at her face. Her head hurt like a son of a bitch. And why was she wet? She winced as her fingers bumped a tender area on her forehead, and she opened her eyes a slit. Blood painted her hand.

Why was she bleeding?

What kind of partying had she done this time? Oh please, no. Not again. She hadn't relapsed, had she?

No. NO. The price of relapse was too high. People had been hurt because of her and her weaknesses. She blinked and forced her eyes farther open.

The place was a mess, like it had been tossed. Why was she hanging upside down in her seat? Wind whistled like a sick siren, chilling her further. She needed a blanket, a warm wash cloth, and some thick band aids.

Suddenly everything came rushing back. The plane, the threatening weather front. They'd crash landed.

They?

Oh, God. "Skip?" His name screamed in her mind but only came out as a whisper. "Skip," she said louder. The wind stole her words. She couldn't see him or the pilot and wiped at her face with her sleeve again. She wouldn't panic. They always say head wounds bleed a lot. Who the hell were they anyway? Her head hurt, she was bleeding, and it was really cold.

This was Alaska.

It was September, which by anyone else's standards meant winter. They needed help, and they needed it fast or they were as good as dead.

Crap, they were in more trouble if she was the only help.

Wren struggled to release the seatbelt with one hand, the other on the ceiling—er, now the floor—of the plane, helping to brace her weight. She still fell with an oomph when the belt released. She scrambled to her knees, her shoulders bumping into the seats as she crawled forward, wiping at more blood as it smeared her vision now that she wasn't hanging upside down.

"Skip? Jim?" No one answered. A coldness traveled up her spine that had nothing to do with the wind leeching through the cracks and broken window of the plane.

Both men hung upside down in their seatbelts just as she had. They looked somewhat like bats, which had her stifling a hysterical giggle. With trembling fingers, she checked Skip's neck for a pulse.

"Please, God, please." She felt nothing, and a whimper of dread escaped her. She pushed harder. In the cramped space, her knees dug into whatever the hell the manufacturer had placed in the ceiling. Probably never took into account anyone having to kneel on them.

Still no pulse.

She felt around, blindly. "Come on, damn it."

Skip suddenly coughed. "Stop," he said, his voice hoarse. "What are you trying to do? Choke me?"

A relieved sob bubbled up. "Oh, thank God. You're alive."

"Guess you never thought to hear yourself utter those words," he muttered.

She ignored him and turned toward Jim. She didn't have to feel for his pulse. His eyes were wide open, but he would never see out of them again.

"Skip?" she whispered. "Jim...?"

"Yeah. I think he had a heart attack or aneurism. One minute he was there, and then he wasn't." Skip rubbed his eyes. "Damn it. The man had a son. Sixteen I think."

"Mother?"

"Ran off years ago. Drugs." He glanced at her and then away. "Come on. We need to get some things done before that weather front hits." Skip winced as he moved to release his seatbelt. He braced himself much the way she had, but there was more of him hanging on the strap. "I can't get out of this thing. Do you see a knife anywhere?"

Wren glanced around the twisted frame of the plane. She didn't see a knife, but she saw smoke.

"The plane's on fire!" She scrambled back. Where the hell had Jim said the fire extinguisher was? "Will the plane explode?" She didn't want to die that way. Though it would be better than freezing to death.

"Wren! Calm down. Tell me where you see fire." There was an urgency in his voice that focused her panic.

"I-I don't. There's smoke in the tail of the plane."

Skip let out a heavy breath. "There isn't anything to burn back there. The engine's up front, gas is in the wings. It's probably dust or fog from the crash."

She took a closer look. It could be dust, but it sure looked a lot like smoke.

"Help me get down." Skip's words captured her attention. "Find a knife."

"Don't you carry a knife? You're a cop. Aren't you supposed to be prepared for anything, like the Canadian Mounties?"

"Huh?"

"The motto for the Canadian Mounties."

"No. That's, 'They always get their man.'"

"Well, what the hell is the motto for Alaska Wildlife Troopers?"

"Just cut me down. There's a Leatherman clipped to the right side of my belt.

"Then get it."

"I think my arm's broken. You'll have to reach it. The faster the better."

"Great. I'm gonna have to save your sorry ass."

"It's not like I haven't saved yours."

Smoke or dust started to seep into the cabin from the tail of the plane. They needed to get out of here. She didn't trust that the plane wasn't ready to go up in flames at any moment. She'd seen plane wrecks before. She watched the Discovery Channel.

Wren reached around his seat, groping around his hip.

"Too far to the left," Skip said, adding in a softer, sexier voice, "Though I am enjoying your hand there."

Shit.

Good thing he couldn't see her as the heat flaming her face was enough to help her forget about the cold. She blindly found his belt and traced it until she located the Leatherman clipped in its leather case. She released the snap and worked the blade free. She crawled to the left in between the two seats, trying to forget about the dead pilot staring sightlessly forward into nothing. Her fingers shaking, she fought to open the damn blade. The seatbelt was pulled tight with Skip's two hundred plus pounds hanging on it. She slid the knife under the belt where it clicked into place, giving her some space where it wasn't digging into Skip's body.

"Wait!"

Too late, Skip came crashing down in a crumpled mess.

"Shit. I told you to wait."

"Sorry, the knife was sharp. I didn't think it would slice through the belt like that." She regarded him lying upside down on his back, his legs flopped forward. He had nowhere to go in the cramped space.

He angled around on his shoulders, keeping his hurt arm next to his side and used his feet to kick open the door. Wind, bearing teeth, rushed in. It aided in pushing the smoke back.

She grabbed the fire extinguisher Jim had haphazardly mentioned right before they'd taken off, but miraculously, the smoke was no longer there. Skip might be right about that, but she was holding onto the extinguisher until they knew for sure.

"Come on, we need to take a look outside and see what kind of condition we're in," Skip said, his voice strained with pain.

Condition? They were screwed.

Skip struggled to climb out of the plane, and she crawled out after him. He cradled his arm, and her head pounded, but the bleeding seemed to have stopped. They stood outside the plane and regarded the wreckage.

Cushioned somewhat by the mossy tundra, she lay upside down on her wings looking like a squashed bug.

"Guess, I'm not much of a pilot," Skip said.

"I don't know. They say any landing you can walk away from is a good one."

He choked out a laugh. "Thanks for that."

"But I wouldn't fly with you again," she added.

The wind blew at the plane, making it shudder. Good thing it was laying on its wings or the wind would probably pick it up and toss it off the bluff and into the rolling surf below.

"Wow, you could have dumped us into the water." They were seriously within twenty feet of the bluff where the deadly ocean could have swallowed them.

"Yeah, crash landing could have been worse."

CHAPTER THREE

Skip cradled his arm next to his side, knowing it was broken. At least it seemed to be a clean break. He needed to immobilize it. The sooner the better. But first he needed to know where that smoke had come from. He was pretty positive what he'd told Wren was the truth. It made a lot of sense, what he'd been spewing, but he'd been surprised before. Besides, he'd helped Jim load the plane. There was more being flown to Egegik than him and Wren and their luggage. Supplies were back there. Supplies he hoped contained food and nothing flammable.

He nodded to the fire extinguisher Wren clutched in her hands like a safety blanket. "You know how to handle that thing?" Being down to only one good arm, he wasn't much help.

"Uh...yeah." She looked at him weird. "You forgot about that Fourth of July when we lit the garage on fire?"

He barked out a laugh. "Damn, that seems like forever ago." They'd been what? Ten, eleven and had wanted to see fireworks go off in the dark. Alaska's daylight summers were horrible for firework displays. So they'd concocted this idea of lighting them off in the enclosed garage. Almost burning down the house. If it hadn't been for Wren and her quick thinking with the fire extinguisher, the house would have been a goner, instead of just most of the garage.

They walked around the plane, hunching into the wind. It still had enough power to push them back. Wren stumbled around on the mossy ground.

There didn't seem to be any sign of fire. Thank the good Lord. That would nail their chances of surviving for sure. They needed the plane for shelter from the brewing storm.

"Looks as though the smoke was from the landing, but keep the extinguisher close." They trekked back to the front of the plane, the wind blowing them making the trip faster. Nothing seemed to be coming from the engine. But then the nose of the plane was buried deep in the spongy tundra. They climbed back into the plane, both shivering by the time he got the door wrenched closed behind them.

Skip tried not to look at Jim. He didn't have time to mourn his friend. Not when he needed to get help on the way, or he'd be mourning more than just Jim. The radio. Hell, why hadn't he thought of that first. He reached for the mic. "Mayday, mayday, mayday! This is November2195Charlie we are crash landed—" He glanced at the GPS coordinates and recited them, repeating his mayday call twice more before the Coast Guard answered.

The reply came back interspersed with a load of static over the radio. "Condition."

"Three people. Pilot dead, one with a broken arm, another with a bleeding head wound, possible concussion."

More static, and with dread, Skip made out the basics of what they were saying.

"Weather...grounded...buckle down...blows over."

"Roger that." Skip turned off the radio to save what battery they had left. He turned to Wren. "Looks like we are stuck here for a while, tonight, maybe tomorrow."

CHAPTER FOUR

"Tonight? Tomorrow?" Wren said. "Lori's wedding is the day after tomorrow. We can't miss the wedding." That's the reason Wren had gotten on the blasted plane to begin with. "What about your parents? And the wedding guests? They are going to be so worried." She'd caused her friends and family too much worry over her short lifetime. Besides, she couldn't spend the night with Skip out here in the wilds with a dead body, no bathroom, no bed, no coffee!

"Wren! Keep it together."

She took a deep breath, held it until her lungs hurt and released it in a big huff. "Got it. Is there a plan?"

"Shelter. Chances are this front will bring our first snowfall. At any rate, it's going to rain and get really cold."

Colder than it already was? She'd forgotten how hostile this part of Alaska could be when it blew.

"I don't want to sound insensitive, but what about Jim?" Were they going to spend the night next to a dead body?

Skip's jaw tightened. "We need to move him."

What about predators? She couldn't bring herself to voice the thought, giving it power. But it was a serious probability. Who knew what lurked out there? She swung around, trying to see as far as she could with the drooping clouds. The tundra was pock-marked with alder bushes and scrubs. Anything could be hiding out there. Bears weren't to bed for the winter yet.

She shivered and regarded Skip. His arm was swelling, his hand almost twice the normal size. "We need to brace your arm first." She glanced around, took out Skip's knife that she'd pocketed after cutting him down and sliced the seatbelt free from the plane. Now what to splint it with? Planes weren't made of wood. She climbed back into the tail where the luggage was stowed.

A webbed netting held the bags in place upside down. She cut one side and worked her bag free. Tossing it to the middle of the plane, it slid to a stop on the ceiling/floor between the seats. She unzipped it and pulled out her curling iron.

"You got to be kidding?" Skip scoffed.

"It's rigid. Got a better idea?"

In her bag, she also pulled out a water bottle and Tylenol. "Might want to start with this."

"Got anything stronger?" he mumbled before tossing the pills back and shutting up.

"Want to bite down on something?"

"Just do it." He ground his teeth together.

"Fine." She climbed over her bag and carefully took his arm. It was a clean break, as near as she could tell between the elbow and wrist. She knew from experience that if they could immobilize it, the pain would lessen. "Brace yourself, this is going to hurt."

"Talking about it isn't helping."

"Okay." She took a deep breath and tightened her grip on his hand, moving the arm back into place the best she could. Skip did really well until she was almost done, and then he hollered, followed by cursing that was more colorful than anything she'd heard in jail.

She did her best to ignore it and do the job. She was good at that. Tunnel vision, her mother used to call it. Whatever. She focused, and when his arm looked as straight as she could get it, she made quick work of bracing it with the curling iron. But the seatbelt was proving troublesome.

The fabric was slick and didn't want to stay tight. "This isn't working."

"Duct tape," Skip gritted out. He pointed to the back. "There's a toolkit. Any bush pilot worth his weight has duct tape."

"Hold this, and don't move it." She didn't want to go through that again. She doubted he did either.

"Don't worry."

She regarded his pale Aleut skin, the sweat beading on his upper lip. Could you get sick with a broken arm? Infection? What if the bone had cut open blood vessels? An artery?

What if he died on her, too?

"Hey, I'm not going to die," Skip growled.

Had she voiced that out loud?

"We're both going to make it out of here alive. All we have to do is survive the night. We've lived through the worst."

She didn't agree. Surviving the night alone with Skip just might do her in.

"Stop thinking like that."

He couldn't still read her like a book, could he?

Damn it. She'd worked so hard on not letting her emotions play over her face like a movie. She needed space away from him, but the only space she was going to find was out there in the wide open wilderness.

And that would definitely kill her.

CHAPTER FIVE

Skip loved the vivid expressions on Wren's face. He'd forgotten how fun it was to talk with her, be with her, and love her. She'd been the most open, emotionally free woman he'd ever known.

He wanted her back.

He'd needed alone time to do that. Being stuck somewhere on the bluffs of Bristol Bay in a plane wreck was more than he'd counted on. He certainly didn't appreciate Jim's death giving him that time.

Jim.

They needed to do something about him, but first they needed to see to Wren's injuries. She finished duct taping the curling arm to his arm, using his knife to cut the toe off one of her socks to protect his skin from the adhesive.

"I need to check that cut on your forehead," Skip said, his fingers reaching up to smooth her hair back.

"It's okay." She jerked out of his reach.

He curled his fingers with regret that she didn't want him to touch her. Surely, things weren't that bad between them.

"The cut needs to be cleaned and bandaged."

"I can take care of it." She tightened her lips.

"How?" He gestured with his good arm, hitting the top of the seat hanging above them. "You see a bathroom? A mirror. Don't be stu—"

"Don't call me stupid." Her expression shut down.

Ah crap. His tone was sorry when he spoke again. "I wasn't calling you stupid. I was going to say stubborn. You're stubborn as hell, Wren, but never stupid." He remembered her dad and his constant verbal abuse. Skip had even confronted the bastard when they were teenagers, and her father had gone after Wren with words that sliced and stomped her struggling spirit. She'd been called stupid so many times in her life that she'd begun to believe it, which Skip believed was the reason she'd looked for an escape. And drugs had been her vehicle.

Wren's gaze dropped to her hands. He wanted to reach out and enfold them in his. Maybe that would stop their shaking. But she had that prickly wall around her so he changed the subject back to the cut on her forehead. "Hand me that first aid kit, and let's clean you up." This time she didn't argue.

She unclipped the first aid kit from where Jim had pointed out its location before they'd left King Salmon. That seemed days ago rather than mere hours.

She set the kit between them and opened it. He reached in and found the antiseptic wipes. Only problem was that he couldn't tear the plastic to get to the wipes. She didn't say anything when he handed her the package, but her look spoke volumes. While she used the wipe to clean the dried blood off her face, he rummaged through the kit looking for anything that would help cover the wound. He laid out bandages, gauze, Neosporin, and tape. Wren finished with one wipe and went to grab another, but he was quicker and got to it first. "Let me."

"I can do this." She ground her teeth.

She really didn't want him to touch her, but he was dying to get his hands on her. Even in this impersonal way. "You can't see everything I can. Come on, there's a lot we need to do. Arguing is a waste of time. It's already getting darker than I'd like."

29

She glanced out of the windows, noticing the black clouds smothering what daylight remained. Night would be coming early, way before they were ready for it. He just hoped the snow would hold off until they could get things situated for the long, cold night ahead.

"Fine." She huffed out a breath that fanned across his face, bringing the scent of mint. She must have chewed gum before getting on the plane. Did she still suffer from motion sickness? There was so much he wanted to reacquaint himself with about her.

He reached up with the wipe and began slowly cleaning away the dried blood around the cut. Since he'd somersaulted the plane, most of the blood had flowed into her hair. Without running water, there wasn't a lot he could do about her hair. The blood melted into the dark strands, blending in. He concentrated on the cut. It was a few inches long, traveling back into her hairline. She'd have a scar, but one that would be easily hidden by her hair. The bleeding had stopped, coagulating over the cut, until he attempted to clean it, then it started to seep again.

"You really need stitches." He glanced down at the first aid kit. It was stocked with the supplies he needed to stitch her up.

"No way am I letting you stick a needle in me." She moved back out of his reach.

"Don't think I could sew you up right with only one wing working anyway. See if there aren't some adhesive strips in there or super glue." Many a time he'd super glued a cut closed. Worked great when you were constantly around the water and not close to medical facilities.

She rummaged through the contents, as he held the wipe over the seeping cut and tried not to be distracted by the faint scent of lemon verbena. She must still use the same body wash. He loved knowing she hadn't changed so much, gave him hope that he might be able to reach her.

"I found them." She tore open the package and held the strip up to him. He exchanged the wipe for the strip and, using his teeth to take the covering off the adhesive, placed one over the cut. He reached for another one that she had ready and did the same with the next.

"Neosporin."

She handed him a gauze pad with Neosporin already on it, anticipating his needs. She could always do that, knowing what he needed before he asked. He'd never been so in tune with a woman before, or since.

That insight of hers had been amazing in bed.

He placed the bandage over the cut, reaching for the length of tape she had ready for him. Once the cut was covered, he became aware of how close he was to her. His head bent over hers, his fingers lightly stroked the strands away from her face. She glanced up at him, her eyes wide.

He was helpless not to lean in. Her breath caught, and her eyelids fluttered. Her lips parted, and her tongue nervously wet them.

He groaned.

The sound gallivanted her into motion. She jerked away, scampering back out of his one-armed reach.

Damn it. He'd been so close to tasting her again. Now she looked at him as though frightened. What reason did she have to be frightened of him?

"Wren—"

"We need to get things done before the storm hits."

He wanted to say to hell with everything, grab her and yank her back into his arms where she never should have left. If she hadn't—

No point in going down that road.

Time to get things battened down. Once their shelter was secure, and Jim taken care of, they had all night to become reacquainted.

He glanced out the window. "We're going to need a flashlight." He'd also need Wren's help with Jim. One handed wasn't going to get a two hundred pound-plus man, dead weight, out of this plane. "Did you see a tarp or anything back there?" Skip asked. They needed to cover Jim with something. Even though, the body was a shell, and Jim wouldn't feel the cold, it went against everything in Skip to just lay the man out in the storm. He hoped Jim's spirit was someplace warm and comfortable—nestled in the loving arms of his ancestors.

Skip was almost jealous of Jim as another blustery gust, this one carrying needles of rain, shook the plane.

Wren glanced at Jim, still hanging upside down in the pilot's seat. She swallowed hard. "I'll check."

He had to give it to her. Most women would be squeamish over what they were about to do. But Wren didn't show any signs of it, and he was watching her every move. This new, stronger, confident woman intrigued him more than his memories. If he wasn't careful, he'd get caught staring.

"How about this?" She held up a Mylar blanket she pulled out of the survival kit. "There are four, enough for us and...him."

"Okay." Unconventional, since a survival blanket was beyond helping Jim, but then this was Alaska. The land of the unconventional.

Wren handed him the small folded silver blanket and then crawled back toward her suitcase and began systematically going through the contents.

He caught a glimpse of black underwear and a hot pink bra before she found what she was looking for.

"I knew I'd need these." She held up a pair of Under Armour.

"Good thinking." Question though, was she going to strip in front of him to get them on under her clothes? She wouldn't get the full effects of the garment unless it lay next to her skin.

Man, what he wouldn't give to lay next to her skin.

"Could you, um, turn around?" She did a cute little circle motion with her finger.

He didn't want to turn around. He did, though it was a struggle in the small confines of the plane, and was rewarded with her image in the broken window. He really should shut his eyes. But he wasn't that much of a gentleman. Hell, he wasn't even close. She whipped off her sweatshirt and the sexy navy tank top underneath, her nipples hard beads against her icy blue bra. Her honeyed skin had him licking his lips. She covered up too quickly. He wanted to see more and had to bite his tongue to keep from asking. Then she shimmied out of her jeans and his mouth watered.

Hips rounded and lush, soft and creamy thighs, little dimples at her knees. He wasn't going to make it. She wiggled into the tight black Under Armour and followed that with her jeans. He really shouldn't have watched. Now he ached to touch.

"Okay, you can turn around."

No he couldn't, not with the kind of wood he had branching out. "I need some fresh air." And the arctic wind would do the trick of settling things back down to size. What the freaking hell was he doing?

He had a broken arm.

Like that would stop him. Okay, they were in a fight for their lives. One of them was already dead, sharing the same breathing space. Well, his and Wren's breathing space anyway. God, he was fucked up.

He should be more concerned with how they were going to get out of here instead of how he was going to get inside her.

Chapter Six

"I still think predators are going to be a problem," Wren said as she struggled to stay on her feet against the wind's impressive attempts to knock her off them. Even though she now lived in Anchorage, she was by no means a city girl. This was Alaska. Predators outnumbered people.

She was cold and hungry and wet and now exhausted after dragging Jim's dead body across the tundra. And her head pounded like a son of a bitch.

"That's why we moved him so far from the plane," Skip explained as though he was speaking to someone slow on the uptake. He struggled alongside her, having a tougher time against the wind as he was a bigger target and unable to put his arms out for balance. She'd zipped his jacket up with his arm tucked into his body. With the brace, it wouldn't fit through the sleeve.

"We should have tossed his body over the bank." It would have been a hell of a lot faster as the bank was twenty yards from the buried nose of the plane. She had no idea why she was pecking at him about this. It was done. The body was covered and secure and probably a hell of a lot warmer than she was right now. Blasted icy rain.

"It's Jim. His family is going to want his body for burial, and the ocean would have taken him. I couldn't do that to a friend."

"You had no problem tossing me in jail, and I was more than a friend. Or so I thought since we were banging each other."

He stopped cold and glared at her. Pain bracketed his face. "What the hell is your problem? Are you spoiling for a fight?"

Hell, yes. Someone needed to pay for how miserable she felt. Skip owed her for a lot of things. Crash landing the airplane and putting her in this situation was just the latest of many.

Besides, she didn't want to get into that plane with him, be alone with him all night, just the two of them needing to keep warm.

Jim had been there before. Dead or not, he'd still been there between them, putting a damper on what could happen. Now that they'd moved Jim clear across the tundra what was going to keep her from doing something stupid?

She remembered all too well what could happen when she was alone with Skip for any length of time. That's how she'd lost her virginity at sixteen. Not to mention her heart. She'd still like to have that back. Her heart, not her virginity. She'd been glad to lose that thing.

The icy rain suddenly turned to shards of icy snow and started to slice at their exposed skin.

"Can we at least fight inside the damn plane?" Skip spit the words through his chattering teeth. "I'm freezing my balls off out here."

Maybe they should stay out here a little longer.

She doubted he'd be in an amorous mood if he lost his balls. But then again she was assuming a lot. He hadn't made a move on her. What if the attraction was one-sided? Could it be just her who was still attracted? Maybe he'd moved on. No, she would have heard. The little village of Egegik had a healthy gossip line.

"Do you even remember where you crashed the plane?" She glanced around trying hard to see through the thick, and getting thicker, onslaught of sleet.

"Of course, I remember where I crash—" He huffed a frustrated sigh and trudged forward bent into the wind. "I'd forgotten how much of a pain in the ass you could be."

Hey, now that's something she hadn't thought of. Skip could keep his balls, and they could get out of this storm, all she had to do was be a bitch. Yeah, surprise. She was up for that.

"And here I'd thought I'd left you with a lasting impression," she said.

He stopped again and turned toward her. "You're pulling out all the stops, aren't you?" His eyes narrowed, either because of the biting wind or because he was really angry with her remembering that last impression. "I'll have to show you the scar you left me."

Scar? She thought she'd only left him with a scratch. It wasn't like she'd meant to hurt him. She'd only wanted to get him to release her. Wasn't her fault he'd underestimated how high she was or the lengths she'd go to be free of him in that state. She hadn't even known until she'd awoken, hung over but sober, and listened to the list of charges against her at her arraignment.

The memory silenced her inner bitch.

What else would happen to him because of her? He already had a broken arm. Granted, she hadn't done that, but she was nagging him when he obviously hurt. They were both wet and cold and probably hungry. She certainly was. Hunger could explain her bitchiness. She hadn't had breakfast because her nerves had been too jittery knowing she was going home, and there was a good chance she'd see Skip. Lunch had consisted of the measly peanut mix and a small glass of artificial punch the airline from Anchorage to King Salmon had given everyone.

God she hoped he knew where the plane was. Her feet were so cold she was in danger of losing digits. Then suddenly there it was. So close she almost ran into the door Skip opened for her.

"Hurry. We don't want it wetter inside than we can help."

She scampered into the upside down plane, having to crawl around the seats in the cockpit. Skip struggled to follow her. He shut and latched the door, but the wind whistled through the broken front window.

"Get out of your wet clothes," Skip said, following behind her, shrugging off his coat. "See if you can find my bag. If we don't get dry, I don't have to tell you how much trouble we'll be in."

Hypothermia. Number one killer in the state of Alaska.

She headed into the tail of the plane. "What does your bag look like?"

"Blue and gold."

She should have known. Trooper colors. Also the colors of the state flag. "Eight stars of gold on a field of blue." She bet his uniform was in his bag. Damn he looked good in his trooper uniform. She'd never admit it, but her good intentions would weaken to mush when he was all gussied up. Hell, who was she kidding? She'd never had good intentions back then. She barely had them now.

She found his bag, and under it were boxes of food. Lots of food. Someone had gone to Costco!

"There's food!" Her stomach growled. She turned and tossed Skip's bag toward him and then swiveled back to the food.

"Change your clothes first," Skip said.

She glared at him from over her shoulder. "You knew there was food?"

"Yes." He bent, and one-handed, unzipped his bag.

"You couldn't have said something?"

He paused and looked at her from under his brows. "Been kinda busy with other things."

"But I'm hungry."

"You're cold too. You're probably so cold that you don't feel it anymore. Now, get out of those wet clothes, or I'll have to warm you up myself. And there will be nudity."

A fiery blush heated her cheeks. She shivered, and hoped it was the cold and not the image his words invoked. She knelt, or fell as her knees gave out, next to her suitcase and rummaged through her clothes. She needed layers. Lots and lots of layers. She didn't care that he was watching her this time, didn't even ask him to turn around. The blush must have jumpstarted her thermostat because her body started to shake, and her teeth to rattle. She was freezing. Thinking of them naked, next to each other, started to sound very appealing. And not just in a survival nature.

She whipped off her jacket, tossed it aside, and lifted her sweatshirt. Her Under Armour felt dry so she went to put on another sweatshirt.

"Take it off," Skip said.

"It's dry."

"If any part of it is wet, your body won't warm up. So, be safe and take it off."

Was it wrong that there was a big part of her who wanted him to say that in a less impersonal way?

"Fine." She struggled out of the Under Armour. The cold sucked the breath out of her. She shivered into a long-sleeved t-shirt and followed that with another sweatshirt. Her jeans were next, and the Under Armour pants. Goose flesh was red and splotchy on her legs before she covered them up with a pair of black heavy sweats with Bristol Bay printed down the side of one leg. Wool socks followed. She was feeling much better when she turned to face Skip.

He was a mess.

Much like a two-year-old who'd just learned to change himself, his jeans were off and he was struggling into another pair. They weren't going on easily with only one good arm and his skin being wet. He still had on his soaked shirt. She should have thought how hard changing his clothes would have been before she'd changed her own. Now she felt like mud on the bottom of his boots.

"I'm sorry, Skip." She reached out to help pull up his jeans. He sighed with what she assumed was relief and let his good arm drop away, letting her take over.

She buttoned the jeans and went to pull up his zipper. Well...he hadn't lost his balls out there in the freezing sleet. Hello. Her fingers jumped away, and she swallowed. "Uh... you're going to have to zip up your pants."

"I can't," he said. Was there laughter in his tone? "Not one-handed. If you hold onto the crotch, I can pull up the zipper."

"I'm not grabbing your crotch." Fire flamed in her cheeks. She wasn't cold anymore. "Your jeans are too small to zip up anyway." Oh God, had she pointed that out? She wanted to die.

"It's the crotch talk." His words didn't have laughter in them now. She recognized that tone. It jumpstarted areas of her body she thought had been put on the shelf.

"Listen. I'm not touching that. You'll just have to leave your pants unzipped until...things are back down to size."

"Things haven't been down to size since I first saw you in the airport." His nostrils flared, and he took a step closer to her.

She backed up, her shoulder bumping into the top of the seat hanging above her. "Not my problem."

"The hell it isn't." He reached out with his good arm and hauled her against him, making sure she felt exactly how she affected him. "Do you have any idea how hard it's been not touching you?"

"This isn't good for your arm."

"I'm feeling no pain in my arm. But there's a serious ache farther south."

"Skip—"

"Just let it happen, Wren."

He leaned down, paused as he looked into her eyes, and then kissed her softly, his lips a perfect fit over hers.

She shuddered and leaned into him. This was like coming home. Oh, how she missed this. Being held by him, loved by him. The rich earthy scent of rugged outdoors, cool ocean breezes, with a hint of salmon berries infused her lungs as she breathed in his essence. How did he smell the same after so long?

The heat of him seduced her closer. He groaned and breached past the seam of her lips, his tongue hot and devastating as he deepened the kiss. He pulled her into his hardness, ground against her and groaned again. His breath became choppy, his fingers digging into her hip as though he needed to be part of her.

Blood surged in her veins, and she became dizzy. Her breath caught as his hand slid up and under her sweatshirt, bypassing her layers, and finding her skin.

Heat, delicious heat infused her body, killing any chill she had left. She wanted to feel that heat everywhere. Get naked with him and—

Wait a minute. What the hell were they doing? His shirt was wet against her front. He was kissing her, more like devouring her, and they hadn't seen each other in five years.

Her hands came up and pushed against his chest, creating a little space to break the kiss. "We can't."

He met her eyes, his unfocused, clouded with desire. "Yes, we can." He leaned in to kiss her again. She pushed harder against him. His eyes narrowed and cleared a bit as he took a moment to study her. "It's the dude, isn't it?"

"Dude?"

"The contractor dude you've been seeing."

Stunned, she relaxed her hands until the words connected in her muddled brain. "Contractor? You mean Christopher?"

"Yeah, him."

She pushed out of Skip's hold. "How do you know about Christopher?"

"I know a lot of things about you."

"H-have you—" No, he couldn't. He wouldn't. "Have you had me under surveillance?"

He looked guilty as hell.

"For-for how long?" She slapped his good arm when he didn't answer her right away.

"Since you were released from jail." He shrugged his shoulder as though her slap had stung. "Actually, the whole time you were in jail too."

"You've been spying on me for the last five years?"

"When you say it like that, yeah, it sounds really bad."

"It is bad. It's restraining order bad. Why? Why would you do that?"

"I sent you to jail—"

"No, you didn't. It was my fault. My consequences. I broke the law."

He took a step toward her. "Wren, it killed me to send you there. I had to know that you were all right."

"So, what, you've kept tabs on me since I was released to make sure I wasn't using again?"

"No. Yes. Kinda." He shut his eyes and rubbed the back of his neck. "Shit. This is all coming out wrong. I had to give you space to work through your rehab, get clean, stay sober. But I had to know you were okay. I couldn't lose hope."

"Hope?"

"That someday we could be together again. Then you started taking up with the contractor dude, and I thought you were over me and moving on with your life. I had to stop that."

"Stop me from moving on with my life?"

He clammed up, rolled his lips over his teeth and refused to continue. It was her turn to narrow her eyes.

41

"So you laid in wait until you thought I was ready? Ready for you to come charging back into my life to pick up were we left off?" Her tone continued to rise. "Where we left off was me standing over you after I shot you with your own gun."

CHAPTER SEVEN

"So we have some relationship issues to work out. An apology wouldn't be out of order either." He rubbed the upper shoulder of his broken arm, where the bullet had grazed him. Maybe if he acted like he was in pain, she'd cut him some slack. It wouldn't be much of an act with his aching broken arm. "That bullet really hurt."

"I sent you an apology."

"One your therapist probably told you to write."

"It was part of the program."

"You were still angry with me."

"Yes. I heard you went to the judge and testified against me. I'd already pled out. You made sure I was sent to jail."

So much for cutting him some slack. "There wasn't any other way I knew that would get you off the drugs." He reached out to take her hand, but she linked them behind her back. His attention was caught by her breasts as the action lifted them front and center. God, she had beautiful breasts. What he would give if she let him...

The scowl on her face deepened. This wasn't helping his cause either.

"Wren, I'd tried everything, but nothing worked. You were going to kill yourself if something drastic wasn't done."

"Sending me to jail almost killed me."

That tore his attention away from her generous breasts. "What are you talking about?" Dread settled into his stomach. He'd had people looking out for her, keeping tabs, reporting back. He hadn't heard of anything life threatening happening to her inside.

"Nothing." She turned away from him.

He grabbed her arm and swung her around. "Tell me."

"Get your hands off me." She yanked her arm free of his grasp.

"You didn't mind them a few minutes ago."

"A few minutes ago I was out of my mind with cold and hunger."

"You're still cold and hungry."

She growled. "Would you quit twisting my words?"

"Then be honest with me, and tell me what happened, damn it."

"I almost ended it, okay."

"What?"

She ran a hand through her hair, wincing as she brushed the bump on her head. "It was too much. The withdrawals, the confinement, not having you—it was just too much. One night, I tried to hang myself with the sheets from my bed."

He sucked in a breath as his heart missed a beat. "Why wasn't I told of this?"

"Probably because it didn't work. I'm still here, aren't I?" She arched a brow and folded her arms across her chest.

Well, shit. He remembered that look all too well. He shouldn't have reminded her that he had spies in the jail reporting back to him. Maybe if they ate, figured out a way to warm up this busted plane, she'd be a little more open for sharing, talking. He wasn't going to get anywhere with her and their relationship if he didn't at least try.

A gust of wind, heavy with sleet, shook the plane. He shivered, realizing he still had on his wet shirt and his pants zipper wide open. He really needed the use of his other arm. To hell with his zipper. It didn't bother him to be hanging out. But the shirt needed to go.

He struggled with the buttons, one-handed.

"Oh, for hell sake." Wren brushed his hand out of the way. "You're more work than a two-year-old." She quickly freed the buttons of his shirt. She didn't spare him a glance as his naked chest was revealed.

That was an ego buster. He'd worked hard on his body since they'd been apart. Building muscle had been his focus, that and his job, which the muscle came in handy for. And she didn't even look. He had pecs, damn it, and abs.

She helped him peel the shirt free from his good arm and then carefully inched it over his broken one. She didn't pause in what she was doing until the fabric fell away from his bullet-grazed shoulder.

She gasped, her fingers lightly tracing the area where her bullet had cut into him.

"See, I told you there was a scar," he softly murmured, enjoying the delicate touch of her fingers on his cold skin.

Her eyes narrowed to slits.

Shit, he said the wrong thing again.

"You chose this scar and it's not a scar. It's a tattoo. Of a wren."

And here he thought she'd appreciate the gesture.

"It's a sight better than the ragged scar you left me with. It was damn hard to explain at the gym that my girlfriend shot me. If I'd gotten it in the line of duty, that would have been different. So I got the tattoo to camouflage it." And it hurt a hell of lot worse than the bullet had.

"Of a wren?"

"Well, yeah. It was your mark, after all. Your brand." He shrugged. "I liked it. Seems poetic in a way. Like you're always with me."

She briefly met his eyes, hers showing surprise and maybe a little wetness. He couldn't tell for sure since she bent to rummage through his bag, yanking out a dry shirt. She found another button-down one, which would be the easiest—if not warmest—to get into with his broken arm.

He wanted to look into those expressive eyes again. "Wren."

"Can we get you dressed so that I can eat something?"

She refused to look at him as she inched the fabric carefully over his broken arm. But he caught the rapid blinking. Was she crying? Had he chipped through that icy shell she'd been encased in since they'd boarded this doomed airplane?

CHAPTER EIGHT

Why had he tattooed himself with a symbol of her? What kind of man does something that?

She'd shot him.

Didn't he hate her for that? She hated herself for what she'd done to him. What did this all mean?

And, damn it, why did he have to look so good?

He'd been fit and lean before. Now he was mouth-watering. Her fingers begged to trace each definition in his rock-hard body. Did the man even have body fat? How could he with all that delicious muscle?

Holy Mother of Pearl. She was toast.

Something had to be stirred up between them, or she would have him for dinner. She wriggled the soft flannel shirt over his shoulders and faced him to button it up. She concentrated hard on the task at hand, not how enticing he smelled, or how his breath lightly blew wisps of her hair. He was the perfect height for her. His chin easily rested on her head. She missed how he'd tuck her into his side, and she'd snuggle her face in the crook of his neck.

She finished the buttons and smoothed the fabric down his front without thinking. He sucked in his breath as her fingers brushed over the ridges of muscle on his stomach.

She shouldn't have done that.

"Wren," he groaned, his fingers brushing hair away from her face.

"Oh, you need your boots tied." She dropped to her knees and grabbed the laces before she did something really stupid and grab him. She thought he groaned again, but maybe it was the wind. She tied his Timberlines and glanced up.

She shouldn't have knelt at his feet.

Her face was even with his gaping zipper and what was pressing hard through the opening. She closed her eyes and bit her lips before she could lick them.

Or lick something else.

What was wrong with her? It was like she hadn't had sex...well she hadn't had sex in a really long time. But sex with Skip would really fuck things up. And they were really fucked up to begin with. Hell, they were fighting for their lives. Unbuttoning his jeans and freeing that thick bulge wouldn't help anyone.

"Yes, it would," Skip growled, reaching for her.

Oh, no, she didn't! Not again. She was such a mess. She couldn't control her thoughts or what came out of her mouth. This was worse than the out of control feeling the drugs had given her. At least they had numbed. She wasn't numb. She was a freaking live wire.

She scrambled back like a crab and jerked to her feet.

"Are you afraid of me?" Skip asked, his eyes ablaze with need. There was enough heat in his gaze to keep her burning all night.

"Right." She gulped.

"You don't want to be alone with me. Afraid of what I'll do or what you'll do?"

"You are way off base here, buddy." Hell, he was right on target.

"Am I?" He inched toward her. She inched back. He smiled. She panicked.

"Okay!" She threw up her hands as puny stop signs. "I need some space. I need to think."

"What's there to think about? I want you, and you still want me." His nostrils flared as though the realization impacted him deeply. Did he still care about her? How could he with all she'd done to him.

She was no good for him. He needed a woman who was stable, competent. Who didn't hurt people.

She shook her head. "No. I want dinner. Food." She'd used food as a substitute for sex the last five years and was damn good at it by now.

Though she had a feeling it wasn't going to work tonight.

CHAPTER NINE

"We're sleeping together," Skip said. "Get used to the idea. You're not going to be able to keep the beds apart."

They'd torn the cushions off the seats—well mostly Wren since she had the use of both of her hands—and made a bed of sorts on the ceiling of the plane. The ceiling was sloped so the cushions slid together. Skip was perfectly fine with that. It meant she'd slide into him too.

Wren glared at him, but he knew it was a façade. She wasn't angry, she was scared. He knew she wasn't scared of him. He wasn't the kind of man who would ever jump a woman. He'd never take advantage of her. Unless she asked him to. Didn't mean he was above talking her into being taken advantage of.

He hid the smile that split across his face with a cough. They'd worked hard in the limited light that was left. He'd hung a flashlight off the exposed metal of the cushion-less seats. He'd also done his best to block the wind, rain and sleet, from coming in. With the plane upside down, the windows were low to the ground. Snow was already covering them, insulating the plane more from the elements. They had enough food to feed a wedding party, and the little village of Egegik, so they'd be fine for quite a while. Plenty of time for the Coast Guard to find them. Snow could provide water if they ran out of the four cases he'd brought along. Heat was the main issue.

There was only one way he knew how to get warm without a fire.

Time to play the injured card. Besides, he had to get Wren to calm down.

"Wren, can we just sit? My arm aches like a sonofabitch. Are there any more pain pills? And I'd like some more of those candied almonds." They'd torn open a bag of wedding almonds Wren had found in the groceries he'd brought back for his sister's wedding. Wren hadn't wanted to eat them, but he'd talked her into it since his sister would be really upset if they died out here because they wouldn't eat the wedding food. The almonds had made a nice dessert after the deli meats and cheese in the cooler. He had a pretty good suspicion the wedding cake hadn't survived the crash. His sister was going to be furious about the cake once she was over hugging and crying that they were still alive.

Now if he could get Wren to stop fluttering around the damn plane. She was doing her best to stay as far away from him in the cramped space as she could.

She turned and grabbed the first aid kit from the cockpit where she'd put it earlier. She'd been making a home out of this wreck, finding places for things, making everything as comfortable for them as she could. He understood the need, but now that it was done, she needed to conserve her energy and rest next to him where they could share each other's heat.

"I'm sorry, Skip. I should have thought about your arm. Here." She shook out four pills and handed them to him, her arm fully extended so that she wouldn't touch him.

He enclosed his hand over hers. "I'm not going to jump you. Relax."

A blush flared in her cheeks. "Sorry."

"And quit saying you're sorry. You have nothing to be sorry about."

"I have everything to be sorry about." She tugged on her arm until he opened his hand. She dropped the pills into his palm and offered a water bottle.

He swallowed the pills to keep from venting his frustration. She needed to get over the past. She was a different person. More mature, less fractured. The strong woman he'd always known she could be. Why couldn't she see that?

"We need to shut off the light to save the batteries. So if there's anything you need to do or get before we head to bed, you'd better do it."

"Bathroom," she blurted out. "I need to use the bathroom."

Did she really, or was it another delay? Whether she did or didn't, it was something he needed to address.

"Okay, we'll go together."

"I'm not peeing with you."

"Have you looked out there?" He pointed to the snow plastered windows. "It's a blizzard. You'll get lost."

She rolled her eyes. "I grew up here too. I'm not some cheechako you have to teach the ropes to." She stopped, and her eyes widened. "Rope. I saw rope." She held up a finger in thought. "Give me a second." She sidled past him and climbed into the tail of the plane. "Shine the flashlight this direction."

He tilted the flashlight toward her and was rewarded as her sweet ass caught in the beam of light. He smothered a groan. He wanted that ass snuggled up to his—

"Hey, could you be helpful here or what?"

He jerked the flashlight beam off her becoming backside and shined it where it would actually help her. Geez, where was his head? Get it together man. She's going to think you only have sex on the brain. It was the truth, but he should pretend otherwise. Women didn't like to know the truth about men.

"Got it." She held up some frayed rope like it was a trophy.

"What are we going to do with that?" Tie each other up? Another pump of blood headed south.

"I'll tie one end around my waist, head out there—" she paused and shuddered "—tie the other end to the struts on the plane so I can find my way back in the snow."

He liked his idea better. But hers was more practical though less titillating. "Good idea." She beamed, and he suddenly wondered how many people, him included, had ever complimented her. Yeah, he'd always told her how beautiful she was but never how brilliant. But then she hadn't done a lot of smart things in her life. So many people had relished pointing that out to her. Her father especially.

"Let me go first," he said. He could at least break a trail.

"If you don't mind, I'm about to burst." She grabbed her coat and slid it on.

He reached up and untied the flashlight from where he'd hung it. "Take this."

He handed it to her but didn't let it go when she grabbed it. "Don't drop it."

"I won't."

She tied an end of the rope around her waist. When she was finished, she met his eyes. "I won't go far. Don't worry."

He buried his hand in her hair, and yanked her in for a fast and hard kiss. He'd meant to only kiss her quick, but she did that softening thing again, and he helplessly sunk into her mouth. She moaned into his mouth and slid her arms around his neck. He reached out to pull her closer and tweaked his broken arm. He hissed and released her, pain flared hot and cold, diminishing his desire.

"Be careful," he gritted out, not wanting her to know how much pain he was in.

"I will." She cocked her head. "You okay?"

"I'll be fine once you're back here. So hurry."

"See you in a few." Then she turned and climbed through the cockpit. Opening the door, wind and snow swirled in, and then she was gone, and he was alone in the cold, in the dark, and in pain. But the pain had transferred from the physical to the emotional. He wanted her back. Now. He wanted to follow her out there.

What if something happened? What if she tripped and hurt herself or lost the hold of the rope and couldn't find the plane in the blowing snow? She hadn't been able to see the plane when they had returned from depositing Jim.

Jim.

Holy shit. She was right. They should have tossed him over the bank. Right now, Wren could be fighting for her life against a bear. It was early yet for them to all be in bed. Just the other day, he'd spotted a sow and her cubs. Jim's scent could have brought one close. Bears sense of smell was eight hundred times that of humans. There were wolves running about too.

What the hell had he been thinking to let her go out there alone? She didn't even have a weapon with her to help protect herself. He grabbed his coat and struggled into the one arm. He couldn't get it to stay over his bad one. Frustrated, he tore the thing off and threw it on the bed of cushions.

She'd been gone too long. What if she hadn't tied the rope properly and the knot worked loose with the wind?

That was it. He was going out there.

Wren shuddered in the cold. There was nothing more bitterly cold than baring your ass in a blizzard. She'd finished her business and had her clothing back to rights when a large hulking creature stalked her way.

A chill that rivaled the storm shivered through her. Skip should have listened to her. Jim should've gone over the bluff. She dropped to her knees and inched to the left, where she remembered the plane being.

If the bear caught her scent, she'd lead him right to Skip.

She grabbed the rope and struggled to untie the knot from around her waist, but the bear lumbered closer. Shit. She needed to get free, run. But where? Then she heard her name. At least she thought it was her name. One thing she did know, bears didn't speak.

She squinted against the slicing snow and instead of seeing a bear, the outline formed into a man.

"Skip Kolenka Ozhuwan! You scared me to death. I thought you were a bear. What are you doing out here, and where is your coat? Are you insane?"

"Apparently." He shivered. "You were taking too long. I thought maybe you were in danger."

"It isn't like women can just whip it out and pee anywhere. It takes some finesse. Besides, I can take care of myself."

"I was worried."

"Have a little faith. It's not like I'm out here trying to score a line of coke."

"That thought never crossed my mind."

Suddenly she was ashamed of herself. He'd come looking for her because he'd been concerned, and she was jumping all over him. "I'm about froze to the bone. Can we continue this inside?" But when they returned to the closed confines of the plane, she realized there was no putting off going to bed with him.

CHAPTER TEN

"How many layers are you going to put on?" Skip asked.

As many as it takes. Wren struggled with a second pair of socks.

"I'm cold," she muttered, when in truth she was sweating. How was she going to sleep next to him?

They had unzipped Jim's sleeping bag they'd found in his survival kit and had it laying like a comforter over the cushions that would keep the cold from the ground seeping from the metal of the plane into them. It was actually quite cozy. Over the sleeping bag was a Mylar blanket they weren't going to need.

Wren couldn't find another reason to postpone going to bed. She lay next to him, their shoulders and hips touching due to the slope of the plane underneath them. Her nerve endings sizzled to life, laying the length of him. She tried to move, giving him space, but no matter what she did she ended up touching him.

"Are you going to squirm all night?"

She didn't bother answering him. She just might.

"I'm going to turn off the light."

"Okay." She hated that her voice sounded timid. She could do this.

"Wren, relax."

The light clicked out and darkness closed in.

Right. Like that was going to happen. She clutched the covers to her chin. With the darkness, her other senses picked up on the whistle and moan of the wind, the heavy splattering of the snow in its attempt to bury the plane from sight. Skip's long even breaths, and her choppy ones. How could he be so relaxed?

"We can't go to bed mad at each other," Skip said.

"We're not married." She wanted to retract the words as soon as she said them.

"And whose fault is that?"

"You arrested me."

"Get over it." He turned toward her and lifted up on his elbow. "You left me with no choice."

"I was entitled."

"Entitled didn't make it right."

"You knew what he'd done."

"I still couldn't let you take the law into your own hands."

"Nobody was punishing my dad, and he killed my mother."

"Wren—"

"No, you know it, and I know it. The whole village knew why she did what she did." Wren still saw her mom's lifeless body, having been the one to find her beaten and bruised and dead. "She took all those sleeping pills because she couldn't escape him any other way."

"It was still her choice. Your dad didn't feed them to her."

"He might as well have."

"It wasn't your call to make, Wren."

She knew he was right. He'd been right at the time to take the shovel away from her before she bashed in her father's head. As it was, he'd let her wail on her father's prized truck longer than he'd needed to, before restraining her. She'd been over all this in therapy.

So much therapy.

"Wren, I'm on your side here. If I could have arrested your father and thrown his ass in jail, I would have gladly done so. But you were the one who broke the law."

Yeah, and her old man had pressed charges, more concerned over his precious truck and who was going to pay for the damages than the suicide of his wife and meltdown of his daughter.

He was free of both of them now.

"So...what is he up to now?"

Skip didn't pretend to know what she was asking. "Same. Drinking, fishing, drinking more. At least, the women of the village steer clear of him. He's alone. Fitting punishment if you ask me. Life without you a part of it is hell."

Her heart thumped. Did he mean his life was hell because she wasn't in it?

"Yes, Wren, that's exactly what I mean."

Again. What was with her? It was like she didn't have control of herself. Speaking her mind like this without being aware of it was disconcerting to say the least.

Silence lengthened between them again. She understood it was up to her to make the next move.

Skip wasn't going to.

If she wanted to be with him, it was up to her to let him know. But did she want that? Who was she kidding? That's all she'd ever wanted. She'd always been too scared to reach for happiness. When she was a kid, anything she took a fancy to her father destroyed. Skip was the only person he hadn't driven off. Skip wasn't afraid.

She needed to stop being afraid.

"How's the arm?" she softly asked.

"Bearable."

"Bearable enough?"

He groaned. "Wren, don't tease me."

"You used to like it when I teased you."

He dragged in a heavy breath. "Don't toy with me." There was a pleading quality to his voice that had the knotted strings around her heart unraveling.

She turned on her side to see him better. "What do you want from me?"

His eyes glowed with intent in the snow-lit evening. "Everything."

She didn't want to hurt him. She'd already hurt him more than she expected forgiveness for. "Skip," she whispered.

That's all it took. He reached for her, cradling her head in his palm as his mouth captured hers. He groaned as she curled into him, fully aligning their bodies. They'd always fit together so well. Her breath caught, and she became dizzy from the intense rush of feeling and emotions unleashed.

"Wren, baby, why oh why did you put on so many layers?"

A giggle escaped her, and suddenly everything felt right. For the first time in years, things felt right. His hand snaked under her three shirts and found her skin. "You're so hot."

"Hot as is 'hot' or hot as in heat?"

"Hot. You've always been too hot to handle." His fingers flicked open her bra. "You had to sleep with this on too."

"I needed everything I could think of."

He pulled back. "Are you sure about this?"

She met his eyes, his searching. "Yes, Skip." To prove it to him, she sat up and lifted off the sweatshirt, followed by the long-sleeved t-shirt, and finally the undershirt.

An animalistic sound escaped him as she tossed off her bra.

His one good hand shook as he cupped her breast. "Such beauty." He lifted and took a nipple into his mouth, making her arch into him. It was her turn to express a wild noise. Little pulls contracted her nether regions as his mouth sucked her nipple, lightly at first then harder, flattening the nub to the roof of his mouth. A long drawn out moan followed. He released her and recaptured her mouth, as though he couldn't decide where he wanted to be most. His hand continued to tweak her nipples, one minute cupping her breast the other molding the mounds and intermittingly flicking his thumb over the sensitive tips and rolling them between his fingers.

"God, I need two hands. I need to touch more of you."

No, she needed to touch him.

"Touch away," Skip said. "I'm all yours, baby."

She didn't mind so much that her words had escaped her this time. With a smile, she undid the buttons of his shirt and inch-by-inch revealed those taut muscles she hadn't allowed herself to explore earlier.

"Skip, you are...magnificent."

"And here I thought you hadn't noticed."

"Oh, I noticed."

"I had to do something to work off my sexual frustrations while you were away."

Had he not indulged with other women?

"They weren't you."

Okay, she really needed to curb her tongue. She'd already revealed more than she was comfortable with.

He must have felt her unease for he kissed her again. Thoughts flew out of her head, leaving it empty of everything but him. She'd wanted this for so long. His arms around her, his body pressing into hers.

His fingers unbuttoned her pants, slid down the zipper, and found her. Heat infused her as his finger slipped along her folds, tested her readiness, before diving into her.

Holy Mother of Pearl, it wasn't going to take anything to make her come.

Just a few strokes of his fingers deep inside her, and a few flicks of his thumb against that ultrasensitive part of her, and she was soaring.

CHAPTER ELEVEN

Skip cursed his broken arm.

He needed inside her. Now. This one-handed situation sucked. He wanted to lift her, position her, hold her tight, as he pounded into her. It wasn't enough to have his fingers inside her.

He needed more.

Then she came apart, her nails digging into him, her pelvis grinding down on his hand.

Oh, shit.

He clamped down on his own excitement at watching her pleasure, or he was going to come in his pants. He hadn't felt like this since high school. He tensed, counted to ten, twenty, a hundred, recited the star spangled banner, while she floated back to him.

Her eyes opened and met his, and he caught his breath.

She still cared.

But could she still love him?

Then she was kicking off her pants, fully naked except her double layers of socks, and his heart stopped at the goddess picture she made. Soft and curvy, so much more mature than the last time he'd been naked with her. The drugs had kept her skinny with bones protruding from her ribs and hips. How he wanted to explore this new body of lushness. His mouth watered and he reached for her, and she was there, her hands tearing at his jeans. She grabbed his erection. He hollered with pleasure so intense it pained him to stop her.

"Wren, I won't last." Then her mouth was over him, her tongue sliding down his rigid length, swallowing him, sucking, he grabbed her head, burying his hand in her hair, twisting, trying to pull her off him before he...

Oh, God.

He hollered her name, his hips thrusting into her mouth as she took him, all of him. The night bloomed with iridescence as he exploded.

He lay there, stunned with his inability to control his own body. He'd never lost himself like that. He'd wanted to be inside her.

"Technically, you were," she said her voice husky and pleased.

Had he voiced that?

"Yep. Guess I'm not the only one who has a problem with that."

He chuckled. This is a new development. What other new things did he get to experience with her?

She slowly crawled up his body, her tongue licking his abs.

His penis twitched, hardened with a new rush of blood. Hallelujah. One good thing about abstinence, he was good to go again. He groaned as her mouth traveled up his ribs, took his nipple into her mouth and teased. She was so expressive, wild yet with a balance of calm he hadn't seen in her before. She was the same but more. So much more he wanted to explore.

"How's the arm?" she asked, her teeth closing over the vein in his neck.

"What arm?"

She gave a husky laugh that had him twitching again, reaching for her. She slid over him, parted her thighs, and hovered. Her eyes met his and stayed focused on him in the bluish light of the storm as she slowly, ever so slowly, took him inside the glorious heat of her delectable body.

He gave a long drawn out groan as she took him as deeply as her body would allow. Her eyes shuddered closed as she rose above him and leisurely began to ride him.

He watched in awe at the magnificence of her. Her long black hair trailed down her back, falling forward over her shoulders, over her breasts, to graze his stomach. Such glorious globes of perfection bounced as her hips picked up speed. His hand clutched her hip, and how he wished he could grab both, somehow take control of her movements, but she was in control.

She took him, rode him, devastated him. Her hips gyrated faster, her breathing choppy, as long drawn out cry filled the plane in perfect harmony with the roar of the wind. She was one with Mother Nature. Bringing the forcefulness and beauty of the storm raging outside, inside to consume him. He was all hers to do with as she wanted. He shouted as he gave himself over to her, embraced the rightness of belonging to her, becoming one with her. Her scream of completeness followed, and then she folded in on him, collapsing over him like liquid heat. His broken arm was bumped.

He felt no pain as pleasure wrapped him up in her blissful blanket.

CHAPTER TWELVE

Wren lay in the afterglow, more content than she could remember. This was right. Skip was her past and her future. Even the storm outside seemed to have calmed as though in agreement. She'd only been living half a life without him. This feeling coursing through her body was higher than any drug had given her.

"You okay?" Skip asked.

She laughed. "I should be asking you that."

"Baby, I'm feeling no pain. You were freaking amazing."

She smiled. She'd felt damn invincible.

Now she had to decide if she could trust herself enough to admit her love for Skip. She had disappointed so many people in her life. Especially him. She didn't want to anymore.

"You won't," Skip said, brushing back her hair.

Geez. Whatever this thinking out loud thing was, it was damn annoying.

"Wren. I want a life with you. Have a family."

"A family?" Kids? Her? That meant she'd be a mother. A child totally dependent on her for everything. No, she couldn't do that.

His hand settled on her stomach. "We might have already created a little Ozhuwan."

They hadn't used protection.

"Are you on anything?" he asked.

"No drugs," she choked out.

"I meant birth control."

"Oh. No." She swallowed, but it didn't remove the lump that had formed in her throat. "Skip. I'm not mother material. Besides, I shot you. How can I be the mother of your children?"

"If I can forgive you for shooting me, you can forgive yourself for shooting me."

"It isn't that simple."

"It doesn't need to be that difficult. I've always loved you, Wren. Even at your worst, I've loved you."

"Skip, I'm poison. Everything I've touched I've ruined."

"That was then. You've changed. You're sober."

"For how long? I'll always be an addict, and you are a trooper. Do you know the statistics for relapse? I have a seventy percent chance of using again."

"And a thirty percent chance of not, which gets smaller and smaller every year you stay sober."

"I move back to Egegik, and it will be a hundred percent. There's a reason I haven't been home."

"He can't hurt you anymore. You're stronger, he's weaker. I won't let him near you."

"You can't protect me 24/7."

"We don't have to live in Egegik."

She scoffed. "Right, your entire family is there. Generations of Ozuwans have lived in Egegik."

"A lot have left too." He reached for her hand. "It isn't the same without you. Nothing is. I've waited a long time, Wren. If I need to wait longer, I will."

Tears choked her throat, and she buried her face in the crook of his neck. "I'm not good enough for you."

"Nobody's good enough for me. I'm quite the catch. Besides, I want someone who will challenge me, and nobody challenges me like you do."

"But—"

"No buts. Work with me. Tell me what you are really afraid of. Or have you been lying to me about the contractor dude." He stiffened. "Are you in love with him?"

She gave a short laugh. "There is no contractor dude. Well, there is. But I hired him. He built me some bookcases, and now he's working little by little on my kitchen."

"There isn't anything romantic going on?"

"Nope."

"You haven't slept with him?"

She leaned up on her elbow and looked at him, her eyes serious as the snow now softly falling outside the windows. "Skip, the only man I've ever slept with is you. There was this 'almost' incident in jail where this woman wanted—"

She didn't finish as he reached up and pulled her down to him, sealing her words with a kiss that lit her internal furnace.

When he ended the kiss, he gazed lovingly into her eyes. "There's been no one for me either. Only you."

"You mean..."

"Yep," he said with a silly smile. "The last person I had sex with—not counting myself—was you."

"You haven't had sex in five years?"

"You couldn't tell how rusty I was?"

She shook her head. "Though it does explain the constant hard on," she tried to joke.

"Wren, you were my first, my only. You're everything. Marry me, love me, make a life with me."

Her heart melted, and tears sprain to her eyes. "Skip." Her words shuddered on a sob as the impact of his words sank into her. How could this man love her so much?

"Say yes. It's such a short, simple, happy little word."

She took his face in her hands and gently kissed his lips. "Yes."

"Oh, thank you God." He kissed her, relief and love mixed in with a desire that would never be sated. "Now, give me three little words that I've waited years to hear from your lips again."

"I love you, Skip Ozhuwan. Only you, always you."

They woke the next morning to the sun shining, snow melting, and the whoop, whoop of helicopter blades.

Skip groaned. "Sounds like the Coast Guard found us."

"Do they have to be so damn reliable?" Wren asked with a sexy stretch. "I had plans for this morning."

She leaned over and kissed him. He loved the feel of her pressed against him and the rightness of the moment. The promise of a new day, a new life, with the woman he'd always loved.

He moaned around her kiss, loath to break it off, but they needed to get moving. "Save that thought for later. We need to hurry and get dressed. Not only are they reliable, they're damn fast too."

Sure enough, they heard a man running up to the plane, his boots crunching in the snow.

Wren reached for her sweatshirt, but not before the man opened the door and was halfway inside the cockpit. With a squeak, she grabbed the covers and pulled them up to her chin, uncovering Skip's nakedness.

"Morning!" The Coast Guard crewman greeted. "Glad to see you two made it through the night." He nodded to Skip and tried unsuccessfully to hide a smile. "Officer Ozhuwan, I see you're conducting the correct deferment method of hypothermia." He addressed Wren, "Ms. Wren, nice to see you, and that the two of you are back together again."

"Leroy," Skip said, worried over how Wren was taking all this attention, "give us a few minutes, would you?"

"Yes, sir." Leroy ducked out of the plane.

"Don't tell me, that's—"

"The kid you used to babysit, yeah."

Leroy popped his head back into the plane, his eyes shut. "Sorry, just thought I'd mention your sister and her intended are impatiently waiting in the chopper. She is really, and I mean *really*, worried about the condition of her wedding cake."

"Leroy, you might as well leave us here. It'll be safer for everybody."

Wren giggled, then laughed long and loud, falling into his one-armed embrace, where she'd always belonged.

The realization that he could be waking every morning with her in his arms, had emotion bursting forth. "Wren, before our lives become hectic with this rescue, the wedding, and Jim's funeral, I need you to know that no other woman could impact my soul the way you always have, always will. I don't want to lose you again." He didn't think he'd survive a second time.

The love in her eyes deepened, and she reached up to smooth the worry lines in his face. "You won't lose me. I've missed you so much, Skip. You're not just the love of my life, you are my best friend. Don't worry, I'm strong enough now."

Moisture collected in his eyes and throat. He hadn't realized how afraid he'd been that he'd truly lost her five year ago. Or that after last night and the light of this morning, the reality of a future with him would be too much for her. He shouldn't have doubted his resilient, little wren. "I love you with everything that is in me and as soon as we get through this week, I don't want to wait another day to marry you."

"Do we have to wait until then?" She gave him a crafty smile. "I'm sure your sister has a perfectly good priest we could maybe borrow after her ceremony. Want to elope with me?"

Bet your ass, he did.

THE END

MOOSED-UP

CHAPTER ONE

She was out of her ever-loving mind. Eva Stuart trekked over the forest carpet of lowbush cranberries, wild mushrooms, and who knew what else. Yes, it was beautiful, stunning really, but Chatanika, Alaska? They had said remote. They hadn't said end of the world, or in this case, top of the world. She didn't even know what time of day it was. Just that she was lost. What had she been thinking, taking a walk about town, when there really was no town? It was a freaking village. And she was the only medical personnel here. She thought she'd be working in a medical clinic with a staff of doctors and nurses.

Nope. Nurse Practitioner was all they could afford. She was it. If there was an emergency, and she couldn't save a patient in time, they were out of luck. She'd wanted something completely removed from Cincinnati, but taking a position like this without really thinking it through because her rat-bastard ex-fiancé was banging her best friend was the definition of extreme. Or stupidity. Davis and Jeremy were probably enjoying a fine meal in her favorite Italian restaurant, drinking an expensive bottle of wine, while she was lost in the woods slapping bird-size mosquitoes.

Yeah, she sure showed them.

What did it say about her that she was still more upset with her best friend Jeremy betraying her with Davis, rather than the fact that Davis was obviously gay too? She missed Jeremy. She could always talk to him, go shopping. He *got* her. He was the best girlfriend she'd ever had. And now he was shacked up with her former boyfriend planning to adopt a baby and start the family she'd always wanted.

Rustling in the brush behind her caused her to freeze.

What was that?

She swiveled at the sound of branches breaking behind her and came face to face with a bull moose.

Shiiit.

"Nice Moosey."

His nostrils flared, and his ears twitched. What had the travel brochure said? Moose weren't cute Disney characters. They weren't dumb, and they weren't nice, and they probably didn't like being called "Moosey" either.

The moose lowered his massive head and glared at her from under the shadow of his impressive antlers. Eva inched back, her heart in her throat.

He charged.

She screamed, and ran for her life, twisting through paper birch and sick-looking spruce trees.

Lynx Maiski whipped off his shirt and wiped his face and the back of his neck with it. He picked up the ax and continued to chop firewood. It was a gorgeous, hot summer day. Well, night actually, as it was headed toward ten o'clock, but you wouldn't know it by the sun. He loved it up here in the north.

Plenty to do, plenty of food, and plenty of peace.

"*Heeeelp!*"

He turned toward the scream and caught a glimpse of Eva, the little sprite of a nurse new to town. He wondered how long she'd last. Hopefully a while, since she was the hottest piece of ass he'd seen in a long time.

What was she doing running hell bent for high water like that? Then he heard the thrashing in the brush right before a bull moose appeared.

Oh, boy.

Lynx sunk the ax in the log and took off after the pair. He hollered and waved his arms, making himself appear bigger than he was, in the hopes of scaring off the wild animal. The moose slowed his gait as the trees thickened.

Smart girl, heading into smaller places where your predator couldn't follow. Much like a bird, Eva flew up a black spruce tree.

Ah, now that's not going to work.

The moose, not afraid of Lynx, stopped at the base of the tree. Eva yelped and climbed higher, spindly branches breaking beneath her.

"Don't move," Lynx warned. She was going to break her cute little neck.

"Shoot it!" she yelled.

"It's not moose season."

"I don't give a shit. Shoot it!"

The moose turned his head and seemed to share a look with Lynx over the new cheechako in town.

"Come on, BW, git!" He slapped his hands together, spooking the moose into charging off into the forest. The dang thing was up to no good. Not the way to welcome a pretty girl to town.

"Do you know that moose?" she squeaked.

Crap, he had to watch that, especially with a cheechako. She wouldn't understand.

"You called it BW," she persisted like a badger.

"I think you're hearing things." The branch she held onto started to creak and give way. "Don't move. You can't climb trees like...that."

She tumbled down through the boughs. He tried to catch her but wasn't fast enough, and she dropped to the pine-needled forest floor.

He hurried and knelt by her side, his fingers spread wide over her, afraid to touch in case she was hurt bad. Her big blueberry eyes were wide open, and she didn't seem to be breathing.

"You okay?" *Please be okay.* He'd planned to make a move once he got up the courage.

She sucked in a deep breath and glared at him. "You suck at this hero shit."

"I wasn't ready. Besides, anyone should know with one gander at these trees that they aren't up to holding your weight."

"Are you calling me fat?" Her eyes narrowed.

"Whoa." He had three sisters and knew enough to tread carefully here. "If anything, you need to pack on a few pounds. Winter's coming, and you need a layer of fat to survive it." Or someone hot like me in your bed keeping you warm, he thought. Damn if she didn't look adorable with her feathers all out of whack. He wanted to smooth her down. Maybe he should help her up off the ground first? "Here, let me give you a hand." He reached for her, and she slapped his hands away.

"I don't need any help." She struggled to her feet, took one step and faltered. Luckily he was right there to wrap an arm around her. She sure was a little-bitty thing. Fairy-like really.

"Take it easy. That was a big fright you just suffered. Moose can be meaner than a stirred up porcupine."

She once again slapped his hands back. "I can handle a *fright*. I think I cut my leg when you *didn't* catch me."

He let the 'didn't catch me' accusation slide. "Let me see." He turned her around like she was no more than a doll. Blood saturated her pant leg in the back of her upper thigh.

"Well, guess I get to play hero after all." Lynx swung her up into his arms, against his bare chest, before she could utter an objection. The woman weighed no more than one of his nephew's sled dogs. He probably shouldn't mention that. Her being city folk and all, chances were she wouldn't take nicely to being compared to a dog.

"Where are you taking me?"

"My house. It's not far."

She tightened her lips. Very nice lips. He'd noticed them before, but he hadn't been this close. Now he wanted to get closer. A whole lot closer.

"Quit looking at me that way and watch where you're walking. I don't need to fall again. My backside is already going to be black and blue."

He could rub something on her skin to help with the bruising.

"Don't even say it."

He had a feeling if he said anything right now it would be wrong. His mother would classify Eva as one of those high-maintenance types. But that was okay. He was as patient as the days were currently long.

Lynx walked out of the trees and into his backyard, up the stairs to his deck and into the log cabin he'd built himself.

"You live here?" Eva asked when he positioned her next to the kitchen bar so she'd have something to help hold her up. "I was this close to civilization? I thought I was lost."

"Technically, if you don't know your surroundings it doesn't matter how close to town you are, the minute you step into the trees you're lost." He regarded her pixie-blond haircut, bird-like bones, and shortness of stature. "You shouldn't go anywhere into the forest without someone with you." An eagle could pick her off and feed her to its young.

Something must have shown in his expression. "I'm not a child."

He buttoned up his lips and didn't point out her attempt to outrun a fifteen-hundred pound moose and her non-existent tree climbing skills. Instead, he looked at the tear in her jeans. "That's a pretty bad cut."

She twisted to get a better look, but the area was high on her left leg right under that sweet little ass of hers. "Damn it, I can't see."

"Quit twisting like that. People aren't meant to bend that way." If she was that flexible—

He'd been too long without a woman.

"I need to get these jeans off in order to assess the situation," she said.

If she took those jeans off, they'd have a situation all right.

"Are you just going to stand there?" she asked, glaring up at him. "Or help me?"

"Uh...we should get you to the clinic."

"I am the clinic."

Well, she had him there.

"You'll have to help fix me up." She glanced around his kitchen. "I need a first aid kit, scissors, rubbing alcohol, clean towels, and a mirror." She reached for the button on her jeans and freed it.

His mouth dropped open as she began a slow striptease out of her jeans, being careful as she peeled the material from the wound.

"Get a move on," she scolded. "I don't want to bleed all over your kitchen."

Her tone, more than her words, snapped him out of his salacious, sexual fantasy.

"Right." He turned and exited the room, mentally slapping himself. Get a grip. She's hurt, not looking for a hook-up.

He returned to find her without her pants in the cutest, littlest pink panties he could remember seeing. He swallowed hard as the blood in his brain flowed south.

"There you are." She gestured toward the heavy toolbox he'd set on the counter. "This is a first aid kit?"

He unclipped the latches and opened it up. "Yep, everything you could possibly need is in here." He didn't know how he spoke seeing all that creamy skin on display in his kitchen. All he needed to do was lift her up on that counter, and she'd be the perfect height for him to—

"What do you use this for?" She held up a tranquillizer dart.

"In case I need to put you down." She didn't laugh at his joke. The wrinkling of her forehead increased. "I'm the law enforcement officer for the Refuge," he explained further before she thought he was a loon.

"Huh." She looked him up and down with what he hoped was renewed interest, her eyes taking their time traveling over his exposed chest. Guess, he should put a shirt on, but he might as well enjoy her examination. Packing on these muscles hadn't come easy, and they didn't come from a gym.

"Where's the mirror?" she asked, tearing her gaze away and studying the items he unpacked from the first aid kit.

"Don't have one."

"What do you mean you don't have one? Everyone has a mirror."

He shrugged. He was a guy. What did she want from him? "There's just the one over the sink in the bathroom."

She twisted, and her soft cotton blouse rose up to reveal a flat stomach. "How am I going to sew myself up?" she muttered to herself.

He walked around to look at her backside. "Yep, that's going to need stitches."

"I know that. Geez. I could tell by the amount of blood loss."

"Are you feeling faint?"

"I'm a nurse practitioner. I don't *faint* at the sight of blood."

"I meant from the *loss* of blood."

She gritted her teeth together. "Listen. I need a mirror so I can sew this closed."

"I can sew you closed."

"Seriously?" Her tone said differently.

"Done it many times. What? You think since I live in a small village in Alaska that I don't know how to do stuff?" He met her eyes. *She did.* His ego hit the floor. "Hell, woman. I live in Alaska. Have all my life. I can stitch on a button, sew up a cut, set a broken bone and cook my own dinner. Self-sufficient. Heard of it before?" Besides, not only was he a Fish and Wildlife Officer, he was a certified veterinarian. The injured had been coming to him before she'd arrived, four-legged and two-legged alike.

"Sorry, I didn't mean to insult you."

"Right." He huffed. "We haven't had anyone manning that little clinic for years. How do you think we survived?" He answered for her. "We did for ourselves and each other. You want to fit in, you'd better adjust your attitude."

"I said I was sorry," she muttered.

Yeah, she was sexy as hell, but her attitude was downright ugly.

"Bend over," he said.

"Excuse me?" Her big blueberry eyes got even bigger.

"So I can clean and sew this up. You're bleeding all over my kitchen, and I just mopped my floor. Yeah, I know how to use a mop too."

She slowly leaned over the counter, bracing herself on her elbows, showing her ass off to its advantage. Since she'd gotten him so hot under the collar, he was able to see the wound objectively. Somewhat. She smelled good too. Like some hot house flower. Tropical with hints of heat. Heat that had his blood quickening a trail back down south. He did a better job of controlling his physical responses to her when she was running her mouth.

"So what brought you here?" he asked.

He thought he heard her mutter "stupidity" before she asked, "Could you keep me abreast of what you are doing as you do it? I don't like surprises."

Good thing she didn't have eyes in the back of her head, or she'd be surprised by the hard-on he sported. He'd never sewn someone up with a woody before. This might be interesting.

He surveyed the injury. Luckily, her jeans had kept most of the bark and debris from the wound. It was more of a deep puncture than a long cut. Might take just a few stitches. It looked worse than it was.

"Hey," she said, startling him. "What's your name?"

"Lynx Maiski. Hand me the alcohol."

She passed him the bottle, her butt cheeks clenching as she readied herself for the sting. He wiped the area and quickly blew on it to help lessen the bite. Goose bumps erupted on her skin, and her voice had a breathy quality to it when she spoke again. "As in Raven and Fox Maiski?"

"My sister and nephew."

"Then you're also related to Chickadee, Tern, Pike, Fiona, and Coho?"

"Yep, sisters, uncle, mother and grandmother."

"Pretty much most of the town."

"A good portion of it."

"So why haven't I met you before?"

"Didn't need any medical attention, I guess. But I've seen you around." He sterilized the needle and thread, and knelt behind her for better access. "Ready? This is going to pinch."

Those adorable butt cheeks of hers clenched again, and he had a moment of light-headedness.

She didn't make a sound as he stitched the neatest, smallest, damn stitches he could. It hurt him to know that she'd have a scar on her perfect milky skin, and he wanted to minimize the blemish as best as he could. Four little sutures later, his brow sweating, Lynx clipped the thread and stood.

"There. Take a few Tylenol as needed for pain and see me in six to seven days for removal."

She turned to face him. "Very funny. How would you like your bill paid?"

The answer was on the tip of his tongue as he was lost in those eyes of hers, but luckily he bit it back in time.

"Sorry for being such a bitch earlier." Was her voice huskier? "As you've probably guessed, I haven't quite assimilated to the area."

He could help her assimilate.

She stood half naked with the counter behind her and him in front. If he placed his hands on the counter, she'd be caged within his arms.

CHAPTER TWO

Eva dragged in a steadying breath hoping it would slow down the galloping of her heart. Nope. Didn't even come close to calming her down. How did this backwoods bear of a man raise her blood pressure? Her eyes dipped to his naked chest. Hills and valleys of muscle had her eyes traveling lower and lower until she had to jerk her head up to break contact with all that hard, smooth, sun-baked skin.

She was fascinated by the human body. One of the many reasons she'd gone into medicine, but Lynx's body far impressed her over any other specimen that she'd yet to see. Maybe it was the Native Alaskan she could clearly see in him. He was bigger, features sharper, darker, more dangerous than other men she'd been around.

Why hadn't he put on a shirt? Was he messing with her? Did he know how long it had been since she'd had sex?

Hell, she didn't even know, just knew it had been a really, really long time. And good sex hadn't happened in an even longer time. Knowing that Davis was gay explained a lot about their failings—his failings—in the bedroom.

She bet Lynx could satisfy her in the bedroom.

She licked her lips.

Did he just groan?

His eyes were focused on her mouth, so she licked her lips again. There was no mistaking the mix of growl and groan this time.

81

Usually her surly attitude did a good job of keeping the male species at bay. She still hated men for the two who had broken her heart. Maybe she should do something about changing that?

Her eyes connected with his and without thinking it through, she stretched up on her tippy toes and grabbed his face between her hands and kissed him.

For a second, he stood frozen as her lips pressed against his, and then he growled, taking over the kiss and devouring her. His big beefy arms banded around her and lifted her off her toes. Her world tipped.

Oh, baby.

This was a bad idea. One of those really *bad* ideas that felt so *good.* Her hands dived into his thick, inky-black hair. Her legs naturally came up around his hips and cradled the impressive—somewhat worrisome—engorged member. Now it was her turn to groan. Her heart thundered in her ears, lights twinkled behind her closed lids. Oh yes! With him between her legs she wasn't going to need a bedroom romp to satisfy her. She was going to come right here.

"Uncle Lynx?"

Lynx went rigid in her arms.

Eva tightened her hold on him as he tried unlocking her legs from around his waist. "No, not yet."

"Eva," he murmured, his voice peppered with pain. "My nephew."

"What?" *Nephew?* She didn't care about anything except the sensations slipping away from her at an alarming rate.

Lynx carefully pried her off him and set her on her bare feet. She stood in the shadow of Lynx's big body, his breathing ragged.

"Uncle Lynx what are you doing to Ms. Stuart?" Fox Maiski stood off to the side behind Lynx in the doorway of the cabin, a Siberian Husky pup in his arms.

"Uh...examining her?" Lynx clamped his eyes shut and whispered under his breath, "Shit, the kid is never going to fall for that."

"Why?" Fox asked. "Is she hurt? She doesn't look hurt."

Oh, she was hurting all right.

Eva took a long deep breath and held it in until spots started to show and then let it out in a rush. She needed to get dressed. By her estimate, Fox was like nine or ten. She was showing way too much skin for a boy of that age. Hell, any boy. Including the big boy in front of her. What was she thinking? Sure, nudity had never been a problem for her. She was a nurse practitioner and saw nude bodies all the time. But maybe not nude as in sexually aroused nude. Geez. She was going to hell.

"Fox, why don't you hang back a minute? Ms. Stuart and I need to finish—

Boy, did they ever.

—bandaging her stitches."

"'Kay." There seemed to be a smile in his tone though his face was stoic. "I'll be outside on the deck."

After Fox exited, Eva leaned in, catching a whiff of forest and man that curled her toes. "Isn't it like after ten o'clock? Why is he running around this late?" She dragged a shaky hand through her mussed up hair.

"We're Alaskans. The sun is up. We'll sleep come winter."

"Where's his mother? It's not safe for him to be out wandering alone. Look what happened to me."

Lynx tried to bite back a smile. "Fox is wilderness savvy. It's almost uncanny. Like the animals watch out for him."

Right. She needed to get dressed and out of here. She grabbed her pants and hitched them up her legs.

"Wait. Let me put a bandage over your stitches."

She held her breath as she stood there trying not to rub up against Lynx like the cat he was named for as he reached over her to grab the gauze and tape on the counter. He had her caged between his big body and the counter. And surprise, surprise, she didn't mind.

What was wrong with her? Seriously, women went without sex for longer than she had. They didn't go around acting like they were in heat.

He cut tape and handed her the strips. "Here, hold onto this. Now turn around."

Her heart leaped with a thrill of excitement with the way he looked at her and spoke in that sexy growl. She normally didn't like to do anyone's bidding, but found herself turning and bending over, and wishing that his nephew wasn't just outside, waiting.

Lynx carefully laid the gauze over her stitches. Would he kiss it and make it feel better? The hair rose on the back of her neck. She swallowed, her breathing coming in short little gasps.

"Tape," Lynx instructed.

She held out the tape for him and closed her eyes as he smoothed the adhesive over the edge of the gauze pad onto her skin. Goose bumps erupted on her over-sensitized flesh.

She needed a cold shower in the worst way.

"Tape."

How in the world could bandaging someone be such a turn on?

"There." His heated palm cupped the gauze pad just below her butt cheek. "How does that feel?"

Get real. Like she was going to tell him that if he would just breathe on the back of her neck she'd rocket off into the midnight sun.

"Fine," she squeaked.

He chuckled, leaned over, and whispered in her ear, "If my nephew hadn't shown up, you'd be feeling more than fine."

Oh, God.

"Are you free tomorrow?"

She had a feeling she'd be free any time this man wanted to see her. Oh shit, she wasn't that easy was she?

"Yes."

"Want to have dinner?"

Was that have dinner or have him for dinner? Either way she was fine with it. Okay, she needed to create some distance, because she wasn't thinking clearly. Hell, she wasn't thinking at all. She didn't even know who this man was an hour ago. Did she want to get to know him or just have sex with him?

She was so messed-up.

She bent and grabbed her jeans and hiked them onto her hips, making him wait for her answer. "Where would we have dinner?"

He took a step back when her elbow connected with his abs as she buttoned her jeans. "I'd like to suggest here, but maybe the lodge would be a better idea?"

The Chatanika Lodge was a combination hotel, restaurant, and general store for the little town. Everyone hung out there, including most of his family, since they owned it.

"Or we could drive into Fairbanks?" he suggested when she didn't say anything.

Fairbanks was thirty miles away, but it took an hour to drive the windy, frost-heaved road. She'd be stuck in a car with him, and what if they didn't have anything to say to each other? What if this...chemistry was just her over-stimulated hormones or something?

"The lodge will be fine." She took a couple of more steps away from him toward the door leading out onto the deck.

"Six o'clock?"

"Sure. I'll meet you there." Now that she wasn't standing so close to him, the reality of what could have happened between them flushed through her system in a fiery blush. "Thanks for, uhmm, everything."

"You're welcome. See you tomorrow night."

Her heart flipped in her chest at his sexy half smile.

"Right. Tomorrow." One last look at all that muscled skin on display and she let herself out of his cabin and into the bright sunlight, softly shutting the screen door behind her. She squinted, trying to focus. Fox sat in a lounge chair, the black bandit-painted puppy asleep on his lap. What did you say to a kid who had caught you in a compromising position? "Hey."

"Hey, Ms. Stuart."

"Call me Eva." He'd seen her in her underwear with her tongue in his uncle's mouth. He could call her Eva.

He smiled, his dark eyes all-a-twinkle. "Okay, Eva."

"What's your dog's name?" There, that was a good safe subject.

"Kiski. She's the runt of the litter and finally strong enough for her vaccinations." At her frown, Fox continued. "Uncle Lynx is going to give them to her."

Uncle Lynx opened the screen door, and stepped out, having put on a snug-fitting t-shirt in dusty blue. "Okay, I'm ready for my next patient." He bent down and rubbed Kiski's ears. She perked up and licked his hand.

"Eva? Why'd you need stitches?" Fox asked with the tilt of his head, looking a lot like the adorable puppy in his lap.

"She's been moosed-up," Lynx said before she could offer anything.

Fox nodded as though he actually understood the term and that it was a common occurrence.

Lynx took pity on her. "Moosed-up is when you've been messed-up by a moose. It's just faster and easier to say moosed-up."

"Oh. Well. I'll let you tend to your patient then." She followed the steps down from the deck and went to turn left, the way she'd come.

"Eva." Lynx leaned over the railing, his elbows taking his weight, making his shoulders seem even wider than they were. "Head right about three hundred yards and you'll come to a road. You'll find your way home safe enough in that direction." He gave her a knowing smile and then disappeared inside the cabin with Fox.

She traipsed off in the direction he indicated, exiting the forest onto the road that led to the clinic and her small apartment attached to it.

Well, shit. Lynx Maiski was her next door neighbor.

CHAPTER THREE

She shouldn't be here.

Eva traced the lines of filigree on her silverware. Why had she agreed to have dinner with Lynx? And here, where his family and friends could all keep tabs on their date? Pike, Lynx's uncle, kept looking at her through the cutout behind the bar where the kitchen must be. He was another good looking man for his age. Tall, thick salt-and-peppered hair, with dark eyes that didn't miss much. They sure did grow them big and muscled up here in the Arctic. Lynx would probably look a lot like his uncle when he got older.

Not something she needed to be thinking about. Davis was a handsome man, but more metro-sexual than mountain man. He'd dressed impeccably in suits and designer menswear, which should have given her a clue. He could color-coordinate better than any woman she knew.

She picked up her water glass and sipped. It was now half empty. She glanced at her watch again.

Lynx was late.

How long should she wait for him? Why was she even waiting for him? Because they'd shared spit, and she didn't want to be one of those easy women. Meeting him tonight did not guarantee that they would be returning to his place or hers to have sex. No matter what last night's impression had given him.

Tonight was about getting to know each other and then hopefully moving onto sex. Soon. She wanted him bad. Had thought of nothing else but being in those arms again and having him between her legs.

"Would you like to order an appetizer while you wait?" the young waitress asked.

Eva hadn't caught her name. She looked for a tag, but there wasn't one. She wore a simple white t-shirt and comfortable jeans, with a short apron tied around her waist.

She needed more liquid courage than food right now. "How about a drink. What can you suggest?"

The waitress cocked her head, pointed with her pencil to the empty seat next to Eva." You waitin' on Lynx?"

"Yes. How'd you know?"

"Word gets around."

Had word spread about her legs clamped around Lynx too? She felt a blush start at the base of her neck. "Well, then, how about something with a kick?"

She tucked her pencil into her amber ponytail. "I got just the thing. Be right back."

Eva watched her hips tick back and forth like the second hand of a clock. She took in the group of diners enjoying their evening meal. She'd purposely showed early and taken a seat in the back corner so that she could watch Lynx arrive. The big windows gave her a view of the parking lot. Now she felt trapped as all eyes routinely flicked her direction. Everyone in this damn village knew she was Lynx's date.

Were they the Saturday night entertainment for the little town?

The waitress returned and set a drink in front of her. "We call it the Ugly Moose. Basically, it's a bold and spicy Bloody Mary made Alaskan style. The celery stalks, bleu cheese stuffed olives, and slices of venison sausage are supposed to look like an ugly moose. It will also give you something to snack on until Lynx gets his butt here."

Eva took a sip around the stalks of celery. "Wow, does that have a kick." It tasted yummy too. She took another sip.

"So what's your name, and is Lynx often late to dates?" Now why did she go and ask that?

"Name's, Bree. One thing you need to know about Lynx is that he's easily distracted. Not that he has ADD or somethin', well maybe just a touch." Bree shrugged her shoulders. "He'll have a good reason for being late, or at least an interesting one." Bree smiled and patted Eva's shoulder. "Let me know when you're ready for somethin' else."

Eva fished out one of the olives that represented an eye of the Ugly Moose and ate it. Interesting name for a drink. She systemically ate all the pieces of the moose and then drained the glass. Yeah, she was a fan. She glanced at her watch again. Lynx was now forty-five minutes late. She'd never been stood-up before, but forty-five minutes had to be in the stood-up range.

To hell with Lynx. And sex.

She ordered another drink and then ordered dinner. She'd have Ugly Mooses—Meeses?—and good food. Both were great replacements for sex.

Sort of.

She ordered a triple berry pie for dessert.

Damn poachers.

Lynx had been called out on a report of poachers. He'd been after this bunch for a couple of weeks with no leads. A Dall sheep had been shot and its head taken, leaving the rest of the meat to waste. Burned him up something awful. He'd been able to snap some pictures of the crime right before a mama bear and her two cubs cornered him.

Now he was stuck up here on the bluff overlooking the scene, waiting out mama and her babies as they feasted on the meat. Well, mama bear feasted, while the rambunctious cubs had their fill and were now tearing apart his four-wheeler.

Not the tires.

Damn little heathens. They were cute as heck as they mauled his four-wheeler, shredding the leather seat, pulling and chewing on wires, and puncturing his tires with their wicked sharp claws and teeth. Lynx snapped some pictures of the destructive tykes for his insurance company.

Well, he wasn't getting back to town with that thing, and he wasn't about to take on the hungry mother. Some things weren't worth fighting nature for.

Hiking out looked like his only option. He checked his GPS. Roughly eleven miles. Great. His cell phone was no use. He had only his GPS spot locater to push that he was OK or not. If he indicated he wasn't OK, the troopers in Fairbanks would be notified. He'd have Search and Rescue out looking for his sorry ass. As a law enforcement officer for the Yukon Flats National Wildlife Refuge he'd never live it down that bear cubs got the best of him. It was his own fault, his mind occupied with thoughts of Eva and what tonight might bring, rather than his surroundings. He knew better.

Now he'd be late for their dinner date. He looked at the time again. Hell, he'd be more than late. He'd be a no-show.

He wondered how understanding Eva Stuart was.

Chapter Four

Not very understanding at all.

Lynx stood there on Eva's doorstep, staring at the door she'd just slammed in his face. Not the type to give up easily, he knocked again.

"Go away," her muffled reply carried through the plank of wood.

"I have a really good excuse."

"You aren't bleeding."

"My four-wheeler is. Let me in so I can explain. Please. I brought breakfast."

There was a long pause. "What did you bring for breakfast?"

"My mother's homemade cranberry muffins, oatmeal with fresh berries, and coffee that will grow hair on your chest."

The door opened. "Give me the coffee." She reached out a hand for one of the large cups he held and took a long sip. She closed her eyes on a sigh, her head tilted slightly back, and he was dumbstruck by the sensuality of the simple action. His heart thumped hard in his chest like it was waking up for the first time.

"Come in, if you want." She turned and walked into the darkness of her apartment as though she didn't give a damn if he followed or not.

Obviously not a morning person, or she'd come in contact with too many Ugly Moose at the lodge last night. He'd already been dressed down by his mother and Uncle Pike for standing up the cute little nurse. Most likely he'd be hearing it from the townsfolk next.

Eva was dressed in a knit top and form-fitting jeans with bare feet, her toes painted a glittery purple and her blond hair spiked.

The place was dark, all the curtains closed, like a cave. Eva dropped into a seat at the little dining table and motioned for him to bring the sack of food over.

He put the food in front of her much the way he'd approach a wild animal.

Cautiously.

Everything about this woman made him alert, all his senses on high octane.

She opened the bag and took out one of the muffins. Biting into it, she moaned over a mouthful. "Your mother can sure cook." She looked up at him and frowned. "Take a seat or I'm going to get a pain in my neck looking up at you. Lord knows you go on forever. How tall are you anyway?"

"Six-three." He sat feeling as though he'd been granted an audience with the queen. She was sure demanding for such a little thing. Would she be demanding in bed? The thought sent a pump of blood to his nether regions. "Listen, Eva, I'm sorry—"

She cut him off with a dismissive motion of her hand. "Just tell me why you didn't show up. And for the record, I've never been stood up before." Her bloodshot eyes met his. "Never."

He took a moment to study her. She seemed slightly hung over. Either because she'd had her feelings hurt and tried to silence them with alcohol, or embarrassment had gotten the best of her since he'd left her sitting in a restaurant where everyone in attendance knew they'd had a date. He hoped it was hurt feelings. That meant their kiss had meant something to her too. He'd never been knocked back like that before from a mere meeting of lips. Never had a woman occupied his every waking thought and dreams like she did.

He launched into his story of destructive bear cubs and the long trek back to town not leaving out one little detail.

She abandoned her muffin halfway through his explanation, and cradled the coffee cup in her hands. When he finished, she took a long draw of the coffee before setting the cup on the table.

"That's quite the story. Do you seriously expect me to buy that?"

He paused. He never thought she wouldn't believe him. But then she was from Outside where things like this weren't the norm. "Yeah, I expect you to buy it. Remember you were chased by a moose yesterday."

"You do have me there. So, what is it that you actually do?"

"I'm an officer for the Yukon Flats National Wildlife Refuge."

"Like what? An animal cop?"

"It's a lot more complicated than that." He tried not to take her comment as an insult. She was uneducated in Alaska. And he planned to educate her. In many things. "I police the Refuge. I'm in charge of conserving fish and wildlife, international treaty obligations, subsistence uses, which is a big part of my job with so many people who depend on fish and wildlife in order to survive. Safety of people using the Refuge, and assisting with Search and Rescue when needed, which is called on more than I'd like." He'd come close to being another statistic himself. "I monitor commercial activities on the Refuge, and Alaska is rich in oil, gas, and gold this far north. Way more politics than I signed up for," he muttered under his breath.

"How big is the Refuge?"

"Yukon Flats is about eight and a half million acres, spanning an area roughly two hundred and twenty miles east to west and one hundred and twenty miles north to south."

"How many officers do you work with?"

"It's just me." He continued when her mouth fell open, "I have other law enforcements agencies that I can call on if needed. But, basically, it's just me."

"How do you patrol something that...big?"

He shrugged getting uncomfortable talking so much about himself. Wasn't that a red flag where women were concerned? But then if she was asking questions, she was at least talking to him and not slamming a door in his face. "By any means necessary. Horse, four-wheeler—which I'm going to need a spare until I get my other one back and repaired—plane, snow machine, dog team, you name it. Whatever it takes to get the job done."

"Huh." She picked up her coffee cup and studied him like bacteria in a Petri dish.

Uh-oh. He *had* talked too much. She didn't have that glazed over look that some women got, but she was from a big city. This had to be boring her to death. "How about I show you a part of the Refuge? It's supposed to be nice today." Which could change faster than a woman changed her mind. "I could take you on a tour, so you can get a feel of the place you are now calling home." When she didn't look like she was going to agree he added, "Show you the lay of the land so that you don't get turned around so easily, and find yourself lost in your own backyard again." That did it. He saw the shift in her eyes as she accepted his challenge. So she was the type who couldn't turn down a dare. That was handy information to have.

"How long will we be gone?"

"A few hours. I'll pack a picnic lunch. After all, I do owe you dinner."

"That you do." She smiled.

The movement focused his gaze on the lips he couldn't stop thinking about.

"Okay, you're on," she said.

Now who was laying down a challenge?

CHAPTER FIVE

"I thought you said 'land'?" Eva asked, staring at the canoe beached on the bank of the Chatanika River.

"Best way to get a feel for the place is by boat."

"This isn't a boat." A boat had a motor not a paddle, and seats not planks.

He laughed. The sound and the way he tipped his head back charmed her in a way that she couldn't explain or begin to understand. He was so different from any other man she'd been attracted to. But then the others had never measured up when it counted. He was big enough and tall enough that he could probably measure up to anything.

She glanced back at the paint-scraped, dented, weary-worn canoe. Yeah, she'd give this a chance. Just like she realized, she'd give him a chance.

"Okay, what do I do?" she asked.

"First—" he held up a yellow lifejacket "—you have to put this on." He held the vest out for her like a gentleman holding a coat for her to slip into. Once she had the lifejacket on, she faced him, looking down at the zipper and clips, not knowing what to snap, zip, or buckle first. Turn out that wasn't something she needed to worry about as he went about securing the lifejacket tightly to her torso. His hands were all business until he finished with the belt around her waist, then they fell to her hips and just stayed there warming her from the inside out. His eyes met hers, and heat simmered between them. Just like that her internal temperature rose, and she wanted the jacket off. Wanted to strip all her clothes off and his too.

His nostrils flared, and he leaned closer, stopping just before his lips would have taken possession of hers. "If I kiss you, we won't be canoeing."

A large part of her was perfectly fine with that. Another, the more sensible part—*damn it*—insisted she step back. "So..." She bent down and picked up a paddle. "Show me how to work a canoe."

He cocked his lips in a smile that had her wishing she'd taken him up on that kiss instead of the canoeing. But if she was going to live here in the wilds of Alaska she needed to know a few things. From what she could tell, people did a lot of outdoor activities.

Like canoeing.

"Second rule of thumb. Do not stand up in the canoe. When you feel comfortable enough with everything else, I'll show you how that can be safely accomplished. Just know that if you stand up, you will most likely dump us both in the water. Third, we don't want to be dumped into the water. Average temperature of the river is roughly ten degrees above freezing this time of year. By the end of summer it might be fifteen degrees above freezing."

"I have no plans to get wet."

"I've heard it before. Let's just plan it now and hope for the best."

"I'm not an idiot. I know what hypothermia is, and I have no plans to experience it first hand."

"Good. Fourth—"

"How many rules are you going to name? This is going to take all day."

"You want to learn as we go?"

"At least we'll be going somewhere," she muttered.

He pursed his lips.

Guess she'd pissed him off. She was good at doing that. Impatience was one of her strong suits.

97

"Here." He handed her a can of bug spray.

"There's DEET in this thing. Have you heard the statistics of what it can do to you?"

"Less harm than the mosquitoes you will encounter today."

"You've got to be kidding me?"

"One of the ways they used to punish a criminal back in the gold rush days was to tie the perp naked in a canoe and launch him on the Yukon. The man would jump into the freezing, silt-filled water with his hands tied behind his back, knowing full well he'd drown, to escape the mosquitoes."

She arched a brow in disbelief. "That's some tall tale."

He stared at her for a long silent minute, and then stepped back and sprayed himself down, adding a healthy coating to his hands and wiping the stuff onto his face and neck, making sure he covered his ears too. She started to rethink her need for bug spray. He did live here. He wouldn't be messing with her, would he?

"Fine, give me that." She exchanged the paddle for the can and gave herself a light dusting.

He smirked and packed the can in the backpack he carried. "Let me know when you need some more."

"What? Are there vamp mosquitoes out there?" Geez. She wasn't that naive.

He ignored her and positioned the canoe to launch. "Go ahead and get in. Face the front, and I'll give us a push."

She climbed in, her arms flaying wide when the canoe rocked under her feet and quickly took a seat. She gulped. Maybe this wasn't such a good idea.

"Here's your paddle." Lynx handed it back to her. She took it not knowing what he expected her to do with it. Maybe she should have let him finish his never-ending list of rules.

But how hard could it be? People canoed all the time.

Lynx stepped in behind her. She dropped the paddle as the canoe rocked back and forth with his movements. Luckily it landed between her legs and not into the river.

There was a sound of them sliding on sand. She glanced back to see him using the paddle to push them out into the rushing current. The canoe easily flowed with the water and picked up speed. Her hands tightened on the edges.

"Grab your paddle," Lynx said from behind. "Don't tell me you're one of those women who expects the man to do all the work."

She arrowed him a look, and he laughed when she picked up her paddle and dipped it into the water.

"The water's fairly calm here, so get the feel of how stroking the paddle directs the canoe. Stay on the right," he instructed when she picked up the paddle to stroke left. "Think of this like sex." His voice purred, raising goose flesh on her arms. "Sex is best when we find a rhythm and stroke deep."

She swallowed hard, visually seeing him above her, her hips finding his rhythm as he stroked deep within her. He had to purposely be doing that. He didn't teach everyone to canoe using words like that. Just how many other women had he canoed with? He'd said that awfully smooth.

"We need to work together or we'll just spin in circles. I'll stroke from the back left, you front right. Find the rhythm."

She began to feel the difference when she wasn't fighting him and matched him stroke for stroke.

"There you go."

She felt a thrill at his words, and the hair rose on the back of her neck. He had such a seductive voice, and with him behind her giving her instruction, it left her feeling vulnerable, needy. Normally not something she liked. She liked being in charge. Hell, taking charge. But it was actually nice knowing he was back there, directing them. Steering them on the correct course.

She began taking in her surroundings. The water lapped by the base of the canoe, the cutting of the paddles causing eddies to swirl in the clear water. She thought she saw a fish swim by and wondered what kind it was. Birch leaves tinkled like jewelry as they brushed each other in the slight breeze. A huge bird soared not making a sound as it glided above them.

"Is that—?"

"A bald eagle. You'll see lots of wildlife on this trip. The Chatanika River is prime habitat for birds and animals."

He set an easy pace, one that gave her the chance to see what was flowing by them. The air was crisp. The sun warm on her skin, and there didn't seem to be another soul around but them. The beauty of the place stole her breath.

"Stunning," she whispered.

"Yeah," he agreed as though he was in church. But then this was spiritual in a way. God's church. "Look left."

She followed where he pointed and saw a beaver rush up the bank, slapping its flat tail as though to scare them off. She laughed, realizing as the sound escaped her that it had been a long time since she'd felt this free.

The water slowed more.

"Rest your arms," Lynx recommended.

She turned to see him with the paddle straddled across the canoe.

"When we flow around that bend ahead the water is going to speed up. Not a lot of rapids in this river but there are a few. Just don't panic, and we'll be fine. One other thing. The Chatanika is famous for its sweepers."

"Sweepers?"

"Low hanging trees where they have been uprooted because of the flow of the ever-changing river. Break up around here can be quite turbulent. So watch your head. See." He indicated such a tree hanging across the river. They ducked and smoothly floated under it.

The next one came up faster. She tried to steer them around it.

"No. Let me steer. You keep paddling left. Eva, left."

The water had picked up fast. One minute calm, almost lake-like, and the next rushing like a faucet. A tree was suddenly there. She paddled hard right getting confused and overwhelmed all at once. They hit the roots of the tree. It banged the canoe hard enough to cause it to bounce upriver a few feet, swinging them into the rapids Lynx had been trying to avoid. The canoe rocked and bounced as they sped up, and she panicked.

"Stay put. Eva, don't move like that. Duck!"

A sweeper swept her right out of the canoe.

CHAPTER SIX

Lynx grabbed the branches overhead and tied a rope to secure the canoe so it didn't float downriver.

Eva gasped and splashed as she fought to swim against the current. "Help! I'm drowning!"

"Eva, stand up." He tried to fight back the laugh bubbling to the surface and lost. The woman was so out of her element, she was adorable. Her spiky hair lay plastered against her skull, her violet eyes went from filled with fear to fury as she stood up and the water came to her upper thighs.

She planted hands on her hips and narrowed those livid eyes at him, and he laughed harder. His sides hurt with it. If the woman could zap him with a spell, he'd be a horny toad right now. Actually he was already horny, had been since he'd picked her up. Scratch that. Since he'd carried her back to his place when she'd been moosed-up.

There was something about her that fired to life every one of his need-to-mate receptors.

"Help me out of h-here you...you b-big moose." Eva shivered, her hand shaking as she slicked back her wet hair.

Ooh, now she looked sexy and mysterious like some exotic European model.

He remained seated and braced his legs on each side of the canoe so that helping her back in didn't tip him into the river. He reached for her and pulled her in. Even soaking wet, the woman weighed nothing. He helped her to sit in the bottom of the canoe, facing him. She cradled her knees

102

to her chest and shook. That sobered him up. She was cold and probably miserable. He'd save his laughter until later when he was alone and maybe retelling this story to Fox. Right now, he needed to get her warmed up. The thought shouldn't please him so much. He took another look at her and decided warming her up might not be as pleasurable as he'd hoped. Not with the blame shooting his way.

He untied the canoe and picked up the paddle, easily navigating them away from the nest of sweepers and the rapids until he reached a pool of water where he could bank the canoe. He jumped out and secured the craft to a tree, reaching back to help guide Eva to shore. She was shaking so badly that he gave up and swung her up into his arms.

She slapped his shoulder. "P-put me d-down."

"Make me," he fired back and tried not to laugh again. He got another slap for his comment. He carried her to a clearing blooming with wildflowers and set her on her feet then proceeded to unstrap her from the wet lifejacket. He tossed that to the ground and went for the buttons on her shirt.

"W-what are you d-doing?" She knocked his fingers away.

"We need to get you warmed up."

She narrowed her eyes. "It's a nice day. I don't think I'm going to f-freeze to death. In fact, the m-madder I get, the less cold I feel."

She should be smoking hot then.

He bit back the reply and instead asked, "Did you pack what I told you to bring?"

She bared her teeth and growled.

He blinked.

Damn if she wasn't the most adorable woman he'd ever laid eyes on. He couldn't stop himself from grabbing her upper arms, lifting her up, and kissing the mad right out of her. She sputtered when he set her back on her feet. He gave her a goofy smile. "Be right back."

He left her to stew and headed to the canoe for their backpacks. When he returned she'd shed her shirt and wore a wet tank top.

Oh, he was in trouble here.

Her nipples beaded like small stones through the tissue-thin, white material. The lace of her bra was defined through the soft fabric. She glared at him as she struggled to get her tennis shoes off. "Stay away from me."

Yeah, not going to happen.

The more time he spent around her the more he wanted to be around her. Who would have thought he'd fall for a pixie of a woman with an Amazonian temper? She went for the button of her jeans next and slowly peeled the wet material down her hips and thighs, until she stomped free of them, wearing only her tank top and lacy pair of electric blue panties.

He took a step closer.

"Stay right there!" She pointed at him with her finger, and if it had been loaded he'd be dead right now.

She really wasn't happy with him. And why did that please him so much?

Probably because she wasn't afraid of him. Most people saw his size and either figured he was as dumb as a musk ox or a man to be feared. Women tended to think the latter and a few men had been educated in the former. Eva was a breath of fresh air he hadn't known he needed.

He stayed rooted to his spot and focused on her every move. The woman was perfectly fine with being practically naked in front of him. He was just grateful. She gathered up her wet clothes and laid them over tree branches to help them dry. He took in her creamy skin, so different from the brown of his, and couldn't wait to join the two of them together. She bent over and fluffed her hair in the breeze. He groaned. She was just messing with him now.

"How are your stitches?" he asked, eyes rooted to her ass.

She turned and looked at him over her shoulder, her back arched in a pose worthy of Playboy.

The minx.

Did she have any idea what she was doing to him?

"They seem fine." She started to wring the water out of her socks.

"You seem warmer now."

She lifted her face to the clear blue sky and closed her eyes. "This sun is just glorious."

It wasn't the only thing. "Would you like your backpack," he asked, his voice husky. She turned and gave him a full frontal view. With the sun behind her, she resembled a mystical faerie sent to sexually enslave him.

Where did he sign?

If he didn't get her covered up, he was afraid of what he might do. There was only so much temptation he could resist.

A hungry man was going to eat.

CHAPTER SEVEN

The look in Lynx's eyes had Eva faltering in her actions. Maybe she'd pushed him enough. She'd gotten drunk on the power. Never had a man devoured her like he was currently doing. It was heady and something she could definitely get used to.

Served him right for dowsing her in the river. So, it wasn't really his fault, but he'd laughed, so therefore the man had to pay.

She figured she'd tortured him enough. Besides, she'd just been bitten by a mosquito. She yanked her backpack from his grip and tore into it, grabbing the hoodie she'd stuffed into it early, believing she wouldn't need it. He'd said a full change of clothes, "just in case." She should have listened. All she'd put in here was the hoodie.

Chalk one up for the mountain man.

She covered up. The sweatshirt ended just past her hips.

"Is that all you brought?" Lynx asked. He looked as though he was in pain as he stared at her bare legs.

She slapped her upper thigh and gave it a scratch. Crap. These damn things were going to suck her dry. "Can I have the bug spray again?"

Chalk two up for the mountain man.

He offered her the can of spray. No light coating this time. She bathed in the stuff and did the same thing he'd done with wetting his hands and rubbing the smelly spray on her face and neck. She swore she could hear them buzzing inside her ears.

"Seriously, you need to put some clothes on," Lynx said.

"This is all I brought," she admitted.

He opened his pack and pulled out a blanket and tossed it to her. "I'll be right back." And then he disappeared into the woods.

She was suddenly alone.

Really alone.

She glanced around. A raven sat on a spruce tree branch. Its beady eye met hers and it cawed, the sharp sound making her jerk. Then it flew off in a blur of black and blue feathers. The clearing was roughly the size of her apartment. Trees crowded in from all sides. She couldn't even tell what direction Lynx had vanished off to.

She sat on a rock and took in her surroundings. No longer was she finding the beauty and tranquility of earlier on the river. Now there seemed to be eyes watching her from the shadows. A rustling to her left had her jumping back to her feet. Her heart in her throat, she waited to see what would appear.

What did she do if it was a bear? She didn't have a gun to protect herself with. She could get back into the canoe, but no way could she out paddle a bear, and didn't bears swim? Nothing ventured from the darkness beyond what she could see. She shouldn't have pissed off Lynx. Why would he just leave her like that?

What was she going to do if he didn't return?

She rotated in a slow circle, scanning the thick trees. She didn't even know which way was home.

Who was she kidding? This wasn't home. It was another planet and all the people here, aliens.

She'd chosen to move here. She could leave.

Not for another two years. She'd signed a contract in exchange for an impressive bonus and the cost of being moved up here. She really needed her head examined.

Another rustling and this time her eyes went wide with fright.

There was something out there!

She hadn't imagined those eyes. It was a dog...or a wolf. Oh God. Was she going to be eaten?

"Hey." Lynx appeared from behind her.

She screamed. He jumped a few steps back.

"What was that for?"

"T-there's a w-wolf out there." She pointed to the trees. He followed her finger.

"Well, he isn't there now. I doubt there's any wildlife within a hundred miles after that scream."

He stuck a finger in his ear as though to help with the ringing.

She tossed him the blanket and grabbed her jeans off the branch. "Get me out of here." She struggled into the damp denim, but by God she got them on. Her socks and shoes were next.

"What about lunch?"

"No way. I'm not taking the chance of being lunch."

"Eva, calm down. There is nothing out there."

"Where the hell did you go, anyway?"

"I needed a...minute to cool down."

"Are you freaking kidding me? You left me here alone in the wilds because you needed a minute."

"Yeah." He tightened his lips. One hard look and he gathered up her lifejacket, tossing it at her and grabbing the backpacks. "Fine, I'll take you home."

CHAPTER EIGHT

"The woman is nuts," Lynx said, slumping on the barstool in his sister Raven's kitchen. It had been a few days since the failed canoe trip, and he needed to figure out a way to get Eva talking to him again.

Much like his house, Raven's was built of logs, with a loft above the kitchen area, leaving the living room open with a cathedral ceiling. But her place overlooked the Chatanika River with floor to ceiling windows. She had a stunning view. While his cabin was more nestled in the trees. Cozy and hidden.

"Really?" Raven raised a brow over the mug of tea she held to her lips, her long black hair pulled up into a clip. She was dressed in jean overalls with smears of clay all over the fabric. She supported herself and son Fox with her pottery and spent a good portion of her day in the studio connected to the cabin. "Is she nuts or driving you nuts?"

"Both."

"Hmm."

He hated it when she did that. "What's that supposed to mean?"

"I don't think I've ever seen you worked up like this over a woman. Heck, over anything."

She had a point. He was normally a very patient kind of man, but he could have wrung Eva's neck the other day.

"You know, you shouldn't have laughed," Fox piped up from the couch.

Lynx had thought the kid was playing a video game or something. He knew better than to underestimate that Fox could keep track of a conversation while he fought some virtual war in a far off galaxy.

"You should have seen her." Lynx chuckled at the memory, all his anger evaporating into nothing. "Damn, she was cute."

Fox set down his game controller, shut off the TV, and turned to face Lynx. "You need to apologize."

"Me?" He glanced from Fox to Raven.

Raven smiled and patted his shoulder. "Fox is right."

"B-but—"

"You laughed, making her feel like an idiot, and then you left her alone," Fox pointed out. "She's not from around here. She's probably never been alone like that in her life."

Damn, the kid made sense. Lynx wasn't going to get into Eva's bed with her mad at him like this. Not that he needed to tell his nephew that.

How did he apologize? She wasn't talking to him. He'd tried when he'd dropped her back at her place, but all he'd gotten was the door slammed in his face again.

"Take her some chocolate," Fox suggested, and then went into the kitchen and lost himself in the contents of the refrigerator.

Raven shrugged. "Couldn't hurt."

"What kind of woman doesn't like *chocolate*?" Lynx shouted through the slammed door.

"The kind of woman who likes *caramel*," was the muffled—though impressively loud—reply from Eva.

Lynx stood there on the doorstep, one hand clutching the box of chocolates he'd bought in Fairbanks. Did she have any idea how much time he'd given to this venture? Shouldn't he get points for that?

If he could just get her to open the door long enough to get close to her, kiss her, shut up that mouth of hers, he might be able to apologize.

Instead, he turned and stomped off her porch, tore open the box of chocolate and ate all of them on the short walk to his place. He liked chocolate just fine. And he'd done a great job picking them out. They tasted rich and dark with all manner of nuts. No creams for the lady he was lusting after.

Hell, he'd failed on the chocolate and didn't even know enough about her to know if she liked nuts. And he wanted to know.

It wasn't just lust he was feeling or he wouldn't care. She fascinated him, and not just sexually, though that did occupy a large part of his day. He wanted to know little things too. Like why she moved to Alaska. Did she have family? Did she want a family?

Whoa. This was getting serious if he was thinking kids.

Yeah, he loved kids. Loved his nephew Fox and wanted a bunch of rug rats running around. He'd always thought that would be for someday. Could someday be here?

Could Eva be his someone?

His stomach churned. He shouldn't have eaten so many chocolates. The sugar overload wouldn't help him with all he needed to think about.

He'd cut through the trees and came out of the woods into his backyard. He could see that a path would be worn between her house and his before whatever was between them was resolved. He climbed up on the back deck and found Fox with the ever present puppy, Kiski.

He rubbed Kiski's ear and let her gnaw on his hand for a bit before taking a seat next to Fox.

Fox indicated the empty box of chocolates. "I take it they weren't a hit?"

"Turns out she doesn't like chocolate." He tossed the empty box aside. Kiski scrambled out of Fox's arms to attack it.

"Hmm, well that's a new one."

Lynx harrumphed in agreement.

They sat quietly watching the puppy destroy the box. At least one female enjoyed the box of chocolates. And this one a real bitch.

"What's your next step?" Fox asked.

Next step? He was at a loss on how to deal with Eva. Alaskan women loved him. A few international ones had too. But this spitfire from the Midwest left him stumped.

"I don't have a clue what to do with Eva." And he shouldn't be confiding in his ten-year-old nephew. But it was either that or the woodland creatures.

"Have you told her how pretty her hair is?"

"Uh...no."

Fox made a tsking sound. "Women like to be complimented, to know they are thought of."

"So then what do you suggest I do? I can't get her to keep her door open long enough to tell her how pretty she is."

"Take her some flowers. How hard is this?"

Hell, no. "I'd have to drive back to Fairbanks to buy her flowers." With his luck she'd hate roses. Would she prefer daisies? Lilies? Ugh, too many choices. Flowers were way more difficult than chocolate. He'd never survive it.

Fox pointed to the field of wildflowers that made up Lynx's backyard. "Pick her some flowers."

"Huh, would you look at that." He reached out and ruffled the boy's hair. "How'd you get so smart anyway?"

Fox shrugged. "Mom watches a lot of chick flicks."

CHAPTER NINE

Eva felt a ping of guilt for not letting Lynx in earlier. She could have been nicer. Not yelled at him as much. Maybe not slam the door as hard as she had. But damn it, she was still mad. A part of her realized the mad came from being scared, and he was to blame for that too. She liked control, and he'd left her in a situation where she'd had none. Granted, she might have driven him to leave her.

Seemed she was good at that too.

Hadn't she driven Davis into Jeremy's arms? Or was it the other way around? Not that she'd wanted to keep Davis, but she sure missed Jeremy. He'd know what to do about Lynx. He'd want to know what the hell held her back from partaking of such a beautiful man.

A bittersweet smile played at the corners of her mouth. Maybe she should pick up the phone and check in with Jeremy?

She reached for her cell and then set it down. No, that part of her life was over. She was on to new and better things.

New, yes. Better? That still remained to be seen.

Though she had to admit, she'd been happier in the short time since arriving here in Alaska than she'd been in Cincinnati. She might be considered a cheechako, but she was learning, making new friends, discovering new things daily. But the one thing she really wanted to experience was sex with Lynx.

It wasn't healthy to go this long without sex. Her mouth watered with the thought of being with Lynx. He made her feel desirable.

Lynx was so big and manly, she felt like a woman, all fragile and feminine around him. Not something she'd had a lot of experience with around Davis. With Davis, she'd been the man in their relationship. Funny, she hadn't figured that out before she'd found him and Jeremy in her bed.

Lynx made her feel desired.

That's it. She needed to apologize to Lynx, and the best way to show her sincerity was to have her way with him.

Plan decided, Eva quickly went and changed her clothes, slipping into sexy under things that would make Lynx stutter. She followed the lingerie with a low, snug-fitting violet top that let the lavender lace of her bra peek over the edges of the material. That would drive him crazy. She added a blue and purple glass pendant on a long silver chain around her neck to help draw his eye to her pushed up cleavage. Just in case he missed it.

Slipping into a floral skirt in pinks, blues, and purples that ended just above her knees, she hoped she wasn't going too far. She hadn't noticed a lot of skirts being worn here in Chatanika. This was Carhartt and Timberland country. But the day was nice, with the sun hot and high in the sky. Besides the skirt would allow her freedom of movement and quick access to Lynx when she got him horizontal. That thought had her inner muscles clenching with excitement.

She stepped into red-hot strappy sandals, knowing they would to be murder to walk in on the gravel driveway, but they completed the look and did great things for her legs. She wouldn't be walking long in them anyway. She planned to drive over to his house. No more trekking through the forest until she got her bearings or bought a handheld GPS.

She stood in front of the full-length mirror and shared a satisfied smile with her reflection. The man would have to be dense as wood not to understand her intent.

Eva picked up her purse, opened her front door, and skidded to a stop. A surprised squeal escaped her before she could cover her mouth. A bull moose chomped the grass that needed to be mowed in her front yard. It was so close to the house there was no way she'd be going anywhere. The moose glanced up.

Hey, she recognized that look in his eye.

It was the same damn moose who'd chased her up a tree last week. Was he the town mascot? Welcoming committee? That would explain one reason for the small population. A rogue moose chasing people off.

"Shoo!" she hollered and received a bored blink for her efforts.

"Get!" she tried again. This time the moose took a big step toward her. She squealed again, and jumped back into the house, slamming the door. Her heart pounded, and her breath came out in loud gasps. What did she do now? She ran to the window and looked out.

The intimidating animal was still there. She'd slammed the door hard enough to sway the trees and yet he still stood there. He turned back to his lunch and continued grazing as though he had no intentions of leaving.

Was this a common occurrence in Alaska? Could you be held hostage in your own house by a moose? She did not want the headline of The Daily News Miner to read: *Woman expired as a bull moose held her prisoner in her house.*

She wasn't dying this way.

And she wasn't dying without sleeping with Lynx first.

This was ridiculous. She needed something to scare the thing away. A gun was a thought. It was the second time she'd had that thought, so she'd better look into it. First, she had to learn how to shoot one so she didn't accidentally kill herself or someone else. She headed to the kitchen. There had to be something in there that she could use.

Knives? Right, get serious. Pans? No, she liked her pans. They'd come with her from Cincinnati, and it wasn't like there was a Williams Sonoma down the street, or probably in the state. Nope. Not taking that chance. She saw the bowl of fruit and reached for the apples. Maybe she could scare him away with these. She didn't want to hurt him, just startle him into scampering off.

She returned to the window to see him munching away as though he had nowhere else to be. Slowly, she cracked open the front door. His ears twitched, and his head came up. She let an apple fly. It hit him on the front flank and bounced off. The moose blinked again and then ambled over to where the apple had rolled to a stop. It sniffed and then ate it in one bite. His head came up with what she could assume was more interest. He took a step toward her, and with his long legs, his step was considerable. She screamed and threw all the apples at him. He bobbed his head and went after each one. She slammed the door.

That wasn't the smartest thing she could have done. She'd fed a wild animal.

Yeah, you sure taught him.

So much for taking care of this problem herself. She prided herself on being smart enough to realize when she needed back up.

CHAPTER TEN

Lynx stuffed his phone back in his pocket. "Gotta go, kid."

"Poachers again?" Fox gathered up the scraps of cardboard Kiski had torn into little pieces while she currently investigated a butterfly.

"Nope. BW has Eva trapped in her house. I've been called to play hero again." This time he wasn't moosin—messing it up either.

"Take her flowers!" Fox hollered as Lynx jumped the last three steps from the deck.

"Right. Thanks." That kid was a freaking genius.

Lynx yanked flowers in his sprint to Eva's. She wouldn't slam the door in his face this time. He exited the trees with a handful of sweet-smelling wildflowers intermixed with some weeds. While he approached the moose, he attempted to clean up the mess and rearrange the blooms. BW was doing a fine job of mowing Eva's front yard.

Maybe he should mow it for her. Chances were she didn't have a lawn mower. There wasn't much of a lawn either, more like forest carpet than grass.

"What are you up to, BW?" Lynx slowly drew near the big bull moose, glancing around the opening, suddenly conscious that he had a handful of flowers and was talking to a moose. There was no sign of Eva, but he could feel eyes on him and knew she watched from the window.

Now how did he talk a moose into leaving an all-you-can-eat buffet of sweet greens?

At the sound of Lynx's voice, BW bobbed his head a few times, much like a horse that was happy to see him.

"You can't keep doing this," Lynx tried to reason, knowing he was setting himself up for a psych evaluation. He hoped Eva couldn't hear him. It was bad enough she was witnessing this. On the phone, she'd demanded he come bearing arms. "We want her to stay, and while this is one tactic, it's going to backfire."

BW took a step closer and extended his head, his nostrils quivering. Then quick as an owl snatching a shrew, BW chomped the tops off the flowers Lynx had picked for Eva.

"Ah dude, you are not helping my cause, here."

The moose bobbed his head again, nudged Lynx playfully in the chest, throwing him back a few steps, and then walked off without a care in the world, blending into the trees. The breaking of branches was the only proof he was still out there.

The door opened behind him. Lynx turned to see Eva, and his mouth hit the ground.

"What was that all about?" Eva asked.

What was she wearing? She looked all womanly and stuff.

"Lynx?" A scowl appeared on her forehead as she studied him.

He needed to tread carefully or that door would be slammed in his face again. There was no way in hell that was happening, not with her all gussied up. He couldn't remember seeing a woman so beautiful before. He remembered Fox asking him if he'd given her any compliments.

"I like your hair," he blurted out.

"Huh?" Her scowl deepened, and then she shook her head as if to clear it. "Explain to me what just happened here. How did you get that moose to move on so easily? And don't tell me I didn't hear you right this time. You called him BW."

Uh-oh.

If he told her how he'd gotten BW to move on, she wouldn't let him into her bed. That door would be slammed in his face for the last time. And by the looks of her, he wasn't getting anywhere unless he did something fast.

"Here, I picked these for you." He held out the munched stems with a few remaining limp flowers.

She didn't seem impressed. "Why did you call that moose BW? And why did it look like he was 'friendly' with you?"

"Can we talk inside?" His eyes bugged when he caught sight of the lacy bra peeking up to say hello under her form-fitting top.

"BW stands for Bullwinkle, doesn't it?"

Damn, why did she have to be so intuitive? "Uh, maybe."

She folded her arms pushing her breasts up and deepening the cleavage that was already blood-starving his brain cells.

"Tell me why when I yelled, waved my hands, and threw apples at *BW*, he didn't scare off until you *talked* to him?"

Oh, no. "Tell me you didn't feed him apples." BW wouldn't leave her alone now.

"It's not like I had rocks in the house or a gun."

She didn't need a gun, not with the heart-stopping punch she packed in that get up.

He needed to do something quick to change the subject, get her focused on something else. "God, how I want you."

"Huh-what?"

He tossed the chomped steams aside and advanced. "Where were you headed?" He reached out and fingered one of her dangling earrings. What perfect little ears she had, elfin-like really. He wanted to nibble.

"I...uh, was actually coming to see you."

He stepped back so he could see into her eyes. "Why?" He liked her suddenly uneasy around him.

She shrugged, and swallowed. "Well, I got to thinking. Maybe I'd been a little rough on you. The chocolates were a thoughtful gesture."

"I'm sorry about the other day, Eva. I shouldn't have left you alone." He realized that he should've apologized first, before trying chocolates or flowers.

Her wary eyes met his. "Why did you? Leave me alone, that is."

"If I hadn't taken a minute to get blood back into my head, I would have taken you against a tree like a wild animal."

A switch seemed to go off at his words. "Next time, take me against a tree." She reached out and grabbed the fabric of his t-shirt, fisting her hand in the soft cotton. Pulling him down, she kissed him.

His heart leaped, and his blood raced. He growled and yanked her into his arms. His hands snaked under the soft knit top and tugged it up and over her head, revealing the sexiest bra he'd ever seen. Lacy, with thin straps and the color of wild lupine, it cupped her perfect breasts, pushing them up for his eyes to devour.

He wanted it off. "What are you wearing?"

She smiled, her magical eyes bewitching him, daring him. "Hardly anything at all."

It hit him then. She'd been on her way to see him, dressed like this for him, so he could do all manner of naughty things to her.

He reached behind her and flicked open the clasp of her bra, letting it drop to where her blouse had fallen. Her breasts were perfect. Small, rounded, and perky with extended rosy nipples. His hand cupped her breast, while his heart swelled with something that made his breath hard to catch.

What was she doing to him?

"Lynx?"

He took in her beauty and knew deep within his soul she was the one for him. This pixie of a woman had somehow, with her sharp tongue and daring spirit, captured his heart.

How did something like that happen in so short a time? He remembered the telling of his parents' short courtship. How his dad had taken one look at his mom and absconded with her. From that moment on there had been no other woman for Fox Maiski Sr. She'd remained the love of his life until his untimely death when Lynx had been nineteen.

"Lynx?" Eva called his name again. "Are you okay?"

No, he wasn't. He was falling in love with a woman who could easily break his heart and destroy him. A woman who didn't understand all there was to know about him and when she did, she'd probably hightail it right back to her former life in the lower forty-eight.

He had to stop that from happening. Somehow he needed to bind her to him. The only way he knew to do that was to follow his animal instincts.

They'd saved his sorry ass many a time.

He lifted her right off her feet, carrying her into the house, and kicking the door shut with his boot. It felt powerful to be on the inside of her door. Her legs came up and circled his hips, and he nearly hit the floor. There wasn't much between him and her besides his jeans and the laughable barrier of her panties. He could feel her heat pressing into him as she ground herself against his erection.

"Bed," he growled.

"Second door on the left." She tightened her arms around him and held on, her lips nibbling down his neck.

He tumbled her onto the bed, her skirt riding up, showing a flash of more lavender lace.

Chapter Eleven

Eva caught her breath at the predatory look in Lynx's eyes.

He'd gone from perplexed, to worry, to decision. And his decision had gooseflesh rising up all over her body.

He stood at the end of the bed and never broke eye contact. Sprawled on the blankets, she didn't breathe as he untied his boots and toed them off. She wanted to smooth the skirt down her legs from where it was bunched on her upper thighs, but was almost afraid to move, worried that if she did, he'd pounce.

She thought she'd been ready to be taken, but by the sweet, thoughtful man who had brought her chocolate, and picked her wildflowers.

This man was someone different.

Wild, hot, unpredictable, looking a lot like the feral arctic cat he was named after. He was so far out of her realm of experience, for the first time in her life she didn't know what to do.

Her eyes widened as he jerked his t-shirt off, and then unbuttoned and unzipped his jeans, taking his plaid boxers off with his pants, leaving him completely naked at the end of her bed.

Oh, she was in trouble.

He was glorious...and huge.

His penis pulsed forward, thick and long, and fear strangled her excitement. There was no freaking way. He'd render her in two.

She scrambled up the bed, but he grabbed her ankles and yanked her back down, holding her spread out before him. He growled, and she let out a startled squeak, feeling like a mouse caught in the clutches of a cat. A thrill she didn't want to put a name to strangled her vocal cords and had her breathing in short, choppy bursts of air.

He stripped off her skirt in one yank, leaving her wearing only the thong, and strappy heels. His eyes blazed amber at the thin, lacy, thong she wore. A raw, inhuman sound traveled up his chest and vibrated out his throat. He crawled up her body, all six feet and three inches of him. Toffee smooth skin, swathed over rock-hard muscle, caged her on the bed. His considerable weight pinned her to the mattress. Her hands came up to push against his immovable chest, to no avail. She might as well be pushing against a concrete dam.

He settled in the apex of her thighs, his hands grabbed her legs spreading them farther apart for the breadth of his hips.

She braced herself for what was to come. The little piece of lace that covered her wouldn't bar his penetration. His fingers tore the lace in two at her hips. The friction of lace grazed her clitoris in a long delicious abrasion as he slowly pulled it free of her body. Her legs clenched around him, her hands falling away from pushing against his chest and grabbed at his hips, as her lower body tried to seek more.

She was totally naked except for her shoes and jewelry, and she'd never felt more vulnerable...or more alive. More in tuned to Lynx's every move, every touch as he knocked her off balance with every second that ticked by.

Sex with Davis had taken place in the dark, under the covers, probably so he could fantasize that she was someone else.

It was daylight, she had no idea what time it was, but the sun was full and bright, and Lynx was big and bold, taking charge of her, reminding her with every heated look and touch that she was a woman, physically weaker and softer than him. There was a dangerous element to being anchored under him that she shouldn't admit thrilled her, just a little.

Scared her, too. More than a little.

"Do I need a condom?" he asked, as though forming words pained him.

"Uh...yes." She nervously licked her lips. His eyes watched her tongue, and then he claimed her mouth, making her forget about protection and everything else.

It was a brand more than a kiss. He plundered the depths of her mouth, his tongue dueled and conquered hers as though he were giving her some insight of what to expect. He tore his lips free of hers and met her eyes for a long moment as though to see if she got the message. Then he clamped his mouth over her breast, his teeth taking her nipple, so his tongue could flick back and forth over the tip.

On a startled screech, her back arched like a bow, and his arm snaked under her, pulling her closer to him, if that were possible. Overwhelmed with sensations that she'd never felt before, Eva squirmed, seeking out his erection, wanting to ride his thick shaft as he sucked and tormented her nipple.

"Please," she begged, not believing what she was asking. She'd seen that thing. Knew there was no way they would fit together, and yet she didn't care. She'd never felt this way before, like she wanted to sink her teeth into him, and then she found herself doing exactly that.

He growled, as her teeth bit into his shoulder, the sound more of a snarl as he moved his hips lower out of the reach of her questing need. He released her nipple and turned to the other one. Grabbing both of her hands in one of his, he anchored them above her head.

She was caught, laid out for his pleasure and dark urges. Liquid heat flared her insides to an out of control inferno.

This man, what was he?

He purred against her nipple as he sucked it into his mouth. Her inner muscles quivered as they contracted around emptiness, wanting him inside her. Then his fingers were there, tormenting her, testing her, twisting and flicking the sensitive nub that had suddenly become her universe.

Her hips arched off the bed as he inserted one finger, then two, then three inside her, stretching her. A rumbling of what she thought was satisfaction pulsated from him at finding her wet and slick with want.

He slowly moved his fingers in and out of her while his thumb did a titillating dance with her clitoris. Her hips gyrated with him, arching, meeting the thrusts of his hand. His mouth continued to play homage to her breasts as he worked her like an instrument. Seeming to know just what she needed when she needed it. How hard to push, when to let up, until she flew. Her world burst into little sparks of color as it imploded around her.

She lay there gasping and tried to understand what had just happened. She'd climaxed before, mostly by herself, and never like that.

But he wasn't done with her yet.

Lynx inched off her and stood at the end of the bed, if anything looking more predatory than he had before. There was a glint of satisfaction and craving in his gaze that had her sucking in air for what would happen next. She worried her lower lip with her teeth as she once again took in the man before her. If anything he was larger, thicker.

He grabbed a condom from the pocket of his jeans, and with a rip of foil, sheathed himself.

How was she going to do this?

The question was taken out of her hands when he confused her by gently picking up her foot and taking off her shoe, kissing the sensitive skin on the inner part of her ankle. Who knew the area of her ankle was so sensitive?

Apparently he did.

In turn, he did the same with her other shoe and ankle. He knew other places too, farther up her calf, then behind her knees, the inside of her thighs. His lips nibbled, and his tongue licked and teased erogenous zones she had believed in medical school to be a myth. Lord knew no other man had ever found them on her body.

Until now.

He took his time exploring, letting her float in a sea of sensation that was more enticing and seductive than any drug. She was his to mold, to have, to do with what he wished. There was no objection, no voice willing to work as his mouth found her. He spread her open for him to feast, his tongue circling, stabbing, sucking. His lips nipping, his teeth grazing.

Inserting two fingers inside her this time, he growled in appreciation as she moaned with pleasure. He took his time, but it wasn't long before stars exploded before her eyes again. Her world tipped as she soared to the heavens.

Boneless, she floated back to earth. With no strength left to brace herself for his penetration, she was beyond caring if the act killed her. At this point, she'd die with a smile on her face.

Positioned at her opening, he slowly and relentlessly entered her. He gave no quarter, and held her down with his hands on her hips keeping her from moving. His taking was deliberate...and perfect. He filled her as no man ever had or, she doubted, ever would again. If he hadn't made her come twice already, prepared her body to receive him, she didn't think it would have happened.

He groaned and closed his eyes. "You feel so fucking good."

His words thrilled her. They were naughty and dark and promised things she couldn't wait to partake of. Then he was seated so deep inside her she couldn't breathe. He waited, giving her time to adjust to his size.

It was perfect, so deliciously perfect. She'd never felt so in tune with another man, so much a part of him and him with her. Just as slowly as he'd entered her, he pulled out and entered her again. Each thrust gathered force and speed until he began to hammer into her. The tension rose, became too much. She twisted on the bed, her legs locking around his waist.

He wouldn't have it and pulled her legs from around him and stretch them farther apart as he bucked into her. A hoarse cry tore from him, and he bared his clenched teeth. Veins roped in his neck as his shoulder muscles bunched.

Heat climbed in her again, this time becoming a viral thing that consumed and demanded her ultimate surrender. She screamed as the orgasm ripped through her.

His body arched and shuddered. He gripped her hips and pulled her even tighter against him as he pulsed deeper within her.

Spent, he slowly collapsed on top of her, and she gave into the darkness.

CHAPTER TWELVE

What had she done?

Eva lay on the bed, not knowing how long she'd drifted. Had she blacked out? Lynx lay next to her, one leg draped over hers, his arm wrapped around her middle as though not willing to let her go.

That had been intense. It had been more than just sex. They'd mated. And with mating all sorts of implications were attached.

She wasn't ready to love again. Especially since she didn't really know the man resting silently next to her. Was he sleeping? Most men snored after sex, dropping right off.

Lynx was as quiet as a cat. Too quiet to be sleeping. He laid in wait. For what she didn't have a clue. This was all new territory to her. And she didn't like it. She felt unbalanced, as though at any moment the floor would open up and swallow her. She needed to gain back control, but how did she do that when he'd showed her how easily he could strip that control from her?

"You're thinking too much," Lynx's voice rumbled next to her.

She turned toward him and found it disconcerting to see him watching her with those dark eyes of his. They'd returned to a more sated espresso color instead of the glowing amber of earlier when he'd taken her.

"I can't seem to stop," she answered.

He reached out and fingered the glass pendant still around her neck nestled between her breasts. "Did I hurt you?" His wary eyes flickered back to hers.

A fiery blush heated her face. She was sore, and knew she'd feel what they'd done for a while. But hurt? No, if anything, she tingled everywhere. She shook her head.

"Are you sure?"

This time she nodded.

"I don't usually get so carried away. There is just something about you."

There was something about him too. But there were too many unanswered questions between them. First and foremost, how had Lynx talked BW into leaving? She couldn't believe she now thought of the rogue moose as BW. Maybe this midnight sun was frying her brain cells.

Had Lynx used sex as a reason not to answer her earlier questions? Or had their coming together meant as much to him as it had to her? Either way, she needed to know.

Now.

What was she thinking?

Not now.

That was the quickest way she knew to scare off a man. Did she want to scare off Lynx? Her body still hummed with the tune he'd made it play. While she really wanted to feel like that again, she wasn't ready for what shown in his eyes. What she needed was a moment to herself and time to think.

"I'm going to take a shower," she said.

"Would you like some company?" Lynx asked.

"No. I...uh...need a few minutes."

He nodded. "Just don't think too hard while you're in there. There's something special here, Eva."

She climbed off the bed and grabbed a blanket to wrap up in. It wasn't lost on her that she had no problem being half-dressed or even naked in front of Lynx before, and now that he knew her intimately, she needed to cover up.

As she entered the bathroom and started the shower, muscles that hadn't been used in a while ached for a soak in a hot tub. She didn't have time for that kind of indulgence with Lynx still out there. Part of her wished he'd be gone when she finished. The other part called her a coward. Was she really hiding in the bathroom because the sex had been too good?

God, she was messed-up.

Lynx covered his face with his hands. He should've handled that better. Damn it, he'd scared her. He'd come on too strong, too extreme. It had been too soon to take their relationship into the bedroom.

Hell, what relationship?

He'd stood her up on their first date, dunked and abandoned her on their second, and couldn't talk her into keeping her door open long enough to get a third.

So what was he doing here lying on her bed? Something had to be going his way, and it wasn't BW's involvement.

Could she care about him too?

Women didn't usually have sex with men unless their heart was somehow involved. At least, that's what his sisters always said. He didn't know what to believe. He'd been with women who wanted him because he was the big Alaskan Native. Women could be as callous as men. But Eva didn't fall into that category, he'd bet his life on it. She was shaken up. What had happened between them had blown her mind too.

He sat up and looked around the room. Clothes were flung everywhere, the bed a rumpled mess. Since he'd done most of the flinging, he could straighten up.

One thing for certain, he wasn't leaving until they ironed out where they both stood with each other.

Whether Eva liked it or not.

CHAPTER THIRTEEN

Lynx was dressed and in the kitchen when Eva entered wearing a short, azure silk Japanese robe that complimented the violet of her eyes. She hastily tied the belt when she saw him, which answered his question if she was naked under it or not. He wanted the woman who had no problem stripping down in front of him when she needed stitches.

"I thought you left." She fluffed her damp hair.

"Not until we talk." He flipped the grilled cheese sandwiches he was cooking and tried not to feel the sting of her frown. "Besides, while I'm here, I might as well remove your stitches." Her eyes widened and he had to bite back a smile.

"No, that's okay. I can take care of it."

"Eva, you can't reach them."

"Seriously, I can do it."

He moved the sandwiches to the plates he'd set out earlier, turned off the gas stove, and faced her. "I stitched you up, therefore, I'm duty sworn to remove them." Besides, he didn't want anyone else seeing her sweet backside but him.

"Fine. Can we eat first? I'm starving."

Once again he bit back a smile. While he enjoyed the ballsy woman he'd first met, this shy and cautious woman charmed him too. He'd taken control by sleeping with her. Now she was the one off balance. He brought the plates to the small table and remained standing until she took a seat.

She adjusted the hem on the robe to cover more of her legs as she sat, but the silky material slid back up her thighs.

131

Rather than fight the fabric, she scooted her chair farther under the table. He sat across from her, wondering what she was going to do next. He was at a loss of what to do with himself. It would help if he knew more about her.

She picked up a triangle of her sandwich that he'd cut into fourths and met his stare. "You are sooo not my type," she blurted out, before taking a bite.

Well, he could have done without knowing this. "What is your type?"

"I don't know." She dropped her sandwich and buried her hands in her hair. "I thought I did, but all the men I've loved have turned out to be gay."

Did she love him? Had that been a slip?

"You are not gay," she continued. Though this wasn't a question, it sounded tentative as though she wasn't convinced.

"Damn right I'm not gay." He was willing to prove it over and over again until she had no doubt in her soul. Skeletons were rattling in her closet, and usually this was the time he stood up and made his excuses, instead he nudged opened the door. "Tell me about them."

She did. He learned all about Davis, the douche bag, and Jeremy, the man who had really hurt her, the one she still mourned. He reached out and held her hand until she ran out of words. He wanted to hold her but was afraid she'd stop talking if he made any sudden movements. So he just held her hand like they were high school sweethearts.

When she finished, she met his eyes and gave him a slight smile. "Sorry about that, guess I had some feelings bottled up."

"Explains why you needed a change of scenery." Something he'd been wondering about. But would she stay?

"What's going on here, Lynx?" She released his hand and slumped back in her chair. "What we did in there—" she gestured toward the bedroom "—I've never experienced that before. I don't know you well enough to have lost myself like that. Who are you? What are you?"

"I'm just a man, Eva."

"I don't buy it. Clarify what happened earlier with BW."

He let out a deep breath. She'd been honest with him, but he couldn't return the favor. To do so would ruin another chance at a relationship. He shrugged and didn't meet her eyes. "Maybe he was finished mowing your front yard and decided it was time to move on." He hated lying to her, but wasn't willing to risk losing her so soon. Then again he wasn't really lying, just not telling the full truth. It still wasn't the best foot to start a relationship on. He was torn, and it must have shown in his face.

"That wasn't how it looked to me."

"How did it look?"

"As though you were talking to him. He acted as if he 'liked' you. Even in captivity moose aren't 'friendly'."

He held his breath. He couldn't go there with her, not yet. She wouldn't understand, and if he came clean now, she'd walk away just like the others had.

Her eyes narrowed as she studied him. Then she came to some sort of decision. "Want a cup of coffee?"

His heart skipped a beat. She wasn't throwing him out. Coffee meant caffeine, talking and sharing and staying up all night. "I'd love one."

Eva stood and entered the kitchen, motioning for him to stay seated. "Instead of coffee, how about a bottle of wine?"

A bottle?

"Okay." He watched her work, gathering glasses, wine from the refrigerator, and a corkscrew. She seemed comfortable in the kitchen, which shouldn't be a turn on in this day and age. He completely believed in equal rights and a woman's choice to do what she wanted, whether it was a doctor, trooper, or cook. He came from a very strong matriarchal family, with his grandmother and mother calling the shots, and if there were any decisions left to be made, his three sisters eagerly took charge. He'd spent most of his time growing up getting out of the way. But if any of them needed him, he was there and could protect and defend better than any grizzly bear.

Eva popped the cork from the bottle and poured two glasses of red wine, handing him one, and then setting her glass and the bottle on the table.

She sat, crossed her legs, the hem of her robe riding up higher on her bare thighs. "So, what now?"

He tore his gaze away from all her creamy flesh, and adjusted himself. Oh man. This wasn't going to be easy. In fact, things were getting harder and harder the longer he sat across from her, catching her scent that was more prevalent to him now that he'd tasted her, and seeing all that soft skin and knowing how it felt to sink into her. She probably didn't want to know what he'd like to do now.

He gathered a deep breath and let it out in a whoosh. "I'd like to keep seeing you."

She took a long sip of wine. "Does that mean we are just dating?"

"No." His tone was sharper than he'd meant it to be. Well, hell. In for a pound and all that. "I want to be exclusive." Isn't that the word women used? What he really wanted was to move her in with him and never let her go, but that might have her packing and running for the Canadian border.

"Like boyfriend and girlfriend?"

More like husband and wife. "Yeah." He'd take what he could get at this point. And having her call him husband might be a stretch this early.

She seemed to roll the idea around as she rolled the wine around in her glass. She lifted the wine to her lips and drank, then set the glass down and stood. "Okay. Let's take out my stitches."

So was that an agreement? Now who was off balance? Just like that, she'd taken the back reins. He bet she killed at chess.

His chair scraped the floor as he stood to follow. Instead of taking him to her bedroom or bathroom, she opened the door that entered into the back of the clinic. A stab of regret hit his heart. She might want this to be impersonal or clinical.

Well, she wasn't going to get it.

Eva opened an exam room and set the instruments needed to remove her stitches on a tray.

He was keeping something from her.

She wasn't ready to have him touch her again. Not when her emotions were still reeling from his lovemaking. Why had she agreed to be his girlfriend? She wasn't in high school or college for that matter. The man was keeping a secret from her, and she detested secrets. Why was she willing to do it, just because he was a God in the bedroom? Could she really be that easy?

Apparently.

He was so...much. More man then she'd ever dealt with before.

"Ready?" Lynx asked, having stayed back by the door as she prepared the room.

How long had she been standing there staring off into the photo of the northern lights hanging on the wall? "Yes." Once the stitches were removed then she could show him the door and take the emotional breather she needed.

He came up behind her, and what air she had left in her body lodged in her chest. Just having him close, had her resolve scattering.

He held out his hand to help her up on the examining table. The protective paper crinkled loudly in the stillness of the room as she lay on her stomach. She adjusted her robe

135

so she wasn't lying on the material, and he could easily raise it to get to her stitches.

"Ready?" he asked again, his voice deep, dark.

She nodded, knowing she wasn't up to speaking.

He dragged the silk over her skin to reveal the stitches. His breathing turned heavier, and she gritted her teeth to keep the moan from escaping from the sexiness of his caress.

She turned her head to the side so she could watch him. His brows knitted together in concentration, and she heard metal rasp as he picked up the cutters from the tray. He took a seat on the rolling stool, and his left hand cupped the cheek of her bottom, pulling the skin taut. She shivered.

"Are you cold?" he asked.

"No." Cold, she was not. If anything she wouldn't mind a winter squall blowing through the room about now.

Very professionally, he clipped each stitch and pulled them out. Total time couldn't have been more than a minute. Yet, her nerves were so on edge she was sweating when he finished.

"Got a mirror?" he asked, his voice husky as his fingers smoothed over the scar.

"Counter." She pointed to the hand mirror standing next to the sink. She rose on her elbows to get off the table.

He placed his hand in the middle of her back and held her down. "Not yet." He grabbed the mirror and positioned it for her to see. "Take a look."

She squinted and then squinted some more. "You're good." There was hardly a scar to speak of. Someone would have to be really close to find it. As close as Lynx currently was.

He set down the mirror, his long arm easily reaching the counter while his body stayed next to her, his other hand still on her lower back keeping her in place. Then he lowered his mouth and kissed her.

Right on the scar.

A moan escaped her. No. She wasn't going to do this. Not here. That's why she'd brought him into the clinic. What said no sex better than an exam room? Okay, maybe wrong choice of words as he proceeded to examine her.

"Lynx, we can't."

"Oh, yes, we can."

"I work here. I can't have sex here."

He laughed, his lips moving up her backside, uncovering her bottom completely. "Haven't you always wanted to play naughty nurse to sexy woodsman?"

Damn, he was sexy, and he had plenty of "wood." She was torn.

"I have appointments tomorrow. Little kids, I think. Vaccinations."

His hands snaked under her to cup her breasts, and he pulled her back against him. The exam room table was the perfect height for him to enter her from behind. "Just say the word, Eva, and I'll stop." He nipped the back of her neck.

Damn, he didn't play fair.

Oh hell, she didn't care. She could put the room back to rights, and no one would be the wiser except her. "Take me."

And he did.

Chapter Fourteen

Eva stretched and woke to the sun shining bright in her window like it was midday. She glanced at the clock in panic and then breathed easier when it revealed seven in the morning. Would she ever get used to this midnight sun? At least she'd slept last night. A marathon of sex would exhaust most, but a Lynx marathon put her into a coma. She'd vaguely remembered him kissing her goodbye some time around five, saying he'd been called out on a report. She'd have to have him clarify that later. He'd told her what he did for a living, but she still didn't fully understand it.

She groaned as she headed for the shower. No, make that tub. This morning she'd take the time needed for a hot soak in the bathtub. Otherwise she wouldn't get through her day of appointments. Maybe she should up her exercise routine. Who was she kidding? Lynx had upped it. It would just take a while to strengthen muscles she'd never used before, muscles she planned to use a lot in the future.

The day was a weird one. Either everyone was being affected by the twenty-four hours of daylight, the summer solstice coming up, or she wasn't privy to a town "language" that everyone else was. She tried calling Lynx, hoping he was free to have lunch with her, but had to leave a voicemail when he didn't answer.

When there was no word from him at the end of her day, Eva decided to head to the lodge for dinner.

She nodded to a few people on her walk as the lodge was only a mile from her place. Nice thing about small towns, most things were within walking distance. She'd probably only need her car to travel to Fairbanks, or to explore farther than the village. It would sure save her a lot in gas money. Besides, it was calming and beautiful to walk outside in the fresh air and sunshine. In Cincinnati she was always in the car from work to home to store. It was an effort to spend anytime outside because she was always rushing somewhere. This was a nice change of pace she hadn't known she needed.

She stepped up on the plank sidewalk of the lodge and entered the restaurant section. The lodge was the town hub. Part hotel, part restaurant, and part country store. If they didn't have what she needed, Fairbanks or the Internet was her only hope.

"Hey, Eva," Lynx's uncle Pike hollered from the kitchen. "How's life treating ya?"

"Great. Just great."

"So I heard." He saluted her with his spatula and a smile, returning his focus to the grill.

What did he mean by that?

She took a seat at the same table she'd waited for Lynx the night he'd stood her up so she could see out the windows, which were wide open to let the cooler air in. She'd be hard pressed to find any building in Alaska with air conditioning.

"Good to see you again, Eva," Bree greeted, setting a water glass in front of her. "Looks as if you and Lynx made up. Is he meeting you?"

"No. It's just me." Did everyone know they were a couple already? Who had Lynx been talking to? She hadn't told anyone. Not that she had many friends to tell. She hadn't made more than acquaintances as of yet.

There weren't many people in the restaurant as it was early for the dinner crowd. A few tourists at one table and two old sourdoughs sitting near the window, one with bat-winged brows and another with a snowy beard that would give Santa a run for his money. She half listened to the conversations going on around her as she studied the menu. She was starved after the night she'd had.

"Now, that there ain't no Fred Meyer bra," Bat-wing Brow said around a mouthful of food. "That's one of those fancy Victoria Secret numbers."

How would they know what kind of bra a woman was wearing under her clothes? Eva centered more of her hearing on their conversation. Beat the one with the woman tourist discussing the merits of different bug spray brands to her husband who looked like he was ready to bug out.

"Bet you a cord of wood that's a citified garment," Bat-winged Brow said.

"How in the hell do you know that?" Snowy Beard asked.

"No way is that boulder holder going to keep the titties warm come winter. I guarantee you that."

"Like you've seen any titties in the last two decades," Snowy Beard said, shoveling mashed potatoes in his mouth.

"Now don't be spouting off about things you know nothing about," Bat-winged Brow said. "Granted it's been a few seasons between the lovelies, but by the looks of the bra BW is sporting, I'd lay ten to one odds that bra is our new nurse practitioner's."

Eva jerked up from the menu and looked out the window at what the men were talking about.

There was BW grazing on wildflowers alongside the road with her lavender bra hanging off his antlers.

Holy shit.

How had that moose gotten a hold of her bra? She sank into her chair and raised the menu to cover her face. Her heart thrashed like a hummingbird's as she tried to think it through.

Lynx had taken the bra off her last night along with her top while they were still outside her door. Come to think of it, she didn't know where her top was either. She hadn't given her clothes a thought, not when all she could think of was Lynx. Embarrassment flamed up her body in waves.

"No way am I taking that bet," Snowy Beard said. "But I'll think I'll make an appointment with the little gal. How do you think BW came about such a lovely garment?"

"I wouldn't put it past Lynx to have found a way around her mad for standing her up the other night. That boy never did stay in trouble for long."

"Yep, he sure does have a way with the ladies."

Eva sank farther behind her menu. *A way with the ladies? How many ladies?* Maybe he wasn't as invested in their relationship as she realized she was.

Had she jumped from one doomed relationship to another? You couldn't call what she'd done a pattern because she hadn't fallen for another gay man. Lynx was as straight as a birch tree. But could he be just entertaining himself with her? And where the hell was he anyway?

"Have you decided what to order?" Bree asked, trying her hardest to keep a straight face. She'd heard those old sourdoughs too. Damn it.

Eva slapped the menu down on the table. It wasn't in her to hide like some simpering female. "I want the moose steak. Rare."

CHAPTER FIFTEEN

Crap, there were three of them.

How was he going to take down three poachers? Lynx settled back on his haunches, hiding deep within the diamond willow and watched. He needed to catch them unawares, and so far they'd been pretty damn aware.

He should have known it was Chad Diamond bringing in hunters on Refuge land. Damn idiot, he knew better than to risk poaching. They'd put him away for good this time. The other two men Lynx didn't recognize. Knowing Chad, he was hiring out as a guide and charging a king's ransom.

One man was big, well over six feet, probably as tall as Lynx was, somewhere in his forties, but that beer belly would slow him down. The other worried Lynx a little more. About ten years younger than Beer Belly, he had a military stance and comfortable manner in which he held his rifle as though it were an extension of his limbs. He wore camo cargo pants with a big knife strapped to his belt, along with a handgun. Lynx figured he probably had a smaller one strapped to his ankle. Yeah, he'd be the one to worry about. Chad would most likely run for the hills.

Lynx had found their truck where his informant had said it was and parked right next to it. Not leaving anything to chance, he'd disabled the late 80's pick-up by taking out the distributor cap and hiding it in the woods. He snapped pictures of the butchered moose head already lying in the bed of the truck, sickened over the needless waste for a fucking trophy to hang on some idiot's wall. He'd tracked them into the woods from there. Now he sat, ignoring the protesting of his muscles as he blended into the foliage around him.

The evidence indicated a snatch and grab. The trio had no camping equipment, and didn't build a fire to cook their lunch as they rested and ate MREs.

Lynx slowly slid his cell phone from his pocket. One bar. Pretty soon he wouldn't have that. He texted his trooper buddy in Fairbanks and sent his GPS coordinates. Chances were this would be all over with by the time Nate could get here. Lynx was on his own, but that didn't really bother him. He did most of his job alone.

He waited. One thing about stopping for lunch, their next step would be to relieve themselves. Then he'd catch them with their pants down.

Beer Belly was the first to stand, spitting and hiking up his belt.

"Fucking-a, Pete," Beer Belly said. "As soon as we bag that other moose I'm going to get me some of that honey at the Lodge. Did you see the lips on that native? They're going to look might purty around my pecker." He turned to Chad. "Whatdaya say her name was?"

"Raven," Chad answered, tearing off another bite of jerky.

Lynx steeled himself to remain where he was and not gut the man where he stood.

"But if I were you, I'd leave her alone," Chad continued. "She's got a badass of a brother who also happens to be the Refuge Officer."

Whom they were about to meet. At least Chad was showing some sense. Dumbass. Breaking bread with these men.

"Naw," Pete said, relaxing his stance a little. He'd yet to sit. "You can go for the native, Big Bart. I want a taste of that sweet little blonde nurse. Bet she's a hellcat in the sack."

Yeah, he had to die.

"You can't be dipping your wicks in Chatanika," Chad said, with a shake of his head. "Bad enough you've been hanging out there. We bag that second bull moose, and you get the fuck out of town, and forget you were ever here. No dawdling."

"Relax, Chad," Big Bart said. "We're savvy enough to bag more than one trophy on this trip." Big Bart gave a raunchy laugh along with a few hip thrusts. Pete joined in with a more sedate chuckle while Chad shook his head again.

Lynx almost felt sorry for him.

Pete looked around and then seemed to relax his guard and took a seat on a fallen log.

Yeah, get comfortable with your surroundings, Lynx thought.

Big Bart grabbed his rifle. "I'm going to go give Mother Nature a what for." And headed off into the trees.

Lynx readied himself, inching quiet as a cat, in the direction of Beer Belly Bart.

"Don't be taking all day," Pete hollered. "I want to be in that blonde's bed by sundown."

Asshole. Sundown wasn't happening until sometime in July, and no way was Lynx letting him get close to Eva.

"No sundown, remember," Chad pointed out.

"It's an expression," Pete responded. "You're strung too tight."

"Let's just get the moose and get out of here." Chad looked around. "Something doesn't feel right."

Pete stood, drawing his gun, scanning the clearing. A porcupine swaggered slowly by. "It's just a rodent. You need a woman worse than we do."

"What I need is to get this over with."

Not to worry, Lynx thought. It will be over with soon enough.

He skirted the clearing, staying deep within the shadows. The forest seemed to hold its breath as he headed in the direction of Big Bart.

The man was whizzing on a poor bush of wild rose-hips. Lynx snuck up behind him, Glock already palmed, and placed the barrel at the base of Bart's head. "Don't move," he growled softly.

Bart squeaked.

"Shake it off, and put your hands in the air," Lynx said.

"Shit, man. I need to shit."

"Not my problem, dumbass. Come on, zip it up." Lynx waited until the man did what he said. With his hands in the air, Lynx searched him, finding a hunting knife, pepper spray, and another firearm. He was packing more than Lynx had given him credit for.

Never underestimate your prey.

Big Bart's rifle leaned against a tree too far out of range. First rule of the forest, you never put your rifle out of arm's reach even while answering a call of nature.

"Hands behind you," Lynx said.

"Come on, man, all I was doing was taking a piss. Don't tell me there's a law against that?"

"I'm sure the rosehips would like to file a charge. You know what this is about. You picked the wrong place to poach. Alaskans take the crime of poaching seriously."

"P-poaching? Man, we're out here for a nature hike."

"Right. Hands behind you."

"Give me a break," Bart whined. "I can't get my hands behind me."

That was a problem. The man's girth started at his shoulders and worked its way down to his gut, his legs looked fairly trim, causing him to resemble an ostrich.

"Fine, in front then." Though Lynx preferred the off-balance of a prisoner's arms behind him, the man would still be restrained.

Big Bart gave a deep sigh and put his hands together over his stomach. "I could really make this worth your time if you would forget I was here."

"I can't be bribed, but I'm happy to add that to the list of charges." Lynx zip-tied Bart's hands together while he read him his rights. All the while Bart bitched like a PMSing woman.

"Yo, Big Bart, what the hell's taking you so long?" Pete hollered.

"Run, Pete! I've been snagged by a trooper," Bart bellowed.

Shit.

The problem was Pete didn't run.

Before Lynx could blink a fist slammed into his face, followed up by another to his gut. Air whooshed out of him, and he fought to stay on his feet with stars blinking over-head. He blocked another hit, but not the one to the back of his head.

Damn. Chad, the weasel, had snuck up behind him.

The midnight sun set behind his eyelids.

CHAPTER SIXTEEN

Eva sat in wait for BW.

She'd get her bra back from that reputation-ruining moose if it was the last thing she did. She'd bought apples at the lodge's market and laid a trail back to her place. With her kitchen shears in hand, she watched BW munch away and wondered how stupid she really was to sneak up on him and cut her bra free of his antlers.

Where the hell was Lynx? The man had tranquilizers that would come in real handy right about now.

There had been no return calls from her messages. Yes, she was upset with herself that she'd actually left more than one. All right three. Lynx hadn't seemed the type of man to sleep with a woman and then forget her the next day. She hadn't figured him for a player. But then, she didn't have the best track record with men either. So what the hell did she know?

Case in point, she was stalking a moose with a pair of scissors.

She crept up on BW. His ears twitched, one facing toward her, the other facing back. This damn moose was determined to make a headline out of her. Instead of her being held hostage in her house, she was now going to be known as the cheechako in a tug-a-war for her bra, which would bring up questions of how she lost it in the first place.

This was so messed-up. Or fucking moosed-up. Yeah, she completely understood the terminology now.

She inched a couple of feet closer to BW. His head stayed down as he munched the pieces of apples she'd sliced with her newly purchased pocket knife—also from the lodge—while on the trek back to the clinic.

She bit her lips to keep from uttering, "Nice moosey" again. Last time that had gotten her chased up a tree. A few more inches closer, and suddenly BW raised his massive rack and pierced her with his deep, knowing brown eyes. There was intelligence there, probably more than she possessed. Her very expensive, lavender, Victoria Secret bra—the sourdoughs knew their lingerie—swung from his antlers.

They stared at each other. Eva didn't breathe as she slowly raised her hand with the scissors.

"What are you doing?"

Eva yelped, jumping back and dropping the scissors while BW took off into the woods, spraying her with clumps of dirt, her lavender bra waving like a flag as he navigated the trees.

Damn it.

Eva swung around to find Raven behind her.

"Are you nuts?" Raven asked. "What did you *think* you were doing?"

"Trying to cut my bra off his antlers." Wasn't it obvious?

Raven paused and then started to laugh, holding her stomach as she bent at the waist and gave into the belly roll.

In disgust, Eva gave a longing look in BW's direction. No sign of him. Who knew how long it would take to coax him back, and how many apples? She'd have to drive into Fairbanks since she'd bought out the lodge.

She picked up the scissors and took a seat on the stairs while Raven laughed. Raven eventually sobered, wiping her eyes of tears, and joined Eva.

"You should have seen yourself. I thought you were going to stab him or something."

"I'm not that much of an idiot. Besides, if I want to stab someone, I have much sharper instruments in the clinic."

"So, it is true. Want to tell me how BW came about wearing your undergarments?"

"One undergarment. And would you buy that I'd hung clothes to dry, and he got tangled in the clothes line?"

"No, not when I see how Lynx looks at you."

"Does everyone know?" This small town stuff was going to take a lot of getting used to. She never thought she'd miss the anonymity of the big city.

"Yes. They're taking bets."

"Bets! On what?"

"Well, the first—and this was set when you arrived in town—how long you'd last. The second, and more interesting, is whether or not you'll tame Lynx."

"Tame Lynx? As in...?" She couldn't bring herself to utter the word.

"Yes, marriage." Raven laughed all over again at Eva's shocked expression. "Relax, the invitations haven't gone out. Yet." She giggled again, wiping at the mirth tearing in her eyes. "Damn, but you are fun."

"We aren't even technically dating. He stood me up, and after sleeping with him last night, he hasn't returned any of my calls."

Now, why had she said that?

"Ah, I knew there was a good story on how BW got a hold of your bra." Raven suddenly got serious. "How do you feel about Lynx?"

"Uh." Did she share with this woman? While they had been friendly since she'd arrived in town, they weren't really confidants. She hadn't had a confidant since Jeremy. Did she want to risk developing another one? Yes, as it turned out, she did. "Can we talk?" She dropped the scissors on the stair next to her and clasped her hands between her knees. "I really could use another woman to talk to."

Raven met her eyes and studied her for a long uncomfortable minute, as though really sizing her up. "You realize he's my brother?"

149

"Can you be impartial?"

"I think so."

Eva gathered her courage. Courage that she used to have buckets full of until Davis and Jeremy had emotionally beaten her up. She set all that aside. This was a new life, a new beginning, and Raven, a new friend.

"I think I could really care for Lynx. What am I saying? I already care too much for him."

"And the problem?" Raven's lips flirted with a smile.

"I don't know him," Eva said. Raven cocked a brow, and the heat of Eva's blush belied the fact. "Okay, so I might physically know him after last night." And very much wanted to *physically* know him better. "But I've never fallen so fast into bed before. I usually take a long time getting to know a man before taking that step. I'm off balance."

"Isn't love all about being off balance? Explains that tingling in the belly and dizziness. That's why they call it falling in love."

Could she really be falling in love? So fast?

"There is no time frame for love," Raven continued, having correctly read the panic Eva felt. "You can't put logical parameters on it. Love just is."

"But what about Lynx?" Was she the only one hanging out here on the proverbial limb?

"I don't know what he's feeling, but I will tell you this. I've never seen him make a fool of himself over a woman like he has you."

"Then where is he? I haven't heard a word from him since he left earlier this morning." She hoped she didn't sound as desperate as she felt, but was very much afraid her desperation had vocalized itself loud and clear.

"Did he say were he was going?"

"Something about a report of poachers he'd been tracking."

"Hmm." Raven swung a long wing of black hair over her shoulder. "His job is one of those where he can be gone for days. Once even a few weeks."

"Weeks?"

"He's usually good about checking in when he can. He has a GPS spot tracker on him if he's out of cell range, which is most of the time. He's in charge of a big area, and it requires a lot of his time." She paused and slightly narrowed her eyes. "Are you one of those women who need a lot of attention?"

Eva paused wondering if that was some sort of insult and then decided it was an honest question, trying to get to know more about her. "No. I don't mind being alone, and Lord knows men get underfoot when they are around too long, but when I share myself with a man for the first time, I wouldn't mind a return phone call."

"Totally understandable. And knowing Lynx, he'd call if he could."

"You don't think he could be in danger, do you?" The thought had the power to paralyze her if she let it.

"I don't know many men who can handle themselves in the woods like Lynx can. It's like he's one with the animals. Don't worry, I'd know if he were in trouble."

"How?"

Raven waited another long minute before responding, and Eva got the impression she was letting her in on a secret. "I'd feel it."

CHAPTER SEVENTEEN

He was going to feel this for days.

Lynx lay on his side, pretending he was still unconscious as the three men argued about what to do with him. He took stock of his injuries and decided he was bruised but not beaten. Nothing broken, nor internal bleeding, but damn he was going to hurt. He'd make them hurt as soon as he could get out of his *own* restraints.

They had found his zip ties and had his hands secured behind his back and his feet restrained together. He'd never live this down if his fellow officers found him like this. He'd have to make sure that didn't happen.

"We can dump him in the river," Pete snarled.

That got Lynx's attention off his injuries and back to the conversation these dumbasses were having. He slowly cracked open one eye. No one paid any attention to him. Were they really thinking of killing him? That was so not going to happen.

"We can't k-kill him," Chad sputtered. "He's a trooper. And I know him."

"You want to go to jail?" Pete got up in Chad's face.

Chad cowered back. "No. But I'm not going to be a part of murder either."

"You're either with us or against us," Big Bart added. "Guess what happens if you're against us?" He belly laughed when Chad paled. "Got that right." Big Bart slid a shifty look Pete's way. "You know we could try a whole other type of hunting?"

Pete shared a look with Big Bart and then a smiled. "I haven't done that since Iraq."

Lynx's blood shivered through his veins. Chad paled even further and backed up a few more steps. Then he ran for his life.

Pete threw his head back with sick laughter. "Let's do it! But I want the trooper."

Big Bart had an unnatural gleam in his eyes. "Just remember our motto."

"Shoot, shovel, and shut up," they quoted together following with a fist bump.

Big Bart grabbed his rifle and gear and traipsed after poor Chad.

Pete paced toward Lynx. "Been awake a while, I see."

"You two are whacked." Lynx struggled into a sitting position.

"There is nothing that makes you feel more alive than taking a life, whether big game or human. But hunting someone who I can pit skill and brains against is another high all its own."

Lynx kept his mouth shut and let the idiot talk himself into his own grave.

"It's actually more sporting for you this way. I could just leave you here to die, dump your body in the river, or give you the chance to kill me while I attempt to kill you."

Lynx knew without a doubt how that scenario would turn out. This idiot was fertilizer.

"So what's the game plan?" Lynx asked. "How sporting is this going to be?" Would the dumbass actually cut loose his ties?

"Think you have what it takes to take out a marine?"

"You're a marine? Funny, all the marines I know have honor. There's no honor in this."

Pete smirked. "If I had no honor I'd shoot you where you sit. Instead, I'm going to let you go, and then hunt you down."

"You are warped." And it would be Lynx's pleasure putting this bastard away.

"Just living on the edge." Pete flipped open his switchblade. "Turn around."

Like he would give this psychopath his back. Instead Lynx moved his restrained hands to his hips so Pete could cut the zip tie.

Pete chuckled. "This is going to be fun."

Next he cut loose Lynx's feet. Lynx fisted and released his hands, trying to pump blood back into his arms. He didn't make any sudden moves as Pete had his rifle trained on him with one hand as he flipped the switchblade closed and pocketed it with the other.

"Are you going to leave me my weapon?" It galled him to know that this piss-ant had gotten the jump on him and had his Glock tucked into the waistband of his cargo pants.

Pete looked at him under hooded eyes. "That knock on your head must've fucked up your brains." Pete took Lynx's Glock out of his waistband and hefted it up and down. "Nice piece. I'll keep it as a trophy of your kill as I can't really stuff and mount you on my wall." He laughed at his sick joke. "But to make it more sporting, I'll give you a ten minute head start." His lips smirked into a cruel smile. "Promise."

No way in hell did Lynx believe him. Slowly, he got to his feet, feeling the soreness from the hits to his gut and head. He wanted to rush Pete, take him down like a linebacker, but not when he held all the weapons.

Lynx inched back into the forest, not taking his eyes off Pete. When he felt more blended with his surroundings, he took off at a run for Chad. The idiot wouldn't survive these fuckups. And he'd make damn sure the fuckups didn't survive him.

Lynx became one with the forest, listening to her breathe, the animals converse, focusing on the subtle clues on which direction Chad and Big Bart had headed, all the while not leaving a trail for Pete to follow.

It didn't take long for the crashing up ahead to alert him to Chad bumbling through the undergrowth. Then the cackle of Big Bart's laughter taunting him.

"Dude, please, I've got me a wife and kids," Chad begged for his life. Lynx had to give him props for trying. The man was as single as Lynx was. Scratch that. More single, since Lynx no longer considered himself unattached, not with Eva holding his heart.

Lynx snuck up on them, and peered through the thick brush. Chad was on his knees, his hands in the air, and Big Bart had his rifle trained on him.

"I really hoped you would've made this more sporting," Big Bart said. "I hate it when they beg."

They? How many times had these two done this?

Pete burst through the trees. "Fuck. I lost him."

"The trooper? Are you shitting me?"

"Just finish this, and help me track him down. He just disappeared. No trace of him at all. Never seen anything like it."

"Better let us go," Chad said. "Lynx Maiski is different, he's more."

"More what?"

"They say more animal than man."

Shut up, Chad. Lynx positioned himself to make a grab for Pete.

"Right," Pete scoffed.

"No, listen, man. You don't mess with the Maiskis."

"Well, since you aren't one of them we can dispose of you right here," Pete said, raising his rifle. "Take your shot, Big Bart, or I'll do it for you."

Lynx rushed Pete from behind, taking him down to the forest floor, and getting Big Bart's attention off Chad and onto them. They struggled, Lynx getting in a few lucky jabs, to repay him for the sucker punches of earlier, grabbing his weapon back in the tussle. He was too close to Pete to do any real damage, and vice versa. It was more of a wrestling match that Pete started to lose.

"Shoot the fucker!" Pete yelled, grunting as Lynx got an arm around his neck.

Lynx rolled him just as there was the repeat of the rifle going off. Pete's body jerked, and then went still.

Lynx whipped his gun around, and Big Bart froze.

"Put the gun down," Lynx said in a deadly voice.

"Oh, thank you, God." Chad raised his face into the heavens, his hands together while he prayed.

"Pete, man, talk to me," Big Bart pleaded.

"I said put down the gun," Lynx hollered, standing and inching toward Big Bart.

Big Bart blinked at Lynx. "I shot him."

"Yeah, you did. And I'm going to shoot you if you don't lay down your goddamn weapon." The resolve in Lynx's voice must have gotten through that thick skull of his, because he slowly lowered his rifle to the ground.

Lynx didn't take his eyes off him as with one hand holding the Glock, he searched Big Bart's pockets and located his zip ties. He secured his weapon in its holster, grabbed both of Big Bart's arms and wrenched them behind his back.

"Shit, man, you're killing me." Big Bart groaned in pain.

"Uh, Lynx," Chad said.

"Shut up, Chad. And don't you dare move. I'm so fucking mad at you."

"But, man—"

"Shut the hell up." Lynx finished restraining Big Bart with the zip tie, and searched him for weapons. He shoved him down to his knees. "Don't even blink."

Then he turned to Chad, his eyes scanning the area. "Where the hell did Pete go?"

"That's what I was trying to tell you," Chad said. "He crawled off that way." Chad pointed north.

Shit.

"Hands behind you, Chad."

"Me? What did I do?"

"Brought these poachers onto my Refuge, and I suspect you were responsible for the other kills I've found in the last few weeks."

"Oh, man. Come on, don't arrest me. Think of my mother."

"I'm sure she could use the break from your constant screw-ups." Lynx restrained Chad the same as he had Big Bart. Searching for weapons and finding him clean, Lynx grabbed his elbow and helped him to his feet. "You really are a dumbass."

"I know. I promise to change. Can't you just let it go?"

Lynx looked him in the eye until Chad glanced down at his feet. "Uh, guess not," Chad said.

"You cooperate and I'll tell the judge. That's the best I can do."

Chad had enough smarts to give up on the matter.

He turned to Big Bart and yanked him to his feet. "Now, listen up. We are going to hike out of here. You two don't want to give me any more trouble, because I'm really pissed off." He read them their rights as he picked up Big Bart's rifle and had both guns trained on them, marching them out of the forest, keeping an eye out for wounded Pete.

"Pete's gonna get you," Big Bart said. "You're a dead man."

Lynx nudged him to move faster as he opened up all his senses, scanning for anything that would warn him of Pete's whereabouts. He should have made sure Pete was restrained rather than thinking he was dead. He knew better than to assume anything in his job. Assumptions got you killed.

Strung tight, he hiked his prisoners to the place he'd parked his truck.

Ah, shit.

His truck was gone. Pete had taken his keys when he'd gone through his pockets.

"Climb in the back," Lynx said to the two, lowering the tailgate of the truck he'd disabled. Next time he'd disable his own, too, in order to safeguard against this happening again.

"I'm not riding back there with that," Big Bart said, gesturing with his head to the severed moose they'd already poached.

Lynx prodded him with the end of the rifle. "Move."

Cussing, Big Bart rolled into the bed of the truck, trying to stay clear of the blood and flies already gathering on the rotting, exposed flesh.

"Chad."

"Seriously, dude."

"Seriously. Get up there."

There wasn't a lot of room with the huge pointy rack of the bull moose.

"Backs together," Lynx instructed, looking around the clearing just in case Pete laid in wait after moving his truck. There was nothing but silence. Even the forest creatures were quiet as they took time out to watch the entertainment. Lynx set down the rifle and holstered his Glock. Grabbing the rope laying in the bed of the truck, he secured the men together and then tied them to the moose carcass.

"Oh, man," Chad complained.

"I'm sure this falls under cruel and unusual punishment," Big Bart said.

Lynx smiled and made sure the knots were tight. He then hiked back into the forest and grabbed the distributer cap that he'd hidden. Making quick work of putting the part back and then using the keys he'd taken off of Big Bart, Lynx started the truck and headed to Chatanika. He called Nate, who it had turned out hadn't received his previous text, and told him he needed backup, giving him Pete's description and that he'd commandeered his U.S. National Fish and Wildlife Refuge vehicle.

Yeah, he'd have a tough time living that down.

Chapter Eighteen

Eva heard Lynx's truck pull up outside and tried to calm the beating of her heart.

What was she, sixteen again?

She rushed to the front door and forced herself to slow to a moderate pace. It wouldn't look good for her to swing open the door and greet him before he even got out of his truck. That would give away too much of what she was feeling. Give him more power over her. She stood on the inside of the door, waiting instead. Hearing him shut the door to his truck and walk up to the path to her door, his gait sounded tired, and she wondered for the umpteenth time what he had been out doing all day. She glanced at her watch. It was headed on eleven. With this crazy sun, there was no way she'd be able to tell night from day without her watch.

As Lynx shuffled up the stairs, she couldn't wait anymore to see him. She swung open the door, and found herself staring into the barrel of a gun.

"Hey, blondie," the man greeted. "Do as I say and you won't get hurt. Now, back up. Slow like. That's my girl."

Eva's heart skipped and then lurched with panic. "Where's Lynx?" That was Lynx's truck this dirty, gun-wielding bastard had gotten out of.

"Don't worry about him. Worry about yourself and what I'm going to do to you if you don't follow my instructions."

Eva swallowed her panic. She needed to keep her head about her, somehow deal with this piece of trash, find Lynx, and make sure he was okay and that this asshole hadn't hurt him.

"What do you want?"

The man smiled, kicking the door shut behind him as he continued to back her up with the gun in her face. "Let's start with the more pressing issues." His smile turned creepy as he looked her up and down, licking his lips. "Then we'll move on from there."

She read that look. No way were they moving into that territory. Blood coated the side of his shirt.

"Let's go into the clinic," she said, "and I'll take a look at your injury."

"I do like an agreeable woman."

Agreeable? She couldn't wait to go all psycho bitch on his ass. If he hurt Lynx, she'd do worse than that. First, she needed to get the gun out of her face.

"Can you lower that thing?" she asked, as she backed up to the door that entered into the clinic.

He sized her up and down again, and lowered the gun to his side, seeming to find her harmless.

His mistake.

She showed him into the exam room across the hall from where Lynx had removed her stitches. No way could she use the same room, not with the memories still floating around in there from the night before.

"Get up on the table, and take off your shirt," Eva said.

He climbed up, setting the gun next to his hip and slowly unbuttoned his shirt. The man was packed with muscle, not as much muscle as Lynx, but enough to render her useless in a struggle. He winced as he pulled the bloody fabric loose from his left side.

"Ooh, that's nasty," she said, carefully inching in for a closer look. Blood bubbled out from the wound. "I'm surprised you made it here without passing out." Now there was a thought. She prayed he'd lost enough blood to do exactly that.

"It's fine. Just close it up." He took his eyes off her to look at the wound, his skin paling.

She reached for a drawer and the gun came up in her face lightning-quick.

"What are you doing?" he asked.

She had to swallow past the fear in her throat in order to respond. "Getting gloves and supplies so I can assess the situation."

The gun wavered, and then he dropped it back to the exam table. Was it getting heavy for him to hold?

"Tell me everything you're doing before you do it, and we'll get along just fine."

"Okay. Just relax." Stupid Neanderthal. She snapped gloves on, never happier than right now not having actual skin to skin contact with someone, and grabbed a handful of gauze pads. She held up the gauze for him to see before wiping blood from the wound for a better look.

"Tell me how you got this wound."

"No."

Her eyes flicked to his. "You realize I need to know what happened so I can figure out the best way to treat you."

"Just patch me up and stop the pain."

She tightened her lips and examined the wound. She'd only seen a bullet wound once, but that was enough to know exactly what this was. She hoped to God, Lynx had been the one to shoot his sorry ass. But what if he'd gotten to Lynx first and he lay bleeding to death out there right now while she was wasting time nursing this guy?

"Ouch! Watch what the hell you're doing."

She jumped back when he'd hollered. "There is no exit wound."

"So."

"I know this is from a bullet. You need to go to the hospital."

"I'm not going to any fucking hospital." His hand tightened on the gun, and he pointed it back at her, resting the butt of the weapon on his thigh. "Now fix me up."

Oh, she'd do that all right. "You want me to dig the bullet out, or sew you up with it still inside?"

The direness of his situation finally dawned on him, and he swore.

"You could have internal bleeding," she said, piling on the bad news. "I'm not equipped for surgery here."

He swore some more. "I'm going to kill that fucking bastard."

Did that mean Lynx was still alive? Her heart swelled, and she had to glance away or chance revealing the rush of feelings coursing through her.

"Can you tell where the bullet is?"

She met his eyes. "It's going to hurt if I probe in there, but I'll be able to tell fairly quickly if it's something I can treat or not."

He studied her for what felt like another endless night. "Do it." He released a deep breath out of his nostrils.

She placed gauze pads over the wound to help with the bleeding. "Here hold these in place, and could you put the gun somewhere else? I don't want you to 'accidently' shoot me if I hurt you." And she planned on hurting him.

"Don't hurt me, and I won't shoot you."

"Seriously? What's your name solider?" She'd recognized the marine tattoo. That seemed to get her somewhere with this redneck.

"Pete."

"Okay, Pete. How about you let me give you an injection. I have locals here for stitches and such. Nothing stronger than that." She lied when he went to shake his head. "This is a small clinic. I can't have hard drugs here. People would be breaking in all the time." She said that with enough deadpan that he bought it.

"Do it."

She pointed to the cupboard above her. "I'm going to open the door and grab medicine. I should give you a shot of antibiotics too."

"Yeah. Good idea."

She relaxed her breathing, trying to show a calm she didn't feel as she turned and opened the door, slowly going through the vials of medication, looking for something that would knock this douche bag on his ass. She couldn't go for anything that he'd recognize or anything that would take too long, since he'd feel the results and probably shoot her dead before the drugs completely took affect.

"Nice ass," Pete hummed. "The higher you reach the better your ass looks."

Oh yeah, he was going down. In the back, she found what she was searching for.

Ah, that would do nicely. She opened the other cupboard and pulled out a vial of penicillin. "Are you allergic to anything?"

"No."

It seemed the more medical in nature she kept the conversation, the more he lowered his guard.

"I'm grabbing a syringe."

"Let me see the meds."

Holding her breath, she carefully picked up the bottles and showed them to him. He studied the bottles, barely glancing at the penicillin which was clearly labeled. "What's this?" He pointed.

"A common local, used to deaden the area so that it doesn't hurt when I dig into you with tweezers looking for that bullet."

He winced at her words, and then gestured with his hand. "Get to it then."

She turned back to the cabinets as relief flushed through her in a hot rush. Her hands shook, readying the two syringes. She faced him again, placing the full syringes on the tray next to the table. She carefully peeled back the gauze pads to see the angry wound. Yeah, this wasn't going to be pleasant for either of them. Him, it was going to hurt, and if she wasn't careful, he'd kill her for hurting him. Talk about a sticky situation. She bit her lip and wiped the area with alcohol. "This is going to pinch," she warned before sticking him with the needle.

He hissed through his teeth.

She depressed the syringe watching the narcotic disappear into his body. She'd doubled the dose not taking any chances on it not being enough. He was a big man, probably tipping the scales at over two hundred with the amount of muscle on display. The double dose might kill him. But, surprisingly she was okay with that. Served him right for hurting Lynx and threatening her, besides if she didn't get him under control, he'd kill her or worse.

She finished injecting him and set the empty syringe on the tray. "I need to inject the penicillin in your behind."

He grunted and leaned over so she could reach his ass.

She stabbed the needle into him, really loving her job when he swore.

"Shit, woman."

"Sorry." She pulled out the needle and didn't rub the injection site like she usually did with any other patient. No way was she touching him any more than she had to.

"Now what are you doing?" he hollered, when she turned back to the drawers.

"Sorry, gathering instruments to probe the wound."

He winced at her choice of words, which is why she'd chose them. No reason to sugarcoat anything.

She took pleasure in dropping the wicked sharp, long tweezers on the tray and enjoyed his skin paling when she next picked up a scalpel.

"Whoa," he said, the gun rising again. "Is that a knife?"

She glanced down at the scalpel in her fingers. "I guess you could call it that." She looked at him as innocently as she could, praying she was pulling it off. "I might need it to make the entry site bigger in order to dig out the bullet."

"Shit." He nodded, and she noticed his head seemed to flop more than it should. "Put it on the tray, but don't reach for it without asking me first."

"Okay." Slower, she added disinfectant, sutures, needle and bandages. "I'm going to need you to lie on your side."

He looked at the door and around the room, much like a cornered animal who wasn't willing to lower his guard. "No."

"Listen, Pete." She used her most convincing nurse-maid voice. "I need the light in order to investigate the wound. Your body creates a shadow. It will be more comfortable for you to lie down, and I'll be quicker."

He seemed to war with himself, and then gave in and lay on his side, keeping his arm free with the gun still glued in his hand. She noticed his eyelids dip and stay closed longer than normal.

Come on drug, do your thing.

"What are you looking at?" he demanded, when he opened his eyes to find her watching him.

"Nothing." *Keep working, Eva.* Don't give him a reason to suspect that you shot him up with narcotics. He was feeling the effects. She needed him to think of another reason to explain the tiredness that would hit him any minute. "We really need to get you to a hospital. You've lost a lot of blood."

Maybe she'd taken it too far or he'd finally wised up. "You bitch. Whatdaya give me?"

The gun came up, and she knew she was toast. With nothing to lose, she made a grab for the gun. It went off, putting a nice hole in her ceiling, and had plaster raining down on them. They struggled, and she fell on him, making sure her elbow dug into his wounded side. Pete screamed, and she freed the gun from his hand.

The door to the room slammed open against the opposing wall, and Lynx rushed in, his gun raised with another armed man in a navy and gold trooper uniform right behind him.

Reflexes had her swinging the gun toward the new interruption.

"Eva, honey, hand me the gun," Lynx soothed, reaching out his hand.

She stood frozen for a moment, the gun still trained on Lynx as Pete threatened and cursed her heritage.

"Eva, hand me the gun." Lynx slowly inched toward her, letting the guy standing behind him cover Pete in case he decided to give them any trouble. Lynx's hand enclosed hers. "That's it. Let go. I've got it." He talked to her in a calming voice, like he was talking down a jumper.

She didn't realize how tight she was strung until Lynx had Pete's gun and yanked her into the warmth and safety of his arms. Then she started to shake like a dried, golden birch leaf ready to fall.

"You got this?" Lynx asked the uniform over her head.

"What's to get? Your woman took him out."

Eva disengaged herself from Lynx's comforting arms. She wanted to stay and never leave the protective circle, but she still had a patient.

"I drugged him up. We need to call an ambulance or air flight him to Fairbanks. I might have overdosed him."

"You are quite the woman," the uniform said with an appreciative look. "No wonder Lynx is ready to call bachelor life quits."

"Nate," Lynx growled the warning through his teeth.

"What? You haven't finalized the deal yet?" Nate turned toward Eva and gave her a smile that twinkled. "Hi, I'm Nate Lewis. And if you'd like to have dinner with me, I'd love to feed you."

"Back off. She only eats dinner with me."

"I've yet to eat dinner with you," Eva said. "You stood me up, remember? Besides, I don't belong to anyone."

167

Nate choked on his laugh, and Lynx's expression darkened. Then he grasped Eva's arm turning it to see better. "Are you bleeding?"

She shook her head. "It's not mine."

"Nice," Nate said.

"Let's get this dirt bag out of here," Eva said. "He's mudding up my clinic." Eva turned back to Pete. He was out cold but still bleeding. She moved to stanch the blood, but Lynx grabbed her arm.

"You don't have to do this. He held you hostage."

"I'm okay."

"You might think you are." He held up his hand when she went to interrupt. "I can bandage him until the paramedics get here. I'm a registered veterinarian, and he's basically an animal."

"Let me help. I'll be fine. Seriously. I can do this."

He smiled at her with what she interpreted to be pride, and it made her heart swell with that teenage excitement. She did her best to tamp it back. There was too much going on to let an infatuation with this man stay in the forefront. "After we take care of him, and you get him out of my clinic, I need an explanation on what the hell this was all about."

CHAPTER NINETEEN

Lynx returned to Chatanika after delivering the poachers to the jail in Fairbanks. The paperwork had seemed endless, and a new day had begun by the time he was finished. Pete was handcuffed to his bed in the Fairbanks Memorial Hospital with a guard stationed outside his room. Last Lynx had heard, Pete had come to cussing about the demon nurse in Chatanika. Lynx liked the description, so proud of Eva and the way she'd handled herself, though he never wanted to see her in danger again.

That was one woman with a level head on her shoulders. And a very pretty one at that. He passed the clinic on the way to his place, badly wanting to pull in and see her. But a shower, shave, and a few hours of sleep would do him some good. He tended to get a little stupid when he didn't get enough sleep, and he'd need all his brain cells for the conversation he knew they'd be having later.

He parked and got out of his truck. He'd have to get it cleaned, since Pete had bled all over the front seat. For today, he'd grabbed a tarp from the precinct and covered his seat. Climbing the stairs to the deck, he felt the many hours he'd gone without rest, and entered the unlocked cabin to find Eva curled asleep on his couch.

His heart flipped seeing her sleeping in his place. It was never clearer to him than right now that she belonged here with him. Quietly, he walked over to the couch and knelt down. She'd tossed and turned during her sleep. The blanket she'd covered herself with pooled at her waist, probably due to what she'd endured the night before. He should have had Raven come and stay with her so she wasn't alone. He tugged the blanket up to her shoulders, tucking the edges in around her.

Her eyes fluttered open, and his heart did that stuttering thing again. He loved this woman.

"Hey," she greeted.

"Hey, yourself."

She went to smile, doing a half stretch when she caught site of her surroundings. Everything must have come crashing back to her, for she sat up quickly and wrapped her arms in the blanket, keeping it close to her body.

"I'm sorry for making myself at home. It's just after you left, I couldn't stay at my place."

"I understand. I'm glad you came here. I should have called Raven, or gotten you a room at the lodge."

"No. I would have been mortified if everyone knew I was freaked out."

"Eva, you were held hostage, threatened at gunpoint. I don't know of any civilian who could've handled themselves better than you did. You kept your wits about you and defeated the bad guy. Pretty ingenious of you too. Nate's singing your praises. So am I."

She glanced down, her fingers plucking the material of the patchwork quilt his Grandma Coho had made for him last Christmas. "Thanks for that."

He tilted his head toward the bedroom. "Want to catch a few more winks with me in a more comfortable place?"

"Uh, about that. We need to get some truths out in the open before whatever this is between us goes any further."

"What kind of truths?" This is not where he wanted to go. He wanted to lift her up in his arms, carry her to his bed, and after loving her, fall asleep in her arms.

"You're keeping a secret from me," she accused. "The past has taught me one thing very important, never to abide secrets."

He really could have used some sleep before this confrontation. But he could see in her eyes how serious this was to her. How did he tell her without making her run screaming from him? He took a seat on the couch, faced her, and covered her hands with his. Looking deep into her eyes, he told her the truth. "I can talk to animals."

She rolled her eyes. "Can you be serious?"

"I am."

"What, you're like a Dr. Doolittle or something?" she scoffed.

He winced. It wasn't the first time he'd been called that. Didn't help that he'd first gone into veterinarian science.

"You're being serious?" she asked as though she'd been waiting for the punch line to a joke.

He nodded and quietly waited her out as the dots connected.

"Okay, then why is BW stalking me?"

"Near as I can tell, he thinks you look like a pretty flower. He's partial to flowers."

"He told you that?"

Lynx couldn't tell if she was humoring him or giving him the benefit of the doubt. Maybe a little of both. "It's more of an image or feeling than actual words exchanged." That would be crazy. "And then I went and told him I'd like to get to know you back when you first came to town. I believe he thinks he's helping me." This was going to sink him. He should just shut up.

"So, he's playing *matchmaker?*" Her eyelids lowered, and she freed her hands from his.

"Kinda." He rubbed the back of his neck and decided he might as well jump in with both feet. She could obviously see if he wasn't telling her the whole truth. "BW and I go back a ways. I rescued him when he was born. His mother died giving him birth, and I, well, raised him."

"You're the moose's daddy?" Her brows rose in disbelief.

"No. Maybe. He's fond of me. He likes to check in and hang out every now and then. I asked him to stay close to town because of the poachers."

"You realize this is a moose we are talking about?"

"I know." Any minute now she'd vow never to see him again. Or worse, pack her bags and head back to Cincinnati.

"Do you talk to more than moose?"

He could talk to all of them including the birds in the sky. "Yeah, but I can't seem to reason much with mama bears or wolverines." He shrugged. "Listen, Eva, I know this sounds crazy, especially to someone from Outside, but if you live here long enough, this doesn't seem so weird. Alaska is a magical place, and I come from a long line of Native Alaskans. Athabascan with some Tlingit mixed in there. There is...enchantment, for lack of a better word, in my lineage."

"Are you saying all of the Maiskis can talk to the animals?"

"No, we each have our own gifts, and they manifest themselves in different ways."

"Fox?"

"We don't know yet. But he's a hell of a lot smarter than most ten-year-olds." It was downright unnatural. "I know this is a lot to comprehend, but I really like you Eva. More than like you. I'm falling in love with you." Already fallen and landed hard. He didn't think she was ready for all that until she'd digested his "gift."

She shook her head. "One thing at a time." She rubbed her face and stood up. "I need caffeine. Lots of it."

"Eva—"

She held out her hand to stop him as he got to his feet and reached for her. "I don't know what's worse. Loving a man who loves men or loving a man who thinks he talks to animals."

He took the one-two-punch like a prize fighter.

"I'm not ready for this." She splayed her hands wide. "All of *this*. It's too much. I've only been in Alaska for a month, and I've been chased up a tree by a moose, stabbed by the same tree, swept out of a canoe into a freezing river, eaten by mosquitoes, had my undergarments stolen and paraded around town by the same stalker moose, and held at gunpoint. Now you say you're falling in love with me. In my book, that means marriage and me agreeing to live here, permanently. It's too much, Lynx. I might not survive next month." She paused to breathe. "I need time to decide what I really want. I'm sorry, Lynx, but would you please leave."

He swallowed and stuffed his hands in his pockets. "It's my house."

"What?"

"You're in my house. Let me walk you home." He couldn't give her a ride in his truck. The reminder of Pete would probably be that last straw that would send her packing.

"Oh." That seemed to take the steam right out of her. She glanced around the log cabin. "Okay, I'll leave, and I'll walk myself home. It's daylight, what can happen?" She laughed, the sound a little hysterical.

"Eva," Lynx called her name when she opened the door. "I never figured you for a coward."

Her spine shot straight as a broomstick. He'd just thrown down a dare. That's how he'd gotten her to go canoeing after he'd stood her up. He hadn't forgotten either.

"That won't work with me this time. Not over something this important." She walked through the door and quietly shut it behind her.

173

Eva followed the path to the clinic from Lynx's cabin. She shouldn't have crashed at his place. But after Lynx had left her last night with one quick, hard kiss and a, "We'll talk when I get back," she hadn't wanted to wait for him at her place. The clinic wasn't home, not after being invaded by Pete who'd threatened to rape and kill her. Lynx's cabin felt more like home. Or was it because Lynx lived there?

She was so confused.

What did she do with what he'd told her? Her logical brain was telling her to pack and get the hell out of here, but her heart wanted to believe everything Lynx had said.

When BW had her trapped, she'd done her best to scare him away and gotten nowhere. All Lynx had done was talk to him, and after what looked like an affectionate nudge, the moose had moseyed off into the woods. She glanced around the dense forest hoping not to come across BW or any other wild animals. She picked up her step.

Could Lynx be telling the truth?

And if he was, then what?

Alaska was like another planet, and she hadn't even seen a winter yet.

Chapter Twenty

It had been two days, and Eva hadn't seen hide nor hair of Lynx. Boy, did that saying have more meaning living in Alaska. Fox and Raven had stopped by to check on her and invited her to go shopping in Fairbanks. She'd enjoyed herself even though she'd figured Lynx had called his sister and asked Raven to keep an eye on her. It made her heart hurt knowing he was thinking of her even though she'd basically called a halt between them.

Her patient load had been heavy, but a lot of that had been townsfolk wanting to get to know her better now that she'd "proven" herself a member of the community by taking down a bad guy. After half a dozen patients, she'd closed the clinic, taped a note on the door of where she'd be, and showed up at the lodge to tell her story over many Ugly Moose drinks so that they all could get back to business. The sharing had been mutual, and she felt more accepted in the small town.

One thing she hadn't been able to ask anyone was if Lynx had been stringing her along or not. She didn't want to voice it, and she didn't want to "out" him in case everyone wasn't privy to his animal talking abilities.

When she returned to the clinic, she'd found her lavender bra hanging from her doorknob. She picked it up and glanced around. She knew BW hadn't left it for her. There had been no sign of him the last few days either. Lynx probably told him it was okay to return to the Refuge now that the poachers had been caught.

What was she saying? She was starting to believe him.

And if she were to believe Lynx, the return of her bra was a good indication that he could talk to animals. How else would he have gotten her bra off of BW's antlers? She had been out of her mind trying to cut it off him with a pair of scissors. The bra wasn't that worse for wear. A good washing and no one would ever know the adventures it had taken.

When she entered her place, nothing but silence greeted her. She used to like the silence. Not so much anymore. She headed for bed. At least with the many Ugly Moose she'd drunk, sleeping promised to be easier tonight.

CHAPTER TWENTY-ONE

He'd given her three days. Now he was getting his woman back.

Chocolate hadn't worked, neither had flowers, but there was no way Eva would be able to turn away a puppy.

Lynx didn't care if this wasn't playing fair as he was way past fair.

With the cute little pup in his arms, he felt very confident that he'd get inside Eva's door. That was until Eva opened her door and his heart pounded at the sight of her, and his carefully planned speech floated off into the atmosphere.

"Hi," he managed to say.

"Hi," she returned.

The puppy squirmed in his arms, bringing him back to his plan and off how pretty Eva looked in her silky blue blouse and sexy short skirt. He wondered what color her undergarments were today.

"This is Kiski." Lynx held up the runt puppy Fox agreed was more suited as a pet than one of the dogs he trained for sledding. "You need someone to help you navigate this country. She's a good start. I'd be better, but she'd go a long way in helping you with the local wildlife."

When Eva didn't say anything right away, he rushed on. "Dogs come in handy. She'll make a good companion, and bears don't like the sound of their barking."

"What about moose?" Eva bit her tongue to keep from smiling. How did one resist a big man holding a little puppy? A puppy that wasn't going to stay little for long. Not with those saucer-size paws.

"They're not too fond of them either."

She held her hand out to Kiski, who lavished her fingers with her pink tongue. How could she resist the blue and brown-eyed pup with the bandit face? Turned out she didn't want to. "Okay, I'll give her a try."

"You'll have to take my word for it, but she likes you and would like us to make a home for her. Together."

"She told you this?"

"Kinda." He looked down at the puppy in his arms who was currently trying to eat the buttons off his shirt. "So what do you say? Remember, she wants us both as her parents."

Eva let the smile spread over her face. The man was too damned adorable. "Depends. Are you house broken?"

He set the puppy down, who promptly began chewing on the laces of his Timberland boots. "I'm house broken where it counts." He started to hope. "Do you feel better about what I told you?"

"I don't understand why I do, but I believe you. But before we go any further, there's something you need to know about me. I drive men off." She lowered her eyes and muttered, "Or drive them gay."

"Eva, I'm not going anywhere, and no way in hell will I ever turn gay. I'm willing to prove it over and over and over—"

"I get the idea." She huffed a deep breath and tried again. "You haven't seen me on my bad days."

He cocked a brow in jest. "It gets worse than this?"

She made a startled, insulted sound. "Are you taking me seriously?"

"No. You're talking nonsense and on some level you know it. Eva—"

"Listen, I'm about the only available woman in town who isn't related to you. I'm convenient."

"Fairbanks isn't that far away. I'm not attracted to you because you're close. There are easier women to be attracted to."

"Hey."

"Well?"

"Okay, so that last one might have been a stretch."

"Don't insult us both. You need me. You love me."

She sucked in her breath, and he waited her out. "We haven't known each other long enough."

He grabbed her upper arms and pulled her in close for a kiss. Her toes curled in her high-heeled sandals before he was finished.

"Time means nothing. Sometimes you just know. Forget everything and just tell me what's in your heart."

Eva searched his eyes and saw nothing but love and sincerity. This man really loved her. And she hadn't shown him the best side of her either. If he could love the worst of her, they were bound to make it.

"I love you, Lynx. Every crazy thing about you."

He closed his eyes and rested his forehead against hers. *"Thank you."*

She pulled back. "Thank you? I just told you I loved you. Reciprocate, mountain man."

He swung her up into his arms. "Oh, I plan to, woman."

Lynx carried her inside, with Kiski trailing after them trying to attack his boots. Lynx tossed Eva onto the bed, sacrificing his broken-in Timberlands to the pup, and then proceeded to show Eva in detail how very much he loved her.

THE END

DREAMWEAVER

CHAPTER ONE

Gemma's lips trembled apart on a moan of pleasure so intense her body shivered with it. Synapses fired behind eyes she dared not open for fear he'd leave her wanting again.

Last time, he'd taken her right to the brink of release before disappearing, leaving her writhing with hunger. Not this time. This time he'd better take her all the way, damn it.

Her body came alive under the tutelage of his skillful hands. The way he knew just how to caress her, tease, and torment, until she wept, threatened, and begged for more.

Her hips arched off the bed, seeking, wishing for more, but once again he strung her out until she was mindless with need.

Oh, please, please. Quit dinking around and take me, already.

He chuckled as though able to read her thoughts, while his hands breezed over her breasts, the heat of his mouth hovered over her nipple, until she sunk her teeth into her lower lip to keep in the whimper. Sensations flooded her, tightening her muscles, and her hands clenched the sheets beneath her as little cries escaped her bitten lips, betraying her.

A growl of satisfaction vibrated from him, pouring into her body, pushing her closer to that delirious edge.

The alarm blared in her ear, jerking her awake.

"Nooo," Gemma groaned. Her sound of distress battered around the empty bedroom. "Not again." Would her dream man ever truly make love to her?

She opened her eyes and found herself alone. Of course she was alone. He was just a dream, part of her imagination. Her very creative imagination.

But he *felt* like more than that.

For weeks now he'd been visiting, always in the deepest of night. That magical time where the world slept and passions awoke.

She threw back the covers, the chill hitting her nakedness.

What the—?

She *never* slept naked.

A quick glance around the room showed her flannel pajamas tossed to the floor, along with her pink polka dotted cotton underwear.

Huh? She knew she'd crawled into bed last night fully clothed, including her hand-knitted woolen socks currently hanging off the top of the dresser. Her copy of *The Three Musketeers* lay face down, where she'd placed it before turning off the light. She'd given up on her love of romance books once the erotic dreams had started, not needing the added stimuli. She'd hoped reading the classics would settle down whatever the heck was going on with her subconscious mind while she slept.

She grabbed a robe hanging over the back of a chair and slipped into the warm terrycloth. It was springtime in Alaska and just like Johnny Horton was famous for singing, it was currently forty below.

No one in their right mind slept naked.

And she was very worried that she was no longer in her right mind.

He'd almost had her.

Lucky Leroy Morgan fell back onto the sweet smelling grass, his hands fisted, his jaw clenched, and aching with sexual frustration down to the cellular level. No, that was no longer true.

Not since he was dead and trapped in this fucking paradise.

He roared up at the perfectly blue skies, his back arching, and his lungs emptying of pent up emotions, praying the sound reached farther up into the Heavens from where he was currently trapped.

If he didn't know better, he'd think this was hell.

She'd been so close. He'd literally brushed her soft skin this time. Smelled her, and she'd smelled like high mountain Himalayan Impatiens with hints of rich, dark coffee.

What he wouldn't give for a cup of coffee.

He sat up, his hands tearing at the lush grass beneath him, and came to face to face with Hansen.

"Failed again?"

Nothing like stating the obvious. "Fuck, yes."

Hansen glanced around and lowered his voice, "Reverence, man."

"I don't give a shit. I shouldn't be here."

"You aren't going anywhere with that attitude."

"Fuck you too."

"She got to you this time, didn't she?" Hansen gave him that knowing smile. "You're starting to care, to fall in love." Nothing seemed to ruffle the calmness the man radiated. That used to impress him.

Lucky Leroy Morgan came by the nickname "Lucky" naturally. He loved women. Not just one. Many. And caring this much about one woman freaked him out.

"You're running out of time," Hansen said. "If you can't get her to accept you before these strong solar storms are over, you're stuck here, my friend."

"Like I don't know that." Lucky clawed his fingers through his shaggy, sun-bleached hair. Here wasn't that bad, for a spirit detention hub so to speak. A lush valley full of sharp-painted wildflowers intermixed with the sweet smelling grass all framed by purple snowcapped mountains jutting into an azure sky. Puffy, porcelain clouds floated by without a care in the Universe. When he'd first arrived, it had been one more adventure. More mountains to climb, a different world to conquer, but the thrill had quickly lost its appeal when he'd realized there was no risk.

He was already dead. What more could happen to him? The worst had already happened. What he needed was to get back to the land of the living.

And Gemma Star was his ticket.

CHAPTER TWO

Gemma flipped the sign to open and unlocked the doors to Chinook Books. Of course, her mother Siri and her Aunt Rosie were the first ones to breeze in.

"Did you see the Aurora last night?" Siri asked after Gemma shut the door behind them.

Siri was garbed in her traditional winter woolen dress pieced together from a variety of rainbow recycled sweaters serged in a haphazard design. Added to the outfit were clashing arm warmers with just her fingers uncovered. Silver rings fitted every finger, and her painted nails shimmered with a glittery crimson today. White bunny boots and a royal purple coat, that was more of a cloak, completed the ensemble. Rosie helped Siri out of her cloak, while Siri stared at Gemma.

Oh Lord, she hoped her mother wasn't off her meds.

"Mom?" Gemma prompted. "You okay?"

Siri blinked her dark blue eyes rimmed with thick black lashes. Her shocking red hair was long and curly and had yet to fade with age.

Gemma glanced at Rosie who shrugged. Aunt Rosie was the complete opposite of Siri. Her brunette hair had been left to gray naturally, and cut in a no-nonsense bob. She wore jeans, a man's flannel shirt and a sensible parka that she shrugged off, along with removing her gloves and knit hat. She resembled Gemma's father who had died when she was eight that it sometimes hurt to look upon her. Gemma took their coats and hung them up behind the counter.

She turned back to find Siri's eyes burrowing into her, as though trying to see into Gemma's soul.

"Gemini Star, what have you been up to?"

She hated it when her mother looked at her like that. "What do you mean?" She'd better clarify. She'd learned early not to volunteer information.

"You've been touched by a Dreamweaver." Siri continued her slow sweep, traveling up and down Gemma's simple brown slacks and cream cable knit sweater. "Tell me you haven't given yourself to him."

"What? No. What are you talking about?" A premonition prickled up Gemma's spine, and she tried to suppress the sudden need to shudder.

"You mustn't do it. Do not invite him in. Your soul will be compromised."

"Huh? What? Mom, you're talking nonsense." But it didn't feel like nonsense. Sometimes the things her mother said were downright freaky. Her dream lover was just that, a dream. No more. Unfortunately she knew enough having been raised by her New Age mother not to completely discount the supernatural. There was too much out there left unexplained. But a Dreamweaver? What the hell was that?

"Siri, let's get you a cup of tea." Rosie shared a here-we-go-again glance with Gemma.

"Yes, tea. Must have tea, and then we'll consult the cards," Siri said.

"Mom—"

"I'm reading your cards today, Gemini. You can't stop me. I'll find out what's going on."

Oh great.

"Siri, you have a full day of customers scheduled today," Rosie said. "Let's concentrate on them first. What do you say?"

"Fine. You're right of course. But if there's time...."

Gemma mouthed "thank you" as Rosie turned Siri toward the café. Amie, the barista who had been with Gemma for years, already carried a tray with a brewing teapot, along with matching cups and saucers to Siri's favorite bistro table right in the middle of the room. No disposable coffee cups for her mother. Tea was a ritual and needed to be respected as such with purified water and a specialized Silver Tip White Tea imported from Sri Lanka.

"This looks charming, Amie, thank you." Siri adjusted her skirts as she sat. "So, Amie, when are you due?"

Amie looked at Gemma, her eyes wide with panic and then back to Siri. "No, ma'am, I'm not pregnant." She smoothed down the fabric of her apron as though to show off the flatness of her stomach.

"Hmm, interesting. I see a new baby in your immediate future." Siri shrugged and helped herself to one of the shortbread cookies also on the tray.

"Amie, I'm going to need a brownie this morning," Rosie said, attempting to get Amie's attention off her nonexistent bump.

"Coming right up." Amie undid the ties to her apron and wrapped them around her front, tying them tighter around her middle as she walked back behind the counter to get Rosie's brownie.

Gemma hurried across the café and whispered over the dessert case, "You know not to take anything she says to heart, right?"

"Yes, I know that," Amie said. The mass of bracelets on her thin wrist jangled as she slammed open the bakery case. "But I'm *late*. Gemma, I can't be pregnant, I just can't. Drew hasn't even asked me to marry him. And I don't know if I *want* to marry him. A baby? What am I going to do with a baby? I'm not ready to be a mother."

"Stop. It's nothing. *Nothing.*"

"But you heard her," Amie's voice rose in worry.

"Yes, and last Tuesday she told Mrs. Halverson that she'd find cockroaches. This is Fairbanks, Alaska. Have you ever seen a cockroach?"

Amie took a deep breath, closed her eyes and let it out. "Right. Okay, but you know I'll need to leave early so that I can buy a pregnancy test to put my mind at ease." Amie put Rosie's brownie on a plate and took it to her.

Gemma studied Amie's trim figure. It was just as fit and petite as it was when Gemma had hired her right out of high school. No way could she be over a hundred and ten pounds. She just topped five feet. With her dyed black hair, multiple ear piercings, coupled with her kohl rimmed eyes and dark purple lipstick, Amie fit more into Chinook Books than Gemma did.

The eclectic bookstore used to be hippie central when Siri ran it. Incense had burned at the counter. Brownies could be ordered "organic" instead of the dark chocolate, nut-filled ones Gemma stocked. And customers hung out all day gazing up at the celestial ceiling her father had commissioned for Siri's birthday. There was still a New Age vibe, and the ceiling still received a lot of oohs and ahhs, but the more years that went by, the more Gemma had lessened the influence. Though she hadn't been able to get rid of Tarot Tuesday, or what she secretly referred to as Trial Tuesday.

When Gemma's perky part-timer, Callista, reported to work at noon, Gemma grabbed a book on dreams and hid herself in the back office. She let Callista run the book floor while Amie continued to fret about her possible pregnancy in the café. Siri was too occupied with her Tarot readings to pay attention to what Gemma was up to.

She wished she could just ask her mother what she meant about the Dreamweaver comment, but she'd learned a long time ago not to show too much interest in her mother's "second sight." At least medicated, Siri didn't talk to people who weren't there and predict the future or the sex of unborn children. Well, as much.

She hoped Amie wasn't pregnant. Maybe she'd run out and pick up a pregnancy test to put both their minds at ease. Until she could get away, she had some investigating to do. She opened the book she'd swiped on dreams and found the table of contents.

The chapter on "Astral Sex" leapt off the page.

CHAPTER THREE

"Well, you look awful," Tern Maiski said, entering Gemma's little back office.

There wasn't much room for more than a desk in the closet-like space. Gemma had tried to lighten it up from the multi-colored rainbow arching across the walls her mother had painted to a much more soothing sage green. Though the rainbow still bled through in the right light as if refusing to be covered up.

Gemma planted her elbows on the old walnut desk that had been her father's, and rested her chin in her hands. "I'm having astral sex."

Tern sank into the chair opposite. "You're having *what?*"

"Astral sex."

"Before I draw any wrong conclusions, explain exactly what astral sex is." Tern shrugged off her stylish black wool coat that reached to her calves and unwound a hand-painted red silk scarf from around her neck. Tern owned the Arctic Tern Art Gallery just down the street, and they had a standing date to eat lunch together on Trial Tuesdays.

"Here, read this." Gemma held up the book for Tern, her head still spinning with the otherworldly implications.

Tern took the book and read the passage Gemma indicated. She glanced up. "You're having sex dreams? What a relief. I thought—never mind what I thought."

"Geesh, Tern. I'm not even seeing anyone special and you thought I'd—holy balls, just keep reading."

Tern followed the passage with her finger. "Astral sex— damn but that's funny to say—is the theosophical belief, belonging to the ethereal region that is believed to exist at a higher level than the material world. Personal auras are said to have non-corporeal sex with astral playmates." Tern leaned forward, the book cradled to her chest. "So you have a spiritual playmate."

"Be serious for a minute."

"I am being serious." Tern's Athabascan skin glowed under the harsh fluorescent lights, picking up the auburn strains highlighted in her thick ebony hair. But it was her dark almond eyes looking grave that had Gemma swallowing.

"Don't tell me you buy into this?"

"Of course I do."

"Come on, I was counting on you to bring me back to earth." At Tern's lift of an eyebrow, Gemma added, "Ground me at least. I need to talk to someone and I can't tell anyone out *there*." Gemma gestured wide with her hand to include all the occupants currently in Chinook Books who believed what the pretty painted cards told them.

"Your mother probably has more information on the subject than this book." Tern held up the Dreamology Dictionary.

"I've been trying my whole life to get away from this kind of stuff. Don't tell me you believe in it?"

"There is a lot I believe in." Tern's tone more than the words had Gemma feeling ashamed as she remembered Tern's close call with death last summer. "There's so much we don't understand," Tern continued. "It's arrogant to discount the unexplained."

Wow, nice way to put her in her place. "Help explain this to me then. I'm so confused."

"Tell me what's happening."

"I'm having the most intense, sexual dreams. It's like he's there. I can feel him, smell him, hear him until I open my eyes. Then he's gone and usually before I ...well, you know."

Tern's lips twisted into a smile. "No, I don't know."

"Don't make me say it."

"Yeah, you're going to need to say it."

"*Come* on, Tern."

"Well, I guess that's close enough."

Gemma felt the blush heat her face.

"How long has he been 'visiting'?" Tern asked.

"Three weeks as of last night."

"Every night?" Those brows of hers arrowed in thought. One brow was split at the apex by a scar giving her a somewhat rakish look for a woman. Very becoming on her and said more than words that she held her own.

"Except two days ago," Gemma admitted, though leaving out how despondent she'd felt when her dream man hadn't put in an appearance.

"So you have been having astral sex—damn, I love that phrase—for three weeks and you haven't orgasmed?"

Gemma's blush flamed, and she couldn't respond.

"You might have to help yourself out for your own peace of mind."

"Forget all that. How do I get rid of him?"

"Your astral partner?"

"Will you quit saying that word?"

"Nope." Tern shook her head and laughed. This time it was full-bodied, and Gemma couldn't help being pulled into the magic of the melodious sound.

"Oh my hell, what am I going to do?"

"Figure out why he's sought you out and vice versa."

"Me? I haven't sought him out. How would I even go about doing something like that?"

"Your subconscious has. Maybe you need to have a talk with yourself and figure out what is missing in your life that you're seeking in the astral plane."

"Well, the obvious. I must be sexually frustrated."

"Are you?"

"I didn't think I was until *he* started visiting me every night."

"Wait, you said he didn't visit two days ago. That was Sunday. So why not Sunday? What was happening that was different that night?"

"Nothing really. The bookstore was closed, so I took care of errands and cleaned the house. I did meet up with Cub and had dinner."

"Oooh, how did that go?"

"Eh. He's good looking, that's for sure." Jacob "Cub" Iverson resembled a Norse god. Cool blond looks with ice blue eyes and muscles that bore witness to his ancestors throwing tree trunks. She should be climbing all over him from the moment he'd moved to town six months ago. "But there wasn't any spark."

"No, spark with Cub Iverson? My goldfish lights up when he's in the room. The man was made for worshiping."

"Don't let Gage hear you talk like that."

"Just because I'm married doesn't mean I can't appreciate art when I see it. So why no spark? Did he kiss you?"

"Yeah." Gemma sighed. "It was nice but not as nice as my Dreamweaver's."

Tern's smile fell, and she became very still. "What did you just call him?"

"Dreamweaver." A shiver skittered across her skin. "Why?"

"Pull up the weather report for the last three weeks." Tern pointed to Gemma's laptop. "Come on. Do it."

Gemma did as Tern instructed while Tern came around the desk to see the results. They quickly scanned through the past weather reports for the last month. Fairbanks had actually fared well for March. Other than the snow storm Sunday night, they'd had cold but clear weather and amazing Aurora Borealis displays due to the record solar flares.

"I don't want you to freak out with what I'm about to say," Tern said, slowly retaking her seat.

"You're already freaking me out."

"Well, hold onto something then. Your Dreamweaver is using the Northern Lights as a conduit to travel between the astral planes. If you aren't careful, he'll snatch your spirit and take you back with him. You need protection."

"Really? You'd think having astral sex would be the ultimate solution for having unprotected sex. You can't get pregnant or catch anything."

"Don't joke about this. There is so much you can lose." Tern tightened her lips. "What's the forecast for the Aurora tonight?"

Gemma glanced back to her computer screen. "Intense."

"Don't go to sleep. Promise me." Tern waited until Gemma promised. "Okay, you wire yourself with caffeine. I'll talk to Gage."

"Gage? Tern, no." Gemma rose out of her chair as Tern stood and hurriedly slid her coat back on. "I don't want anyone else knowing about this."

"We're going to need his help. He works for the Geophysical Institute, remember. He's an Aurora genius. We need to know what we're up against if this 'thing' is using the Northern Lights as a stream into our world."

"This sounds like *Star Trek*," Gemma muttered rushing to catch up with Tern as she exited the office onto the book floor.

"Until I get back with you, it wouldn't hurt to find out what Siri knows. She might have some other ways of protecting you."

"I can't talk to my mother about this." She'd wished now she hadn't talked to Tern.

Tern stopped and faced her. "Your soul is at risk. Talk to her. And no sleep." She held up her finger when Gemma went to interrupt. "No naps either."

"You've got to be kidding?"

"The Aurora is out there even during the day. We humans can only see them at night." Tern took Gemma by the arm and steered her toward the café. A few tables were taken by regulars who liked to hear Siri's readings. Siri was currently deep in the middle of another reading for Mrs. Halverson who never missed a week.

"Amie, large coffee with a double shot of espresso for Gemma," Tern ordered. "I want you to make sure she drinks enough of those to make her twitchy."

Amie, paler than when Gemma had left her, pointed at Mrs. Halverson. "Did you see Mrs. Halverson's cockroach?"

Gemma followed Amie's shaky finger. There on Mrs. Halverson's pink lapel jacket was pinned a huge emerald cockroach.

Siri stood, holding the moon card in her hand for Gemma to see. "Dreamweaver," she whispered.

CHAPTER FOUR

Gemma's eyelids closed and then blinked open. It was two in the morning. The television was playing a marathon of *Star Trek: The Next Generation* at top volume. She'd turned the heat down, and the inside temperature of her house was currently sixty-five degrees. She was freezing and tired, and almost to the point where she didn't care anymore if her Dreamweaver visited.

At least he'd keep her warm.

She had to be careful that the temperature in the house didn't drop enough that her water pipes were in danger. That was taking this astral stuff too far.

Who was she kidding? It had already gone too far. She'd let a bunch of people scare her with nonsense. This was ridiculous. Dreamweavers didn't exist. There was no real proof. But then if spirits were sexually enslaving souls, would there be proof?

Probably just a lot of sexually satisfied women who didn't give a flip if they were enslaved.

That's it. She had to work tomorrow. Enough was enough.

She readied for bed, washing her face, brushing her teeth, and donning a UAF sweatshirt, knee socks, and drawstring sweats that she double knotted around her waist.

There, let's see if an astral spirit can untie knots.

After adjusting the thermostat to a more comfortable level, she headed to bed.

Before slipping under the covers, she glanced out the window and caught her breath.

The snow glistened with neon greens, electric blues, and hints of violet reflected from an unearthly sky as wave after wave danced across the firmament. Maybe she should make another pot of coffee. No. This was crazy. The Northern Lights did look otherworldly. Magical even, chilling with their dramatic display. She'd seen it all before. Though the last few weeks had been the most impressive of her twenty-five years. Still, enough. Sleep called. She was probably too exhausted to engage in anything anyway, even if her dream lover did visit.

And if he did, it was about time she learned the guy's name.

Finally.

Lucky watched as Gemma adjusted the covers under her chin. He'd been here all night, actually been able to follow her throughout most of her day with the powerful solar flares from the sun storm.

The need to get close to her, smell that combination of sweet-spiciness laced with hints of dark coffee, was making him crazy. He'd seen her guzzle back cup after cup and was hungry to see how she'd taste.

"Come on, Gemma. Go to sleep." The sooner she entered the REM cycle, the sooner he could take a sample and find out.

Suddenly she sat up in bed and looked around. Her wide and searching eyes were the color of an arctic night with sparks of emeralds and sapphires shining within their depths.

He froze on instinct even though he knew she couldn't see him. But had she heard him? That was the first time he'd spoken out loud today.

"Gemma?"

"Who's there?"

Holy shit!

Gemma scrambled out of bed, grabbing the heavy book on the side table. The light clicked on, and he almost laughed at the sight. She looked like a stirred up polar bear wearing all those layers.

He'd gotten her naked before. He had no doubt he would again. But maybe he ought to keep his mouth shut. A spooked woman was not a relaxed one. And he needed her relaxed.

Gemma searched the room, peeking around the closet door and then checking the bathroom. She exchanged the book for a hockey stick that she had standing guard in the corner and headed for the rest of the house.

Great. She wasn't going to sleep any time soon if she was scared off her ass.

He always was his own worst enemy.

Lucky admired Gemma from behind as she methodically searched each room in the small clapboard house, double-checked that all the doors and windows were locked and then headed back to bed, grumbling under her breath, "I am *not* going crazy."

He stifled a chuckle. The woman was delightful. Cute, yet sexy in that ruffled up kitten sort of way. The kind he wanted to cuddle with but knew at any moment the claws might come out. He kept silent this time as she snuggled back into bed. She left the bathroom light on, and it gave a soft glow into the bedroom, bathing the bed with a copper cast, highlighting her skin and hair with gold dust.

He'd always been attracted to shiny things.

She expressed a loud sigh and settled deeper under the covers. He advanced onto the bed, freezing again when her head came up, and she swept the room.

"Too much caffeine," she muttered. "There is *nobody* here." But as though to make sure, she took the adjacent pillow and laid it lengthwise, right over him. His non-corporeal body took the smothering of the pillow and rose above it.

He didn't dare breathe—didn't really matter if he did or not, but he liked going through the motions—for fear that she'd sense more of him. How was she picking up on his presence?

Did it have something to do with the Northern Lights or were these visits actually creating a connection?

God, he hoped it was the latter.

He needed her. Not just spiritually. She was his ticket back to the physical.

Gemma drifted in that place where she wasn't completely asleep yet couldn't fully wake up.

He was here.

She could feel him...breathe?

Spirits didn't breathe. But then he was more than a spirit. He was a Dreamweaver come to weave an enchanting spell over her, enslave her into giving up her soul so that he could take over her body. She'd read a little more today after everyone had made such a big deal, and now she didn't know what to believe. Just knew she wanted to curl into him.

He smelled like fresh mountain breezes with undertones of earth and pine.

Heavenly.

She mentally giggled at the thought. Of course he smelled heavenly. Wasn't that where he was from?

But what if he was from that other place? The one she dared not mention in case she invited a darker element into her life. One otherworldly spirit was enough.

Could she be a spirit magnet?

Her mother had raised her on a steady diet of natural organic foods, and homegrown herbs and berries with enough supplements to ensure she lived forever. It was a hard habit to break. Her first fast food hamburger and fries had been at the age of fourteen, and she'd promptly thrown it up. She was pretty healthy without a lot of toxic chemicals, though like most women, she had an addiction to chocolate. Pilates was her exercise of choice, and weather permitting, she took full advantage of all the outside activities living in Alaska provided.

Yeah, her system probably was real attractive to the body impaired.

"It isn't your body that attracts me," a husky whisper said before lips nibbled the side of her neck. "At least, not just your body, which is smoking."

Funny, wouldn't a dream lover say all the right things? He'd kind of stumbled over that.

She needed to make him go, but instead found herself arching her neck to give him better access. If she could only open her eyes, he'd disappear. But her eyelids were so heavy. She reached up her hand and laid it on his cheek.

Her fingers dived into the softest, silkiest hair. She had a picture of sun-bleached wavy strains left too long without a trim.

This was different. More interactive.

He groaned. The sound vibrated throughout her like a plucked guitar string. "Yes, touch me," he said. "It's been so long since someone has touched me."

She could feel him, hear him. He was more than just a sensation this time. "How is this possible?"

"Don't question. Just do."

"Who are you?" *Please don't say Dreamweaver.*

"Lucky."

What did that mean?

His hand, large and calloused cupped her bare breast and her nipple pebbled, stealing her breath. How was he doing this? And was she naked again?

"Yes." There was a smile in his voice as he switched attention from one nipple to the other.

"Okay, how?" Did she really even care as his clear expertise in seduction ratcheted up her need for him?

"That's a loaded question, Gemma." His lips traveled lower over her collarbone.

"I need some answers." Boy, did she ever. And quickly, before her mind gave up and let her body embrace the sensations he enticed her with.

"I know. But could we just...enjoy each other first?"

He did have a point. *A very impressive point.*

"Why thank you."

"Are you reading my mind?"

"Sorry, bad habit I've recently gotten into." His lips traveled to her breasts, and one rogue hand ventured lower. Much lower. Any articulate thought evaporated.

He gave a husky laugh. "Good to know."

He went to church, worshipping, lavishing her nipples while his fingers teased and tormented until everything inside her melted with wanting. Why was he doing this to her?

"Because you're the one."

"The one what?" She needed to stay coherent, present, and not drift with him.

"Not what. Who. You and I were meant for each other, Gemma."

"How do you mean?" A shiver of unease intruded.

"You were my future."

"What do you mean 'were'?"

"We are destined, Gemma." His mouth traveled lower, and she started to see stars.

"Wait...what?"

"Do you really want me to stop and explain?"

Nooo. Yes.

She didn't know what she wanted. She wanted him. Wanted to be filled, consumed, and thoroughly loved by him.

"I'm here willing to do it all, babe."

203

Babe?

"Gemma," he rushed to cover.

Had that been a slip? Most men called women 'babe' as a cover because they couldn't remember the woman's name. "How many other women do you visit?"

"There is only you." There was a long pause. "But to be honest, there have been many. Before."

"Before what?"

"Before I...died."

CHAPTER FIVE

Gemma rushed to let Tern inside the bookstore. They had an hour before anyone would be reporting to work, and before the store was scheduled to open.

"I stopped and picked up cinnamon rolls from Bun on the Run." Tern held up a bag. "Not that the café food isn't great, but I'm sure you get tired of it."

"Bless you." Gemma relocked the door and led the way to a little bistro table in the back of the café. If people saw them from the large plate-glass windows, there would be knocking and begging for her to open early. Coffee goers were a wired group, as she was learning herself. Never had she been this agitated. When this "situation" was over with, and she cut back on her consumption, the caffeine withdrawals were bound to be legendary.

But that wasn't today, and she needed the hit, feeling more zombie than human. Gemma veered toward the café to pour mountainous cups of coffee, adding a few too many shots of espresso to hers. Getting through today was going to be an experience.

"So, tell me what happened last night? You didn't sleep, did you?"

Gemma placed their coffees down on the table and sat. "Uh...some." Not that it was enough sleep to count since she'd been participating in other activities at the time.

"Did your Dreamweaver visit?"

"Yes."

"Gemma!"

"I tried to stay awake. I really did, but after two in the morning, I gave it up." Thinking she was crazy to be afraid of going to sleep. Boy, had she been proved wrong.

"So what happened?"

Gemma's face heated. "Okay, first off—I feel nuts for talking about this—but, Tern, you have to understand. He is really sexy and *really* adept at seduction."

"How far? Was there inter—"

"No." But it had been close. So close.

"Did you get his name?"

"No." What did Tern think of her? She sounded so easy to her own ears. Some random guy, spirit, or whatever, shows up and puts the moves on her, and she just lays there and takes it. Participates, even.

"Gemma, if he shows up again you *have* to get his name. There is power in a name."

She'd tried, hadn't she? It was all a bit fuzzy in the light of day. "Okay, if I see him again, I'll get his name."

"Good. I talked to Gage. He's in Poker Flats with all his fellow cronies from around the world. They haven't seen solar displays like this since the 1960's. It's like geekville out there. While he doesn't believe in all this Dreamweaver stuff—scientist —" she shrugged "he did say that the intense solar flares are interfering with radio transmissions and satellites. He's going to keep me updated with the forecast." Tern reached over and laid her hand over Gemma's, her eyes solemn. "He also said it's going to get more extreme in the next few days based on the sun's flares in the last twelve hours. The most recent flares from the sun are like nuclear bombs."

Great. Gemma peered into the black liquid of her cup. If that was the case, she'd need something stronger than coffee to stay awake.

"I haven't had a decent night's sleep in three weeks. And last night, might as well count as no sleep. I'd just dropped off when he was there. In fact—" she shook her head "—no never mind."

"Tell me. The littlest thing could give us a clue on how to stop him."

Gemma thought about it, realizing that Tern wasn't going to think she was crazier. She leaned in even though she knew they were alone and no one could overhear them. "Before I fell asleep, I could have sworn I heard him."

"While you were awake?"

"Yes, and later when we were, you know, we talked."

"Like communicated in your dream?"

"No, actually talked. He could read my thoughts though, come to think of it. But I *talked* to him. I *heard* him."

"Hmm."

"What does that mean?" She sat back in her chair.

"I think we need to talk to your mother."

"No. Tern, you don't understand. Mom is barely there. This will send her right over into that other world of hers and there won't be enough medication to bring her back."

Tern seemed to shelf that argument for another time. "How did you stop, you know, both of you? Did the alarm clock go off like last time?"

"No, I was able to call a halt."

"How?"

"You know how I said we could talk? Well, he's enough of a man—Dreamweaver or not—to step in it. He called me babe."

"Babe?" Tern narrowed her eyes. "He called you babe?"

"Yeah, can you believe it?"

"How do you mean? Like an endearment in the heat of the moment?"

"No, more like when a guy calls you babe when he can't remember your name."

"I don't know. Babe isn't all bad."

"Seriously?"

"I had someone special who used to call me babe. But it was sweet and so like him, you know?" Tern gave her a bittersweet smile. "I was going to introduce him to you when we returned from..." Darkness clouded her features. "Never mind. We're getting off track." She cleared her throat. "Okay, let's plan on what we're going to do."

Tern's mood shifted so quickly that Gemma had trouble catching up. She knew Tern and Gage had been through hell last summer.

"What are your plans tonight?" Tern asked. "Gage will be in Poker Flats probably for the next few days. Do you want to crash at my place?"

"Actually, I kind of have another get-together with Cub."

"Ooh, that's perfect. Sleep with him tonight. I doubt your Dreamweaver will be able to put in an appearance if you're getting busy with another man. If he does that might be...crowded."

"I am *not* sleeping with Cub."

"Why not? What if you've brought this on yourself because you're sexually frustrated? Maybe that's the reason this Dreamweaver sought you out. Like a succubus."

"Ew. No, he said we were destined. That I was his future...that is, you know, before he died."

"Hmm."

"You have to stop with the hmms. They wig me out."

"I need to do some more research. If you don't want to talk to Siri, my Grandma Coho probably has some insight."

"No more people. I don't want everyone to know that I'm having astral sex with some Dreamweaver." She sounded nutty enough.

"Then talk to your mother. If destiny's involved you could be in real trouble."

CHAPTER SIX

Gemma strapped her kayak onto the roof of her car and drove to meet Cub.

It was technically still winter, even though the calendar said spring was around the corner. But the rivers and lakes were frozen and there was enough snow on the ground to call a snow day in most cities of the lower forty-eight. To keep in kayaking form, and be ready once the ice broke up, Gemma had joined a group of diehards who met one night a week at the Hamme Pool. They paddled and practiced rolls, exercising muscles that wouldn't get that kind of a workout in a gym.

It was also where she'd first met Cub.

He was an avid river kayaker, famous in these parts. He could probably compete on a world stage if he felt so inclined. But as far as she could tell, his biggest competition was himself.

"Hey, Gemma," Cub greeted as she climbed out of her Outback Subaru and began unstrapping her neon green river kayak. He made quick work of getting the kayak off the roof of her car. She wasn't short, more average than tall, but Cub shouted his Viking heritage with Norse god good looks to his big feet and towering six-four foot frame. She'd never believe the man could fit into a whitewater kayak if she hadn't seen it so herself. And while she plunked, more than slid into her kayak seat, Cub melted into his like butter on toast. There was something admirable about a man who was so comfortable in skin.

"Thanks, Cub."

He handed her the boat one-handed and picked up his own that he'd set on the ice-packed blacktop in order to give her a hand.

"Hey, I've been thinking of that kiss we shared the other day."

She flicked a look at him from under her lashes, wondering where he was going with this subject. So out of the blue too. They usually discussed technique, certain rivers they wanted to traverse, or the weather, while walking in to the pool to meet the five to seven other people who took advantage of the "evening kayaking."

"Okay, what about the kiss?"

"I think we should try it again." Cub stopped, and while he couldn't really face her with each of them holding a kayak, he did pretty good job of nailing her with a look that had her swallowing a sudden—surprising—kick of curiosity. "I wasn't really on my game the other night, and I think we should give it another go."

She hadn't thought there was anything between them besides common interests and friendship. But, hey, why not. Cub made a lot more sense than her Dreamweaver.

"I'd like that." She shared a smile with him, and they continued into the building, Cub holding the door open for her.

He was sweet and thoughtful and had a corporeal body. And he wasn't hard to look at either.

Suddenly she was glad that she hadn't pushed off tonight since she was so tired. She was also glad she'd downed that Rock Star.

Lucky didn't feel lucky at all. He'd been talking all damn day, but Gemma, by all accounts, hadn't heard a peep from him. Similar to the day before, he'd been able to follow her around feeling like an attention-starved puppy, his heart weeping at seeing Tern. Hell, how he'd missed her too.

He missed everything.

He'd mentally salivated watching Gemma partake of each bite of cinnamon roll from the Bun on the Run. He wished there was some way he could experience what she smelled, tasted, felt. Definitely what she felt. How she felt.

Touching her while she dreamt was thrilling, amazing. Sensual on a level that he hadn't been with a woman before—no shit—but he still missed that human contact. The pressing together of warm flesh, the thrusting of groins, entering the heat of a woman. Entering Gemma.

Holy hell, did he want to enter Gemma.

Should he be saying holy hell? All right, holy heaven. There, that felt somewhat better. Or more appropriate. Listening to Tern and Gemma discussing all the implications of him visiting from another plane, kind of freaked him out too. They didn't understand that he wasn't out to harm Gemma. He wanted to give her pleasure. But that wasn't his only motivation. If one thing death had taught him, it didn't do any good to lie to one's self.

Was this a particular hell he'd been sent to because of the free-living lifestyle he'd engaged in while alive?

Too may questions.

For now, he'd learn more about Gemma. Knowledge was power. He was beginning to realize she was his soul mate. She was beautiful, smart, adventurous, and fit. So physically fit.

But who the hell was this guy she was with?

Lucky didn't like the way she looked at him, staring too long when he tore off his shirt and revealed muscles that even made his mouth drop open.

Gemma stripped down to her sunset-orange bikini. Where the hell was her life jacket? Those perfect breasts, which had left Cub speechless, too, needed to be covered up and buckled down.

Cub sidled up to Gemma, and on instinct, Lucky tried to push him aside. He went flying through the man, didn't even cause the guy's perfect hair to stir.

This was no good. He was losing steps that he'd gained. "Here, let me help you," Cub said, wrapping his hand around Gemma's upper arm, his fingers way too close to the sides of her breast that the tiny scraps of material barely covered. Damn the man, he brushed the exposed globe of goodness with a slight caress of his index finger. Lucky couldn't really fault him, but how he wanted to gut him on the tiled surface of the pool for touching his woman.

Yeah, this was hell.

He didn't like seeing another man's hand on his Gemma. He'd never been the jealous sort. Back to that free-living lifestyle. And he didn't like feeling this way at all.

It was cruel. Torture. He wanted to return to his spirit prison. That would be better than watching Gemma enjoy another man's touch. He didn't miss the goose bumps or the becoming blush of her skin at Cub's smooth maneuver.

Gemma climbed into the kayak, and with a push from Cub, slid into the water of the pool. Lucky watched with awe at her form as she paddled across the water, getting to the deep end and rolling the kayak. Wow, the woman was skillful. What else did she like to do? So far, he'd mainly been concerned with how she liked to be touched. Did that make him some sort of ass? Or pervert?

Of course it did.

Cub slid his kayak into the water and quickly caught up to Gemma with a few powerful strokes. Now Lucky was in awe of the power the man possessed just in his shoulders. He missed pitting himself against what nature had to offer. Granted there wasn't a lot of nature here in the Hamme

Pool, but it wasn't a stretch to see how both Gemma and Cub would perform in the outdoors paddling down the world class rapids of the Nenana River.

A lump formed in his chest and spread throughout his soul. This wasn't fair. If you were dead you shouldn't be able to hurt like this.

"What would you like to drink?" Gemma asked, as she let herself into her house. Cub had followed her home after two hours of cavorting about in the pool. "I don't have much more than cooking wine for spirits as I don't drink much. But I can make you some tea, hot chocolate or coffee."

"I don't think you need any more stimulants." Cub blushed, making him appear boyishly adorable. "I mean, no more caffeine. Don't take this the wrong way, but you look dead on your feet. Maybe I should leave and let you get some sleep."

She was dead on her feet, but not willing to fall asleep. Not with what had happened yesterday. "How about some hot chocolate? I always get cold going from the heated pool to twenty below." At least it had warmed up, gave her a little faith that spring was indeed around the corner. To be honest, she was more chilled at the stunning display of Northern Lights gyrating across the sky than leaving a heated pool. They were so luminous and alive, trekking from greens, to purples, to reds and crackling with energy. After what Tern had shared with her, she hadn't been surprised to find her radio full of static on the way home, though a tad concerned.

"I haven't been sleeping well," Gemma confessed. Afraid she would crash as soon as she got home had been one of the reasons she'd decided to ask Cub over for a drink. With the Northern Lights lit up the way they were she was apprehensive about being alone, fearing she wouldn't be alone for long.

A brush, like a hot breath, swept over the back of her neck.

She'd stacked her wet hair on her head after showering at the pool. A shiver that was anything but chilling, fluttered through her body. She glanced behind her and found no one. Cub had pulled out a chair and sat at the table a good ten feet away. She swallowed hard, and added a heaping table-spoon of instant coffee to her hot chocolate.

"You okay?" Cub asked. "You seem a little on edge. I'm not going to jump your bones."

He might not, but she had the feeling there was more than the two of them currently in her kitchen.

"Just a little spooked, I guess." She handed him a mug of hot chocolate and took a seat across from him, taking a sip from hers. "I've never seen the Northern Lights this vibrant."

"You know the Native Alaskans used to fear that the stream of lights were their ancestors coming back to earth to snatch their souls."

Great.

"The Scandinavians believed that when red appeared it was a sign of war," he continued. "Even the Native Americans thought they were a conduit between worlds. Some still think that's true. It wasn't until the nineteenth century that we learned they were solar activity. Makes you wonder who is really right? Scientists whose theories are less than two hundred years old, or our ancestors."

"What do you believe, Cub?"

"I like thinking there is a connection between our world and the Heavens. To think that we are totally cut off, or that our loved ones who have passed before us are completely out of reach, is sad."

Grief flickered across his expression, and she wondered who he had lost. His grief seemed fresh as though the claws hadn't quite let go. Cub gave the mystical display out her window another look and then settled his starry-blue eyes on her. "Enough of that. How's the bookstore?"

She snorted a laugh. Cub had a way of jumping subjects that she appreciated. "Lots of reading and recommending. With all the changes in the way people like their reading material, we seem to be holding our own. But that might have a lot to do with Siri's faithful followers. How are things at Search and Rescue?"

"Challenging."

There was a long silence while Cub's blue eyes studied her. The air seemed to thicken as he set his hot chocolate down. Gemma suddenly found it hard to swallow.

Cub stood, taking her hand, and helped her to her feet. "Now, about that kiss."

CHAPTER SEVEN

Gemma licked her lips. "I should make this clear. I didn't invite you over so we could sleep together." Oh no, why had she said that?

"Good to know." Cub bit back a smile. "So why did you invite me over?"

"You make sense." No sleep made for one stupid girl.

"Excuse me?"

"We like the same activities. The same people. I've even heard that you've been known to read the occasional book."

A dimple winked at her as he grinned. "And here I thought it was because I was so damn cute."

She answered his grin. "Yeah, there is that too." Might as well take stupid a step farther. "I thought you were going to kiss me?"

"Sure put the pressure on."

He took her hand, a sweet understanding smile curving his lips. "Come here." He sifted his fingers in her hair. "Close your eyes."

"If it's all the same to you, I'd like to leave my eyes open."

"By all means, leave them open then."

His head lowered, but before his lips would have taken hers, his mouth grazed her cheek, his fingers tracing the angles of her face as though learning her. His hands framed her face, and he slowly took her mouth with his.

The kiss was soft, questioning, almost innocent. Like she was back in high school being kissed for the first time, though not awkward. Awkward had been last time they'd tried this.

Cub applied more pressure, pulling her closer to him, and deepened the kiss. This was nice. Sweet.

"Your hot chocolate tastes way better than mine," Cub murmured.

"I, uh, added a little something."

"Let me take another—" Cub's mouth took hers more aggressively this time. His arms wrapping around her, lifting her off her feet and closer to his body. Her stomach did a surprising little flip.

Wow, he had such big...hands. His arms were long enough to envelop completely around her, his hands splayed around her back, with his fingers brushing the undersides of her breasts.

A groan vibrated from him, and he broke contact, seeming startled by the sound. "That was much better than the other day."

"Much," she whispered. Maybe sleeping with Cub wasn't such a bad idea after all.

A chill blew into the room.

Cub looked around the kitchen. "Do you have a window or door open?"

"No."

He set her back onto her feet and turned. "Did you feel that?"

"Feel what?" Oh, no. She was awake right? She pinched herself. Yep. Cub's kiss had been real. She hadn't dreamt that. Neither had she dreamt the sudden drop in temperature that sent more than just a shiver through her body this time.

She followed Cub into the living room where he double-checked her front door. It was still closed and locked from when they had entered the house.

"Where's your thermostat?"

"Down the hall." She led the way, realizing for the first time how close the thermostat was to her bedroom. She had a short hallway. Her bedroom was at the back, a guest bathroom on the left, and second bedroom on the right across from the bathroom. They were now just a few feet from her open bedroom door. Her queen size bed was a temptation she didn't want to resist.

But for sleep or some other reason?

"Your thermostat seems fine." Cub adjusted the settings and the heat kicked on. "Must have been a freak thing." He glanced at her unmade bed and then back to her. "Nice sheets."

"They were a gift." It was hard to admit to this big man, who was currently biting the inside of his cheek to keep from laughing, that she'd trekked down the Star Trek sheets for herself. And they'd been hard to find.

"A fan?"

She shrugged. "Somewhat." She didn't want to scare him off with the truth.

He pointed to the autographed picture of Leonard Nimoy framed and hanging on her wall. "I think more than somewhat." He cocked a brow. Not as impressive as Spock's famous questioning brow what with Cub being all blond and blue-eyed...and hot. "Don't tell me your bedroom is 'where no man has gone before'?"

"Oh, you're funny." She reached around him and shut the door.

"Guess that was the wrong joke to make?"

She folded her arms across her chest.

"What if I admitted that I'm a huge *Doctor Who* fan?"

"Nope. Gotta do better than that. *Everyone* is a *Doctor Who* fan."

He choked out a laugh. "Okay, if you really want to get personal—"

"You laughed at my sheets."

"Personal, it is then." He cleared his throat. "My favorite movie of all time is...*Titanic*."

Her arms dropped to her sides. "'I'm the king of the world' *Titanic*?"

He gave her a sheepish look. "Too soon?"

"Yeah, I think so." It was her turn to bite back a smile, which she lost. "It's hard to see the big man in front of me, who it's been rumored to have stared down a bear, so in touch with his feminine side."

"Once. I stared down a bear once. Don't ever want to do it again, and it was more of a case of being too scared shitless to move than actual bravery. Besides, I thought women liked men who were in touch with their feminine sides."

"To a point. Men still must be able to defend hearth and home, kill spiders, and pay attention when picking out paint colors. But we don't welcome your opinions differing from ours. And above all, there is nothing manly about crying during a chick flick."

"Good to know. I'll be covert when I take you to see the new Nicolas Sparks movie. What do you say?"

She glanced at him from under her lashes. "So you want to move our relationship beyond the pool?"

"I'd like to get to know you better, Gemma. You have very impressive paddling skills." He angled his head to the side. "Did that sound dirty to you?"

"A bit."

"Good. So, you want to take in dinner or a movie sometime?" He leaned in closer. Her back was literally against the hallway wall. But she didn't feel trapped.

"On one condition," she said.

His finger tucked a loose strand of hair behind her ear. "Name it."

"We see the new Joss Whedon movie instead."

He leaned back. "Don't tell me you're a *Buffy* fan?"

She nodded. "Diehard fan of not just *Buffy*, but *Angel*, *Firefly*, and *Serenity* too."

He shook his head. "Should have known by the Trekky sheets." He gave a deep, pretend sigh. "I guess if you can overlook my love for *Titanic*, I can see past the geek in you."

She let go of the laugh. It had been so long since she'd flirted like this.

Another cold breeze swirled around them. Gemma rubbed her arms.

Cub looked around, tapped the thermostat, and shook his head in confusion. "I think you have a draft somewhere."

She had an idea of where that cold breeze was blowing in from.

Her Dreamweaver needed some boundaries.

CHAPTER EIGHT

"She's calling you," Hansen said, munching on the biggest strawberries Lucky had ever seen. He also knew, from experience, they were the tastiest too. Which was weird since if you were dead, how did you taste things?

Was it all an illusion?

Gemma wasn't. And neither was that claim jumper Cub. What kind of name was "Cub" anyway?

"Lucky? Did you hear me? Your woman is calling for you." Hansen shook his head. "You always were a lucky bastard."

Hence the name. That was until he was murdered.

"Are you going to answer her or what?"

Lucky stopped pacing for a minute and faced him. Hansen reclined on a boulder with the bottomless basket of strawberries. His legs crossed at the ankles as he took in the splendor Limbo had to offer. Hansen might be content to stay here and not move on to that place others before them, and after, had chosen to enter. But Lucky wasn't. He wanted to move back. And he couldn't figure out how to get there. He thought he had been on the right track with seducing Gemma. Could he have been wrong? He didn't like what he felt now. Like he could kill someone.

"So what happened to have you hiding here away from that pretty woman?"

"She kissed a guy named Cub. *Cub.*"

"Yeah, you already told me that."

"She kissed the same guy. *Again.* And this time they both enjoyed it."

"Wow. That sucks for you." Hansen bit into another apple-size strawberry. "So why then is she calling you?"

"She's not happy with me."

Hansen set the basket of berries down on the vibrant green grass. "What did you do?"

"Nothing big, just tried to cool them off."

"Chill in the air?"

Lucky nodded. More like an arctic wind.

"You aren't to interfere if she chooses someone else."

"She can't choose someone else." He was already feeling more for her than he had for any other woman. And since he'd glimpsed his future and seen their life together, how happy they'd been, the little people they'd created, he wanted it all. He'd been robbed of too much.

Damn it, he was owed.

"You know that this isn't a sure thing," Hansen cautioned.

"I know." Boy, did he know. That's why he was trying his damnedest to make a solid connection with Gemma. And he'd been doing a pretty good job of it until Cub had kissed her tonight. Flirted with her. Made her laugh.

"Do you really think ignoring Gemma is going to get you further with her?"

Ah, man. "Love has never been this complicated for me before," Lucky grumbled.

"Sure, when you love and leave 'em it isn't complicated. It's convenient. Everything you're trying to do with that woman has complicated written all over it. But I will tell you one thing about women. You give them the silent treatment, and they will freeze your ass out. No one does revenge better than a woman."

Lucky rubbed his neck. Didn't he know it. "All right. Don't wait up for me."

Lucky found Gemma pacing a path in her carpet, dressed again in another sweatshirt with Rink Rats and opposing hockey sticks on the front, sweats, wool socks, and an expression that could freeze geothermal hot springs.

"Last time I'm calling you," she hollered at the ceiling. "Get your ass down here, Dreamweaver!"

"Call me Lucky."

She jerked and slowly turned toward his voice, muttering under her breath, "I'm not crazy. I am not crazy."

"You are not crazy, Gemma."

Her eyes traveled over him. "You're really here?"

"Yes."

"Why can I hear you but not see you?"

"I don't know. I'm not up on how all this works. Like you, I'm learning as we go."

"Why are you...visiting me?"

"For the reasons I told you last night."

"I was your future?"

"Yes. My wife, my lover, my friend, and the mother of my children." He heard the catch in his voice and tried to man up. He remembered her amusement with Cub about men being in touch with their feminine side. He got the feeling she preferred a man's man. While he'd been light-hearted and full of Zen in his first life—he hadn't felt that way in a long time—no way would he be caught watching *Titanic* again. Though he had to admit, Kathy Bates was the best thing about that movie.

"Whoa. Wife? Mother?" She dragged her hands through her hair. "Seriously?"

"We were to be introduced, but I didn't make it back. If I had, that would have been it. As it is, I fell in love with you the first moment I saw you."

"After you were already dead?" She backed up a step.

"Yes."

"How? Who?" She shook her head, closed her eyes and took a deep breath. When she opened them, she seemed less flustered. Not much less, but a tad.

"Gemma, talk to Tern. Tell her my name is Lucky Leroy Morgan. She'll fill in the rest."

"*What?* How would Tern know?"

He lifted a hand and caressed the side of her face, glorifying in her response as she closed her eyes again and leaned into his touch. "I don't have any more time, babe. Snow's coming. Get some sleep." He kissed her, trying his hardest to erase Cub's touch from her mouth and memory.

His spirit slowly disintegrated in her arms as the snow outside turned heavier, blocking out the magnetic waves from the sun.

CHAPTER NINE

Gemma didn't care that it was after midnight. She called Tern. There was no way she was sleeping after what Lucky had told her.

"'ello," Tern mumbled into the phone.

"His name is Lucky, and he said that you would explain everything. So. Explain. Oh God, you've *got* to explain all this to me. I know I'm not crazy. *I know it.* Mostly know it. Holy balls, Tern. Tell me!"

"Gemma?"

"Yes, of course it's me. Who else would call you up in the middle of the freaking night ranting like a possessed woman?"

"You'd be surprised," Tern muttered. "Hold on, *what* did you say his name was?"

"Lucky Leroy Morgan."

"Holy shit. I'll be right there."

"Tern?" Gemma looked at the phone, and sure enough, they were no longer connected. "Well, hell." How was she going to wait out the time it took for Tern to get here? Gemma glanced out her window. Snow fell in fat flakes. Tern was roughly ten minutes away on a clear day. Maybe she should call her back and tell her not to come?

The phone rang once before Tern answered, sounding much more awake than before. "I know it's snowing. I'm still coming."

"Be careful then."

"Put on a pot of coffee. The ramifications of this...are huge." She disconnected again.

Gemma went back into her kitchen, cleaned up after her and Cub, and had the coffee ready by the time Tern pounded on her front door.

When Gemma opened the door, Tern entered in a rush of snow flurries, wearing pajamas with cute little puffins on them. She shrugged out of the parka and toed off her snow boots.

"I never pictured you for flannel," Gemma said, pointing at Tern's comfortable choice of sleepwear.

"What did you think I slept in?"

"Never really thought about it until now. But satin and lace, I guess, based on your fashion sense."

"Nobody *sleeps* in satin and lace. Besides, Gage is still gone. And I get cold at night without him." Tern followed Gemma into the kitchen, taking a seat, and a fortifying sip of the coffee Gemma poured for her. "Now start from the top and don't leave *anything* out."

Gemma started speaking, and Tern never took her eyes off her. Tears welled and threatened to spill by the time Gemma had finished.

"Give me a minute." Tern sniffed and wiped at her eyes.

Gemma grabbed a box of tissues and a half empty bag of M&M's. By the looks of Tern, who was normally a rock, they were going to need more than coffee. Maybe she should get out the cooking wine?

"Lucky was, is—oh God, I don't know the correct tense to use." Tern hopped to her feet, went to the kitchen sink, and splashed water on her face. She gazed out the window where the snow was silently, almost reverently, falling in feathered puffs. "I loved him. Still do. He was a world famous mountain climber. He'd conquered Everest. And Denali twice—the second time during the winter. Nothing scared him." She took a heavy breath, shuddering as it left her body.

"Where you two ever...."

"Yeah, this was before Gage and I met." A bittersweet smile appeared. "Man, he'd been fun."

Gemma squashed the jealousy that suddenly rose within her. If Lucky had been with Tern, why was he wanting to be with her? Tern was so exotic, confident, and accomplished with that extra something that was hard to put your finger on.

"I never loved him the way that I love Gage," Tern continued. "Lucky was fun, daring, a gambler in all aspects of the word. Unfortunately, he lost that last gamble."

"How?"

Tern was suddenly all business as she retook her seat. "Last summer. Things were bad, and he was killed." That seemed to be all that she could reveal about the horrors she'd been though. "Gemma, we need to figure out how to help him. We already know the how and the why. Now let's figure out what we must do to help Lucky break the bonds of death."

"Whoa. Wait." Gemma's hand flew up to stop Tern. "What do you mean *help* him? I thought I had to stay awake, and not let my 'Dreamweaver' seduce me. What about my soul?"

Tern pursed her lips in thought. "It's Lucky. He can't be after your soul. He isn't like that. There's got to be something else."

"How do you know what he's like now? He's dead and wanting to get inside me." Silence filled the air between them, and Gemma flushed realizing what she'd just said. "Won't he take over my spirit and inhabit my body?"

"I don't think that is what this is about. Lucky is a special soul. It isn't in him to be conniving like that." Tern suddenly looked around. "I need to talk to him. Can he talk to me?"

"I don't know. You're the expert."

"No, I'm not. But I know someone who is." Tern nailed her with a look that shouted volumes.

Oh, no. "Not my mother again."

Chapter Ten

"You should have come to me before now," Siri scolded, adjusting her colorful skirts. Today she was garbed in a medieval-style embroidered heliotrope-colored dress with a flaxen-lace kirtle. Where had she bought that? Her red hair was piled on top of her head with long curls intertwining with her purple feathered earrings.

Gemma felt drab in her simple slacks and black sweater. But then she'd always felt drab next to her mother. As a child she'd gone out of her way not to draw attention to herself, which hadn't been hard as Siri had garnered most of it.

"Siri, what can you tell us about Dreamweavers?" Tern steered the conversation to what they had come for. After depositing their coats, boots, hats, and mittens they were sitting around Siri and Rosie's living room, which was draped in scarves from India with colorful cushions that weren't much higher than the floor. A low hand-carved ironwood table squatted in front of them.

Aunt Rosie lowered a tray of tea and poured them each a cup. She was dressed much the way Gemma was in no-nonsense jeans and a sweater. Tern was as colorful as Siri, but classy and fashionable making a statement with her choice of clothing rather than being one.

"We need to see what the cards tell us." Siri settled a look on Gemma.

"I don't want my cards read," Gemma quickly interjected. She'd had enough of having her cards read. Growing up, whenever she was upset or had a problem, Siri always consulted the cards.

"Not yours. His." Siri's surprising crystal gaze locked on Tern's. "Did you bring them?"

"Yes." Tern opened the big leather bag and laid a charcoal-colored Polartec jacket, a scratched and dented compass, and a picture on the table.

Gemma slowly reached for the picture. "Is this him?" she whispered.

"Yes, when he was in Africa," Tern said. "Right after he climbed Kilimanjaro."

Lucky and another man stood together with grins that were big enough to bring one to Gemma's lips in response. They looked like they had just conquered the world with their hair tossed in the wind, and the skin on their faces red and chapped by the elements.

She knew his face though this was the first she'd laid eyes on an image of Lucky. But she'd drawn her hands over his cheekbones, his strong jaw, kissed that smiling mouth. His soft, warm bedroom eyes were so happy. So alive. An ache spread, enveloping her heart.

"Who's the other guy?" she asked, trying her best not to trace Lucky's image with her finger. That would give away too much in front of her mother.

"Hansen. He was a climbing buddy of Lucky's. He was killed not long after that picture was taken."

"How?"

"Climbing accident. Lucky had a hard time dealing with his death. I don't know if he ever came to grips with it."

"Let's get started," Siri said. "The mood is shifting in the room. Rosie, would you please light some frankincense to help clear and calm the air?"

Rosie moved to the old drawer-stacked desk in the corner. It was full of little cubbies that were filled with all kinds of incense, aromatherapy oils, herbs and dried flowers, and little things her mother collected. Rosie pulled out the incense and lit it, resting the stick on a piece of pottery made just for that purpose. A twist of smoke curled upward.

Scents of balsamic and sharp pine with hints of lemon filled the air. Gemma found it strong and offensive, but breathed deep hoping the aroma would calm her.

Siri picked up the deck of Tarot cards and handed them to Gemma to shuffle. She did not want to do this, but one look from Tern had Gemma taking the cards and shuffling them. She gave them back to Siri who spread them out onto the table.

"Pick." Siri pointed to the perfect fan of colorful cards.

"Why do I have to do this?" Gemma asked.

"You know why," Siri said. "You're closest to the Dreamweaver."

"Wouldn't that be Tern?" They'd been lovers and friends. Gemma hadn't even met the physical Lucky.

Tern prodded Gemma. "He sought you out, and I'm not the one having astr—"

"Okay, fine," Gemma said quickly. She swallowed, gathered her courage, and picked the first card, right from the middle.

The Six of Wands.

"Balance and harmony is the Sixes." Siri indicated Lucky's picture. "An illustrious career as an adventurer, but he needs to let go of the past in order to achieve spiritual victory. He has been adored by many, but needs to beware of staying too long."

"Staying too long? What does that mean?" Gemma asked.

Siri flicked a glance at Gemma from under her lashes. "I don't know, but I'd wager the longer he stays on this plane, the more chances he's taking of being stuck there and unable to move on. Pick another card, and we shall find out more."

"Fine." She picked the next card, trying to tap down the trepidation she'd felt since last night.

The Hanging Man.

Both Tern and Rosie gasped, even Gemma knew this card was a biggie.

Siri drew in a deep breath and slowly released it. "This card represents his conflict. He dangles between the mundane world and the spiritual one. He is caught between them, and time is running out. Something must happen soon or the time for action will be lost." Siri sat back in her chair. "Sacrifices he has made in the physical world give him freedom and power in the spiritual world. He's been blessed and sees things with new eyes."

"Seriously?" *Are you freaking kidding me?* Goose bumps shivered over Gemma's skin.

"You know how this works," Siri said. "You are guided to draw the cards. I merely explain what they mean. There is no cloak and mirrors here, Gemini."

Gemma strengthened her resolve, and studied the cards, picking from the left this time.

"The Two of Swords." Siri paused taking the card from Gemma and lay it down for everyone to see.

There was a striking image of a woman blindfolded with her arms crossed and holding a sword in each hand.

"There are two sides fighting. He is faced with a decision, and if he waits too long it will be made for him," Siri said. "Or he is fighting with himself because of something he didn't finish while on earth." She looked to Tern. "Could this be why he is hanging onto the physical plane?"

"No, I don't believe so. Lucky was always one to jump in with both feet, come what may. As far as I know, there isn't much he regretted. He lived a good life. Not always the best decision maker, but he didn't shirk the consequences either. He lost his life too soon. So maybe that is why he can't or won't move on?"

Rosie had been sitting quietly sipping her tea until now. "Don't they always say, 'Heaven is where your heart is'? Maybe his heart is with her."

"Rosie, that isn't helping." Siri jerked her head toward Gemma.

Like she wasn't going to pick up on that.

"A fair reading, Siri," Rosie said. "Just because you're scared for Gemma, doesn't make it right."

"Mom?"

"I'm doing my best to stay neutral." Siri's mouth tightened. "But I don't like this. Another card."

Gemma pulled the Hermit from the pile.

"He's restless and walks from dusk until...damn."

"Holy shit, this is getting freaky," Tern said.

No kidding. Gemma had never seen a reading so...*in tune*.

Siri fidgeted, picking at the embroidery threads on her skirt. "He peers at whatever takes his fancy, seeing things that he's missed out on during his lifetime. His answers will not be found in the physical world. He will only get them inside his own spirit. There are powerful choices to be made, requiring much change and commitment. He *must* stay in the spirit world." This last bit sounded different than the rest Siri had revealed. She suddenly grabbed Gemma's hand, her nails sinking in. "Gemini, you must promise me. You can not let go of the physical plane. No matter how enticing he is. You must stay grounded *here*."

"Don't worry," Gemma reassured Siri, not liking the crazed look that had returned to her mother's eyes. This was the mother Gemma feared. The one who'd stripped naked and danced at her high school graduation. "I wouldn't even know how to do that."

"Never learn."

Gemma shared a look with Tern, expecting to see her just as confused. But Tern was serious as the grave. Maybe not the best analogy she could have thought up. They needed to get this over with.

She picked another card.

Seven of Cups.

"This is his present," Siri said, seeming to have shaken off her 'spell'. She was back to business, taking the card from Gemma and placing it in line with the others. "He's been given a strange and wonderful gift, but beware, there is hidden danger. Don't get lost in daydreams."

"Danger?" Gemma swallowed.

"The Seven of Cups also represents temptation, addiction, jealousy and emotion." Siri looked directly at her. "To lie with him, Gemini, will create consequences that will be life lasting. Don't get lost in your cups. The snake is on the card for a reason."

Why did she have to mention snakes? She hated snakes.

"Siri, don't put your own prejudices into the reading," Rosie said. "Tell her what that really means."

Siri's sorrow-filled eyes fell on Gemma. "I don't want you hurt. He could steal you away into a place we can't reach you. Dreamweavers are tempting seducers, and it's easy to get caught up in their passion." This sounded less instructional and more like she spoke of personal experience.

"That is not going to happen. There is power in belief, right Mom? Haven't you always told me that?"

"Yes, and you don't believe, do you Gemini?" Siri smiled as though expecting the same answer Gemma had always given.

"This is a crap shoot, Mom." But she was beginning to consider that there might be something to all this, and it scared the holy hell out of her.

The next two cards reinforced what was said before. The Ace of Wands and the Chariot spoke of decisions to be made, with not a lot of time allowed in which to make them, stressing the need to embrace the chaos and focus emotions.

Then Gemma pulled the Tower.

The only sound in the room was the clicking of the second hand of the clock hanging on the wall. Rosie sat back in her chair while Tern covered her lips.

"What does this mean?" Gemma asked.

"He is a creative and disruptive force. The Tower is grounded in the earth but reaches into the Heavens." Siri pointed back to the picture of Lucky. "Hasn't he always reached for Heaven, driven in life to climb all those impossible peaks? But he will land on the jagged rocks of reality and be shattered by a truth he didn't recognize."

"Wait," Gemma said. "I don't get it."

Siri went to explain again but stopped and turned to Rosie. "Tell her in words she'll understand."

Sure, dumb down the New Age speak for the non—somewhat—believer.

"In *Star Trek,* when the space-time continuum is disrupted, reality as we know it changes," Rosie said. "When you called earlier, you said Tern *had* planned to introduce you to this man and that he'd seen your future had he not died." Rosie waited for Tern's nod before continuing, "He died, therefore, both of your futures have been changed."

Well, what do you know, Gemma understood that perfectly. And it made her suddenly sad. She wanted this over with and pulled another card.

Nine of Cups.

"This is a wish card. He wishes to be satisfied on all levels. But an overabundance of physical pleasure can lead to intoxication and illness. Balance transferred to a spiritual level enters peace and harmony. This man has had many relationships, Gemini, and has played free with the life he'd been given."

"Last card," Tern said, as though the weight of the reading weighed heavy on her.

Gemma went for one card and then felt the need for another. She closed her eyes, and slowly pulled the last card from the many.

"The Fool," Rosie and Tern whispered together.

"Interesting," Siri said. "The Fool is busy playing sightseer, imagining the possibilities. But if he isn't careful, he won't see the edge of the cliff he's about to tumble over."

"There is another side to that, Siri," Rosie said. "Give her the rest."

Siri narrowed her eyes at Rosie. "I was getting to it." She huffed and adjusted her skirts before speaking again. "There also must be a leap of faith or ultimate gamble that is required for a new beginning." She sat back as though the reading had taken a toll.

"We need to think on this," Tern said.

"I can't think anymore." Gemma rubbed at the headache that had become a constant throb behind her eyes. "I'm so tired." So extremely tired.

"What you need is a good night's sleep," Siri said. "I believe I can help you with that." She pulled a sandwich bag out of her pocket with a half a dozen small white pills and handed it to Gemma. "Don't panic. They're just sleep aids. But they will put you in a sleep so deep your unconscious mind will also rest. He will not be able to reach you."

CHAPTER ELEVEN

"Wow, that's some heavy shit," Hansen said, relaxing on his favorite rock.

"Freaky, if you ask me," Lucky answered, worrying the back of his neck. He'd just returned and reported everything he'd heard about "his" Tarot reading to Hansen, hoping the man could help him figure out his next step.

"She pulled *all* those cards on you. There wasn't anything that you did to *help* the situation?"

"That damn storm left me with only enough strength to eavesdrop. Besides, I know nothing about the Tarot. Chakras are more my speed."

"How does Gemma's mother know all this? Know so much about you?"

"I think the woman's been 'touched'."

Hansen got a calculating look in his eye. "Maybe I ought to dream weave a little myself and find out."

"Dude, she's like over fifty."

"Yeah, so? Age is just a number. Besides, from how you've described her, she sounds kinda hot."

"I think she's in a relationship."

"What's a little dream loving? Doesn't hurt nobody."

"Speak for yourself," Lucky muttered, dropping to sit on the grass that never seemed to need watering. He lay on his back and gazed up at the puffy clouds. It never rained. He missed a good hard rain. Damn, but he itched to get out of here. Turns out there was something to the saying, "Too much of a good thing."

"That's okay," Hansen said. "I wasn't really serious about dreamweaving anyway. I'm happy here. What's not to love about Paradise?"

Lucky raised his head to debate the reasons but stopped. He had a feeling Hansen hadn't moved on because of him. Hansen had always been a supportive sonofabitch. Lucky was going to miss him. That is if he wasn't stuck with him for all eternity.

"So what's your next move?" Hansen asked.

Hell, if he knew.

So help her God, if another person asked for a book, and they didn't know the title or author, she was going to scream. The earlier Tarot reading twisted around in her head, so Gemma had dived into work, hoping that would help her to compartmentalize.

It wasn't working.

Gemma gritted her teeth and plastered on a fake smile as she turned to greet another customer. "Oh hi, Cub." Gemma's fake smile flirted with the real thing at seeing him.

Cub stopped cold. His eyes widened, and he looked like he'd been caught doing something he shouldn't be. "Hey, Gemma. I thought today was your day off?" He stuffed his hands into the front pockets of his jeans. She couldn't help but notice how the fabric fit across his hips.

"Normally it is, but I couldn't stay away. You know how it is when you own your own business." So, he wasn't in here to see her. Her fake smile returned at full-wattage. "Is there something I can help you find?"

"Uh...no." Cub clearly looked uncomfortable as his gaze flitted around the store landing everywhere but on her. "I'll just look around."

"Okay." Awkward. "Let me know if you need anything."
She made a beeline for the café and left the book floor for
Callista to manage. The young English major seemed better
at it lately anyway.

The store had been hopping all day. Bad weather always
brought in the customers. A lot of them were hanging out
in the café with their laptops, drinking their daily water consumption in coffee. Lately, she'd been no different.

"Large coffee with a double shot of espresso, Amie,"
Gemma ordered.

"Are you sure?" Amie asked, sending a worried look
her way. "You've been downing the coffee at a terrible rate.
You're going to eat through your stomach lining if you keep
this up. Maybe some tea would be better?"

"Not strong enough," she mumbled.

"Hey, can I talk to you about your mom?" Amie asked
as she went about making Gemma's drink.

One of the very reasons she needed copious amounts
of caffeine. She was lucky she didn't drown her life in a bottle. "What about her?"

"Remember when she said I was pregnant?"

Oh, no. Gemma braced herself for the news.

"Well, she was half right."

"Come again?"

"Siri's words had hinted that a new baby would be in
my future. Well, I'm not pregnant. Seriously, not pregnant. I
took six pregnancy tests in the last week and then you-know-
what decided to put in an appearance and relieve my fears
for good. But Drew came home with a new puppy. So your
mom was right."

"A new puppy?"

"He's way cute. And puppies are babies. Dog babies."

That they are. Maybe she should add something stronger to her coffee after all? She was having trouble keeping
up. Amie handed her the hot drink. Gemma took a large sip
not giving it time to cool, and burned her tongue. She jerked

the cup away from her mouth, spilling drips of coffee on her sweater. She swallowed the burning liquid as Cub came up to her.

"You okay?" he asked, holding a bag with his purchase in one hand, the other still locked away in his pocket. Guess he found what he'd come in for.

She grabbed a napkin and blotted her mouth and the front of her sweater. What was wrong with her? She knew better than to guzzle fresh coffee. Good thing her sweater was black.

"Here." Amie set a cup of ice water on the counter for her.

She mouthed a silent 'thank you' and took a drink, letting the cold water cover her scorching tongue. Swallowing, she answered, "I'm fine." She concentrated on getting the words out past her swelling tongue.

"Can we...sit for a minute?" Cub indicated a table in the corner next to the window.

"Actually, I really need to get back to work. It's time for me to cover Callista's lunch. But would you like something to drink?" She gestured to Amie who patiently waited to see if Cub needed anything, taking in every word exchanged between them.

"Hot chocolate?" He reached for his wallet, and Gemma stayed his hand.

"No, it's on me."

"That's twice now you've treated me to hot chocolate. Can I treat you to dinner Sunday night?"

Dinner? When he was clearly uncomfortable with seeing her here today?

"I really enjoy your company, Gemma." He leaned in and whispered, "And the kiss we shared the other night."

She couldn't stop the heat from illuminating her face. Amie's quirky smile confirmed she'd heard everything.

"Okay." Gemma figured agreeing to dinner would get Cub out of the store faster and away from probing eyes and the questions Amie would no doubt demand answers to.

"Good. I'll pick you up at your place at seven."

"How about I meet you?"

"Actually, I'd really like to pick you up. You know, like a real date."

Amie's smile was ear to ear now. But if Cub picked her up, that meant he'd be dropping her off at home too. It could mean another kiss, maybe more. She suddenly needed to hold the cup of ice to her face.

"All right. Seven then. Dinner," she clarified if not for him, for herself.

"Great." Cub paused and then leaned in and kissed her cheek. "See you Saturday."

She watched him saunter out of the café and into the blustery outdoors.

"Wow, can that man wear a pair of jeans," Amie whispered in awe.

Yep, he sure could.

Gemma took a long drink of the ice water.

Callista joined them. Her waist-length, flaxen hair lay in a braid down her back. Little silver-rimmed glasses perched on the bridge of her nose that Gemma knew she only wore to help downplay her stunning looks and make her appear smarter. She wore gray slacks with a simple white blouse as another camouflage of sorts. "Are you seeing Cub Iverson?"

"Uh...kinda. Maybe?" They were just friends, really. But there was a date planned, and they'd shared a kiss, but wasn't she seeing...

No. She *wasn't* in a relationship with Lucky Leroy Morgan. You couldn't be in a relationship with a dead person. Unless he was a vampire.

Oh, balls. She needed some sleep.

One thing she did fully comprehend in her sleep-deprived state, Cub was very much alive.

"She has a date with him Sunday night," Amie shared, leaning over the counter. At least she hadn't said it loud enough for the all café guests to hear.

"I'm so glad. I was heart-sickened to hear about his wife."

"Wife!" Gemma and Amie said together.

A few eyes turned their direction.

"I thought you knew?" Callista stepped in closer. She continued when both Gemma and Amie shook their heads. "Cub lost his wife a year or so ago. I'm so relieved to see him moving on. He was depressed a long time after he lost her. They were high school sweethearts and were married right after graduation."

"How'd she die?" Gemma asked, words suddenly hard to speak and not because of her burnt tongue.

"Breast cancer."

"Oh, no. That's awful," Amie said.

Gemma had a sinking feeling in the pit of her stomach, and it had nothing to do with how much coffee she'd drunk today. "Callista, what book did he buy?"

"Uh...'Your First Time: A Guide to Loving After the Death of a Spouse.'"

CHAPTER TWELVE

"Are you really going out with him?"

Gemma jumped, and the pile of sci-fi books in her arms scattered to the floor. She glanced around, even though she knew there was no one else in the store but her. Everyone had headed home for the night since the bookstore was currently closed. She should have done the same, but had prolonged her workday not wanting to face her empty house. Not with sleep beckoning and her seducer waiting for her to fall asleep. Was he tied to her or the house?

"I'm tied to you, and going out with that other guy will really complicate things," Lucky's voice rumbled over her.

"And you don't think my life isn't complicated already?" She was talking to dead guy. Basically a ghost, and since he'd shown up here didn't that mean he was haunting her?

"I'm not a ghost, and I'm not haunting you."

Holy balls, she forgot about that mind reading trick of his. "You have to stop doing that." It was bad enough he knew so much about her, she didn't want him inside her confused, messed up mind too. What woman would like the man she was attracted to knowing her every thought?

"I love how you think. You're refreshing and honest. Your thoughts are as beautiful as you are."

The man could seduce merely with words.

He gave a chuckle that did crazy things to her insides. "You should see what I can do with my—"

"Okay, stop." She threw her hands up.

"You say stop, but what you'd really like is for me to—"

"No more reading my mind."

"It's hard not to when you project so easily. You have such charming thoughts, Gemma."

Project? Did she have a part in this?

"You're like a beacon in a storm. A hot, fervent place promising shelter where I want to—"

"Beacon or not, I don't want you in my head." It was tough enough being *alone* with her own thoughts.

"I can't promise. I'm not the most disciplined."

That, she believed.

Gemma bent to retrieve the books she'd dropped and found them missing. She swiveled and discovered the books stacked on the shelf where she'd meant to display them. "Did you do that?"

"It was my fault for scaring you. Helping you clean up is the least I could do."

Yeah, but unnerving as hell. She shook off the shiver. She hadn't even seen the books move. Explained how he could so easily get her undressed.

"Definitely a perk."

"Hey."

"Sorry. I can't help it. Just like I can't help this."

He tucked strains of hair behind her ear that had fallen out of her clip, and she swore he nuzzled the side of her neck.

Her heart skipped. *Now don't get excited*, she tried to chide herself. She was supposed to be downplaying her attraction to Lucky not building on it. After all, there was only so far this—whatever it was—could go.

A wave of sadness enveloped her, and she suddenly felt lonely. She'd never been one to feel alone. It was more than melancholy she felt. It was desolate isolation with the promise of eternity. Could she be picking up on Lucky's feelings?

"Now that is interesting," Lucky murmured. "I'm not up on all the rules. Rules have never been my thing." She imagined him shrugging. "But somehow I must be transferring my feelings to you."

Her knees wobbled. She might need to sit down for this. Instead of falling into a horizontal position that her body so badly craved, she returned to the customer service desk for the other stack of books awaiting her attention. She felt him shadow her. What she wouldn't give to see him. There was another wave of understanding that she interpreted as him wanting the same thing.

She grabbed a pile of "Hot New Romances" and carried them to the endcap in the romance section. She placed the books in the already set up Plexiglas holders and then looked them over to make sure the display seemed balanced. She turned to get the next pile of books to fill in and found them floating in the air.

She froze.

"Did I freak you out again?" Lucky asked, the stack of books lifting as though he were offering them to her. "I'd just like to help."

"Don't move," she whispered. With him holding the books, she knew exactly where he was. What if she put something on him? "Seriously, stay right here and don't move." One last look to make sure the books were still suspended in mid-air, she ran for the café and grabbed one of the clean aprons Amie had hanging in the kitchen. She rushed back to find the books floating where she'd left them with Lucky presumably still holding them.

"What are you doing with the apron?" There was a distinct frown in his voice.

"I want you to wear it."

"Not very manly. How about *you* wear the apron and nothing under it?" Though she couldn't see his eyebrows waggling, she'd bet good money by his tone they were.

"You're such a man."

"Thank you."

"Now put on the apron."

"If I have to wear that thing, the least you can do is put it on me yourself."

The challenge lay between them. A challenge she didn't have any problem accepting.

"Divide the books in both hands," she ordered, fascinated as the stack of six books suddenly became a pair of three, each held about four feet apart. She reached up and felt solid shoulders under her hands.

Lucky moaned. "Your hands are so warm."

"Shh." If he kept talking like that her willpower would dissolve like sugar in a sea of water. The books moved closer to her as though he intended to hold her. "Nuh-uh. Keep the books in your hands. And no dropping them. Enough merchandise has been bruised tonight already."

She looped the apron over his head a little astonished when it stayed. Next, she stepped closer and brought the ties around to knot behind his back. If she closed her eyes, it was like wrapping her arms around a flesh and blood man.

He was here. He was real.

Yet, he wasn't.

Lucky groaned as though in pain. "Do you have any idea how good you smell and how badly I want to hold you?"

"Stop that," she said, though her voice held no conviction. She swallowed hard and stepped back. In front of her was a floating dark green apron with hovering romance novels on each side. She shook her head. "Stay put. I have another idea."

She ran to the office, hurrying back with her wool scarf and knit hat.

"Purple really isn't my color," Lucky said. "Besides, the scarf will clash with the hunter green of my apron."

She giggled, surprising herself with how much fun she was having. She reached up and with one hand felt for the top of his head, her fingers diving into thick, soft hair. It was her turn to groan. By her calculations, his hair was just shy of shoulder length, wavy and soft as goose down.

"Gemma." He moaned her name, the books inching closer to her in her peripheral vision.

She shushed him again. When they'd had these stolen moments before she wasn't fully awake and always came away wondering how much of what she remembered had really happened and what was just a dream. But she was awake, aware, and more involved than she wanted to admit.

"Close your eyes," Lucky whispered.

"No." She gasped. The desire to close her eyes was unbearably hard to refuse. If she did that she'd be lost again. And she badly wanted to give in. So she didn't. She grabbed the hat and placed it on his head, next she wrapped the scarf around his neck. She stepped back to view her handiwork.

He looked a bit like a scarecrow.

"There is nothing sexy about a scarecrow."

"I don't know. The scarecrow was always my favorite character in The Wizard of Oz."

"Well, I am brainless with desire." The humor in his voice was back and made her smile. She realized how much she'd laughed tonight. What fun they would've had together if he'd lived.

"Aren't we having fun now? Can you only enjoy things when you're alive? I'm proof that isn't true."

She sobered as the improbability of their situation cleared all the laughter out of her.

Her heart was in danger.

"Gemma—"

"I know." She shook it off. Tonight. She'd steal tonight for herself. "Do you like to dance?"

"I'm a fan of anything that gets my body flush against yours."

And just like that her despondence was gone as laughter bubbled to the surface. "Hang tight. I'll be right back." Once again she returned to the office, picked out her favorite music to play, and lowered the lights in the store, flipping the switch for the mural on the ceiling. Before her dad had died, he'd installed lights that resembled the constellations. Gemini being the brightest. It had been too long since she'd lit them up.

She walked out of the office into a magical land of light and color. The plate glass windows at the front of the store reflected the greens, reds, and purples of the Northern Lights, while her ceiling sparkled with stars and the fluid streams of the Milky Way. She found Lucky, having placed the books she'd been making him hold, onto the display. He'd even moved the books around so that the colors on the covers popped and balanced the promo. There wasn't anything about what he'd done that she'd change.

He seemed to get her in a way that no man had before. As though he could see into her soul.

He turned as she approached and for a moment she thought she saw more than an apron, hat and scarf. He seemed more outlined in the dim light. If she squinted, she thought she could see details of his frame.

The hat cocked to the side. "Fleetwood Mac?"

"I'm a hippie child. Some things you don't outgrow."

"I'm a big fan of Stevie Nicks and of the hippie lifestyle."

"You're not just saying that?"

She felt the touch of his hand on her check. "One thing you can rely on with me, Gemma, I will never lie to you." She felt his other hand on her waist, just above her hip. "Dance with me."

She slid into his arms as though she'd always belonged. His hips brushed hers, as they moved into a rhythm as natural as breathing. He led her across the book floor under the twinkling lights of the constellations as the smoky voice of Stevie Nicks sang "If Anyone Falls in Love." It was like they danced on clouds as each step fell into step with each other. He twirled her around the bookcases, from romance to mystery to sci-fi, they glided.

The song changed to the slower ballad "Silver Springs," and Lucky wrapped both of his arms around her, pulling her in close to his body. She sighed, resting her head on his invisible shoulder. This felt so perfect, yet made no sense.

"Babe, just live in the moment."

His bedroom voice rumbled under her ear, and the scent of fresh mountain air twined around her. She didn't even mind his use of "babe" as she had the other night. This time her insides melted with the endearment. His hands caressed up and down her back, as his hips brushed tantalizingly against hers.

He slowed their movements until they were basically standing in place, holding each other and swaying to the music.

"My mother read your Tarot cards today."

"I know. I was there. I couldn't communicate due to the storm, but I heard every word."

"How close did the reading come?"

"Damn freaky. Your mother is one woman who is tuned into the Universe."

"How much do you believe?"

"Just the fact that I'm here with you now has me believing everything."

"What's the time limit that the cards spoke of? And the choices you must make?"

"The Northern Lights dictate the time I can be with you. Once they settle back down to normal, I won't be able to return to this plane. Unless...."

"Unless what?"

"I must choose to stay or to move on."

"If you choose to stay how would that work?"

"Much like a spirit who is tied to his life."

"And if you move on?"

There was a long pause as he slowly turned her in a small circle. "There is no place that I would rather be than in your arms."

"We are talking Heaven here, right? You want to give up Heaven to be with me?"

"Gemma, when I'm with you I feel more alive than I did when I *was* alive."

"But you climbed mountains, lived on the edge. How does being with me, like this, compare to all that you have done before?"

"Don't you realize that love is the biggest adventure of all?"

Did that mean he loved her?

"Yes."

"You're supposed to stay out of my head."

"That is too important of a question not to hear...or answer."

She stopped swaying and stood still within his arms. "What do you see as a future for us?"

"I don't know." His arms tightened around her as though he was afraid she'd break their embrace. "All I know is that love is the most important thing out there. Love traverses life and death. Close your eyes, Gemma. Let me show you."

Part of her wanted to do exactly that. Close her eyes and be lost in the fantasy of this man. But wouldn't that be opening herself for heartache to come? Of course it would.

"Gemma?"

"I need some time to think." This was not the ideal relationship. What kind of future would they have together? Her always alone except for her "imaginary" friend. While she believed he was real, others would not. They might do to her what they'd done to her mother and commit her to the mental ward of the hospital.

"Gemma?" Lucky prompted again. "You aren't crazy. I'm real, just physically impaired. We were meant to be together."

Meant to be or not, what about children? She wanted them. Had always dreamt of a big family. She'd been an only child. Children needed siblings to play with, plot with, and help care for their parents. She wanted at least four kids. And no way could a dead man get her pregnant. That she was pretty damn positive about.

"We can figure this out. Together."

But the deeper her heart was involved with Lucky, the harder it would be to let him go.

Under her hands she felt taut muscles, and smooth flesh dusted with fine hair. What she wouldn't give to actually see him. Her eyes slid shut and there he was in her mind. The adventurous man from Tern's picture. Real, vibrant, and so alive. She pressed her body harder against his and glorified in the moan of pain and pleasure that seemed torn from him.

"I've never had a woman affect me like this. Never felt desire so deep."

Neither had she.

One of his thighs thrust between her legs, and it was her turn to moan as she made more room for him, straining against him. His hands cupped her behind and lifted her. Swinging her around, he pressed her against the bookcase of Divination and Prophecy. A few books hit the floor, and she didn't care. All that occupied her mind and body was Lucky and how he coaxed the wicked little flame inside her into a greedy fire.

"Gemma, Gemma. I can't get enough of you. I need you. To be part of you."

She felt the release on the button of her slacks and the zipper slide down. Why, oh why hadn't she worn a skirt today? Her clothing was too restrictive.

He gave a soft chuckle. "Oh, babe, you are the sweetest thing I've ever known."

Her head started to buzz as everything inside her pooled into a wave of unquenchable thirst. He'd been stringing her along for weeks, with her waking just before diving over the edge into bliss.

But tonight she was awake.

She felt the bookshelves dig into her back, the tight band around her upper thighs as he held her still, positioning her perfectly for the rubbing of his engorged erection through the constraints of her clothing. The need to have him deep within her, now, caused her ears to ring.

The impatient peal of the phone rang throughout the store, clashing with Fleetwood Mac's "Rhiannon."

"Ignore it," Lucky murmured, his tongue doing amazing things to her breasts. She hadn't even realized he'd gotten her sweater off and the front closure of her bra undone.

"Please," she whispered but didn't know if the plea was for him to stop so she could silence the blasted phone or to keep going so she could finally climb that peak he'd been driving her toward since that first dream visit.

His rough hand cupped her breast, holding her prisoner as his tongue lavished her erect nipple. The phone went silent, and she gave a groan of relief that quickly turned to a sound of pleasure as he took her nipple into his mouth. Her inner muscles contracted as he sucked, nipped, and licked. She might be able to clamber over the crest just on the attention he showed her breasts.

But she wanted more. She wanted all.

The phone pealed again, seeming angrier than the last time if that were possible. Who was she kidding? She was having the most intense make out session with a corporeal impaired being. Of course phones could ring with emotion.

"Holy balls, you've got to be kidding," she said. *The damn thing was not going to shut up.*

"I've never had a woman refer to my balls in a religious context before. I like it," Lucky said, humor in his voice.

She choked on a laugh, but sobered when she opened her eyes and caught the definite outline of the man in front of her. Her breath caught. "Don't move."

"What's wrong? Besides the phone."

"I can almost see you," she whispered.

"What?"

While his image wasn't fleshed out, she could see where he was, like a mirage in a desert. He was there and yet he wasn't.

The phone started up again. It obviously wasn't a customer wanting a book put on hold. "I'd better get that."

"I'm not letting you go." Next thing she knew he'd carried her to the information desk in the middle of the store so that she could reach the phone. She didn't take her eyes off Lucky, afraid if she did, his image would dissolve. Blindly, she reached behind her for the receiver.

"Chinook Books," she answered breathlessly.

"Oh, thank goodness I reached you," Rosie said. "Siri's been arrested."

CHAPTER THIRTEEN

Gemma drove to the police station mad at herself for being so dang distracted that she hadn't realized what day it was and how her mother would celebrate the spring equinox. Siri had, no doubt, demonstrated some pagan ritual naked.

How many times had she bailed out her mother?

Rosie had apologized profusely for not watching Siri closely enough. The clever, conniving woman had begged off dinner, saying she was feeling poorly and needed some sleep. Rosie had bought it and got lost in her favorite BBC TV series.

That's all it took. A few minutes and Siri was gone, stripping down to her birthday suit in the middle of the Bentley Mall. At least she was inside and not baring all outside in cold enough temperatures sure to cause frostbite.

Gemma pulled into the Troopers Station off Peger Road. "Lucky?"

"I'm right here," he said in the seat next to her.

She didn't know if she should feel relieved or more stressed that he'd insisted riding shotgun. The fabric of her life seemed to be unraveling thread by thread.

"It will be all right, Gemma." He took her hand in his and squeezed before releasing her.

She took a deep breath and stepped out of the car. The brisk air helped to clear her head. As she reached to open the door to the building, it swung open presumably by itself.

"Maybe you should stay in the car," Gemma said.

"There is no need for you to handle this alone."

"I have many times before," she muttered under her breath. "If you're going in there with me, no more opening doors. We're talking Alaska State Troopers here. They're a suspicious lot, and magically swinging doors are going to produce some questions."

"Got it."

Gemma managed the second door in the Arctic entryway and walked up to the desk where a young trooper, who looked to be just out of the academy, sat on the night shift. His badge said Trooper Cooper.

"Hi, I'm here for Siri Star."

"Good. The woman is driving us batty. I almost called the psych ward."

Gemma blanched. Not the psych ward. The last time had been rough. Lucky placed a supportive hand on her back, and knowing that she wasn't alone in this situation felt so good that tears popped to her eyes.

"Stop right there," Trooper Cooper said, his voice stern but lost its effect with his baby face. "I don't do tears." He jumped to his feet and hurried to usher Gemma back where her mother was being held.

Siri sat completely naked in the middle of the cell in the lotus position, her arms out to the side, thumbs and forefingers together as she hummed some incoherent mantra.

"Holy Jesus, Mary, and Joseph." Trooper Cooper threw up a hand to shield his eyes. "We gave her something to wear. The woman was fully dressed last time I saw her." He shook his head as though that would help wipe Siri's image out of his memory banks.

There was one thing about her mother, she left an impression.

"Mom?" Gemma walked up to the bars, her hands wrapping around the cold metal. The concrete floor had to be freezing. "Mom," she called again, but Siri continued with her mantra. Then she abruptly stopped.

Her eyes flew open and nailed Gemma on the spot. "You brought your *Dreamweaver.*"

How did she know Lucky was here?

Trooper Cooper unlocked the cell, holding it open for Gemma to enter, keeping his back to Siri the whole time. "Get her dressed, and I'll speed up the paperwork."

"Thank you."

Gemma entered the cell. "Mom, we need to get you dressed."

"You need to get your Dreamweaver the hell away from me."

"Mrs. Star," Lucky said besides Gemma. "I come in peace."

Siri stuck her fingers in her ears and began chanting louder.

"Mom." Gemma knelt on her haunches in front of Siri and put her hands on her shoulders, giving her a hard shake. If she didn't get her to stop the trooper was bound to call in the guys with the straight jackets. "When was the last time you took your medication?"

Siri stopped chanting and glared at Gemma. "I don't need any medication. I'm not crazy." She narrowed her eyes in Lucky's direction. "And it's Ms. Star."

"Right." Gemma redirected Siri's attention. "Then tell me why you are naked in a jail cell after being arrested for public lewdness."

"It's the equinox."

Like that explained away everything.

"Mom, we need to get you dressed."

"Not with him here."

See, crazy. "Shouldn't you be more concerned that you're naked in front of Lucky than getting dressed in front of him?"

Siri flattened her lips in a stubborn line.

Gemma let out a frustrated sound and got to her feet to reach for the orange inmate uniform that Siri must have shed as soon as she was left alone. But Lucky beat her to it, holding the clothes suspended behind Siri. She sent him a mental thank you and took the uniform. "Hands up," she ordered Siri.

Siri grumbled, but like a two-year-old, she raised her arms above her head and let Gemma yank the top down. Siri continued to mutter nonsense as Gemma pulled her to her feet and had her step into the cotton pants.

"Why have you not heeded my warnings?" Siri asked, once fully covered. "Dreamweavers are nothing to fool around with. Your soul is at stake here, Gemini."

Rosie suddenly appeared, holding up a bag filled with prescription bottles. "I found her pills. She's been stashing them in the couch cushions." Rosie shook her head. "By my calculations, she's been off her meds for two weeks."

"I'm not taking them." Siri crossed her arms over her chest. "And you can't make me."

Oh great, she was once again the parent of a middle-aged toddler. Gemma breathed a tired sigh.

A hand massaged the muscles at the base of her neck. If she turned, she'd see nothing, but she felt Lucky silently offering support. She'd give anything to be able to lean back and let him help her take care of things. How she wanted to just sleep. Lay her head down and check out for a few days. But with Siri's latest shenanigans, sleep was the last thing she'd be able to do.

She'd been alone for what seemed like forever. Her dad had died when she was eight, and since that time she'd been the main decision maker. It had been up to her to make sure they'd eaten. Left to Siri, Gemma had gone days without a real meal. Eating whatever she could scrounge. She'd learned fast how to procure groceries, cook dinner, and hide money to pay the bills. She'd been an adult for a long time. More years than her twenty-five years. Being able to lean on some-one was more seductive than the hottest kiss.

Thankfully Rosie had moved in with them after Social Services started visiting. A teacher had become concerned when Gemma had worn the same outfit to school for more than two weeks. She'd been clean, well as clean as an eight-year-old could be washing her own clothes.

Aunt Rosie had taken pity on the both of them and promptly taken over. That had helped. And had kept Gemma out of foster care. Barely.

"In ancient times your mother would have been revered for her talents," Lucky said, obviously trying to soothe.

"I don't need some Dreamweaver standing up for me," Siri said. "Though, thank you for that."

Witnessing her mother naked for all the world and God to see would scare off most suitors—though her mother still looked dang good at fifty. The scary thing was the brightness of her eyes and the crazy stuff coming out of her mouth. She seemed high on something. Gemma had seen her high many times with all the "organic" foods her mother baked—when she had baked. But she'd hoped between her and Rosie they'd nipped that. Trooper Cooper didn't seem to suspect narcotics or she was sure a blood test would have already been performed and Siri charged with more than indecent exposure.

"Wait a minute. Mom, you can hear him?"

"Of course I can." She gave Gemma a look that questioned her intelligence.

Gemma turned to Rosie. "Can you hear him?"

"Hear who. I have no idea what the two of you have been talking about since I got here. I've been contemplating whether or not I should take Siri's meds."

"Just an idea," Lucky interjected, "but you might want to move this conversation somewhere more comfortable and with less institutional ears."

"Your Dreamweaver has a point," Siri said. "Besides, I'd like some tea. The floor of this place was mighty cold on my nether regions."

"A shower might be in store too," Gemma said. Who knew the things that had walked across this floor? "Rosie, if you can stay with her—" and make sure she stays dressed, she silently added, "—I'll go see what Trooper Cooper needs from us so that we can leave."

"Trooper Cooper?" Rosie smirked. "Bet the poor soul takes a few ribbings on that name."

Whether he did or not, Gemma planned on being sweet as the Bun on the Run's cinnamon rolls in order to get out of here fast.

She signed the papers Trooper Cooper had prepared, paid the bail money, and took the copies of the arrest with the court date. Wonderful, another day in front of the judge. Somehow she had to keep Siri on her meds and out of jail. Maybe it was time to get Rosie some help. Gemma sure didn't want to move in with either of them. She'd fought hard for her independence.

Gemma returned to Siri with Trooper Cooper who acted very relieved to see her fully dressed. They did the checking out—since Siri had been brought in naked there were no personal effects to claim—and then Rosie and Gemma escorted Siri to Rosie's Jeep Cherokee.

"Gemma, there is really no need for you to see us home. I can get Siri cleaned up and in bed. I'll make sure she takes her meds, but getting her an appointment with Doc Walton Monday wouldn't be a bad idea."

Gemma nodded, too tired to think straight. "Thanks, Rosie."

"I'm just so sorry she got away from me tonight. If I had been thinking straight myself, I would have figured she was up to something."

"Don't be too hard on yourself. You weren't the only one not thinking straight."

"I really hate it when you guys talk about me like I'm not here," Siri chimed in.

"Well, I really hate bailing you out of jail."

"Yeah, I can see that." Siri stared at something to the left of Gemma. "Leave my baby alone. Her soul is not yours to take."

"I'm not after her soul," Lucky said. "I'm after her heart."

"Her heart is not available to you either."

"Mom."

"Gemini, he will break your heart and leave you a shell of your former self. I know what I'm talking about. I was fool enough to dream walk once."

Chapter Fourteen

The night shone bright and clear, and Gemma watched Rosie's taillights as she drove out of the trooper parking lot. Deep in thought, she made her way to her Subaru. Her feet crunched on the snow, sounding super-loud in the silent night. Blue-green celadons with hints of violet reflected in the snow. She was afraid to look up or even glance sideways. Ever since their shared dance, she'd caught the outline of Lucky in her peripheral vision. But when she'd looked directly at him or where she assumed he was, he disappeared again. And now with her mother's cryptic comment about dream walking, Gemma didn't know what to think.

She'd tried to get details out of Siri, but she'd jumped from subject to subject much the way a distracted child on a sugar rush did. There was no getting information out of her until she leveled out, and even then Gemma doubted Siri would fill her in or remember what she'd said.

The evening had warmed up from the blustery afternoon. Everything was quiet as though old man winter had decided to give up the fight and let spring elbow her way in. Could Siri's naked dance have wakened spring from her slumber?

Gemma shook her head, not believing the direction her thoughts had taken. Sleep. She needed sleep.

She drove the short distance home, white-knuckling it as the roads were icy from the rising temperatures. She fishtailed as she took one of the turns on Riverview Drive.

Lifting her foot off the gas, and turning the wheel to compensate for the skid, Gemma regained control of the car just as it would have headed into the ditch. Heart pounding, she slowed her speed. Her reflexes were too slow. If she didn't get some sleep soon, she'd have to stop driving. She heard somewhere that driving drowsy was worse than driving drunk.

She pulled into her driveway, parked in the garage, and slowly released her grip on the wheel. Home. But she was suddenly apprehensive about entering her own house.

"I won't hurt you, Gemma," Lucky whispered next to her.

She jumped, slapping her hand over her heart. "Don't do that. You have got to figure out a way to make some noise."

"Sorry, I didn't mean to scare you...or overwhelm."

"You were so quiet that I assumed you left. Have you been here the whole time?" She half-turned trying to catch his image in the dim light. There. She had to swallow. A vague outline, but he was there.

"I never left your side. You seemed to need time to think. By the way, nice driving back there."

"I can almost see you. How is this possible?" What was she asking? How was any of this possible? It was freaky to say the least.

"I don't know. I'm just grateful for whatever is out there in the Universe that lets me be near you." His hand captured hers, and held it, linking their fingers together.

She stared down at her hand. And saw nothing. No tendons, knuckles, or fingers other than her own. She squeezed her fingers, and his hand gave her a squeeze back.

She didn't want to have astral sex with him.

"Gemma, we aren't going to do anything you don't want to do."

She wanted to have *actual* sex with him. The hot, sweaty, break-the-bed-frame kind of sex.

A strangled sound came from him, and his hand suddenly clenched hers.

Time to get out of the car.

She released her hold on him and opened the door. Somehow she needed to control her thoughts since he couldn't seem to stop listening in. A deep breath did nothing to clear her mind or the raging need to be touched by this Dreamweaver who had somehow burrowed his way into her heart.

She dropped her purse on the table and entered the kitchen. "I need to eat something. Would you like—?" Yeah, well, that was stupid.

The phone rang, saving her. She glanced at the clock. Almost midnight. Had Siri given Rosie problems? Relief filled her to see it was Tern. "Hey." She'd yet to get Tern's impression of the Tarot reading earlier that day. Had that been today? Afterward Tern had seemed more shell-shocked than Gemma and had quickly made her excuses.

"I know it's late, but I finally talked to Gage." There was something in Tern's voice that Gemma couldn't quite put her finger on. "The man is going crazy nuts with all the data from the solar storms."

Opening the fridge, Gemma stared at the contents. Mayo, mustard, and wrinkled fruit of what kind she wasn't sure. She really needed to make time for grocery shopping. She grabbed the mayo and mustard, found a jar of pickles and set the items on the counter. She was pretty sure she had a can of tuna fish somewhere. She hadn't eaten since lunch, and that had been a brownie and a cup of coffee, not enough fuel for dancing with a Dreamweaver and bailing her mother out of jail.

"According to Gage, you'd better buckle up," Tern continued. "There's a weather disturbance that is supposed to move in sometime in the early morning for about eighteen hours and then you're in for a freaking ride."

Gemma shut the cupboard, setting the forgotten can of tuna fish on the counter and listened to Tern rave over the projection of record solar energy directed at the earth's poles for the next week.

"Gemma, do you think Lucky can talk to me?" Tern asked when she'd finished her solar report.

"Uh...I don't know."

"Would you ask him?"

Gemma swallowed and pushed the makings of her dinner aside, not hungry anymore. "Tern, you don't sound as though you're warning me off anymore." If anything she sounded excited.

"It's Lucky. He wouldn't hurt a fly. There was one time when we were geocaching in the Chugach Mountains, and Lucky refused to kill a spider. He's very into his Buddhist beliefs."

Gemma didn't miss the change in referring to Lucky in the present tense. "Tern, just how close were you and Lucky?" Had it just been a fling with them or more? Please not more.

There was a pause and then the truth came at her hard. She didn't have anyone to blame as she'd asked the question herself. Still the truth was hard to swallow.

"If Lucky hadn't been so much of a gambler, with a weakness for other women, and Gage hadn't come along, I would have happily waited for him."

Weakness for other women?

What the hell did that mean? Could he be playing her?

"No," Lucky said. "She didn't mean it that way. Actually she might have. I do have a love for the ladies. Did. When Tern and I were together it was one of those open kind of relationships. I was free to see other women, and Tern was free to see other men."

Gemma held up her hand to get Lucky to stop speaking. She couldn't comprehend it all.

"Are you in *favor* of me seeing him now?" she asked Tern. One minute her soul is at stake and the next she's being pushed to accept her Dreamweaver?

This day had been too long already. Sleep. She had to get some sleep.

"Yes," Tern said. "I don't know why or how this is possible but any chance to have Lucky back, no matter the capacity, I'll take. He was robbed of his life. And...I owe him."

"Tell her she doesn't owe me anything," Lucky's voice came from her left this time.

She jumped. "You have *got* to stop doing that." The man needed to stay put and quit floating around.

"Gemma? What's going on? Is he there?"

"Uh...yes. He said you don't owe him anything."

"Of course he would say that. But he's wrong. Tell him I love him, and whatever he needs from me he has it."

Gemma turned toward where she assumed Lucky still was and went to repeat Tern's message.

"I heard," Lucky said. "Tell her thank you, but she's wrong. My situation is nobody's fault but my own, and the one who has already been punished."

She repeated what Lucky had said, wanting answers herself.

"Oh man, I'm going to cry," Tern said. "Gemma, promise me you'll give him a chance. In fact, get some sleep. The unconscious mind will be open to the astral plane more so than if you are awake."

Right now she didn't want to be open to the astral plane. Gemma wasn't sure how much Lucky could hear from Tern's side of the conversation but didn't want to share this little gem of information. "You know this goes completely against what you and Siri have been saying from the start."

"Forget all that. This is Lucky. You are fated. I'll go and let you two be together." And then she was gone. Gemma had a strong feeling the "be together" wasn't sharing a cup of coffee.

Gemma put the phone down on the counter, looking around the kitchen feeling exposed.

"Lucky?"

"I'm here." She felt his hand on her cheek trying not to freak out that her eyes were open and she could feel him but not see him or his outline in the harsh lighting of the kitchen.

She took a step back, part of her weeping inside at the loss of his touch falling away.

"Talk to me. Tell me what you're feeling."

Couldn't he read her thoughts?

"They're coming too fast and jumbled for me to make sense of them. Gemma—"

He couldn't make sense of them? Try having them. "I think it's best if you go now. I need some time. This is...too much. I can't make sense of anything."

"You're thinking too hard."

"Of course I'm thinking too hard. How do I not? I'm falling in love with a dead man, my mother is off her meds, and I'm beginning to think I need to get on some." She pressed her palms against her temples where her head pounded. She hadn't eaten and now couldn't as her stomach bubbled with anxiety.

"You're falling in love with me?"

"That's what you picked out from all of that?" The question coming out a bit hysterical. "Not the being dead part, my mother nuttier than a granola bar and me following in her footsteps? None of that concerns you at all?"

"Are we about to have our first fight?"

"Holy balls! You would think dying would have gained you some insight."

"I really like how your skin flushes when you're angry," his voice rumbled with arousal.

"Are you *freaking* kidding me?"

"No. Your skin does that same thing when I—"

"Okay, enough. Let me tell you something, yelling in my kitchen, by all accounts appearing to be alone, to a spirit who is turned on by it is not an attraction for me." She suddenly felt Lucky behind her, his hands massaging her shoulders.

"Close your eyes. I can make you forget everyone and everything." His voice purred into her ear, making her want to give in. For a moment she did, closing her eyes and leaning into his body, her blood quickening at his obvious arousal. She wanted to turn and bury her head in his shoulder, grip his backside in her hands and pull him to her. Strip him of his clothes—did he even wear clothes?—at least, strip hers and then ride him until she thought of nothing.

He gave a painful groan, his hands leaving her shoulders to grab her hips, holding her tight against him. "Yesss," he hissed.

All it would take was the relaxation of her body against his. One thought and she knew he'd have her naked and writhing on her kitchen floor. Did she want that?

"God, please say yes, Gemma." His lips trailed down her neck, his teeth grazing her shoulder.

"I can't." The words were torn from her. She so badly wanted to lose herself in him. "Lucky, I can't make a decision like this when I'm this sleep deprived."

She felt his need to push and was surprised when he took a slight step away from her. His hands shook where they still held her hips, but he was no longer pressed against her. Part of her breathed easier, but the other part mourned the promise of his body next to hers.

"Rest, Gemma," he said. Though she clearly heard the implied, "*You'll need it for next time.*"

CHAPTER FIFTEEN

Gemma tossed and punched her pillow. She glared at the digital clock on her bedside table as the minute turned from 1:59 to 2:00 am. How could she not sleep? She hadn't slept more than a few fitful hours in weeks. What the hell? She was alone. Utterly and completely alone. She'd tried a hot shower, needing it after the jail stopover.

Her mind ran circles around her problems, never settling on a course of viable action. Maybe she should talk to someone? Who? A therapist? *Right.* What she needed was a freaking sleeping pill.

And Siri had given her some.

Gemma jumped out of bed and raced into the kitchen. Where had she put them? Her purse produced nothing, but the pocket of her coat proved helpful. There was the small plastic baggie with a dozen or so small white sleeping pills.

Had Siri said how many to take? One, two, four? Obviously not four. Geez. Maybe not even two. She could Google the information if the pills had a name on them. But there was only a number etched into the face of the pills. Should she call Siri and ask? No, it was way too late to call anyone. Besides, she shouldn't even be entertaining the idea of taking medication her mother recommended.

Obviously, she was way past doing anything reasonable.

She needed sleep, and she was going to get some even if it killed her. Okay, probably not the best thought to have.

She'd take one pill. If that didn't work within a reasonable time frame she'd take another. An hour should be good.

Fishing one of the little white pills out of the baggie, Gemma swallowed it whole without water. She stood there waiting, for what she didn't have a clue. A magical stirring of melatonin that promised sweet oblivion?

Clutching the baggie in her hand, she filled a glass of water and headed back to bed. Setting down the glass with the bag of pills next to the bed, she came to a cold stop. What was she doing? Sleeping pills cozying up to a glass of water didn't give off a happy outcome for waking up in the morning. If ever.

It was so hard making decisions—right or wrong—when she wasn't in her right mind. The pills had to go, but suddenly the effects of whatever she'd taken took form. Her legs were heavy, reflexes sluggish. What had she taken? Definitely needed to know that before she'd taken them. Her eyes refused to focus. Things in the room seemed to move on their own or was she swaying? Everything was too much effort, just gathering the pills and hiding them away in her night table—far away from the glass of water—took all the energy Gemma had left.

A few tries and she was able to swing back the covers and crawl under them. Her eyelids locked shut, and her breathing slowed. A sense of peace came over her, and she sighed. Finally, she'd get the rest she'd been depriving herself.

Then suddenly it felt like she'd stepped off the planet. Tripped into nothingness.

One second she was flat on her back in bed, the next transported as though she were on the starship *Enterprise* and Scotty had just beamed her up.

Deeper than sleep. Deeper than a coma. She was gone.

She opened her eyes to find herself not on her bed. Not even in her bedroom. By the warmth, and lush grass under where she lay, she wasn't even in Alaska. The only snow and ice in sight was high atop amethyst mountains in the distance.

Her breath caught on the beauty and tranquility of wherever she was. Colors more vibrant than any palette painted wildflowers that bobbed and swayed in the sweet-scented breeze. She couldn't quite comprehend the snow-topped majestic mountains sheltering the surrounding meadow. A blue ribbon of liquid sapphires sparkled in the sun. If this was a dream it was the most visual and sensual one she'd ever had. Too real. She struggled to her feet, pinching herself even though she had no desire to wake up and leave.

Where was she?

"Limbo. And how the hell did you get here?"

Slowly she turned. There was Lucky in full Technicolor. A tight-fitting t-shirt with some climbing gear company's symbol scrawled across the chest showed off heavy, defined muscles in his torso and arms. He was lean and hard, his skin smooth and golden, his eyes the softest brown. Cargo shorts and hiking boots completed his outfit. Is this how he was dressed when he visited her? The man was a walking advertisement for REI.

"Gemma, what *did* you do?" A scowl darkened his face.

"Took a sleeping pill," she admitted, her eyes devouring the sight of him.

There was a pause. "Sleeping pill or pills?"

"My mom gave them to me. I just took one and ended up here." She looked around again. "Got any ideas how that happened?"

He pursed his lips in thought, the scowl furrowing deep lines in his forehead.

"What is it? You know, don't you?"

"I have a theory."

"I'm not dead, too, am I?"

"No. You and I are connected. Destined." He rushed on when she went to interrupt. "I know you don't like that word, but it's the only explanation for why, after I passed away, that I was drawn to you. I'm thinking taking a sleeping pill allowed your spirit to astral project to where it wants to be. To me."

Astral project?

Hadn't she been warned about that? What had Siri said? Gemma had the sneaky suspicion she was in trouble.

"What are you thinking?" Lucky asked, looking as though he wanted to reach out and touch her but was afraid to move.

"You can't read my thoughts?"

"You're doing that mile a minute thing, but your expression is freaking me out."

"Well, I'm a little freaked."

"That explains it then." He stuffed his hands in the front pockets of his cargo shorts. She followed the movement, and his eyes widened. "Can you see me?"

"Yes." Her throat thickened with emotion. This was so much more real, being with him here, seeing him. She reached out to touch him, and he sucked in his breath.

Softly her fingers traced the bones in his face. His eyes shuttered closed on a groan. "Gemma, tell me you can feel me too."

"Yes," she whispered. "It's as though you're really here with me. Alive." She cupped his jaw, the stubble raspy against her fingers, and placed her other hand on his chest. Unbelievably, his heart pounded fast under her palm. His skin was hot like he had an internal sun heating him from the inside out.

Slowly he grasped her shoulders. "Let me—I have to—" His mouth was on hers, kissing her, plundering, groaning as he yanked her into his arms. She melted into him. All of her soft curves linked with his hard angles, like puzzle pieces always meant to be together.

"Gemma," he moaned. "Please, I need—"

"Yes, I need too," she rushed to finish for him.

"Are you sure?" Warm rich brown eyes stared into hers.

"God, yes."

"I don't know how much foreplay—"

"No foreplay." She flipped the button free on his shorts, besides who knew what kind of time they had together? "We've had weeks of foreplay." She slid his zipper down. "I need to see you. Really see you. All of you. Now."

In a flurry, he stripped off his clothes.

Her eyelids threatened to close from the sheer beauty of this man, but she forced them to stay open, not wanting to miss a minute of viewing his body.

There wasn't an ounce of fat on him. She'd guessed this from feeling him in her dreams, and dancing with him the night before. But in the flesh he was magnificent. Worship worthy. Muscles corded and hardened every inch of his skin. His upper body bunched as though he could easily shoulder the weight of the world, angling down to a solid waist with muscles defined in a way she'd never seen illustrated outside of a book. Her eyes traveled lower, hoping the promise of his torso extended to other parts as well.

A choking sound came from him, and too late she remembered he could read her thoughts when they weren't jumbled. They weren't jumbled now. Call it a one track mind. She had it. Regardless of the blush heating her face, she had to look, and then stared. Her mouth fell open in a silent "O".

His penis jutted out from the V-line of his groin, proud and unapologetic of its size and thickness. He flexed the muscles of his abdomen, making it bob in a playful hello that was anything but reassuring. She'd felt that thickness and length pressing against her. But feeling and seeing apparently were two vastly different things.

"Looking at me like that makes me glad for every damn mountain I struggled to climb."

She licked her lips. She couldn't wait to climb him.

A surprised guttural sound escaped him, and he took a large step back, putting distance between them. "Keep thinking like that and I won't be able to behave."

When had he ever behaved?

He'd snuck into her dreams, seduced her in her sleep. Bewitched her every thought. "I'm not asking you to behave." Quite the opposite, in fact.

"I want this to be special for you, Gemma. Not just a tumble like I've had with so many other women. I want to love you."

"Love me then." The words came out like a dare. "Love me until I know nothing but you. And you know nothing but me," she couldn't help adding. She reached for the hem of her top and whipped it off, her breasts bouncing with the action. Her bottoms went next, leaving her as naked as Eve to his Adam. In this paradise, it was easy to imagine the world barely born and just the two of them existing to love one another.

"Oh, Gemma." A low moan escaped from deep within his throat. His hand clenched around hers, and the space he'd put between them disappeared like it had never been. A low growl preceded his fingers fisting in her hair, and his mouth devouring hers. She'd broken the thread he'd been holding onto, had felt it snap in the air with her last words. With the one hand gripping her hair, holding her mouth prisoner to his plundering, his other hand seized her hip, yanking her flush against him.

His erection searched for entry between her thighs as though it had a mind of its own. That she had no doubt, as the bulbous head found her wet and slick. He lifted her leg around his hip and entered her with one hard thrust, arching her body backward.

Breath whooshed out of her, and she couldn't get it back.

In this position, she was completely at his mercy. Not any man could hold her body this way, and do what he was doing to her, without the strength of steel infused within his very fiber.

Gasping, she tore her mouth free of his, her neck arcing into the bow her body had become. From chest bone to hip bone, they were one as he bent his powerful body over her, in a way forcing her to take everything he had to give. He held himself impossibly deep within her, breathing hard, keeping their bodies flush and tight, his mouth hovering over her collarbone.

Lightly he scraped her skin with his teeth. "Gemma," he groaned. "I've never felt so...so complete as I feel buried within the depths of your beautiful body."

She melted further at his words. A rush of molten liquid infused her body where they were joined, and her inner muscles contracted in a series of hot spasms.

She stretched her arms around his neck and held on as he slowly, painstakingly retreated from the heat of her body, and then thrust in to her again. She'd never been held like this before. Never been made love to like this and didn't know how long she'd last without crumbling at his feet. Muscles strained as sensations snapped and sparked with electrical current.

"Tighten your hold on to me," he ordered, lifting her other leg to hook his hip, his arms wrapping like steel bands around her. In one graceful, measured move, he lowered them to the lush, carpeted ground without retreating from the zenith of her body.

How did a man move like this?

"Yoga," he answered. His mouth stole her breath as his teeth captured her nipple. With a flick of his tongue against the turgid peak, he tugged and released it, only to suck the nub roughly into his mouth as his hips slammed hard into her.

Her arms hooked around his upper torso as she attempted to anchor herself. If anything she found herself holding on more in this position than the last one as he mindlessly pounded into her.

"Oh, God," she began to chant. She tried to slow the reaction of her body, wanting it to last longer, but sensations danced over her like vibrant waves of the Northern Lights. "Oh, my God." Electrical currents charged her with each plunge and retreat. His mouth continued to lick, suck, and nip at her breasts, his hands yanking her closer, spreading her, angling her hips upward, opening her to the sweet assault of his body as he imprinted on hers with voltage too high to contain.

"*Ohmygod,*" she screamed to the Heavens.

His answering shout of satisfaction joined in with the cadence of her cries, clutching her tight within his iron grasp as he emptied his essence inside her.

She imploded into the fabric of the Universe.

Lucky's body settled softly over hers, his weight delicious.

"Oh, God that was amazing," she gasped.

"You gotta quit throwing that word around. Someone will hear."

No way did she have the strength to move even if a crowd of thousands had gathered. "Who will hear?"

"God," he leaned in and whispered, nibbling on her ear.

She giggled then sobered, her wide eyes meeting his. "You're not kidding."

"Kinda. Sorta. Yeah, not really. I haven't seen the Big Guy as I'm stuck in Limbo. But hard not to believe He exists with all this." He lifted his head, looking around them at their glorious surroundings, then back to her. His eyes heated with emotion as he gazed into hers. "And with what just happened between us."

"Do you, uh, think what just happened was okay?" She shrugged. "You know, with Him?" *And you*, she silently added.

"As far as I'm concerned, He made all this possible. You are meant to be here. Now. Like this. Otherwise, you wouldn't be here." He caressed her face with the back of his fingers. "As for me, there is nothing in my life, or death, that compares to what I just experienced with you. I love you, Gemma, more than I ever thought it was possible to love someone."

Tears tickled the back of her throat, making it impossible to speak. Something in the way she looked at him must have satisfied him, for he smiled, and softly kissed her lips. Taking time to treasure rather than plunder.

They held each other like that for a long time, leisurely caressing, softly kissing, as they seemed to float in a moment of weightlessness.

"This place is so beautiful," Gemma murmured, gazing up at the puffy clouds so white they gleamed like pearls.

"Nothing is as beautiful as you are."

She angled her head to look at him, her mind needing to see his reaction, though her heart feared for his answer. "How could you ever leave such a place?"

He smoothed her hair to fan on the grass, before his eyes could meet hers. "It's a spirit prison, Gemma. Doesn't matter how pretty it's dressed up, it's still a prison."

"So if you choose to stay with me, you can leave this place?"

"Yes."

But what kind of hell would that be? In her life but not. A spirit to wander and never die.

"Let's not talk about that." He gave her a hard, quick kiss. "I don't want to waste one moment of being with you like this." His lips trailed down her neck.

"Could I stay here with you?"

He froze, and then his head came up, his eyes piercing hers. "No. Don't even entertain the thought. This isn't living. It's existing. No hunger, yet you can eat if you want to. Everything you think you want is provided, but it isn't real." He released her and fell back on the grass, linking his arms behind his head gazing up at the sky. "At first, I loved it here. I climbed all those mountains, explored endless valleys and hills. Experienced beauty in landscapes like I'd never seen before. But there was always something off. There is no challenge. No change."

"How long will I be able to stay here with you?"

He turned, and his sad eyes meet hers. "You're already leaving me, babe." His finger traced the side of her face, her bottom lip, trailing over the curve of her chin. "I suspect you look to me now, how I look to you. There is translucence about you, and you're fading, fast."

She felt it now, a heaviness pulling her as though she was anchored somewhere and the slack was being pulled out of the line. It must be the effects of the sleeping pill, or whatever her mother had given her, wearing off.

"I don't want to leave you." Not after finally being with him. Loving him.

He kissed her, held her locked within his arms, yet she could feel herself slipping away. His mouth became more demanding, as he gripped her tighter. There was a moan of despair as she was taken from him, ripped from the comfort and love she'd found in his arms.

A cry as if his heart were being torn from his chest ripped through the tatters of space.

Gemma jerked up in bed feeling like the wind had been knocked out her. She was cold, the bed empty, and she was fully dressed in her "I Otter Be Asleep" pajamas. The same pajamas that she remembered stripping out of in front of Lucky.

That *hadn't* been a dream. It couldn't be. She knew it in her core, in her heart. But waking up in her bed made it hard to believe she'd actually made love to Lucky.

Despair threatened to swamp her. She climbed out of bed, and any doubt that she'd been with him evaporated. It had been a long time since she'd been with someone and the physical aches were a pleasurable reassurance that she hadn't dreamt being with him. The night had been magical, what they'd shared had been out of this world.

She chuckled with the thought. Out of this world pretty much said it all.

She jumped in the shower, humming as she got ready for work. It wasn't until she was on the way to Chinook Books that the gravity of her situation hit her.

She'd slept with her Dreamweaver, participated in astral sex, and would do so again if given the opportunity.

And didn't she have the opportunity shut away in the drawer of her night table in the form of a baggie of little white pills her mother had supplied her?

CHAPTER SIXTEEN

Saturdays were always busy, and Gemma was able to lose herself in book recommending, one of her favorite things about running the bookstore. There was a steady stream of customers until about three in the afternoon.

She was in love with a man with no foreseeable way of having a normal relationship. But then who really had a normal relationship? Her parents hadn't. They hadn't even been married, in the legal sense. Siri didn't believe in a legal document proclaiming them married by the government. Instead, they'd participated in a hand-fasting when Gemma had been old enough to be the flower child.

Her father had been the exact opposite of her mother, and he'd loved all the differences. Gemma remembered how he'd looked at Siri with so much love it hurt as though the definition of the Universe was held within Siri's eyes.

Lucky had looked at her like that last night.

A bittersweet smile curved her lips. What would her father say about the situation she'd gotten herself into? Would he warn her off like Siri had, or encourage her to follow her heart?

As logical as her father had been, when it came to love he was as impractical as Siri. One thing Gemma did know, Siri had never loved her father. Not like he'd loved her.

Gemma had checked in with Rosie earlier in the day to see how Siri had fared after her stint in jail. Apparently it hadn't disturbed her one bit. She'd still been asleep. A good sign since when this had happened in the past, Siri would go into a manic phase with days of not sleeping. Kind of like Gemma was doing. Could that be a sign she was following in Siri's footsteps? Should she have made an appointment with Doc Walton too?

But then if she mentioned to Doc Walton that she was seeing a Dreamweaver, taking her mother's sleeping pills, and having astral sex, he would no doubt set her up for an evaluation in the psych ward.

The bells over the door chimed, and Gemma glanced up, her customer service smile plastered on her face. Though with the direction her thoughts had taken she was no longer in the mood to endure customers.

Tern marched in like she was on a mission. Gemma's smile faded. What now?

"I have something for you." Tern glanced around the store to see a few stragglers in the café, Amie behind the counter cleaning up, and Callista occupied at the register with a customer. "Good, you're not busy."

"That's not a good thing for someone who is self-employed."

"You know what I meant." Tern held up a necklace with a deep bluish-purple crystal wrapped in silver wire. "Here, you need to wear this."

"What is it?"

"Indigo tourmaline. It will help open your third eye, the sixth chakra, and strength your ability to transcend your reality. Go ahead, put it on."

Gemma slid the necklace over her head even though she wasn't sure she wanted help "transcending her reality." She jolted when the stone brushed against her heart. Her hand smoothed the tourmaline in place. What the hell had that been? Static electricity in the air? Crystals didn't have magical powers. Did they?

Tern gave her an approving smile. "I've done more research and if you actually have sex with Lucky the act will strengthen your bond."

"*Shh.*" Gemma grabbed Tern's elbow. "Come here." She dragged Tern into the bookshelves of Philosophy and Travel, providing them some privacy where they wouldn't be overheard.

Tern squinted and then gasped. "Oh my God. You've *been* with Lucky. What happened? I need details."

Details she wasn't going to get. But then Tern knew how gifted a lover Lucky was. Jealousy rose up in Gemma. Her friend had been with the man she loved. Experienced the joy Gemma had found in his arms. That was one very important thing that friends should not share.

"How?" Tern asked. "That storm front moved in last night. I would think that in order for Lucky to be able to sustain enough of a presence to accomplish intercourse the solar flares would need to be out of this world."

There was that phrase again.

"He didn't visit me. I visited him."

That stopped her. "*You* made love with Lucky on the astral plane? In his realm?"

The way she said that made it sound bad.

"How did you travel there?"

"Remember those sleeping pills my mom gave me after the Tarot reading? Well, I took one."

"Hmm." Tern tapped her lower lip with her finger in thought. "How did you make it back?"

"I assumed when the effects of the drug wore off. I woke up in my bed."

"And you know for sure that you were there and didn't dream everything?"

"It wasn't a dream. You sound like I need to repent or something." Hadn't Tern been pushing for her to connect with Lucky, strengthen their bond? Wasn't this why she'd given her the tourmaline to wear?

"What is it?" she asked as Tern took a step back to study her, cocking her head and narrowing her eyes. "Tern, what aren't you telling me?" For cripes sake she was tired of people not telling her things.

"You have the same look about you that your mother does."

"What the hell does that mean?"

"The colors in your aura are more vibrant, which is normal after having really good sex, but...you have similar breaks or holes in the layers like the aura that surrounds your mother."

"Aura?" *Dreamweavers, astral planes, chakras, and now auras?* Was her reality anything that she believed? If all this was true, where was her freaking starship? "What do you mean holes?"

"I don't know. Siri probably does."

"You can see auras but don't know why mine would be broken?"

"Not broken. Missing. If you want me to speculate, I'd have to say, part of you is still in the astral plane."

"You are busting through all the rules," Hansen said, standing with his hands on his hips as though bringing judgment. "How did you get her here?"

"It wasn't anything to do with me. And how can I break the rules when I don't even know what they are?" Frustration ate at Lucky. He'd been pacing long enough to actually mow a path into the perfect field of grass. He needed out of here. He needed Gemma, needed to be with her now more than ever, and no matter what he did he couldn't break out.

Each time he'd meditated, he'd been lost in a swirl of snow. He'd been able to visit her before through storms worse than the one currently over the arctic. There'd been bad weather the day Siri had read his Tarot cards, and while he hadn't been able to interact with Gemma, he'd been able to see her, hear her.

Today was different.

Each time he closed his eyes and concentrated, a static whiteout appeared meant to confuse and cage. No vibrant liquid streams of light to guide him to her. It was like there was divine interference. Had he broken some unpardonable rule by lying with Gemma?

Panic chilled him to the soul.

"You're seriously going to choose to be with her." Hansen dropped to his favorite rock. "You're going to give up Heaven for a woman?"

"She is my Heaven." Lucky stopped and faced his friend. "I have never felt more alive, more in tune to a person than when I hold her in my arms. It's killing me, all over again, not to be in her presence."

"How is it going to feel for her if she chooses you but can never truly be with you?"

Lucky raked his hands through his hair, pulling at the roots. He needed to consider that, but the heartache that always followed paralyzed him. "It's a gamble. I love her. There is nothing without her. I have to go all in."

A sudden zinging along his spine caught his breath. There. A thread of energy. "Gotta go."

He shut his eyes and concentrated on that thread as it weaved around him. His spirit reached out and gently gripped the end, letting it wing him across distances so vast he couldn't comprehend it all.

Gemma.

The only thing in his mind, in his heart, and he followed both like a bullet to its target.

CHAPTER SEVENTEEN

Gemma glanced up as Callista rounded the corner of the bookcase where she and Tern were hiding.

"Hate to interrupt, but Cub is here." Callista had trouble keeping the delight out of her voice.

"What's he doing here?" Tern asked, her hands going to her hips.

"They're dating," Callista filled her in. "Gemma, he's waiting for you at the customer service desk. That is one man I sure wouldn't make wait long." Callista swiveled on her clogs and headed back to the register.

"You're dating Cub," Tern said. "And sleeping with Lucky."

She made that sound really bad. "Yes. No." A growl of frustration escaped her.

"You can't do this to Lucky."

"What about Cub? *You* were the one who told me to have sex with Cub."

That tied Tern's tongue for a second, but not for long. "That was before. We need to find a way to get Lucky back here."

"I don't know the whole story between you two, and I don't know if I want to. But I'm freaking confused, Tern. Cub's alive. He's here." Oh God, he was here waiting for her, and she was debating whether or not she was cheating on Lucky with him. "I need to go and see what he wants. Most likely he heard how unbalanced I am and is breaking off our date for tomorrow."

"If he doesn't, you should."

She was beginning to think the same thing. She wasn't any good for him if she didn't have a clue what she wanted.

Gemma tried to get herself mentally put back together while she walked the short distance from Travel to the customer service desk. A cold breeze blew into the store, and her step faltered. It was strong enough to blow her hair back from her face.

She turned the corner of Mystery, and there was Cub waiting for her, standing tall and golden at the desk. He was in jeans and t-shirt the same color of his ice blue eyes. His unzipped Columbia jacket gave him the look of an Olympic Norwegian cross country skier. A dozen red roses were clutched in his hand.

"Hey," he greeted, looking uncomfortable as he glanced around the bookstore.

Gemma felt all eyes on them, especially the ones boring into her back from Tern. She wasn't doing anything wrong. *He* had come to see her. She owned a business. People came and saw her every day. Bought books, coffee, sometimes just popped in to say hi.

"Hi," she responded. "Everything okay?"

"Yeah." He rubbed the bridge of his nose. "I, uh, wanted to bring you these, and let you know—"

Here it came. He was here to break off their date. Relief and regret warred inside her.

"—how much I'm looking forward to our date tomorrow." Cub held out the flowers to her. "I was passing by Forget-Me-Not and saw these." He shrugged self-consciously. "And, well, I thought of you."

Oooh. She slowly took the flowers. A swirl of cold air twisted around her.

Her movements froze, and her heart raced.

Lucky?

She glanced to the side to see if she could pick up any details in her peripheral vision. Nothing. No mirage, no vague outline. Lucky hadn't answered her mental question either. Was she just imagining him here?

The bell on the door rang as it closed behind a few café customers. Well, that explained the draft.

"I hope you like roses." Cub stuffed his hands in the pockets of his jacket. "I know most women do. They smell nice but are kind of clichéd these days, aren't they. The flower shop didn't have a good selection. These were the best of the lot, and I'm talking too much."

Gemma laughed, pushing aside all the crazy things floating around in her head. "Cub, I love them." She took the flowers and buried her nose in the center of the bouquet. They smelled sweet and spicy, and while they wouldn't live long, she'd enjoy them while they did. "Let me put these in some water. Oh, thank you, Callista." She took the vase of water from Callista—ignoring the knowing twinkle in her eyes—and arranged the flowers on the desk. They were a promise of spring, brightening up the dry, always dusty, bookstore. She smiled for real this time. "Thank you, Cub. They're beautiful."

He seemed to blush, and dipped his head in a slight bow of acknowledgment. "I'll see you tomorrow night." Then he leaned in and kissed her on the cheek. "I'll be thinking of you until then," he whispered.

Nice move. The skin on her cheek tingled, and she badly wanted to cover the spot with her hand.

Tern sidled up next to her, her arms folded across her chest as the two of them admired Cub's confident stride as he exited the bookstore. "You are in so much trouble," she murmured.

Yes, she was.

Lucky slammed into Limbo. The thread he'd chased to Gemma flung him back like a broken rubber band.

He lay there breathing heavy, his body stinging as his soul absorbed the abrupt shift from one plane to the next. A few moments passed while the pearlescent clouds drifted lazily over his head.

Why the hell couldn't it rain? He wanted thunderstorms, lightning. A goddamn squall.

Seeing Gemma with Cub, taking his flowers, letting him kiss her had torn his heart out of his chest. Lucky hadn't missed the slight flush to her skin as Cub's lips had grazed her cheek.

He leapt to his feet and ran for the rocky cliffs. The facts of his existence pursued him like arrows.

He hadn't done anything that bad in his previous life other than his part in Hansen's death, though Hansen didn't seem to hold any grievances toward Lucky. It had been a tragic accident when they'd been climbing the north face of Mont Blanc and the rope snapped. Lucky had blamed himself for a long time. After all, he'd been the one who'd checked the gear. He should have seen that the rope had been compromised. But being here with Hansen had reassured him that it had been just that, an accident. A byproduct of living life on the edge.

He started to free climb his way up the sheer rock face of granite that he'd tackled many times before. He raced, not being careful of his handholds, until he'd slid down the cliff one too many times. Even though he didn't have a body to bleed, his soul ripped and burned with each cut of the rock. He needed that now. Needed the physical pain, or as close to it as he could come, to dim the bleeding of his heart.

Oh, God in Heaven, why was he being tortured this way?

He'd spent his life working hard and playing harder. Hell, he'd turned play into his livelihood. While he hadn't gone to church as often as he should—believing that God didn't exist in a building—he'd given thanks. God was in nature. And Lucky had shown his appreciation in all the things that God had created. Including many women, and a few too many beers.

It hadn't even been his fault he'd been killed. At least the killer hadn't been after him, just using him as tool of vengeance against Tern. Boy, had that worked. He'd had his head so far up his ass he hadn't seen that knife before it was too late. But the knife that had ended his life hadn't hurt nearly as much as the blade of truth slicing through him now.

The muscles in his arms burned and bunched as he struggled to free climb, searching for tiny edges and footholds in his ascent to the top.

He couldn't ask Gemma to be his. It was unfair to her. His life was over, hers still in progress. She had a chance to find happiness. Be with a man who could hold her, love her, give her children. Be with her the way a man and a woman were supposed to be together. Not in the spirit of the sense. How could he provide like a man should provide for the woman he loved? It wasn't as if a spirit, ghost—or hell—*Dreamweaver* could get a fucking job.

By all appearances, Gemma would be alone for the rest of her life if she choose to share her life with him. She had Siri and Rosie and many friends, including Tern, but they would pass on or moved on with their lives and she would have no one tangible.

It was the ultimate act of selfishness to ask of her.

He struggled to reach the top of the cliff, his fingers slipping before he clasped the thin cracks within the smooth face of granite. He heaved himself up, his legs shaky, and looked over the wide cosmic landscape below him, his spirit in tatters.

Filling his lungs, he threw his head back, clenched his fists at his sides, and howled out his heartache until his legs gave out and he dropped to his knees. His heartache echoed back at him, the sound distorted by the rocky precipice into a cruel, mocking laugh.

He bowed his head to his chest, drained. There was only one choice he could make.

CHAPTER EIGHTEEN

Her biggest fear had finally been realized. Call her certifiable. Gemma was beyond questioning what was real and what was myth. The facts were she was in love with a Dreamweaver. Truly believed he'd died prematurely and that they had been destined. They'd shared themselves with each other last night, and it had been deeper than any other physical coupling she'd experienced. Her soul was linked with his and her heart freely given.

After Tern had left, she'd decided to call off her date with Cub. But hadn't figured out exactly how she was going to do that without damaging his spirit. Allowing him to think there could be something between them wasn't fair either. She'd tried to connect with Lucky, swearing she'd felt him hovering in the store, but the snow had thickened, and she figured he hadn't been able to break through. Later tonight he would. The skies were supposed to clear up. And the thought of being with him again, no matter the capacity, had her heart skipping.

She'd left the store for Callista and Amie to manage and headed to her mother's. There were some things she needed to know. No longer was she a disbeliever.

Hallelujah and all that jazz, she believed!

Somehow Siri was connected to the world Gemma had visited. She needed to know how, and what were the implications of what she'd actually done last night, and how to make them everlasting.

There was a sense of rightness, freeing actually. Like she'd finally let go of the fear. After all, her biggest fear had been that she'd turn out as bat-shit crazy as her mother. Guess what, crazy wasn't so bad. In fact, it felt downright liberating in a strip-off-your-clothes-and-celebrate-the-equinox kind of way.

Holy balls.

Snow spitting sideways, slowed her progress. The roads had turned dangerously icy. It was a relief to finally park her car in front of her mother's.

Hell, she'd never had that thought before.

Gemma let herself into the house, dusting snow off her hair and shoulders.

"She's been waiting and seems pretty lucid," Rosie said, taking Gemma's coat. "I was able to get her medication into her, but you know how it is. Are you sure you want to do this?"

"I have to know."

Rosie nodded and stepped aside. "I'll leave you two alone." She kissed Gemma's cheek. "Listen with an open heart." Then she disappeared into the back of the house.

Siri sat on the low cushion, in front of the carved table, shuffling the Tarot deck in front of her. Dressed in a caftan of silk saris, she was the bright spot in the candlelit room. Her breath caught when her eyes met Gemma's. "No," she gasped. "Tell me you didn't."

"You can see?"

"Oh, Gemma, my bright star, I did not want this for you." A hitch in her mother's voice tugged at Gemma's heart. It wasn't lost on her that she'd called her Gemma instead of Gemini either.

"Mom, why didn't you tell me?" Gemma knelt down at Siri's feet and took her hands in hers.

"How could I? You would have locked me up for sure." A sad smile curled her lips. "Let me tell you a secret." She leaned in and whispered, "I'm not all here." She tapped her temple. "A big part of me exists somewhere else."

This wasn't news to her. Except for the idea that Siri believed parts of herself existed somewhere else. "Tell me how, please."

"That's it." Siri shrugged. "I can't remember it all anymore. There are vague images, feelings. I was so into experimentation when I was younger. Did things that one shouldn't. Drugs, sex, astral projection when I didn't understand the gravity of what I was dealing with. So many mistakes, thinking I knew it all. There are elements, spirits out there who are not to be trusted. They want to live again so badly that they will tempt and tease you into risking things that you would not otherwise do. Risking your very soul."

"Lucky isn't like that."

Siri sadly shook her head. "They are all like that. Like vampires sucking out our life's essence. Has he talked of how he was robbed, killed before his time? How you are fated?" Siri didn't wait for Gemma's answer, not that Gemma could answer with the lump lodged in her throat.

"I tried to warn you, Gemma. I should have done more to steer you away. It's apparent that you've slept with him. But how many times have you laid with him?"

Heat rushed into her face. *Never* had they talked of sex. As open to experiences that Siri seemed, sex was a subject never to be discussed. She'd been a contradiction growing up, this free-spirit in every sense except one. Gemma was finally getting an idea of why.

"Once," Gemma admitted. "Last night."

"Where?"

Gemma dropped her eyes to the Mosaic rug beneath her. The intricate design of purple, black and blue with shots of gold swirled into a mess of color. "He called it Limbo."

Siri sucked in her breath. "Oh, dear God." Her hands clenched Gemma's. "How did you get there?"

Gemma swallowed. She couldn't tell Siri the pills she'd given her had sent her on a round trip ticket to the one place her mother seemed to fear most. "I don't know for sure."

"How long were you there?"

"Most of the night. Why?" It was her turn to ask some questions. A few answers would be a welcome change of pace.

"The more you share, the longer you astral project, the harder it's going to be to fully return. If at all." Siri pondered for a few minutes, the pupils of her eyes almost totally black. "We can knit back together your aura, given enough time and no more exposure to your Dreamweaver."

What was she, a sweater? And if this could be done, how did they "knit" Siri back together?

"I'm lost, Gemini." Siri answered her unasked question. "There are no threads to lace me back together. I played too long in the astral plane, lost too much of myself to those worlds."

Worlds?

"Your father tried, bless his heart, but the threads of my soul had already been stolen." She hopped to her feet and went to the desk, sliding drawer after drawer open until she pulled out a long silver chain with a ruby crystal hanging from it.

Gemma had a feeling she knew where this was going.

"I should have given this to you before. Where is my mind?" Siri shook her head as though to clear it. "It will help ground you. Your first chakra is the root, here." She motioned to her groin. "I want you to wear this and imagine that it's a grounding cord running from your spine to the base of your tailbone deep into the earth. It will help you draw energy up through the earth and keep you from astral projecting." She handed the crystal to Gemma. "Go ahead, put it on."

"I can't take this. You should wear it."

Siri held up her hand where a ruby winked on her ring finger. "I've always worn this. Your father gave me this ring when we hand-fasted. It does the same and symbolizes who my anchor is. Or was." She gave Gemma a bittersweet smile.

Gemma took the necklace and slipped it over her neck, trying to keep the one Tern gave her hidden in the wool of her sweater. The stone lay heavy between her breasts, clinking with Tern's. "Who was he?" She didn't need to specify that she wasn't asking about her father.

"That's it, I can no longer remember. You see, Gemini, they play on all your desires and leave you none of them by the time they are finished with you."

What should she do?

Thoughts swirled much like the snow flurries the Chinook winds were stirring. Gemma mulled them over on the drive home from her mother's.

Last night with Lucky had been...everything. He'd done just what her mother had said. Delivered on all her desires. He knew how to touch, kiss, press, retreat until she was nothing but a mass of mindless sexual need. Never had she experienced anything like it. Her heart was no longer hers.

Neither was her body.

She couldn't deny that she loved him. But had he weaved a spell to feed on her soul as her mother seemed to claim? And how was it that mother *and* daughter had ended up seduced by Dreamweavers?

There was too much to think about, and all of it fell under the umbrella of crazy. She was glad she hadn't called off her date with Cub. Maybe she needed it. Lucky hadn't been around to answer any questions. The snow had stopped, and heavy clouds were dispersing from cloaking the skies above Fairbanks. She could see the waves of the Northern Lights as they broke through the atmosphere.

It was a harrowing drive. The temperatures had warmed up to freezing. The roads were iced over like frosting on a cake, and Gemma's hands trembled by the time she safely parked her car in the garage.

Spring was in the air, but Alaska did spring like she did everything else. With a vengeance. They didn't call it Break Up for nothing.

She entered into the kitchen, laying her purse and keys on the dining table. What she needed was a long relaxing soak in the rub. She also badly needed to talk to Lucky.

Where was he? He visited before with less of an Aurora display. He should be here.

"Lucky?" she called into the empty house, knowing she wasn't going to get an answer back. The house was like a void. A black hole.

Siri couldn't be right and that Lucky was using her, feeding off her soul like some astral vampire.

The air suddenly shifted in the room, became colder, swirling for a moment before settling. Just like it had in the store earlier. Had Lucky been trying to get to her but couldn't for some reason? She'd much rather believe that than the alternative.

"Gemma."

She swiveled on her heel. And there he was. She caught and held her breath. She could *see* him, yet could also see *through* him. He was more substantial than ever before. Not solid like he'd been last night when she'd visited him, but more. And since she was able to see more, she saw the agony and decision in his bedroom eyes. Dread settled in her stomach.

"What's wrong?"

"I'm sorry, Gemma."

"For what?" It suddenly became hard for her to swallow.

"For everything. I never should have hunted you down. I should have left you alone to live your life, and I should have moved on."

"That's a lot of shoulds." Her knees trembled, and she couldn't help the tears forming in her eyes.

"Don't cry." There was a catch to his voice. "This is hard enough."

"Then why are you doing it?" she whispered.

He held still, only his fists clenching and unclenching as though it took everything for him not to pull her into his arms. "I want you to have what I can't."

"But you can." She took a step toward him, coming up short when he moved back. "I can see you. Every time we are together our bond strengthens."

"Which is why I need to end it now."

"No." The breath she gasped hurt as it burned its way into her lungs. "Don't you get it? I can see you, hear you." She took another step and placed her hand over his heart. "Feel you."

His eyes closed on a moan, and his hand came up to clasp hers hard against his chest. "I can never be a whole man for you. Never give you the family you've dreamt of. Cub can do that."

"Cub?" Confused, she let her hand fall away from him. "You were there? In the bookstore."

"Yes. He likes you. It wouldn't take much for him to fall in love with you." He caressed the side of her face. "It wouldn't take anything for a man to love you."

"What about me? Don't I have a choice in this? What about us being destined for each other?" Had her mother nailed that one?

"Your mother is a gifted woman. There would have been a time when she would have been considered the Shaman or Seer. Listen to her. She will help you through this."

"No," she said through clenched teeth. "You don't get to decide this. I have a stake. This is my heart, my life, my decision. I love you. Why do I have to live without you because you suddenly feel the need for self-sacrifice?"

"I don't *feel* the need. It's what's right. You will forget me in time."

She shook her head. "That will never happen."

He suddenly grabbed her shoulders and gave her a slight shake. "You have to, Gemma. I can't move on unless you do." He dropped his forehead to hers. "Gemma. There will be another time, another life for us. I-I am so very sorry that I couldn't wait until then. Forgive me." His mouth was hard on hers, desperate.

There was a moan of pain as he tore his lips from hers. His eyes burrowed into hers. "If you truly love me, then forget me and live your life in celebration of what we couldn't have. I'm not coming back. I fully expect you to move on... as I plan to."

Then he was gone.

Silent sobs shook her frame until she stumbled and sank to the floor, her arms hugging around her as though it would help contain the pain of her splintering heart.

The Northern Lights ripped through the fabric of the night sky.

CHAPTER NINETEEN

There wasn't a lot of time until her date with Cub. A date she should have canceled. It wasn't fair to spring her newly insane nature on him. But then maybe he could pull her back from the edge she teetered on. Give her that anchor to reality that she felt dragging.

She'd spent most of the night lamenting on what Lucky had said, threatening him to come back to her, even going outside and yelling at the Northern Lights until the dogs in the neighborhood started to howl. When yelling hadn't worked, she'd begged. And then cried until there were no more tears left in her body.

Lucky never appeared.

As a last resort, she swallowed one of the sleeping pills hiding in the drawer of her night table. And slept. No visit from her Dreamweaver, no astral projecting to him. Just sleep. She didn't even think she moved.

He was truly gone. And during the afternoon, after she'd cleaned her whole house, caught up with the meaningless tasks she'd been putting off, she realized Lucky was right.

Her heart wept for him while her mind applauded his willpower and wished she could be as strong. Left up to her, she'd have followed him wherever he journeyed.

Three times she'd picked up the phone to call and cancel with Cub, but Lucky's plea to live her life in celebration of what was taken from them stayed her hand. She'd spent most of the early evening going back and forth over what she should do.

Indecision became decision as evening approached.

It was too late to cancel now. Besides, she liked Cub. They had a lot in common. He was noble, adventurous, and very nice to look at. A good man. One who reminded her of Lucky in a lot of ways.

Okay, she needed to stop that.

Comparing Cub to Lucky wouldn't serve anybody. It wasn't like Cub was looking to marry her or her him. It was dinner. They enjoyed each other's company. Besides, they both needed to eat.

A knock at the door suspended her thoughts. This would be good. A normal evening out with a man. A flesh and blood man. Nervous sweat broke over her body and she waved her hands in front of her face, hoping she didn't have a sheen on her skin.

She opened the door, welcoming the chilly air to cool her overheated body. Cub stood there dressed in dark slacks, a button-down white shirt, and tie, with a dark wool coat left to hang open. The cold didn't seem to faze him. A box of chocolates was clutched in his hand.

"Wow, you look nice," she blurted out. She'd never seen him in anything but jeans, t-shirts, or swim trunks. The man polished up pretty.

"Isn't that supposed to be my line?" Cub said, cocking a nervous smile. "You do, by the way. Look nice that is."

She'd thrown on a black skirt that hit above the knees, and in deference to the weather had added tall leather boots. A simple, form-fitting black sweater topped off the outfit. At the last minute, she'd added a splash of color from the hand-painted sea-green silk scarf she'd bought at Tern's shop months ago. All black didn't always send the best message for a date, since she looked more like she was going to a funeral. But no matter what else she'd tried on that had been cheerier, nothing had worked. She'd left the indigo tourmaline and the ruby crystal on her dresser. Neither would do her any good as Lucky had chosen to move on.

"Thanks." There was a pause as she waited for Cub to do something. Finally, he shoved the chocolates at her.

"I hope you like chocolate. I actually heard of some women not liking chocolate, which has to be like some urban legend, but since I didn't know for sure I thought it was a good bet that you'd be okay with them, and I'm talking too much again, aren't I?"

Here was someone as confounded as her. "For the record, I love chocolate. Feel free to give them to me any time. Thank you." She took the box, noticing they were one of her favorite brands, though the thought of eating one right now made her nauseous. She hoped she'd be able to choke down dinner. "Please, come in." She shut the door behind him and walked to the kitchen, setting the box of chocolates on the counter.

"Did you find that draft?" Cub asked following behind her. "Your house seems warmer today. Or is it because it isn't as cold outside as it was the other night? If you haven't contacted anyone, I know a guy I could call. He'd be here this weekend if you need him. Just say the word." He rubbed the bridge of his nose. "There I go again. I'm messing this up."

"Messing what up?" She turned after grabbing her purse and keys.

"Our date. I'm going to talk you to death."

"I'm not worried." At least one of them would have something to say. She wasn't sure how much of a conversationalist she'd be tonight. Another reason she really should have called this off. Though Cub had been entertaining since he'd shown up, if not rattled. "Why are you so nervous? It isn't like we haven't spent time together before. I'm not going to attack you or anything."

"I'd like you to." His face flushed bright red. "Sorry. I can't believe I said that out loud."

She paused adjusting the purse strap on her shoulder. It was her turn to suddenly feel nervous. "Cub, I—"

"Forget that slipped out." He rubbed the bridge of his nose again. She'd never noticed the nervous action before. But then she couldn't remember if she'd ever seen Cub nervous.

"Okay, what's up?" She had a sneaking suspicion this had to do with the book he'd bought in her store the other day.

"Gemma, I like you." He dragged in a deep breath and let it out in a rush. "I've only dated one other woman in my whole life."

She stared at him. One woman? He had to be close to thirty.

"I married my high school sweetheart. She was the only one I've ever dated, ever loved, ever *made* love to." He pulled at his collar. "I lost her a year ago, and you are my first date."

Oh man, way to put on the pressure. "But we've been out before so this doesn't really count as our first date."

One woman?

"Those other times I wasn't looking at you as a...romantic interest. That first time I kissed you, I hadn't really thought it through. It was a spur of the moment kind of thing. You were there, I've been really lonely, and I bungled it up."

"The second time you kissed me, you didn't."

"I know!" He smiled like a kid who'd scored the winning goal at a hockey game. "It gave me hope that I could move on and experience another relationship."

Oh, holy balls, she needed to put a stop to this. She was going to break Cub's fragile heart.

"I'm doing everything wrong. Everything the book said not to do." He closed his eyes and grimaced. "Can we forget all this and start again from when I knocked on the door. I'm not this much of a basket case."

Good thing, since she was.

"Come to dinner with me, Gemma. Get to know who I am, that is getting to know more about me than just kayaking and my love for sappy movies."

He was like a puppy, all wobbly and adorable. How did she say no? "Where are you planning on taking me for dinner?"

Gemma laughed at the story Cub regaled her with about a particular rescue where the wife had been worried sick when her husband hadn't returned from a hunting trip, and then livid when the husband had been found holed up in the Brooks Range with another woman.

She and Cub ate dinner at Pike's Landing and continued to share stories of work—shying away from family for now—and outrageous experiences that Alaska seemed famous for. Sipping her coffee, Gemma watched the Northern Lights reflect over the snow. She didn't feel Lucky, no brush of fingers on the back of her neck, no cold breeze in the room, no whispered inflections, and knowing he'd never appear again sent pain radiating throughout her chest. She might have to consider moving some place south where the Northern Lights couldn't reach as they would serve as a constant reminder of her Dreamweaver.

"What happened just now?" Cub asked. "You've done that before with me. One minute you're here and the next worlds away."

Worlds away summed it up.

"I like you, Cub."

"Good. I like you too."

"But I'm not good for you." This was way too soon. What had she been thinking?

"Shouldn't I be the one to decide that?"

"I don't want to hurt you."

301

"Ditto. By the way, I'm a fan of the movie *Ghost* too." Cub said it in joking, but Gemma couldn't help the shiver that slid over her.

"What is it?" he asked.

"Do you believe in the afterlife?"

"So, the deep part of the date has arrived." He tried to steer the conversation back to the lightheartedness without success. "Okay, yes, I do." He cleared his throat. "After my wife died, I felt her. She was there, holding my hand, helping me through the worst of my grief. It was so hard to realize that while I worked in Search and Rescue the one person who meant the most to me was beyond my ability to save."

Why couldn't she fall in love with this man? There was so much to love about Cub. And that was before adding in his amazing physique. How had he not been scooped up? Could it be that he'd been so in love with his wife that other women weren't a consideration until now? How had he picked her to begin his journey back to the land of the living? Why couldn't she have met him before Lucky, but then would that really have mattered? She knew Lucky would have stolen her heart regardless at what time in her life he'd appeared.

Where did that leave her?

"I have something to tell you." Unable to stop herself, she let it all out. Everything. Ending with her heartache. Their ice cream melted and was forgotten by the time she'd finished filling him in on the craziness her life had become. Cub regarded her with rapt attention, his mouth partly open in awe.

"So this guy, this Dreamweaver, is real to you?"

She nodded, not believing that she'd really spilled her guts. What must he think of her now? A hot wave of embarrassment flooded her face.

He fell back in his chair, looking a bit stunned. "Really?"

"Yes, really."

"Fascinating." His brows lowered. "And you love this man?"

She nodded again.

"Well, aren't we a pair?"

She choked on a laugh. "Got any advice?" *Other than therapy*, she silently added.

"Since I'm not one who is great at taking advice, I can't really hand it out."

Her laugh came much easier this time. "You really are something special, Cub."

"Yeah, I get that all the time." He motioned for their check. The waiter rushed right over to hand it to him, and Gemma realized they'd been talking a while. In fact, they were the last ones left in the restaurant.

Cub dropped enough cash on the table to cover the tab and leave a healthy tip. He helped her into her coat, his hand guiding her at the small of her back as they exited the restaurant. The ice was slick underneath their feet, and she slipped. He grabbed her arm, holding her close to him as they slipped and skated their way to Cub's truck, laughing like children. She was suddenly very glad she hadn't canceled.

Cub held the door open for her, and she turned before climbing in. "Thank you for dinner. I really enjoyed myself and hope that I didn't dump too much on you."

He glanced at her lips and then back to her eyes. "I'm the one who should be thanking you." His thumb came up and caressed her bottom lip. Slowly, as though to give her enough time to move away, he leaned down to kiss her.

His lips settled softly on hers. They were slightly cold from the night air, but quickly heated as they moved against hers. Wisps of wanting surprised her with the desire to sink into him and forget.

What kind of woman could feel something like this for two separate men?

He moaned against her mouth, and the vibrations did funny things to her insides.

Last time she'd kissed Cub, Lucky had messed with the temperature in her house. Tonight, nothing. Could she be doing this because she wanted to evoke a response from Lucky? Cub's response seemed to all be in working order.

"You're drifting again." He tilted his head up, his startling blue eyes searching hers. "Your Dreamweaver?"

"I'm conflicted."

"So am I. Maybe we can try and move on together?"

Two emotionally taken people trying to make a relationship work? "At least we're on the same page."

Cub chuckled. "Let me take you home." He helped her hike into the huge 4x4 truck, shutting the door after her.

She put on her seatbelt while Cub walked around the pickup, getting in and doing the same. He started the engine and backed the truck out of the parking space, while playing with the knobs on the stereo. "Uh, something else you might need to know before we go any further." He slid her a glance, and she couldn't wait to see what else this man had to reveal. "I'm an Enya fan."

Soft strains of Enya started to play.

She couldn't help herself and laughed. "Now *that* I didn't see coming."

Nor did she see the vehicle slide through the red light at the intersection until it was too late.

Cub swore, swinging his arm out to help brace her in her seat, as he yanked the steering wheel so that his side of the truck took the brunt of the impact as the other vehicle broadsided them. The crash jolted them sideways. Metal screeched, glass shattered, and rubber burned as the black ice on the road, combined with the momentum of the other vehicle, skidded them off into the ditch. The top-heavy truck lifted onto two wheels and rolled.

CHAPTER TWENTY

Gemma lay there, stunned, fighting to breathe passed the impact of the airbag. As it slowly deflated, and the resulting powder settled, the light caught the glitter of glass everywhere. Enya continued to sing her soothing song, but there was nothing soothing about the situation. It took her a moment to realize what had happened.

Cub.

Gemma tried to see him, but could barely move, pinned in place by her seatbelt. Her side of the truck lay on the icy, snow-laden ground. She took stock of herself. Nothing seemed broken or bleeding, but she'd be sore.

"Cub?"

No answer. Gemma struggled to free her seatbelt, and then climb to her knees on the passenger door to reach him. Cub hung awkwardly to the side in his seatbelt, his eyes closed, blood seeping from a cut on his forehead.

"*Cub.*" Panic laced her voice. She wanted to shake him awake, but was afraid to touch him in case of a spinal injury. Carefully, she felt for a pulse in his wrist, letting out a huge breath of relief when she found one strong and steady. The car that had T-boned them had followed them over into the ditch and now squatted on top of Cub's door. The front wheel had broken through the window, and cold air whistled through the interlocked vehicles.

"Hang tight!" a stranger yelled from the front of the truck. "Help is on the way."

Gemma reached out with shaking fingers and shut off the stereo, silencing Enya, and bringing in the other sounds of the accident. Spitting and hissing from the engines of both vehicles, the heavenly sound of Cub's even breathing, and then the welcome sirens of emergency vehicles as they rushed to the scene.

"Come on, Cub, wake up." She didn't like that he was still unconscious.

An Alaskan Trooper struggled to reach them through the snow. "Ma'am, can you give me your condition?"

"I-I think I'm okay, but Cub isn't."

"Cub? Cub Iverson?"

"Y-yes, he works for Search and Rescue." Fairbanks wasn't that big of a town when you boiled it down, and Troopers and Search and Rescue were an even smaller group.

"Hold on, we'll have you out of there soon." He handed her blankets through the broken windshield.

She carefully wrapped them around Cub first and then bundled up in the other. While she wasn't cold at the moment, mainly because of the adrenaline coursing through her body, the shock of the accident would hit her and she'd be freezing. Hypothermia was a serious threat.

The rest was a blur of activity as the emergency crews worked together and helped her out of the truck, working carefully to cut Cub free as he didn't slide through the broken windshield like she had. He had still failed to regain consciousness when they loaded him in the ambulance and headed to Fairbanks Memorial.

"Come on, Cub," she prayed inside the ambulance as the EMTs checked his vitals and hooked him up to an IV. She couldn't lose another man she cared about. She continued to pray as they raced over icy roads toward the hospital.

They rushed Cub into the ER, ushering her toward another part of the emergency room, to be checked over.

As she suspected, other than bruises and powder burns from the airbag, there wasn't anything wrong with her. With his quick thinking and reflexes, Cub had saved her life, or at the very least, saved her some serious injuries. Everyone, nurses, doctors, EMTs, and troopers all commented on how lucky she was.

Lucky.

She couldn't help thinking that if she were truly lucky, she'd be with Lucky right now. Despair over Cub's condition and her own, settled over her as she sat in the waiting room for an update on Cub.

How could she have thoughts like that when Cub was probably in there fighting for his life?

After the troopers had taken her statement of the accident, she'd called and reassured Siri and Rosie that she was okay. Siri wasn't concerned as she'd already "felt" that Gemma was fine. Rosie told her to keep them posted on Cub's condition.

Dr. Macalister, announced by his name tag, entered the waiting room wearing green scrubs and the classic white lab coat. He looked to be in his fifties, trim, of average height, with auburn hair, split heavily with silver. He also sported a pierced ear where a diamond winked.

Gemma stood, surprised when the action made her dizzy.

"Careful, there, Ms. Star," he said, grabbing her arm to steady her. "Take your time standing. You've suffered an ordeal that will be feeling itself physically for a few days now."

"Call me, Gemma. How's Cub?"

"Here, let's take a seat." He steered her back to the chair she'd been planted in and took the one beside her. "He's actually doing great. Strong man, your Mr. Iverson."

She didn't correct him. As soon as they realized she wasn't a family member, or significant other, the information train would stop.

"As far as we can tell, there isn't anything wrong with him. He'll be bruised and sore when he wakes up. Head injuries are tricky things. His CAT scan came back normal. Minimal swelling, so we expect him to wake soon."

"Can I see him?"

"What the fuck, man." Lucky pushed at Cub's unmovable chest. "Get back there. She's crying at your bedside."

"It isn't me she wants."

"What the hell are you talking about?" He'd *sacrificed* everything. "I gave her up for you. So that you could be together. So she wouldn't be alone. Now move your sorry ass."

Cub took in the view around him, obviously stunned by the beauty. Lucky was tired of people enthralled with this place. "I want to stay here."

"Are you fucking kidding me?" Gemma wasn't losing two men she cared about. "No way. There is nothing wrong with you."

"Yes, there is. My heart belongs with my wife. I thought I could move on and hopefully share a life with Gemma." Cub shook his head. "But not now. Not with this chance to be with the one woman who I've always loved." Cub looked around like she'd appear at any moment.

"It doesn't work like that," Lucky muttered. A softening in his heart lessened his anger. This man was as lovesick as he was. "You're in Limbo, dude. You're wife isn't here. She's on the other side of here, and if you choose to enter that place, there will be no going back." He was still here because he couldn't make that final choice. He'd done his best to keep his distance from Gemma. It tortured him as she cried his name, sobbed until her body could no longer weep. The only thing keeping him from saying the hell with it all was this man. Cub-fucking-Iverson. He was supposed to be the white knight. He'd proved he had the right stuff, the way he'd saved Gemma from being hurt in the accident. But what was this shit? "How could you want any other woman besides Gemma?"

"Gemma is wonderful, and without this opportunity I was going to give romancing her my best shot. But as much as you care for Gemma, I care for my wife."

"You're choosing to die. You get that, right?"

Cub met his eyes, and all Lucky could see was hard resolution. "I want to be with my wife. Take my body, and be with Gemma."

"Whoa? *What?*" It was like the very fabric of the Universe held still. "What are you saying?"

"She's coming for me." A smile lit Cub up from the inside. "I can feel her." His very spirit began to glow a golden hue. "I don't have long. And my body will be wasted if you don't take it."

"I can't do that," Lucky whispered, though he so badly wanted to. Didn't even know it was an option. *Maybe it wasn't an option.* Were they messing with things that would backfire in a really bad way? A fire and brimstone kind of way?

"No, Lucky," Hansen said, appearing from wherever he'd taken himself off to, giving a nod as way of introduction to Cub.

Lucky's heart sank. He knew that he couldn't be *that* lucky. Another chance at life, another chance at loving Gemma.

"You don't understand," Hansen said. "Your self-sacrifice the other day has presented this avenue to you."

"What kind of game is this?"

"No game. A test, if you will. You've proven yourself worthy of another life."

"Wait a damn minute. What if this dingbat hadn't come along?"

"Eventually, if you hadn't moved on, there might have been another willing to give up his body to you."

Lucky looked Cub up and down, taking in his well-toned physique. Hell, he'd won the jackpot. Though it would take some getting used to being that tall. "Do you hit your head a lot?"

"No, but you probably will."

"There isn't a lot of time," Hansen said. "The longer a soul is away from the body, the faster it starts to deteriorate."

"How do you know all this?" Lucky turned on Hansen, looking at him as though for the first time. This was Hansen, his carefree buddy, right?

"Go," Cub said. "Just do me a favor and don't tattoo my body or anything."

"He can't come back and push me out?" Lucky asked Hansen, since he seemed to have all the answers.

"No. Once the agreement has been made, there is no going back."

Lucky regarded Cub again. Filled with emotion that brought tears to his eyes, he reached out and enveloped Cub in a bear hug. "Thanks, man."

"The only thanks I need is to know that Gemma will receive the love and care she deserves."

"Count on it."

CHAPTER TWENTY-ONE

They'd sent her home.

Kicked her out of Cub's room and told her she couldn't return until visiting hours in the morning. There had been no change in his condition. The nurses and doctors had reassured her that Cub would probably be okay even though he hadn't woken. Head injures were tricky. She was so sick and tired of hearing that.

Once home, she'd taken a few Advil and a long hot shower for the aches and pains that were making themselves felt. She slipped into her pajamas and went to crawl into bed when there was a knock at her door.

She glanced at the clock. It was after two in the morning.

Another more insistent knock sounded. Maybe it was the trooper who'd driven her home. Did they have more questions? The other driver was still touch and go, but that had more do to with the illegal drugs in his system than the car accident. She peeped through the window and gasped, yanking open the door.

"Cub!"

Soft brown eyes met hers, instead of Cub's striking blue ones, along with the widest smile she'd even seen Cub sport. "No, call me Lucky." He scooped up in his strong arms and spun her around.

She hugged him back, so glad that he was okay. "How— why? Wait! What?"

He set her on her feet, but kept her within the tight circle of his arms. "It took me a while too. I still don't understand it all, but I'm just supremely honored, and humbled, and fucking grateful."

"Why did the doctors release you? How did you get here? And why didn't someone call me to let me know you had woken up?"

A frown appeared on his forehead, where a small bandage covered the stitches he'd received, and for a moment, he resembled Lucky so much that her breath caught.

"Gemma, I'm Lucky."

"I know you're lucky. We were both lucky. But I don't understand the hospital—"

"No, babe, look at me. *See me.*"

He'd called her babe.

Suddenly the room spun, and she kissed the carpet.

"Come on, babe. That's it. Come back to me." Lucky's voice purred over her, and Gemma reached out with her arms to hold him tight against her.

"I've missed you." She buried her face in his neck, refusing to open her eyes in case he disappeared on her. "Don't ever leave me again."

"You are stuck with me, Gemma. Forever and always. Before God and country, say you'll be mine." He kissed her, and everything inside her caught fire as though solar flares were exploding within her. Her body arched into his, and her hands raked through his hair.

His much shorter hair. She stiffened, confused.

"Open your eyes, Gemma, and look at me."

"No," she whimpered.

"Please. There is a lot to explain. A lot to celebrate. Come on, babe. I'm not going anywhere."

Slowly she opened her eyes. She lay in her bed, the light low, but the man above her, holding her was Cub, wasn't he? He looked like Cub, but he also looked like Lucky. Had she completely lost it?

"Right now, I sure as hell miss not being able to read your mind."

She stared. Blue eyes to brown. That cocky grin instead of Cub's bashful one.

Quickly he filled her in on the meeting in Limbo and Cub's choice. And Lucky's fortune. Hers too.

Silence followed his hasty explanation. Then Lucky caressed her face with the back of his fingers. "Are you okay with this?"

"I'm not dreaming, am I?"

He shook his head, his expression stoic as if bracing himself for her next words.

"And Cub is truly happy?"

"Grinning like an idiot."

"And there are no give backs?"

"I double-checked."

She launched herself at him, wrapping her arms and legs tight around him. He laughed rolling over the bed with her. Joy filled the room, followed by hard, quick kisses.

"Damn, but I love you."

"Oh, Lucky, I love you. So, so much."

"Now don't do that. I'm not good with tears. It killed me when you cried over me."

"You were there?"

"I couldn't leave you. I hurt with you. Each tear that fell from your eyes, there was an equal one falling from mine."

"Wait. Your eyes." She pulled back. "How will we explain the changes? There are bound to be questions. You aren't Cub, but you look like him. People will expect him."

"Head injuries. They change people. Especially their personalities. Besides, I'm not worried about other people. Are you going to be okay with the new bod?" he asked, half jokingly. "Good thing the man had the same level of hotness I did. But I gotta grow out the hair. I look like a damn boy scout."

Gemma smoothed her hands through his hair, over his face, tracing his brows. He looked more and more like Lucky as she gazed at him. Lucky's expressions, his inflections came in how he looked and talked. "I see you, Lucky Leroy Morgan. It's you who I love. Though I must admit, I did not find Cub's body unattractive."

"That's a bit convoluted."

"You didn't want me to come out and say I thought Cub looked like a Norse god, did you?"

"I do, don't I?" That cocky smile was back in place.

"What about the eye color? Cub's eyes were blue. Not just blue, but a stunning blue."

"That will be one for science to try and explain. Or I can wear contacts."

"You know Tern is going to flip. There will be no keeping the truth from her."

"Tern will take it in stride. It's your mother who I'm worried about."

"Oh, holy balls."

THE END

BEARING
ALL

CHAPTER ONE

She'd been sent to kill him, and this time she wasn't going to fail.

Donned in head-to-toe white winter gear, blending seamlessly with her surroundings, Kate "No Mercy" Mercer lay on her stomach in the snow and viewed the terrain through white binoculars. She'd been casing the area for days, freezing her ass off.

The Edge of Reason Lodge came by its name naturally. Built on the edge of the Kenai Peninsula in Kachemak Bay, Alaska, the lodge perched on an imposing mountain with a jagged ice-encrusted beach at its feet. The deep, frigid waters of the finger fjord split off from the bay with no outlet, creating a natural defense for the lodge against invasion. There would be no surprise attacks as the only way in was by boat or float plane. He'd see her coming. Which is why Kate had chosen to drop in behind Sadie Mountain and trek in from there. A person would have to be crazy to attempt it. Luckily she was way past crazy.

She'd served in Afghanistan and had thought nothing of conquering the Kenai Mountains. She should have thought again. Hiking the glacier-pocked, steep terrain midwinter had been a bitch. All of it added more motivation to take down Sergei Lavinsky, code name The Bear.

Kate had to give it to Sergei, the man was pretty damn smart for holing up here in the middle of nowhere.

But she'd still found him.

It appeared all of the lodge's occupants were gone, presumably for the holiday. Probably somewhere warmer would be her vote.

Leaving Sergei alone.

All she needed to do now was wait for the perfect opening to move in. It was the day before Christmas Eve. By tomorrow night she planned to be somewhere more hospitable herself.

The temperature dropped fast as the winter solstice sun slid behind the snow-laden peaks. The view was breathtaking, that is if she could tear her eyes away from Sergei, who was currently chopping wood, wearing snug jeans, snow boots, and only a half-buttoned flannel shirt. His sable-black hair swung around his shoulders with each powerful plunge of the ax into the logs. She didn't know why he was chopping wood when there were rows and rows of ready firewood alongside the lodge under the cover of a lean-to. It was almost as if he were teasing her, though she knew there was no way he was aware of her presence. This was the closest she'd dared venture toward the lodge, keeping to the tree line high above the large log structure.

Through the binoculars, she could clearly see the black stubble peppering his jaw and tried to suppress the shiver as she remembered how it felt to have that rasp of beard against her bare skin. She adjusted her position slightly where she lay prone in the snow above him.

She'd planned well, done her homework. Waiting until she knew the lodge would be closed for the season and the owners scheduled to be away, vacationing for Christmas. Only Sergei was left as caretaker. She didn't understand how a man with his skill set was content to play guide, fisherman, and handyman of a rustic lodge in Alaska. Living here, she got. He was, after all, Russian, and Alaska was as close as he could get to Mother Russia in topography after his defection.

Defecting or not, he still had to die.

A final swing and he sunk the ax in the stump he'd been chopping against. Good, she needed that ax out of his hands before she made her move. He stretched his arms over his head, fingers linked as he arched from side-to-side. She tried not to appreciate the breadth of his shoulders as the muscles bunched under the red and black flannel of his shirt. His tanned forearms, revealed by rolled up sleeves, were bigger than her biceps, and sprinkled with dark hair and heavily roped with veins. The cold didn't seem to faze him at all.

He turned and glanced her direction. Hawk-like eyes, arched with heavy brows, swooped over her where she hunkered down in the snow. She caught her breath and held still. His eyes continued to sweep the landscape, not settling on anything in particular. Seeming at ease, he bent and loaded his arms with firewood from the large pile at his feet.

Time to make her move.

She couldn't shoot him from here. It was too far away for accuracy. Besides, this was a personal kill. He needed to know who had taken him down, and she needed to look into his eyes and watch the life drain out of them. She stamped down that little part of her that bemoaned the thought of this big, magnificent man no longer walking the earth. That weak part of her had ended up in his bed when she'd been sent to neutralize him the first time. And if she hadn't, Perry would still be alive.

Stowing away her binoculars, she slowly rose to her feet and crouched toward deeper shadows within the spruce trees. Silently, she crept down the mountainside.

Gloves off and zipped in her coat pockets, she unclipped her 9mm from its holster and clamped it with both hands, ignoring the sweat coating her palms.

Sergei returned to load his arms again, and Kate remained under the heavy snow-covered branches of a spruce. He never looked her direction. No more than a hundred yards from him, she waited as he overloaded his arms, stacking the firewood up to his chin. He gave her his back and headed toward the woodpile. She inched closer, stopping when he paused, and cocked his head as though he heard something. She waited until he resumed his trek and then snuck up behind him.

She raised her gun.

"Hello, Kate," Sergei said, not bothering to turn around and face her.

She jerked at his words. How had he known she was here? And why the hell didn't she just pull the trigger?

Sergei took his time piling the chopped firewood in place before facing her. The impact of him looking directly at her had her locking her shaky knees. No, she wasn't falling for that slumbering, come-hither look of his.

Not again.

"Sergei," she greeted, her voice as cold as the sea foam lapping the shore and icing over.

"Come to kill me again?" He arched a brow.

Why didn't he seem concerned? She had a gun trained on him, and he didn't even seem surprised to see her. It had been two years since he'd turned her life upside down. Two years of planning, of living with regret, and being fueled with the promise of vengeance.

He took a step toward her.

"Stop right there." She raised the gun a little higher, not realizing she'd lowered it a tad. He had however, if the lift of his lips was any indication.

"You don't vant to shoot me." He purred the words and continued his slow cat-like stroll.

She shot off the 9mm toward the empty beach and swung the weapon back to aim at him. The sound echoed over the waters like ice calving off a glacier. Sergei froze. Good, the man needed to take her seriously. She was deadly serious and she wasn't leaving until he was good and dead.

"Katja."

He said her name in that sexy, dark Russian accent of his, reminding her of how he'd trailed his lips over her skin, whispering her name during the midnight hours as his hard, powerful body made love to hers. No, fucked hers. There had been no love between them. She tried to crush the memories of the night that seemed carved into her consciousness. Now was not the time for thoughts like this. They'd just distract her from her mission.

"You know that I'm sanctioned," he said.

"The United States Government might have pardoned you, but I haven't. There are still crimes you must pay, deaths that must be avenged."

"And you've set yourself up as my executioner?"

"Yes."

"Gone rogue, have you?"

"Isn't that what you tried to get me to do?"

"*Dah.*" His dark eyes traveled down her white snowsuit. She doubted he could tell anything different about her by the way she was bundled up. So bundled up to protect herself from the harsh elements she'd failed to take in account that seeing him, talking with him, would have her sweating in the get up. She envied him his casual clothes, with the cold breeze ruffling his half-opened shirt. She could see the definitions of his pectoral muscles, the soft sprinkling of chest hair that she remembered nuzzling her cheek against after experiencing the most intense climax of her life within his protective embrace.

"Rogue looks good on you, Katja."

"Shut up."

"Kill me, then. You've come a long vay to do it." He spread his arms out to encompass the imposing terrain.

Kate squeezed the trigger.

CHAPTER TWO

Sergei ducked and dived for Kate just as she fired. The bullet whizzed by the side of his head. He swiped the gun out of her hand before she could get off another shot and took her down hard to the frozen ground. He had to have knocked the air of her, but damn if she didn't still fight him. She was everywhere, hands, arms, limbs, and feet, getting all nasty with how they pummeled him.

You'd think the woman held no appreciation for him. Not that he blamed her. He'd never treated a woman worse than the one currently under him.

And how he regretted it. Not just because she was here to kill him, but because he hadn't been able to stop thinking of her since he'd last had her beneath him.

"*Oomph.*" His hold slipped as she got in a lucky punch to his kidneys. "*Derr'mo!*"

She scrambled for her gun. He grabbed her feet before she could reach it, and yanked her back to the ground.

She pulled a foot free and kicked him in the chest. This time he was the one fighting for breath. She'd gotten better at hand-to-hand combat.

He was pissed. And impressed as hell.

His hand clamped around her calves, and he crawled up her back, locking her legs down with his and pushing her face into the snow.

"Cool off."

"Go to hell, you bastard," came her muffled reply.

"Already been there, Katja." He flipped her over, grabbing both of her hands and anchoring them down on the sides of her head.

Bozhe moi, she was beautiful. His memory hadn't exaggerated her sexiness. Her hood had come off in the struggle, and dark auburn hair splayed over the white snow beneath her. Her jade green eyes flashed daggers at him. Hate and something else shined in their depths. Rosy, plump lips tempted him to nibble.

He'd better not.

There was only so much of living on the edge he was willing to risk. If he kissed her, she'd kill him for sure. He saw it in her eyes. It was in the lines of her tense body, the anger and hurt infused in her flushed skin.

"Settle down," he said.

She head-butted him.

He saw stars. It was close, she almost knocked him out, but he had one thing going for him that she didn't. Not only was his head harder, he weighed twice what she did. He slumped over her, letting his weight smother her into compliance as he compartmentalized this new bout of pain she'd inflicted on him. He bit down on his tongue, not wanting to say something in the heat of anger that would make the situation worse.

Worse?

She wanted to kill him.

She struggled under him, muttered words that burned his ears with their intent, and then she must have realized she wasn't going anywhere and suddenly became calm. A little too calm. More like she lay in wait for an opening. He gave her a few minutes for the gravity of her situation to sink in. Not that it seemed to do any good.

Somehow he needed to neutralize her without hurting her. The way she was going, they would both end up dead. He'd kill her on accident, and he'd be dead on purpose. There was too much that needed to happen between them before either of them stood before the Pearly Gates. If they'd even make it that far with all their sins.

He let up some pressure, and she inhaled a deep breath, and started all over with her struggling.

"*Hvatit*, Katja."

"Fuck you."

"Keep it up and I vill."

The threat had her swallowing, but she didn't seem as put off by the idea as tempted. Could she still desire him after all he'd done to her? Now that he had her on The Edge, he wouldn't rest until he found out.

Flipping her onto her stomach, he adjusted the contact of his body against her so she didn't feel his sudden hard-on. He needed things back down to size and the thoughts of stripping her bare and taking her from behind out of his head. He kept a hold of her hands and pulled them behind her back, wishing he had something to secure her with. She thrashed in his grip and his hold slipped. Damn, but she was tenacious...and talented. Either he was rusty or she'd been working hard-on her self-defense skills. She hadn't been a slacker in the department to begin with. It had been a while since he'd grappled like this. *Well, never like this.* He'd never been sexually turned on while fighting for his life before.

"Ve're going to stand up and go into the lodge and... talk," he growled in her ear.

She shivered under him.

"Got it?"

She gave a shaky nod.

Slowly, he got to his feet, keeping his hold on her hands, yanking them high up her back, increasing the strain on her shoulders. "To your knees."

She brought her knees up under her. The action raised up her ass. Damn, but she had a nice ass. Even covered in the white snowsuit, it was a shapely ass.

"Let go," she muttered through her teeth. "I'm not going to try anything."

He scoffed. "I don't believe you." Keeping her hands locked behind her, he allowed her to stand. "Take it slow. No sudden moves."

And then he was flat on the ground.

She'd swept her foot behind her, tripped him onto his backside. Tearing free of his hold, she swiveled and kicked him square in the groin.

Son of a fucking bitch. He grabbed his balls.

She gave him a smug smile before twisting around for her gun.

All right, that was it.

He was done playing nice.

Fighting through the fog of pain from where she'd kicked him, Sergei lunged for Kate just as she reached for her weapon. Wrapping his arm around her neck in a rear naked hold, he cut off her oxygen. Her nails scraped his forearms, drawing blood. She sank to her knees, and he went with her, not letting up the pressure of the choke. Frantically she struggled in his grasp, unable to breathe. He held her that way until she slumped and passed out in his arms, her head rolling back against his shoulder. He checked for her pulse, and then cursed with relief and frustration.

Damn, this woman. Would he ever get back in her good graces?

CHAPTER THREE

Kate woke tied to a chair.

Pain sliced through her brain matter like ice in a blender. Head hanging forward, she didn't move, taking stock of her condition and what she could see of her surroundings. She was in a great-type room, with comfy leather furniture to her left and a cheerfully burning fire in the stone-laid fireplace to her right. Glass windows took up the opposite wall overlooking a large deck and the view of the ocean. A thick bear rug lay at her feet.

She sat in a rough-hewn wooden chair made of logs with her hands tied behind her back. Sergei hadn't restrained her feet. The chair was heavy and large enough that she wouldn't be able to stand and use her body weight to break free from it. Hence the reason he hadn't restrained her further.

His mistake.

She hadn't been tied up long because other than the strain in her shoulders, and fighting with Sergei earlier, she wasn't stiff. He'd stripped her of her outerwear and boots, leaving her wearing only black Polartec base layers and Smartwool hiking socks.

Her hair hung loose curtaining off her face from his view. But she knew he was there, watching her. She could smell him. A fiery mix of danger and sex as potent as the Russian vodka he liked to drink.

She remembered everything that had happened in sharp detail before he'd put the choke hold on her. The man had to have balls of steel for being able to function after how hard she'd kicked his privates. Part of her was surprised Sergei hadn't killed her. Maybe he wanted to torture her some more. But the joke was on him. Nothing could hurt her worse than what he'd already done to her.

"I know you're avake," he murmured from her left. "How's your head?"

Slowly she raised eyes to glare at him from under her brows. "How do you think it is?"

"Probably pounding like son of a bitch."

Yeah, that about summed it up.

"I brought you aspirin and vater."

"What is this? Nurse the prisoner back to health so you can break her kind of thing?"

"I don't vant to break you. I love how you are, Katja. How do you Americans say, 'All piss and vinegar'?"

"Very attractive."

He cocked his head, and his eyes turned slumberous as they traveled up and down her form fitting outfit. "I think so."

"Untie me."

"I don't think so."

"Afraid?"

"I don't relish you trying to squash my balls again."

"Coward."

He inclined his head as though giving her a point. "Call it vhat you vill. I have plans for my manhood, and I'd prefer to keep things civilized between us."

She'd yet to experience anything "civilized" where he was concerned. But keeping him talking held his attention on the conversation and unaware of the blade she'd sewn into the modified elastic back-strap of her bra.

Carefully with small movements, she pushed the blunt end of the knife, slicing through the hidden pocket in her bra and her shirt, freeing the weapon from her clothing. She turned the blade, painfully nicking the side of her finger, and started sawing through the bindings.

"Vhat took you so long to find me?" Sergei sat on the low coffee table in front of the leather couch, kitty-corner to her, and flicked two aspirin out of the bottle.

"What do you mean? It wasn't like you sent me an invitation."

"Pretty much, that's exactly vhat I did. Do you really think you vould have found me othervise?" He held two aspirins in the palm of his hand, showing her the bottle to prove he wasn't slipping her something else. Like she'd trust anything he offered her. "Take."

"No, thank you."

"There is no reason for you to suffer."

"I've been suffering since I met you."

He leaned forward and trailed a finger down her jaw line. "Katja," his voice hummed his pet name for her deep from within his chest. "'Tis no good, lying to one's self."

Memories flooded her at his touch. Yearning shook her hands, and she almost lost hold of the blade. She couldn't let him distract her. Her body might crave his touch, but it was mind over matter. And it mattered more than anything for her not to lose herself in him again.

"How long are you going to keep me tied up?" she asked as the first twist of rope gave way. She made sure not to move her arms and reveal what she was doing. She also needed to get him away from her. He was too close. For many reasons.

His eyes bored into hers, as though sifting secrets from her soul. "That depends more on you."

"What do you mean?"

"Still vant to kill me?"

The scathing look she sent him had him smiling. "You'll be restrained until you no longer desire my blood on your hands."

"I'm surprised a big man like you, skilled in all the ways to subdue someone, is afraid of a woman like me."

"Katja, you scare the shit out me."

His response shocked her into asking. "Why?" At every turn, he'd been able to best her. Physically, emotionally, he'd been the master.

His hand dove into her hair, and he tipped her face up, his lips coming within a hair's brush of hers. "Because of this." His words rumbled over her lips as he kissed her. His mouth took hers, his tongue sliding past with no struggle as the shock of his possession, and his need, froze her into responding. She didn't fight, so stunned she almost lost the grip on her blade. She cut her fingers clutching it in her grasp. He plundered, growling like the bear he'd been nicknamed as though he'd waited forever to feast.

What sick game was he playing now? Just as something tingled to life in her stomach—she prayed it was nausea—he tore his mouth free.

"*Bozhe moi.*" He released her, swiveled away, and paced to the fireplace. Bending, he tossed another log on the fire and stirred the coals with a poker. He stared into the flames for a long time before turning back to face her. His heaving chest was the only giveaway to the kiss he'd stolen from her. "You aren't leaving here until you and I come to understanding."

"What would that understanding be?" She held her breath as she severed through the last of the rope, grabbing the bindings in her hands, keeping them tight, so he wouldn't know she was free.

"I care for you, and you care for me. There is more between us than hate, Katja."

"The only thing I care about is killing you."

She lunged.

CHAPTER FOUR

Sergei registered shock as Kate launched herself at him with a knife, and then excitement.

The woman was incredible.

He liked that she wasn't afraid of him. Though this hate of hers needed to be refocused. He couldn't keep defending himself, worried that his training would kick in and he'd hurt her without meaning to. It had bothered him deeply to choke the air out of her earlier. But he was prepared for this attack. Somehow he knew she'd get free even though he'd tied some serious knots.

But where the hell had she gotten the blade?

He'd patted her down after stripping her of her snowsuit and boots. What he'd liberated had more than surprised him. Multiple knives, two other guns, mace, and a retractable baton. Where had she hidden this pretty little beauty? And was there anything else on her person that he'd missed?

His hand blocked hers on the downward stab of the knife. She twisted out of his grasp and flirted away before he could get a better hold on her.

Wasn't she something? Fearless.

He was twice her weight and at least a foot taller. She came at him again, lower this time, and he got lucky and immobilized her knife hand. He yanked her close, wrapping his other arm tight around her, bringing her flush against him, letting her feel every inch of his heavy hard-on this time.

He had his own hidden weapons.

Her eyes widened as she got his point, and she tore herself free of his embrace.

"Nice moves," he commented, his nostrils flaring with anticipation for her next one.

"Why won't you just die?" she gritted out through clenched teeth.

"Vhat vould be fun in that?"

She growled and lunged for him again. This time he used her momentum to swing her past him. She went flying across the room, falling into a bookcase that held an impressive assortment of books. A few tumbled and clattered to the hardwood floor. But she hadn't dropped the knife.

"*Nyet*, Katja. I don't vant to hurt you."

"Well, you'll have to kill me to get me to stop."

She circled him, her hand locked around the small blade, her stance low. The blade was only a few inches long, but razor-sharp. Blood stained her fingers and dripped down her forearm, proving that it was wicked enough to take seriously. The blood angered him. She'd cut herself.

"You really going to fight *me* with that little thing?"

"Anything I have to do I will."

"This vill end badly for you."

Like a dance, they circled each other. Rapid blocks followed. Forearms, elbows, shins. Exhilaration heated his blood. There was no way he wasn't getting "personal" with her in a knife fight. He'd yet to be bested; had, in fact, learned his skills at the hands of necessity on the streets of St. Petersburg.

She advanced, and he fended left, letting her slash at him, getting close, but never close enough. There were many things he could teach her. First, she needed to take the emotion out of the fight. It made her sloppy. This he knew she was aware of, but couldn't seem to stop herself, which gave him hope. It didn't help when his smile widened as her scowl deepened.

She jabbed, and he took a step into her attack, deflecting the strength of her blow, though she did get in a lucky lick of the blade to his forearm. He twisted, wrapping his arm around her middle, hoping to cage her in, but she was quick and side-stepped him, kicking him in the back of the leg. He went down on his knee, and she had him by the throat, her chest to his back, knife at his jugular in one hand and her arm tight around his neck.

"Nicely played," he murmured right before he flipped her over his back onto the bear rug.

Bastard.

This was the second time today Sergei had knocked the wind out of her.

Kate gasped soundlessly like a bear-flung fish hurled onto the shore. And then Sergei's body crushed hers into the fur, his forearms digging into her biceps, his heavy thighs anchoring her legs so she couldn't kick him again.

The ache to fill her lungs consumed her. Her head pounded, her fingers burned with the shallow cuts, and the upper ribs in her back smarted from the toss over his shoulder. All of this was his fault.

"A knife is a very intimate weapon," he drawled over her, his breath a spicy mix of coffee and cinnamon.

Oh shut the fuck up, she wanted to hurl back at him, and would have if she'd had the air to do so. Spots circled her vision, and for a minute she wanted to give in. Fearing she'd wake up tied to a chair again had her holding onto a thread of consciousness.

"Let it go, Katja." His fingers squeezed around her wrist like a vice.

Her diaphragm stopped spasming, and air rushed like a wave into her starving lungs. She gasped, clawing her fingers and trying to cut at his hold on her wrist. He swore as she nicked him, and he twisted the knife free of her bloodied fingers. He flung the blade up to the ceiling where it embedded itself into a log beam.

"Vhat else do you have hidden?"

He cupped both of her hands together in one of his while the other snaked under her shirt. His rough palm splayed over the sensitive skin of her stomach as though daring her to object.

He couldn't mean...and why couldn't she stop urging him on?

"Get your hands off me," she gritted out through her teeth.

"Tell me vhere the knife came from? I patted you down."

Like a spy gave up her secrets.

"Fine, have it your vay." He yanked up her top until it covered her face, sheathing her in shadows.

She could see nothing, but felt the heat of his eyes as they took in her bare torso. Only the custom black bra covered her breasts...then she felt his deft fingers dive into the cups. She squirmed in his hold.

"Stop," she ordered, "or so help me I'll—" Her muffled warning had no effect on him.

"Vhat? You'll kill me? Getting old, Katja." He clicked his tongue when he found the razor blade taped between her breasts. "I knew these things were dangerous."

She growled, and he chuckled.

Carefully, he peeled the tape with the razor blade off her skin, smoothing down the chafed area with his fingers.

Why was he being so gentle with her? The hand holding hers together was locked tight, but not painful. His body restraining hers was heavy and hard, but not smothering. It was like he was doing everything he could not to hurt her, while she was doing the opposite.

She didn't like the comparison.

He was a killer. Dangerous, sinful and sexy in that dark way mothers warned their daughters against. His touch on her breasts as he continued to see if there was anything else hidden, was almost...worshipping. He could have stripped off her bra, manhandled her, bruised her, and yet...he hadn't.

Her nipples beaded, mortifying her.

Don't notice, don't notice.

His fingers brushed over the peak of one and halted.

"Katja," he whispered her name. His fingers hovered over her aroused nipple, and the pebble tightened and hardened further.

She felt him grow heavier on top of her. This was bad. She didn't want to be here again. Didn't want his touch, didn't want to be consumed with him. She...did...not.

Was that the brush of his lips over the flesh above her bra? The caress was so slight she wasn't sure if it was him or a sudden draft in the room. But it knocked the air out of her again.

She didn't want to investigate how it made her feel to have this man desire her, still, after all the time that had passed. He'd pursued her hard in Afghanistan. But that had been to get information from her. He hadn't really been enamored of her. Had he? And why the hell should she care? She wanted him dead...she did. *Damn it.*

He smoothed down her top, and his dark eyes stared into hers. If fire could shoot out of them she wouldn't have been surprised. She'd been unable to catch her breath waiting for him to strip her of her bra and was more than a little surprised that he hadn't. His eyes, with their sultry flecks of amber within the dark coffee depths, hunted for something within hers.

"You have beautiful breasts, Katja. They have haunted me these many years."

That she hadn't expected. She flattened her lips in an inflexible line. What did he want her to say? Thank you?

"You are a pawn being used in a game of not your making." He brushed her hair back from her face. "Don't be such. You must let this go."

"I am not a pawn."

"I saved your life the night you gave yourself to me."

Gave herself to him?

"Just as I gave myself to you," he added in a softer more dangerous tone that rubbed areas inside her she didn't want resurrected.

He had not given himself to her. Those were soft, romantic words, and he was neither of those things.

"There vas mutual loving on both sides, Katja."

She still refused to respond. He confused her, and she didn't like it. Her hate for him had fueled her for a long time. Kept her going when she didn't know if she could go on. She liked it, craved it. Whatever mind game he played, she would not be suckered in.

"You seduced me in order to set me up," she bit out.

"You *let* me seduce you, and I saved your life that night. It isn't me you should hate. It's Perry."

"Sure, attack a dead man. A man who can't defend himself."

"Perry vasn't defendable vhen he vas alive."

"Stop."

"The sooner you realize that the sooner ve can get past this and explore vhat ve discovered about each other in that hotel room."

"There is nothing I want to explore with you. I want you out of my life, and off my radar. I wish you had never come across me."

"Now who is coward?" His eyes turned cold, and she knew she was in the presence of The Bear. The one who killed, maimed, destroyed. She tensed, and then when nothing came, she didn't know what to feel. He wasn't doing anything she expected of him. Was that another way of toying with her? Keeping her off balance?

"Vhen vas the last time you ate?" he asked.

Too long. "I'm not hungry." Her stomach stirred making a liar out of her.

"Right. You've been on the hunt, therefore eating rations or vhatever you could kill. And since, you no doubt, didn't vant me alerted to your presence, you vouldn't have lit a fire and cooked anything."

She hated that he knew so much about her and her activities.

"Since you entered The Edge from behind, you vould have hiked in from either Tutka Bay or parachuted in. Vith your skills, I'd bet on the drop. Either vay, you must be starving. And I can alvays eat." He murmured the last words like it wasn't food he wanted to consume. "Come." Sergei rose to his feet without letting go of her hands. He pulled her to hers, and dragged her into the kitchen.

Birch cabinets lined two walls with stainless steel countertops and a wall of windows taking up the other where a table sat overlooking the bay. There was nothing but black outside the window testifying to the deadly landscape. The ocean was a mirror of darkness, and it took no imagination to think of the souls it had already claimed. Would hers be next? What better way to dispose of a body than to sink it somewhere out here off The Edge, knowing the sea scavengers would digest the remains? No moon was out tonight to help illuminate or soften the harsh landscape.

Sergei sat her in one of the kitchen chairs—grabbing another length of rope he conveniently had resting on the counter—and tied her up.

"Is this really necessary?"

"Vell, let's see. You've shot at me, kicked me in balls, and come after me vith knife. *Dah.* I believe it's necessary." He looked at her. "There are a lot of sharp things in a kitchen, as I'm sure you are vell avare. I've been alive this long for a good reason. I plan. Prepare. Study." He tightened the rope around her hands, this time keeping them in front and then wrapping the rope around her middle, anchoring her whole body to the chair.

Yeah, this would be a bitch to get out of. She had to wonder why he hadn't secured her like this to begin with. Had that been some sort of test?

She could get out of this, too, if she wanted. Being double-jointed came in handy for someone like her. But she'd save that for later. For now, she'd let him relax, which as she looked back on it, was something she should have done before. Now he was on guard—or at least, more on guard—and she had a feeling the man never completely relaxed.

He finished checking her bindings. "Stay."

Sergei disappeared, and she wondered how long he'd be. Did she have time to get loose? She could, given enough time. Only a few people in the world knew she was double-jointed. And most of them were dead. The few who were alive weren't in her life much anymore. She had a martial arts coach who probably didn't remember her, and a brother in prison. Their parents had passed away in a car accident when they'd been in high school, and Kate had entered the military rather than head down the self-destructive path her brother had taken.

She could hear Sergei rummaging in a room not far from the kitchen. Now was not the time to make another move. She should have waited when she woke from the choke hold to cut herself free. The moment of surprise was a precious one, and she'd squandered hers. It was always good to have one's opponent have low expectations of one's abilities.

So she waited.

Sergei didn't keep her waiting long. Again, making her glad she hadn't attempted to get free.

He plunked a first aid kit on the table, swiveled a chair around in front of her, and sat. Taking her bound hands in his, he opened the package of antiseptic wipes. Cursing under his breath, he cleaned the dried blood from her fingers.

Why was he doing this? Some Stockholm Syndrome shit to relax her? She didn't give a damn if her wounds were tended to. But the shock of having him clean the blood off her hands sealed her mouth shut and caused her heart to pound with feelings she refused to put a name to. He applied anti-bacterial cream to the cuts, and then covered them with band aids. She said nothing and neither did he. Once he was done, he doctored the shallow cuts she'd inflicted on him, and then bundled up the supplies, depositing them to wherever he'd procured them.

When he returned, he opened the refrigerator and pulled out a marinating salmon. She could smell soy sauce, brown sugar, and something spicy. Her stomach rumbled again, and he flicked a glance her direction from under his brows. A slight smile split his lips. "I've always vanted to make you dinner. I never figured you'd be my captive audience though."

"Funny man."

He arranged the salmon on a baking pan, preheated the oven while he started rice to cook on the gas stove.

"Coffee?" he asked, pouring himself some in a mug painted with funny moose faces.

Oh God, yes. "I don't care."

That smile reappeared as he set the mug in front of her and poured himself another. He'd tied her in such a way that she had use of her hands and arms, T-Rex fashion, so that she could feed herself and drink, without struggling too much.

How freaking thoughtful of him.

She waited for him to drink from his cup first before picking up her coffee and sipping. She cut off the groan before he heard it. The coffee was dark and rich and strong, just how she craved it.

He seemed satisfied and went about preparing dinner. While the rice simmered, he added the salmon to cook in the oven, and grabbed canned vegetables from the pantry.

"Sorry, no fresh vegetables this time of year and store is too far."

Like she cared one way or the other. She'd been eating MREs. Right now food was food, and she'd gladly eat it, but didn't plan on thanking him for it. If she'd already killed him, she could have raided the pantry, eaten anything she wanted before she was picked up. She had two days to finish this.

But it would be done tonight. One of them wouldn't see morning.

Chapter Five

The salmon was so good Kate wondered if Sergei would give her the recipe. But then every time she cooked it she would be reminded of him and this secluded retreat with its homey interior, the rustic log walls, the million dollar view. He'd lit candles and placed them in the middle of the table, adding a romantic element to the meal that she didn't appreciate. When she'd mentioned it, he'd pragmatically pointed out that fuel and energy were scarce on The Edge and they used them sparingly. Even less in the winter. Darkness encompassed most of the hours this far north.

She hated viewing his chiseled bones, his aristocratic nose, and the close-cropped beard lending him a roughness she found too appealing in the caressing light of the candle. Time slipped away as she ate. She cleaned her plate and didn't object when he filled it again, barely biting back the thank you.

It was hard to measure this man by the one who had killed Perry and seduced her. She'd sent Perry to his death because of Sergei, and that was something she couldn't live with.

By feeding her, Sergei was in fact making it easier for her to kill him. She had to remember this. He was restoring her strength, fueling her. Now if she could separate the assassin from the man in front of her.

Without asking if she wanted any, he set a slice of dense, dark chocolate cake in front of her with wild raspberry compote. She should refuse any more food, but this dark dessert whispered to her like salvation. She hadn't had anything so self-indulgent in years.

"Eat it," Sergei drawled, looking at her as though daring her to. He took a large bite himself, the muscles in his jaw fascinating her for a minute until he arched a brow at her longer than necessary perusal.

She picked up her fork and broke off a piece. It melted in her mouth. Rich, sinful chocolate coated her tongue while the wild raspberries with their tart sweetness stimulated her taste buds. This time she couldn't keep in the moan. He grinned as though he had her number. And in this case, she had to admit he did.

"You couldn't have made this," she accused. No way he was that good.

"No, I did not. One of the best cooks in Alaska lives here on The Edge, and made this especially for me as a gift before she left."

"Where is she now?" How close were Sergei and this cook? And why the hell did she care?

"Vacationing in the Northwest with her children." Another smile lit his face as though he cared for these children. How did a man who killed for a living care for children? It made him seem less heartless, more human, and she didn't like that.

"You talk about them with affection." Who were they to him?

"That is because I do have affection for them."

"I didn't know you liked children."

"There is much about me you don't know," he murmured, taking another bite of his dessert while looking her up and down.

She knew Sergei was trying to converse with her, to lower her guard. The intimate candlelight. Them alone together in the lodge. Feeding her dinner.

It wasn't going to work.

Kate didn't want to go down that sexually potholed-road so turned the conversation to something neutral. "This cook, she's the sister to Mel Bennett?" Mel Bennett, part-owner of the lodge, intrigued Kate what with surviving one of the most publicized kidnapping and rescues.

"*Dah.*" He leaned his forearms on the table, pushing his empty plate aside. "So, Katja, vill I need to keep you tied up all evening? I'm villing to, you understand. Vhile I haven't spent hours in the company of a beautiful voman restrained, for my pleasure, I find I'm not opposed to the idea."

Every nerve, wrong and right, flared to life at his words. How did he do that? He'd done the same thing to her in Afghanistan, which is how he'd gotten her upstairs into his hotel room and in his bed. Just listening to him talk in that dark accent that had whispered equally dark promises to her in the deep of night, had her shifting in her chair. Promises that he hadn't kept since he'd vanished from that hotel room before the sun had risen.

"I am not restrained for your pleasure."

"Though, oddly enough, I'm enjoying it. How long vill you let me?"

"You tied me up."

"You forced me to," he countered. "Are you going to behave? If you promise to, I vill untie you."

Was he really that susceptible? Or was this a trick? "I'm willing to behave if you are." For now.

A grin spilt across his face. "I have bested you twice now. I vill best you a third if you try, and I von't promise I vill contain myself like I have so far."

Really, contain himself? From what?

His brow arched again as if he'd been able to read her thoughts and dared her to ask for an explanation. She didn't want one. Nor, apparently, needed one when her insides heated as his gaze brushed over her breasts, her waist, her hips.

She held her hands out as far as they would reach in their T-Rex knots. "Untie me."

"You must say the vords."

Oh hell, no. She was not saying please.

"Promise me that you vill not try to kill me again until ve have talked. Really talked. Vhere you listen to my side of the story."

"Then I can try to kill you?"

"If you feel the need, you can try."

So the man wanted to talk, attempt to sway her into believing what she knew was wrong. Not with the blood that had painted her hands, the deaths that weighed heavy on her soul.

"Fine. I'll hear you out."

"And?"

"I promise not to kill you until after I hear you out. Better?"

"*Nyet*. But good enough for now." He stood, reached into his pocket, flicked open a switchblade, and came toward her.

CHAPTER SIX

Something else fired in Kate's blood as Sergei cut through her bonds. She held still, barely breathing with him so near, hoping he didn't notice her pulse racing.

"Have you had that blade on you this whole time?" she asked as he freed her hands and went to work on the ropes anchoring her to the chair.

"This blade vas my father's, and I'm never vithout it." He let the reality that he'd been armed the entire time during her multiple attacks sink in.

The last of her bindings fell away, and he slowly gathered up the rope, his eyes never leaving hers. She stood, massaging her wrists. The relief of being free washed over her. She wanted to stretch, bend at the waist and touch her toes, but, much like prey, she kept her eyes on Sergei as he flicked the switchblade closed and stashed it away in the front pocket of his jeans.

"Do you need to use the facilities?" he asked, depositing the rope back onto the counter.

Badly. She nodded.

"This vay." He gestured with his arm into the great room of the lodge, which she took time to catalog.

There was a door in the kitchen that led outside and the French doors off the great room exited onto the large deck. He took her up the stairs that overlooked the stunning two-story room and the hand-laid rock fireplace. Tongue-and-grove pine covered the ceilings where log beams jointed together. Stunning place. One she would love to spend time in.

Sergei brought her into a large bedroom, where he was obviously staying. She stopped at the doorway.

"The lodge isn't in use this time of year. I hadn't planned on any 'guests'. So the only rooms open are mine."

"You live among the others?"

"No. Vhen everyone is here, I stay in bunkhouse. I like my privacy, and I don't require much in vay of needs." His words slid over her like a caress as though if he could have her, his needs would be met.

She didn't want to enter the bear's den. The mammoth king size canopy bed was made of logs. Imposing, much like the man. A quilt in hunter greens and rich browns covered the bed. Books on multiple subjects were stacked on both night tables and piled onto the floor. One window showcased the impassable mountains with nestling glaciers in the distance, while the other looked out over the black cove. The room must be on a corner of the lodge to be able to see so much of the outdoors. She understood why he had picked it.

Had he seen her coming? She'd come from the direction the mountain-side window faced. She could almost map her trail from here. If he had been gazing out of this window, he would have seen her inch down the mountainside. They shared a look, and she hated that he'd known. She was not this predictable. The man had to have a sixth sense.

He cocked his head to the side as she continued to stand in the doorway. "I'm not going to jump you, Katja. Unless you make a move on me first, then all bets are off." He gave her his back as though he didn't fear her in the slightest.

That burned.

It was not a trust gesture. It was I-don't-think-you-are-a-threat-to-me gesture. He flicked on the bathroom light. She ventured into the bedroom, her blood simmering. He gathered up items from the counter, and the drawers. A razor, scissors, dental floss, and spray cologne.

"Feel free to shower if you'd like," he said, carrying the few things he'd grabbed out of the room. "If you need more bandages there are some in the bottom drawer."

Like she was getting naked with him so close.

"The door locks from the inside," he added.

One thing she knew without a doubt, if Sergei wanted into the room, a standard bathroom lock wouldn't keep him out.

He stepped aside for her to enter. "Don't try the window. The drop is too far and the terrain nothing but ice. The fall vould kill you and there is nothing inside here to assist in your descent. You have twenty minutes in case you'd like to shower. I promise not to bother you until the time is up." He shut the door behind him leaving her peacefully alone.

She didn't waste any time.

Sergei heard the shower kick on. He'd give anything to know what Kate was doing in there. Knowing her, she wouldn't lay down her guard long enough to take the shower he'd offered. But she'd surprised him before. Hell, everything she did surprised him. From the first moment he'd "chanced" to meet her in the outdoor market in the eastern Afghan city of Khost.

It was supposed to be a quick drop. Get in, get out kind of thing. That was until he'd seen her, talked with her. He'd fallen right then and there. The woman had an innocence about her he hadn't encountered in years, if ever. What had she been doing as a spy?

In the last two years, she'd lost some of that innocence. A fair share of it at his hands. Part of him regretted the necessary evil of that and another part did not. But what he regretted the most was the pain he'd caused her. Not killing Perry, but not being there for her the morning following their unbelievable night together and the resulting aftermath.

He'd been able to do what he could from a distance, making sure she wasn't court-martialled, by him turning state's evidence. He'd given up his country for her, and she didn't even know it.

She would soon.

The shower shut off. He glanced at his watch. Five minutes until show time.

CHAPTER SEVEN

Kate hadn't been able to resist the shower. It had been a few minutes of heaven to wash in the blue-green, fully-tiled slate shower outfitted with power nozzles and a rain faucet. How she would love to have lingered. A quick wash of her hair, scrub down of her body, and she felt like a new woman.

Revitalized.

She'd gone so far as to wedge towels under the door, not that it would have saved her from Sergei if he'd chosen to break through the lock. But it made her feel better doing something to make it harder to enter the room. The more reasonable part of her decided that if Sergei were initiating a truce of sorts, he wouldn't waste what ground he'd gained by interrupting her shower.

She grabbed a towel and began drying off when a knock came at the door. She froze, and then scrambled for her bra. There were still a few tricks sewn into the garment that Sergei hadn't seen.

"I have a change of clothing, if you vould like. I've left it outside the door."

Wow, he was making her feel right at home, wasn't he?

She listened and heard him step back. Was he still in the room?

"My back is turned. Safe to go ahead and open door."

Seemed as if he'd thought of everything. Donning the bra, which she wasn't about to give up, she wrapped the towel tighter around herself, moved the rolls of laughable barrier away from the door and opened it. True to his word, Sergei faced the bed. She snatched the pile of clothes and relocked the bathroom door. He'd found her a simple pair of jeans, her size, a warm, soft sweater in moss green, and a pair of woolen socks. No underwear. But then she didn't want to wear some other woman's under things. She went commando, rinsing her underwear in the sink and hanging them to dry over the shower's glass door. She smirked, wondering what he'd think of her making herself so at home in his bathroom? Not that it would matter. She wouldn't be here long. She had a stash of supplies in her backpack up on the mountain.

The sweater was roomy and warm. She used his comb and left her hair to dry down her back. Time was up. She reentered the bedroom to find Sergei lying on the bed, his legs stretched out and crossed at the ankles, reading a book. She doubted he was reading. He'd better *not* be reading. That meant he wasn't worried about her in the slightest.

The man had better worry.

Sergei's breath caught at the sight of Kate. No makeup, her deep red hair wet down her back, wearing the soft green sweater that did amazing things to her porcelain skin. Her eyes gleamed like cut stones. She looked soft and cuddly, fresh and beautiful. And dangerous. He wanted to gather her into his arms and tumble her down onto the bed. Stay with her for days, weeks, loving every inch of her. He hadn't had enough time with her last they were together in a bedroom. He doubted a lifetime would be enough time to learn all that he wanted to about this woman.

He climbed off the bed, and didn't miss her need to take a step back. Good.

He made her nervous.

How about he make her a little more nervous?

"Come." He walked through the bedroom door and headed down the stairs to the great room. She paused before following him. He knew he confused the hell out of her. She'd expected him to conduct their "talk" in the bedroom. There was no way he'd be able to concentrate on anything but getting her out of her clothes and into his bed if they stayed there. Best to move the conversation to neutral territory. Plus, she wouldn't expect it of him.

He stoked the fire as she paced around the room looking at everything, all the while keeping him in her peripheral vision. She glided as she walked, and he found he could watch her all day.

"How long have you been living here?" she asked.

"Almost two years." He set the red-hot poker back in the stand, seeing her eyes catalog his every move. He wondered how long it would take her to try and reach for the poker as a weapon to use against him? He hoped long enough for it to at least cool down.

"Why here, other than the obvious comparisons to Mother Russia?"

"I have no love left for Mother Russia," he replied his voice cold. "But I do enjoy the fishing, the wildness, the freedom that Alaska offers me. Besides, your lower forty-eight is too damn varm."

"Why no love for Mother Russia?"

He didn't want to go there. "Answer me a question, Katja. Why has it taken you so long to find me?"

"So the picture was a plant."

"A very good one, I thought." Six months ago Cache Calder, the renowned photojournalist for *World Events,* looking for a "Where Is She Now" story, located Mel Bennett, and Sergei had made sure he'd been partly seen in one of the photographs that had made the magazine's publication. No one else but Kate "No Mercy" Mercer would have the guts to come after him. He'd begun to lose hope she'd nibble on his bait, and had started to consider searching her out. Again, he asked, "Why so long, Katja?"

"Did you miss me?"

"Yes."

She caught her breath, obviously expecting a sarcastic response to hers. She swayed right, away from him, as though retreating from his verbal tango.

He wanted to take her into his arms, lock her tight in his embrace. Press her body up against the wall, spread those long legs of hers apart, and lose himself inside her once again. His mouth watered remembering how they'd exploded together that first time against the slammed door of their hotel room.

Sergei waited her out, until she turned back around and regarded him with distain, those jade eyes narrowed with accusation. "Why did you kill Perry?"

Here came the questions she'd been leading up to. While he'd enjoyed the promenade, it was time to get to the party. "Because he hired me to kill you."

CHAPTER EIGHT

Perry had hired Sergei to kill her?

Kate reached out and grabbed the edge of the book-case shelf.

"I don't believe you." She straightened away from the bookcase and stood strong, though her knees wobbled in her borrowed jeans.

"Part of you does."

"Not Perry. Maybe someone else hired you. I've made a lot of enemies. But Perry was my partner, my mentor. He wouldn't do that."

"I know. But he did."

Sergei stood there next to the fire, the bear rug spread at his feet, his stance relaxed, but his shoulders tight as though this discussion meant everything to him. Why would he care? What did he want from her?

"Katja," he spoke slowly as if to help her understand, "Perry vas a double agent."

She sucked in her breath. "No, he was not. He loved his country. He gave up everything for his country. His family, his wife, there was nothing the man wouldn't sacrifice for his country."

"Including you, but it vasn't love for country that drove him. It vas power, money, and most of all ego."

"He was my partner for six years. I would have known if he was crooked."

"You do know."

352

She shook her head. Was he not listening to her? No way was Perry playing both sides of the fence. He'd trained her right out of Quantico. He'd taken her under his wing and taught her everything.

"Perry told me that you'd slept vith him. He's exact vords to me vere, 'A few Black Russians and she's an easy lay'."

Everything in the room stopped. Even the softly falling snowflakes outside the glass seemed to suspend in mid air. One night. She'd slept with Perry once and it had been after a few too many Black Russians. Nobody knew about that. *Nobody.*

Nobody but her and Perry.

"You refused to drink the Black Russian I ordered for you."

And yet, she'd still slept with him, not needing any alcohol for him to seduce her into his bed.

"You don't get to say bad things about Perry. You killed him."

"I was not the one who killed him."

"You sent the person who did."

"Just as he sent a person to kill you. I vould do it all again too. Everything, Katja. *Everything.* Perry vas not this perfect man that you have raised on pedestal. He vas a very flawed man not vorthy of your love and loyalty. If you can't believe vhat I say, believe yourself. Your 'American' gut. Ask yourself, vhy I vas brought into the operation?"

"You were the Russian spy we were working with."

"That is vhat you vere supposed to think. It's vhat I thought. But Perry handpicked me to keep you occupied and paying attention to me instead of the deal happening right under your nose."

"I am not that gullible."

"I didn't think so, but you are proving yourself othervise."

She snarled at him, faced him full on and he couldn't help the arousal that heated his blood. She stroked his inner beast to life with her aggressive ways.

"Perry brought me in to seduce you," Sergei continued. "In his vords, you like them rough-looking."

That seemed to be the last downward chop of the ax that freed the tree from its roots. She roared through her teeth and came at him, arm raised with a kerambit.

Where the hell had she procured a kerambit?

It was curved and resembled a two-sided cat claw, with finger holds making it impossible to knock out of her hand. The black, highly sharpened blade was more wicked than anything he'd had slicing his way in a long time. An Indonesian weapon, arched to maximize cutting ability, and typically a last resort weapon, but she wielded it with swift finesse and deadly intent. He barely had time to prevent her stab. His armed blocked, but the nature of the knife sliced his forearm as she parried his move.

"Son of a bitch, Katja. *Nyet!*"

"You *nyet.*" Her teeth were clenched, and bottomless pain had tears swimming in her eyes. Sergei deflected another swipe, but not the kick to his instep or the punch to his ribs. The truths he'd been hurling at her had stuck in tender places, and she couldn't accept it. He hadn't wanted the truth to break her. He'd wanted the truth to heal them.

He knew what it was like to be betrayed and had tried to temper his responses to her with that in mind, but the woman was seriously going to kill him if he didn't do more than defend her attacks. Blood from the wound in his arm smeared the hardwood floor. She'd been holding back in their earlier skirmishes. Either that or her rage was a hell of a motivator for his throat.

He took her down, tripping her, but she was back on the balls of her feet dancing away from him, only to sucker punch him from behind.

"*Katja,*" he warned.

He was stronger, but she was faster.

And one of them would regret tonight.

Chapter Nine

Kate had to take her opening.

Twice now she could have taken him out, sliced through his neck, cut open his belly, and yet she hadn't.

What the hell was wrong with her?

His mind games had not worked.

Perry was innocent of all Sergei claimed. Sergei was the dirty one. The double agent. The killer. Not Perry. Never Perry.

Sergei reached for her, and she slid away, and then bounced back in easily. She could have sliced through the upper muscles of his thigh, but she didn't. She growled in frustration as tears blinded her. Then he took her down. It was almost a relief to have him slam her hand to the hard-wood, forcing free her grip on the blade.

He growled as he picked it up and looked at it. Then her. "Ivan made you this?" One arm was across her throat, his other hand locked around her wrist, while his body pressed her into the floor. "How the fuck did you get one of Ivan's kerambits?"

She flattened her lips. He growled again, deeper within his chest, sounding so much like the bear he'd been nick-named by his enemies that fear scuttled up her spine. Still, she refused to answer.

She'd survived water-boarding. What could he possibly do to her?

The dare must have shone in her eyes, because he lost his last thread of control. No longer the cool predator, he was the untamed animal, and she was about to meet his wrath.

He stood and jerked her to her feet. Twirling her around and wrapping his arms around her middle, he hefted her onto his side. From this angle, with both his arms anchoring hers around the middle, and her feet to the side, she couldn't get enough leverage to kick out at him. She squirmed as he mounted the stairs, hoping to throw him off-balance. He squeezed those bands of muscled-steel tight enough around her ribs, preventing air into her lungs. Stars twinkled in her vision as she fought to breathe. Next thing she knew, he swung her onto the bed and followed her down.

Cursing in Russian, and keeping a tight hold of her, he opened the night table and pulled out a length of rope.

Did this guy have rope planted in every room?

"No," she gasped as he looped an end over her wrist and tied it to the log bedpost.

"No is too late," he gritted out, grappling for her other hand as she fought and bucked under him to no avail. He quickly had her other hand tied to the opposite bedpost. He tested the knots, seeming satisfied with her spread before him.

"I vant to see you escape these," he taunted. His dark eyes were mere slits in his chiseled face. His jaw was a rigid line of verdict, and his nostrils flared with exertion. A final growl and he crawled off her.

He didn't speak as he stalked into the bathroom. She heard water running, realizing when a drawer opened and closed with a slap, that he was bandaging the wound she'd inflicted on his arm. A seed of regret bloomed to life, and she did her best to stomp it out of existence. Pretty easy to do with her strung between bedposts like she was. While Sergei was cleaning himself up, she took stock of her situation.

The nylon rope was tight and strong, not giving her any leverage to even move off her back, the knots out of reach of her fingertips.

Sergei reentered the room, not looking any calmer, though no longer bleeding. His brows were a line of condemnation. A few short, determined strides and he was back at the side of the bed.

"When you blame me for this, just know I would never have treated you so given the choice." He reached for her leg, and she kicked at him. "Don't make me tie your ankles, too, Katja."

Her heart pounded hard in her chest. She had to have her feet free or there was no chance of her ever getting away. Sergei fished his switchblade out of his pocket, and her muscles tightened up like wire. How had she forgotten that he still had that on his person? Why were her emotions flying so wild that she made costly mistakes like this?

Hello, she was currently tied to a bed with The Bear standing over her.

He flicked the knife open, climbed onto the bed, and straddled her hips. "Mel is going to kill me for ruining her sweater," he muttered before slicing the cable knit from her body.

She lay there on the bed in her black bra. She'd gotten her breath back, but couldn't draw air to save her life. His fingers grabbed a shoulder strap and sliced through it and the other, then he carefully slid the knife between the valley of her breast and cut through the middle of her bra, baring her breasts. They received a courtesy glance as though he couldn't help himself, but it was the bra itself he was focused on. She squirmed underneath him and he squatted farther on his haunches, anchoring her lower body to the mattress.

He turned the modified bra over in his hands, his fingers searching and finding the other kerambit she'd hidden in place of the underwire. He arched a brow at her. "Ingenious. I don't believe this is standard issue."

She refused to speak. Not that he cared as he investigated further, mutilating the bra with the switchblade. He suddenly went very still, and she knew he'd found the tracking device.

He held up the small round disc the size of a quarter that had been in place of a nipple cover. "Who is monitoring your movements, Katja?" he asked, his voice more deadly than she'd ever heard it.

A chill skittered over her skin and it had nothing to do with being bare from the waist up.

"I need you to answer me," he said.

She met his eyes. "Go to hell."

He stared at her for a very long time. She glared silently back at him. Finally, he dismounted her hips and got off the bed. Crushing the homing device with the blunt end of his switchblade on the end table, he slipped the knife back in his pocket, and examined the remains, making sure they were no longer in working order.

Slowly he turned back to her, his hot gaze traveling over her body, her nipples hardened because of the cool air, not because of the intense scrutiny of his eyes.

"Vhat else are you hiding?"

He smoothed his hand over her knee, down to her calf to her ankle. Her muscles jerked in her legs as one by one he rolled down her socks and inspected them. He tossed the socks to the floor, and then leaned over her and released the button to her jeans.

"Don't," she said, the word more of a dare than a warning.

He met her eyes for a moment, and then they flicked down to her waist as he lowered her zipper.

"Sergei." She hated the want laced within his whispered name and prayed he hadn't heard it.

He shut his eyes, and then tossed his tousled black hair out of them. Both of his hands fisted around the fabric at her hips, and he yanked off her jeans in one hard move.

She'd gone commando.

He cursed. It didn't matter what language he'd sworn in, she knew that word, but somehow he made it sound more dark and seductive than it should have been.

Heart pulsing in her throat, she'd never felt as naked as having this man strip her bare.

CHAPTER TEN

For one glorious night two long years ago, Sergei had worshipped her body, labored over her for many hours, until she responded with just the slightest touch, look, a mere whisper of words.

She lay naked before him again, yet tied to his bed. Defiant.

Bozhe moi, how he loved her. And she'd hate him for what he had to do next. By the green fire shooting at him from her eyes, she already hated him. She'd come to kill him, but she hadn't. There'd been a couple times she could have, and for whatever reason she hadn't taken the kill. Did he dare hope that she didn't hate him as much as she wanted to?

Guess he was about to find out.

When he finished his search, she'd surely hate him afterward. He'd be violating her, but then she'd attacked him time and time again, and the latest attack had been her last. The tracking device had him returning to the bed after stripping off her jeans.

She could have another device hidden anywhere.

The act of touching her naked skin again had blood boiling through his veins and hardening the region of his body he didn't think could get any harder.

He sat beside her on the bed and started with her arms. Slowly he smoothed his palms from her tied wrists up to her shoulders, feeling for anything taped to her skin and examining her for injection sites were a micro chip could have been inserted.

"You don't have to do this," she said. "I have nothing more concealed on me. You've taken it all."

His eyes met hers, and he swallowed at the anger and dread reflected there. "You've forced my hand, Katja," he returned softly.

She looked away. Her skin flushed, turning a rosy hue, and goose bumps appeared under his fingers. Inwardly he groaned as her nipples tightened to buds. Buds he wanted to lick and suckle.

He had to keep this quick, impersonal, clinical, for the both of them.

His hands traveled over her shoulders, around her neck, and under her hair. Even believing that nothing could be planted in her hair, he fanned the strands over his pillow, the red vibrant color like flames against the icy white of his pillowcase. Her eyes shuttered closed as his fingers gently traced where her neck met her spine, and he took a moment of her not watching him to scrutinize her expression. Eyes shut and lips parted, her breathing became shallow as the tips of his fingers tenderly trailed forward from her neck and around the delicate shell of her ears. He spent a lot of time there remembering how sensitive her ears were.

Some things hadn't changed.

Her pulse quickened at her throat, and it was all he could do not to cover the area with his mouth and lick his way down—

He couldn't think this way.

Over her collarbone and down the sides of her ribs, his hands continued as he tried to shut down his physical responses to finally touching her again. Two years had been a long time to go without. Kate had been a hell of woman to try and get out of his system. After a few lack-luster attempts with other women, he'd done some serious soul-searching, and realized how much Kate had meant to him. It didn't matter that they hadn't spent a lot of time together in the classical sense of getting to know one another. Sometimes a man just knew.

Heart recognized heart.

He ventured closer to the sides of her breasts, wanting to cup them, caress them, nibble them. But there was nothing to search that his eyes couldn't see, and she wasn't packing anything around these beautiful breasts anymore. There was nothing tapped or strapped, or pierced to mar the perfection of the aureoles with their tight dusky peaks.

He started to shake.

His hands splayed across her stomach. She sucked in her breath, and he flicked a glance back to her face. Her eyes were wide, her lips swollen from being nervously bitten. He locked his gaze with hers, as his hands caressed over her belly down to the sides of her hips.

What he wouldn't give to grab those hips and thrust his body deep into hers. She recognized the need that had to be reflected in his eyes, for the shock of it had her trembling under him.

He didn't hold anything back. He let all his frustration, his want, his love for her show through, praying that she'd somehow understand and be able to forgive him for what he was about to do next.

Kate hated him.

Hated what he was doing to her, what he made her feel. How could she want him until she shivered with it? Part of her rejoiced in being tied up, the choice he was taking from her. Finally she'd be with him again, experience the ecstasy only he'd been able to call forth from her body.

For the last two years she'd been consumed with him. Vengeance had been her religion. She understood the need for retaliation. This yearning, she did not. She felt betrayed by her own body. If anything, Sergei tying her up and strip-searching her should fuel her hatred and need to kill him. But all she could think about was his touch, how he'd felt between her legs, deep within her body, and how long until he would be inside her again.

His hands clasped her hips, and she couldn't help the slight arch of them. Oh hell, what was she doing? She couldn't enjoy this. What kind of woman did that make her?

An animalistic sound from deep within him reverberated throughout the room causing her blood to burn in her center and melt toward where she wanted him most. Instead of his hands searching her depths, he cupped them under her buttocks, his fingers clenching around them, his eyes closing for a moment, before he splayed his hands up her back. Searching for any abnormalities on her skin that she knew he wouldn't find, his movements brought him closer as he leaned over her, cradling her within his arms as his hands smoothed up her back to her shoulders. His nostrils flared, and her inner muscles clenched in response. His lips were mere inches from hers. The kiss he'd given her downstairs had been shocking. She hadn't expected that he would desire her after all this time. Why would he when he'd already gotten what he'd wanted from her during that night in Afghanistan?

But he wanted her now. She could see it, feel it in the very air vibrating around them, and her body responded in ways she wished she could shut down.

His hands caressed down her spine back to her hips, his fingers curling around the front, pausing before tracing the line from the tops of her thighs to the heart of her sex.

Oh God, she was not going to make it.

Why hadn't he gagged her too? She bit hard on her bottom lip, trying to keep in the appeal for him to take her, ride her hard, give her some sort of release.

His fingers traced her folds before dipping into her wet center.

"*Oh, Katja.*" He groaned as though in torment, his head falling forward, his hair grazing the sensitive skin of her stomach.

Unable to stop her herself, she shifted her legs, giving him more room to probe her further. Deeper. She arched her hips into his hand, wishing for him to deepen his stroke.

"*Fuck.*" He suddenly growled and surged off the bed. Grabbing a quilt that was draped over the leather chair next to the fireplace, he covered her with it before slamming out of the room, leaving her there writhing with want.

Oh yeah, he was a dead man.

Sergei unscrewed the top of the vodka bottle with a shaky hand and slung back a huge swallow.

Bozhe moi, he'd barely made it out of the room without burying himself inside her. He'd had to know that she wasn't packing anything else that could kill or maim him. He hadn't taken into account her body alone was enough to do him in. And what he'd just done set back any chance he had of reconciling with her. That is if there had ever been a fucking chance to begin with.

He took another swallow, relishing the burn of the bitter liquid down his throat. Recapping the bottle, he set it on the table. He'd need more vodka when he returned. She'd had a tracking device on her. There had to be more somewhere. He'd already shredded her snowsuit and boots. And since he'd stripped her bare, after finding her deceptive—brilliantly constructed—bra, that left her base camp.

He opened the door from the kitchen and went outside to gather more wood. The weather had already turned blustery with the storm front moving in tonight. Cold slapped him, dropping things back down to size in a flash. He hadn't bothered with a coat, and wood bark scraped his forearms as he gathered logs. Once back inside the cabin, he banked the fire downstairs to burn slow and even and then headed upstairs.

A deep breath and a stern pep talk to himself not to get near the bed, he entered the room. Kate hadn't moved, but then how could she when she was trussed up like she was? The temptation she offered almost buckled his knees. Her eyes were slumberous, the jade having deepened to granite and heated with fire. She probably wanted to kill him even more now. Luckily the quilt covered her nakedness, but her image was tattooed into his brain, and it took some prodding from him to head to the fireplace rather than join her under the covers.

He started a fire—another fire—the one in his blood had flamed again being in the same room with her, and added more logs.

"The room vill varm soon," he said, standing and facing her. This woman scared the hell out of him. "Is there anything else you need?"

There was a pause as she gave him an incredulous look. "Yeah, you could untie me."

Well, he'd asked. "I am leaving for a few hours. The fire vill keep you varm. Might be good to get some rest. You've... exerted yourself much today."

"Where are you going?" She frowned.

"I need to find your campsite."

"It's dark out there."

"*Dah*, and cold too."

"So, you're just going to leave me here. Tied up?"

"*Dah*."

"I can go with you."

"I don't trust you not to kill me. You'll stay here vhere I know you'll be vhen I return."

"Sergei, you can't leave me tied up like this." She struggled in her bonds, and the quilt slipped, revealing a plump breast that tempted him to either stay and entertain himself with her or untie her and take her with him. Both decisions could be his last. He walked to the bed and covered her up, tucking the quilt in around her, and checking the knots.

She wasn't going anywhere.

"Don't hurt yourself vhile I'm gone. Rest." He smoothed hair out of her eyes and turned to leave.

"Sergei..."

He turned at the door.

He could see the worry in her eyes, but was it for him or herself? Most likely herself.

"Don't get yourself killed," she said through clenched teeth.

"I thought you wanted me dead?"

"I do, but by my hand, not by some wild animal or freak of nature."

"You are not in the best position to still be threatening me."

She narrowed her eyes.

"Tempt me to stay," he threw out before he could bite it back. What the hell. He'd never have her thinking different about him if he didn't bare all that he felt about her. It wasn't like she could hate him more.

"There is nothing at the campsite except my supplies hidden within a backpack. You'll never find it in the dark."

"How about giving me the coordinates?"

"How about I don't?"

His lips twitched. He loved sparring with this woman. Whether physically or verbally, she was a challenge. And he was always up for a challenge. There was another part of him standing at attention too. "Be back soon, Katja. I hope you vill think on vhat ve have done and spoken of vhile I'm avay."

Then he walked out the door before he was tempted to stay and forget the world in her bewitching body.

A smile slid over his face when she hollered his name with insults about his mother and his ability to think straight. He hurried into his gear, knowing she wouldn't do as he'd asked and rest, though she'd need magical powers to free herself of the bonds he'd tied her with.

Just as he would never be free of the bonds tying his heart to hers.

CHAPTER ELEVEN

How dare he leave her here like this? Trussed up and so turned on her vision blurred.

Kate listened hard, past the snapping of the fire he'd started for her—wasn't that fucking thoughtful—and the pulsing of her molten blood rushing through her veins. There was a silence within the lodge that told her she was completely alone. What if she needed to use the bathroom or the lodge caught fire? Or the phone rang? Okay, the last one was a stretch. But, seriously, what if Sergei had decided to leave and not come back?

She kicked off the blanket, and the cold air spanked her bare flesh. If she didn't get free of the ropes, she was now in for an uncomfortable night even with the fire burning cheerfully. At least the chillier air helped cool her over-heated sensibilities.

She craned her neck to look at the headboard and the canopy above her. The whole bed was made of logs, though the canopy rails were quite a bit thinner than the posts. The posts might as well have been tree trunks rooted into the ground. There was no sway, no give in the ropes no matter how hard she strained against them.

She took a moment to think.

Looking around the room she scrutinized what she could reach—nothing—or use to help free herself.

Again, nothing.

Sergei must feel pretty secure that she wasn't going anywhere. She snarled through her teeth in aggravation. She couldn't still be here tied up like this when he returned. What would he do to her then?

Never had she been at the mercy of a man like this. Yes, she'd been captured, tortured, but this was different. This was Sergei, and he had always been able to get to her on a deeper level than anyone she'd ever met.

There was something not right in that the one man she wanted to hate, needed to kill, understood her. Not the person she showed the world, or even the person she pretended to herself to be. He saw *her*. Flaws and all.

That's it. If she had to use the ropes to saw through her wrist, she was getting out of these bonds. She struggled against the ropes. If she could just gain a little extra room... but Sergei had stretched her arms far enough apart that there was no possible way for her to do that.

Maybe she could swing her legs up and bust the rungs? It wasn't like she had anything else to concentrate on. Other than what Sergei had told her about Perry and that was certainly something she didn't want to revisit right now. She was too raw. Her feelings churned under the surface. Any provocation would stir them up into tidal waves she couldn't surf at the moment.

Swinging her legs up, she used the ropes as leverage and the strength of her abs in a way a gymnast would on parallel bars, and kicked at the rails above her.

Shit, that hurt.

Her feet stung with the impact of ramming them into the log rail. She kept at it, though, encouraged by the sound of a crack. A few more non-enjoyable head-banging incidents against the headboard, and she splintered the top rung above her.

It tumbled down on top of her, nailing her upper torso. Oh, yeah, that would leave a bruise.

She wished she could curl into a ball as pain radiated through her upper body. Out of breath and sweating, she took a few minutes to lie there, compartmentalizing the impact before bucking her body and dislodging the wood laying across her ribs. It crashed onto the floor and echoed throughout the lodge. Good thing Sergei wasn't here, because the racket would have brought him running.

One down. The side rungs would be a bitch as she had to kick out at an angle. Grunting with the exertion, she lashed out to the right. She didn't give up as her muscles ached and burned. Finally, she knocked it loose. Luckily this one didn't land on her, but it took out the bedside lamp—killing it—and shredding the pile of books Sergei had stacked, littering them across the floor, and denting the wall before coming to a final stop.

The momentum slid the rope up the post a few inches, and she was able to get her knees under her. She inched her body back toward the headboard, nudging the pillows out of her way. The action stirred up Sergei's scent, and she found herself suddenly sexually frustrated all over again.

Oh, that man was going to pay. And he would pay hard.

With thoughts of tying *him* up and torturing him, Kate slowly shuffled the ropes up the thick log posts, and struggled to her feet. The logs towered a good five feet above her, but if she could get enough of the rope to shimmy up the posts, she'd be able to toss them off. Thank goodness he hadn't tied the rope tighter around them, just made sure he'd tied them fucking tight around her torn and bleeding wrists. That was the least of her worries, not with freedom within her sights.

The strain and pull on her shoulders burned.

Flipping her arm up and rotating it just right in the joint, she was able to slowly gain distance up the post. She worked on doing the same to the other arm. Repeating the action, she kept up the steps, gaining inches and then a foot, only to have the rope fall back down and have to start it again.

But it was working.

Sweat dribbled down her forehead, her hair was heavy and hot around her, creating a sort of blanket.

When she had the rope at the top, she held her breath, edging it over the log post, gasping when it actually came loose. Her arm fell, and she cursed Sergei's name as blood rushed into the limb with relief.

She couldn't believe she'd succeed. She'd refused to hope, and the release of not having her arm pulled, washed over her. She took a minute to baby her arm next to her body, cradling it, before turning toward her other arm, busting the rail free of the post, and easing the rope over the top.

Yeah, that one was considerably easier.

Guess, they didn't make furniture like they used to, or at least, not furniture that could withstand Kate "No Mercy" Mercer.

She collapsed onto the bed, breathing heavy with a satisfied smile. The lengths of rope were still tied to her wrists, but she was free. After a few minutes of rest, she sat up and struggled with the complicated knots.

Where was a knife when she needed one? What the hell kind of knot had Sergei tied?

He'd made it seem so easy as he'd tethered her into place. She studied how he'd secured the rope, hoping to remember how he did it, so she could use his technique herself some day if needed.

Finally, she had the bindings undone. Gathering the ropes, she eased off the bed, her muscles sore and stiff, and opened the grate to the fire, tossing them into the flames.

There, that was better.

The flames greedily attacked the nylon rope, melting them more than burning. The acrid smell assaulted the room, and she huffed a breath of satisfaction.

Tie her up again, would he?

She headed toward the bathroom to clean up. There wasn't a lot of time. And there was lots to do before Sergei returned.

She glanced out the window facing the mountains and the direction he would have taken.

All she saw was snow.

A pang of worry burrowed its way into her heart.

Sergei struggled up the last incline. There was the site. Kate had done an excellent job hiding her tracks, but there weren't many who could hide from him. He had a way of sniffing people out. A sixth sense that his father and grandfather had possessed too. He doubted that anyone would have found where Kate had made camp with how she'd chosen to hide. He found her supplies tucked under the branches of a spruce. Just a little duffel. He liked a woman who packed light. Holding his flashlight in his mouth, Sergei opened the backpack and emptied the contents. Tent, satellite phone, MREs, a few more knives—what a woman—rope, fishing hooks and twine, and a change of clothes.

Those he needed to dispose of. He liked her naked.

He emptied everything, and then tore off his gloves to feel the seams of the pack. It took him a while, but he found another tracking device sewn into the bottom. It was very well hidden, and he'd missed it during the first and second search. He would have given up if he hadn't been positive that another existed. Flipping out his switchblade to cut it free, he paused.

Who was coming for her and when?

Snow began falling in serious flakes. He looked around, his eyes sweeping his surroundings. He needed to head back or make shelter. The storm was going to snow them in and keep whoever was coming off The Edge.

Unless they were already here.

He gathered everything and stuffed it all back into the duffel. Swinging it onto his shoulders, he headed back down the mountain.

Tied to his bed, Kate was in a vulnerable position, and she had a lot of questions to answer.

Kate cleaned up her wrists, grabbed her underwear that she'd washed earlier, and slipped them on. Feeling much more covered with that little bit of fabric, she found the jeans Sergei had stripped off her flung into a corner. She yanked them back on along with the socks. Her bra was ruined. Sergei would have to pay for that. She'd loved that bra. She slipped into one of Sergei's flannel shirts she rummaged from a drawer. This one had a blue and black checkered pattern. It was soft and roomy and smelled like him. She hated that she wanted to snuggle into it.

Did she really care more for this man than just wanting him dead?

A twinge she didn't want to investigate centered around her heart at the thought of him actually dead. She glanced back to the window and the white-out conditions. How much longer would he be?

She shook her head as though to rearrange her scrambled thoughts back into their rightful slots. Why did she care?

Could he be right about Perry? Had her partner set them both up?

She rubbed her hands over her face, twisted her hair into a loose knot and secured it with two pencils she'd located in the small desk by the window. Then she got down to business.

She searched the room, starting with the rest of the desk. There was nothing of consequence. No computer, hidden documents, weapons. Other than the pencils she'd already helped herself to.

She moved on.

She did a full sweep of the room. Nothing. Just clothes, blankets, towels. Nothing personal other than the books that she'd done a good job of destroying. She didn't bother with the bathroom since she'd already been through it once. She left the room and did a quick exploring of the upstairs. Much as she figured, there wasn't anything. The rooms were obviously used for paying guests.

She headed down the stairs on quick, quiet feet, keeping her ears tuned to any changes within the log building. The wind whistled outside, and snow spit at the windows. She couldn't see anything out of them with the blizzard.

He'd been gone a while now. Should she...?

Oh my hell, you are not going out there looking for him.

The kitchen was her first stop. As with any dwelling, the kitchen always housed the most interesting objects. She helped herself to a handful of nice, decent cutlery and one sinfully-sharp Ulu—an Eskimo knife mostly used for filleting fish. It was a third of a circle in shape with a bone handle that fit nicely in her palm. A long curved blade used for slicing muscle meat from the bones of salmon, it was wicked cool.

Yeah, that could come in handy.

The chef knew her knives. As Kate explored the downstairs section of the lodge, she stashed them in places just in case she needed them later. One thing she'd learned as a spy, always be ready to defend yourself.

Her life was all about putting up walls and arming them with deadly things. The filleting knife was hard to let go of as she hid it inside a stunning vase, glazed in the colors of the Aurora Borealis, and displayed upon the large hearth of the fireplace. She hated not having a weapon on her person. Being tied and strip-searched again was not in her future. She really wanted to hate Sergei for what he'd done to her, wanted to use the violation as fuel against him, but was finding that harder and harder to do. Probably because part of her had enjoyed his touch. More than part of her. He hadn't needed to be so gentle with how he'd conducted the search. Leaving her wanting had burned more than the actual act of the strip-search. Probably because if the roles had been reversed, she'd have done the same.

The thought of tying Sergei to a bed and stripping him naked, allowing her hands to search every inch of his skin, had her rooted in place. What would it be like to have free access to his body? To do with him what she wanted?

Oh, so not thoughts she wanted to be having.

Slowly she sank down on the leather couch, her toes curling on the rug, and her hands fisting in her lap. She gazed unseeing out the French doors. Snow had piled up on the deck in alarming amounts. Wind swirled flakes into a mass that became a wall. If Sergei didn't show up soon, he wasn't going to be able to. He'd be stuck out there unable to find his way back. She didn't know how he could see a foot in front of him as it was. It would take nothing to get turned around, step off a cliff and fall to his death, or slip on ice and break a bone, and then freeze to death out there in this.

Why was she more worried about Sergei struggling through the storm than making him pay for Perry's death?

She'd been all fired up to make him pay, had dropped in on The Edge guns blazing and knives slashing after his head. Was that the problem? What if she was really after his heart, since he'd broken hers?

Oh God.

He'd left her in Afghanistan. Abandoned her in the face of betrayal, death, and devastation. His betrayal, or so she thought. The accusations he'd said about Perry had a truthful ring to them. There were things she'd witnessed and for some reason or another had talked herself around to where Perry wasn't in the wrong.

Could *she* have been wrong this whole time? She wasn't gullible like Sergei claimed, but were her loyalties misplaced?

She stood and paced the area of hardwood next to the French doors, searching to see something through the whiteout.

Where the hell was he?

She rubbed her arms and realized how chilled the room had become. She added another couple of logs to the fire, stoking the flames until they burned brighter and hotter. Much the way she burned waiting for Sergei.

She had questions he needed to answer, and he'd better get his butt back here fast.

A clatter coming from the kitchen froze her in place.

Chapter Twelve

Kate positioned herself near the fireplace, the fillet knife within handy reach.

Sergei entered and came to a fast stop at seeing her. He'd already taken off his winter gear but his skin was flushed with cold, his nose and cheeks red, and his hair wet from melting snow. She drank him in, and he stared at her in wonder.

"How did you get free?" His eyes narrowed and slid around the room as though looking for someone else.

She disregarded his question for one of hers. "Where the hell have you been?" It came out accusing as though she were a fish wife demanding to know where her man had been out carousing.

He tossed her backpack into the corner, and wrung his hair back from his face.

Oooh, he looked all European and sexy with his wet, black hair slicked back from the sharp bones of his face. Her heartbeat increased, and she shifted on the balls of her feet.

"Miss me, Katja?"

"Parts of you," she muttered under her breath.

His eyebrows shot up, somehow having heard her from across the room. His gaze heated, and his chest expanded with a quick breath.

She went liquid inside.

"You've been vorried about me," he stated.

"Have not."

"How can you vorry for me vhen you vant me dead?"

"I have not been worried," she lied. "I could care less what happened to you out there." He advanced so quickly, she didn't have time to respond before his chest was right up against hers. So not like her.

"How long vill you continue to lie to yourself?"

A sound of frustration escaped her at his nearness. He'd left her sexually sensitive, and the minute he'd entered the room all those unquenchable needs returned with teeth.

Hungrier.

She grabbed his head and yanked him down, capturing his lips, searing her mouth against his.

A dark and dangerous sound came from him and made her insides do funny things. Heat burned within her as she gave herself over to her desires. Her tongue dueled with his, her teeth scraping. He yanked her flush against him. Every part of him completely engaged with her. She wrapped her arms around him, wanting to embrace all there was about this man. His body, his strength, his heat.

There was no more waiting. She knew the truth. For two years this is where she'd wanted to be. Since the moment she'd woken alone in that hotel room clear across the world, she'd craved his arms around her again. His scent weaved and mixed with hers, creating something that was undeniable. She broke off the kiss and grabbed the front of his shirt, ripping it open. Buttons and flannel flew, revealing the most gloriously muscled chest. Dusted with just the right amount of hair, and defined in the way of a God, Sergei was chiseled, and strong, and touchable.

She tripped him.

He took her down to the floor with him as though expecting the move, their fall cushioned by the bear rug. His hands wrenched the shirt she'd stolen from his drawer over her head, dislodging the pencils anchoring her hair in place. He growled at seeing her bare breasts.

He flipped her over so that she was on the bottom. His eyes searching hers before his hands cupped her breasts. He sucked a hardened nipple into his mouth, and her back arched off the fur beneath her, a startled gasp escaping her.

Oh God. His rough hands were not gentle as he stripped her once again of the jeans. She struggled with the button and zipper of his, not being nearly as adept at the action as he seemed to be. He released her nipple and seemed torn between taking the other one into his mouth or stripping off his own jeans. The jeans won.

"I don't have a condom on me," he rasped out, his breathing choppy.

"I don't care."

"There is protection upstairs in bed table. Plus bed."

Not one they could use in its present condition, and she didn't need protection. "Why didn't you take me up there?" The question was out before she could take it back. She didn't want to talk. She wanted to lose herself in him. Silence these incessant needs.

"Katja." He smoothed her hair away from her face. "I couldn't take you tied to my bed like that."

"Yes, you could have." Seemed as if honesty was getting the best of her tonight.

"You vould have hated me."

"Yes, I would have." She flipped him over and straddled him, rising to view him beneath her, between her thighs.

He was glorious. Such a beautiful male specimen. It was her turn to finish stripping him bare. She didn't waste any time. She wanted him. Wanted him hard and fast and thrusting inside her. Wanted the urgency back where troubling thoughts did not reside.

He reached up, his hands sliding up her back, splaying over her ribs. "How'd you get this bruise?"

"Not important." At least, not now.

He burrowed his fingers in her hair and brought her lips to softly meet his. Her hair tumbled around them, as he reverently explored her mouth. He was getting gentle and tender, and she didn't want that. Her hand snaked down between them and grasped his shaft and squeezed. The untamed sound that escaped him stirred tremors inside her.

He flipped her back over, tore off her underwear, grabbed her hips and positioned himself at her opening. The large tip of his penis just breaching the lips of her sex. "Tell me you vant me. That this means something to you."

She curled her lips over her teeth, not wanting to answer him. Or hear the truth herself.

Her body wept for him. He knew it. He could feel it. Why did she need to say it too?

"*Katja*," he warned, inserting himself partway.

Oh God. "This means something," she snarled, clenching her inner muscles trying to draw him inside her. "It fucking means something to me, okay?"

He impaled her with one hard, deep thrust.

She gasped at the forceful invasion, the sheer fullness and perfection as he lay heavy and hungry within her, undeniably part of her. He expressed a lengthy, painful groan. His eyes never left hers as he slowly retreated from her body and then advanced, taking her hips in his large hands and lifting them to receive his thrusts deeper. Again and again, and then faster and faster, until his name became a broken cry on her lips.

He pounded relentlessly into her, wringing everything from her body, until her very soul shattered with the pleasure he wrought from places she didn't know existed.

His back arched, and his thrusts quickened, the veins in his shoulders and neck roping under his skin. His head fell back on a roar as he surged, clutched her against him, and pulsed deep within her. He stayed like that suspended for a minute as though he couldn't take the pleasure.

Tipping his head, he looked at her, his eyes dark, satisfied, and clearly not willing to give her up. Slowly he enfolded her in his arms, his body flush to hers as he tightened his grip around her.

"Katja."

Her name was like a whispered vow on his lips that broke the chains she'd locked around her heart.

CHAPTER THIRTEEN

Sergei basked in the rightness of Kate cuddled within his embrace. What they'd just done solidified everything that he'd put in place to bring her to The Edge.

"Let me up." Kate struggled with his arms, pushing at his shoulders, kicking out at him, connecting painfully with his shins.

"Vhat?" Had he hurt her? He'd been rough, consumed with her, but she hadn't objected. If anything she'd spurred him on, wanting him hard and fast, not gentle and slow like he'd tried to temper.

"Let me go!" Her voice broke on the last word, and he released her. She scrambled to her feet, grabbing the quilt thrown over the end of the couch.

"Katja?" Alarmed, he hurried to his feet.

"Stay away from me." Her words held no threat. Emotion clouded their meaning, making the words more of a plea. She ran for the bathroom that was located on the first floor. He rushed to follow. The door slammed in his face. Looked as though she'd been free for some time. Time enough to know the layout of the lodge.

How had she freed herself? No one he knew could have gotten loose of those knots without help.

He went to bust through the door, but then he heard a strangled sob. His heart thudded in his chest.

Bozhe moi. What had he done?

He braced his hands on the doorframe and leaned his head onto the wood. "Talk to me, Katja." He had to fix this. Making love with her had been wondrous. Better than before. Right. So very right. She was his mate. His equal. His everything. But had he somehow ruined things, making them worse than he had before? "Open this door."

"Go away."

"Either talk to me or I'm coming in."

"I need a minute." The toilet flushed.

He wasn't buying it. "Katja." He growled.

"I need a few goddamn minutes, okay?"

Hearing the anger back in her voice reassured him, and he straightened back from the door. "That's all you vill get."

"Go to hell."

"Vith bags packed. As long as you follow," he added.

He was infuriating.

Kate splashed cold water on her face. What was she going to do? That had been too intense. She'd lost valuable ground having sex with him again. Somehow he knew she cared. He'd known before she'd known. How? Was the man some kind of sightseer? There had been whispers about him. He sensed things before others, which is why he'd been impossible to kill. They needed someone like her to have him lower his guard. But he'd bested her at every turn.

Two years ago, she'd been told to sleep with him and then kill him. But she couldn't then, and she couldn't now. Though she didn't seem to have a problem with the sleeping part. So what did she do?

Follow her heart or her head?

Quit her job and disappear? She'd have to disappear as in "die" for others not to come after her. Could she chuck everything and finally do what she wanted? Wouldn't that be a treat? She couldn't remember the last time she'd actually done something because she wanted to. That wasn't true. Last time she'd slept with Sergei it had been what she'd wanted. Ordered to or not. She'd never wanted a man like she had wanted him.

And here she was, hiding in the bathroom like some simpering female.

Didn't that bite?

Pull it together, Kate. The longer she stayed in here the weaker she looked. She never ran. The fact that she needed a few minutes after he destroyed her to put herself back together was forgivable. For a bit. Quickly, she cleaned up, shaped up, squared her shoulders, and wiped her expression clean of the turmoil she felt inside.

Sergei was waiting for her as she exited the bathroom. Leaning against the wall in the hallway, he'd dressed in his jeans, and button-torn flannel shirt, leaving his feet bare. His gaze swept her from her bare feet to her body covered in the quilt.

"Are you okay?" he asked. "Did I hurt you?" There was command and concern in his voice that tugged at her heart.

"No, you didn't hurt me." But she couldn't tell him she was okay. She wasn't, and it was about time she quit lying to herself. And him. "We need to talk."

"*Dah*, ve do."

"First, I'd like to get dressed."

"I like you the vay you are." His voice went smoky and dark, stoking sparks to fire inside her again.

"We have to take sex out of this."

"Never." His nostrils flared. "You vant me. I vant you..." He stopped, but it seemed as though there was more that he wanted to say.

"That may be, but it's getting in the way."

He smiled, his eyes softening when she didn't disagree with him this time. "No, Katja, everything else is in *our* vay. Ve need to, how you Americans say, 'clean house'?" He held up the knife she'd stashed under the couch. He must have seen it when he picked up his clothes. She hadn't noticed he'd been hiding it behind his back. "Who are you arming against?" he asked. "Me...or is there someone else you are expecting?"

She swallowed. At least he'd only found the one knife. Good thing she hadn't stayed longer in the bathroom, he would have most likely sniffed out the other four.

"How did you get free? Who else is here, Katja?"

She smirked. "I didn't need help getting free."

"I don't believe you."

"You will," she threw at him.

"Show me."

"It will be my pleasure." As soon as she said the words, realizing she was flirting, she regretted them. So much for taking sex out of it.

"After you then." He gestured toward the stairs.

She didn't want to be in a bedroom with him. But then that hadn't stopped her from having the hottest sex of her life with him on a bear rug in front of the fireplace in the great room of this lodge.

Hell, the bedroom would actually be safer. She'd broken the bed.

"How am I to explain this?" Sergei regarded the splintered logs of the canopy bed. This was a lot bigger than a shredded sweater. Did the woman have superpowers? He looked at the bed, and then at Kate, then back to the bed. He ventured closer to investigate. She'd reduced the canopy to firewood. Gathering up the broken, splintered pieces, he stacked them along the wall. The four-poster bed could be saved with some woodworking, but the canopy was shot. He wasn't up to counting the casualties of his books.

The strength and determination Kate had to free herself was fantastic.

"Impressive," he said.

"Thank you." She attempted to bite back a smile without succeeding. The woman was enjoying this.

So was he.

"You're very provocative, Katja," he said, his voice huskier. His eyes traveled over her down to her long legs peeking out from the folds of the quilt. While she'd gathered up her clothes on their way upstairs, there hadn't been time for her to dress.

He needed to figure out how to keep her naked.

A blush bloomed on her cheeks, and she shuffled on her feet. She held up the clothes in her hand and indicated the bathroom. "I should—"

"No, you shouldn't."

She paused in backing up toward the bathroom.

"Ve vill make love again tonight, Katja. Getting dressed is vaste of time."

"That's presumptuous of you to say."

"Is truth." He turned more fully toward her, ready in case she bolted or attacked. "No more pissy-stepping around."

"You mean pussy-footing."

"Means same, no?"

She shrugged. "I suppose so. Doesn't change the fact that it's pretty arrogant of you to assume I'll meekly fall into bed with you again."

"There is nothing meek about you. I'd never make that mistake. I don't trust you not to ruin another bed if I have to tie you to it in order to get some rest myself. And it's not possible for me to share a bed vith you and not make love to you."

His words lay between them like the challenge they were. He couldn't wait to see what she'd do.

The bundle of clothes wavered in her hand as though they held the weight of her decision. Then she dropped them to the floor. "Fine. But you need to answer some questions for me first."

His heart stuttered.

She'd actually discarded her clothes. Willingly agreed that they were making love again. Tonight.

"Fine," he returned though it was an effort to get words past the hope blooming in his chest and the blood in his body heading south. "I have questions also."

"Why would Perry want you to kill me?"

While she asked the question impersonally, he saw the pain in her eyes, in the way she held her body, so straight as to break if touched.

"The arms deal," he said. "You knew too much. Soon you vould have figured out that he vas double-dealing. You are smart voman, Katja, and asked all the right questions. Therefore you had become liability."

"How were you told to do it? Kill me?"

"It vas supposed to look like you had been raped, strangled, and then left for buzzards. Another unfortunate statistic for vomen traveling abroad alone, unprotected."

She swallowed hard, and her eyes flickered before meeting his again. "When did you decide not to kill me?"

"Killing you vas never in my plans. I needed to use you to trap Perry...but I planned to bed you the moment I met you."

"Bed me?" Her eyes went granite.

"Maybe I messed up translation. English not my first language, you understand."

"Not buying it, Sergei."

It was time to put her on the defensive. "How did you acquire one of Ivan's kerambits?" Ivan had been his comrade, his partner, and had helped set up Perry.

"He personally made it for me."

"And obviously taught you how to use it. Vhy is he helping you?"

"You defected. Turns out he's a bit angry about that."

"So he sought you out?" He didn't wait for an answer before continuing, "And you didn't think it vas coincidental that ve had vorked together and now he vas vorking vith you?"

"All I cared about was getting to you."

"Is Ivan the one coming for you, Katja?"

"Yes, to make sure I do the job."

"And to exterminate you if you haven't."

She nodded. "That seems to be the way these contracts work. Really motivates a person to get the job done."

"Vhen?"

She looked out the window at the storm and then back to him. "Not tonight."

She dropped the quilt.

Chapter Fourteen

The action of the quilt pooling at her feet, knocked the air out of him, and his heart thumped hard enough in his chest to fell a lesser man. She was glorious, standing proud and naked before him.

Strong, curved, and battle-bruised.

Some of those bruises came from fighting with him. How many—seen and unseen—would there be by the time things were resolved between them?

"I vant more than tonight," he said.

"How much do you want?"

If he said everything, she'd run. She was like a skittish wolf venturing carefully into uncharted territory.

"I have vaited a long time for you to come for me, Katja." He stepped close enough to touch her, his voice lowering with intent. "I vant you for as long as you are villing to let me keep you." He had to give her the choice to stay...or go. But if she chose to leave, he didn't know if he had it in him to let her.

"We aren't the best fit, you and I."

His brow cocked. "I disagree. Ve fit very vell together." His fingertips grazed the tips of her breasts, the nipples pebble-hard, and then traced the faint lines marring her body. Many knife scars criss-crossed her arms, and a bullet wound creased her shoulder. He wanted to hear each and every battle. Wanted to kill every person who had caused her pain.

She shivered under his hands. "Not what I meant. Two spies? How would that work?"

"One retired spy and one soon to be retired, I hope. Ve understand each other. And you can hold your own against me. I find that extremely attractive."

He took her hand in his, kissed her fingers. "Come to bed vith me, Katja. Let me show you just how vell ve fit together."

She let him lead her to the bed. He turned down the covers. It wasn't lost on him the difference between having her on his bed like this from just a few hours ago fighting with her, tying her up. Leaving her. He wasn't leaving her tonight. They were snowed in. No one could get in or out of The Edge of Reason.

Finally, they had time.

She lay on the bed.

"Stay." He turned and stoked the fire, lit the candles on the mantle, and snuffed the lights. The glow from the snow, along with the fire, illuminated her ivory skin and turned her hair a darker red. She was stunning, lying on his bed, waiting for him. He had a moment wondering if he'd conjured her. So many nights he'd dreamt of having her here with him. It was hard to believe she was real. Their coming together downstairs, while it had rocked him, it had been frantic and over much too soon.

Tonight would not be the same.

He stripped bare in front of her, loving the way her eyes followed his movements, her breath quickening in the silent room. Only the moaning of the wind and flickering of the greedy flames added a wildness that complimented her the way no other music could.

He crawled onto the bed, up her body and settled his weight on top of her. The pleasure of her bare skin against his caused bliss to settle in his bones. The feeling was one so foreign, emotion thickened his vocal cords. Afraid of what declarations might come from his mouth—declarations she wasn't ready to hear—he kissed her, expressing physically how he felt.

She groaned under him, her hands grasping his hips. He shifted his lower body away from her. The woman had a way of taking him in hand and getting him to lose control, like she had downstairs. That was not happening here.

Here, he was in charge.

She raked her nails up his back and then down to his buttocks, and his whole body hardened under her hands.

Okay, so maybe he wasn't in charge.

His mouth turned greedier even though he did his best to slow things down. He deepened the kiss, while his hands stroked her, trying to be careful, his touch tender, exploring. She arched under him, her leg anchoring over his hip as she pressed against him.

Bozhe moi. How did she fire his blood like this?

His hands rougher than he intended, yanked her hips against his, his shaft riding between her thighs along her slick folds, rubbing the sensitive area that had her wrenching her mouth free on a cry, and sinking her teeth into his shoulder.

He refused to enter her. Not yet.

"*Sergei.*"

How he loved a demanding woman.

His mouth captured the nipple of one breast, his fingers the other as he continued to grind against her.

She growled, losing patience with him, and tossed him over onto his back. The strength it took for her to be able to move a man like him, one who had expected her to make the move, so astonished him that he lay there on his back stunned for a moment.

A moment that was his undoing.

She straddled his thighs. He could see where they would have control issues. They both liked dominant positions. This was going to be fun.

And torture.

Retribution shined in her eyes as her hands teased their way down his body, her mouth following in their wake as she licked and nipped at his chest, his nipples, down the contours of his stomach, to grasp the base of his shaft in her hand.

Her tongue circled the tip.

He snarled, watching her as she took him in her mouth. Heat infused him, and colors painted the room. She knew what he liked, how to run her teeth, her tongue, enclose her lips over his flesh to where if he didn't get her to stop he'd lose himself right then and there.

He had more planned for them.

He grabbed her shoulders and lifted her off him. She gave a startled cry as he tossed her onto her stomach, and twisted to hunch over her. His hands held her arms, his feet locking her legs down to the mattress. In a sense, he'd restrained her again. She couldn't touch, tease, torment, or fight him this way.

"Sergei," she warned, a little apprehension coming through in her tone.

He was beyond speech, overcome with need. He kissed her neck in a vain attempt to express regret for not taking this slower like he'd intended. Next time. Or the time after that. His teeth raked her skin, his mouth trailed down her back, all the while keeping her imprisoned within his dark embrace.

Spreading her legs, he pushed himself heavy between them and penetrated her from behind in one hard, deep thrust.

Air escaped her in a gasp while he growled with the intense pleasure, tightness, and heat as he sheathed himself deeply within her. His hips drove into hers, the power and weight of his body keeping her captive beneath him. He released her hands and burrowed his under her, one banding her chest, his hand holding her breast, the other snaked down her stomach to find and stroke her clitoris.

She screamed as she came, and he still rode her. Not giving any quarter as he took her, forcing one climax after another from her until he could no longer withhold his own.

A guttural sound escaped his lips as he gave himself over to the pleasure that had the power to bind him to her forever.

CHAPTER FIFTEEN

Kate woke up...alone.

Memories of how devastated she'd felt the last time this had happened sank into her consciousness. Quickly followed by the heavy guilt of Perry's death later that same morning. Her shame and culpabilities had been hard to explain to her superiors and herself. She'd promised herself that this wouldn't happen again. And here she was.

Alone.

Sunshine sliced through the windows. The blizzard had blown itself silent much like the fervor she'd had for Sergei's blood. By her calculations, since the sun didn't rise early in Alaska this time of year, it was around noon. The aches and tenderness in her body bore testimony that she hadn't dreamt last night or early this morning. She'd been well used. And had done an equal amount of using herself.

She tossed her hair out of her face and rubbed her eyes. How much ground had she lost? Each time they'd come together, she'd lost more of her heart to him until she didn't know how much of it was actually hers anymore.

The door suddenly opened, and Sergei entered. Her backpack was slung over one shoulder and he held coffee mugs in each hand.

He paused in the doorway. *"Dobriy den',"* he murmured, his tone gritty, slumberous.

"Afternoon," she returned, understanding at least that much Russian. She didn't want to think about how she looked as his eyes drank her in. She'd never cared about her appearance before. Just because this bear of a man stood there all hot and sexy didn't mean she needed to add a bit of make up, though she suddenly felt compelled to do so. Sergei had dressed in another flannel shirt, this one a dark gray. His jeans had been black at one time but were worn more charcoal in color with a small tear above the knee.

How observant was she that she'd slept through his rising, showering, and dressing? She never let her guard down like this. It had only happened one other time, and that had been with him also. What kind of power did he have over her?

She sat up and curled her legs into her chest under the blankets.

He walked around to the side of the bed and handed her a cup of coffee. The dark, bitterness drifted toward her, awakening her muddled senses.

Sergei dropped her backpack onto the bed. "Time to make plan. Company is coming for dinner." He seemed all business this afternoon and less the demanding lover of a few hours ago.

"How do you know?"

"No vay to really explain. I just know."

She wasn't about to question his sixth sense. He'd known she was behind him when she'd snuck up on him yesterday. Had that really only been yesterday? In a mere twenty-four hours her whole life had changed, changed so much she didn't know what was up or down...or who to trust. So instead, she took a sip of coffee and swallowed.

Not only could he make love to a woman until she was ready to reveal state secrets, his coffee was sinfully addictive.

"I like that you are no longer trying to kill me," he stated, taking a long sip of his coffee before setting the cup down on the night table.

Could that be her downfall? She felt as if she was barefoot trying to navigate an icy slope.

His eyes dark and brooding, stared into hers. "Do you have any more transmitters on you?"

"No." That question—demand—she hadn't expected.

He picked up the backpack and handed it to her, not taking his eyes off her. "Check bottom seam."

She ran her fingers along the seam finding a quarter-size transmitter. Could this be one of Ivan's backups in case the one in her bra had been found? But why wouldn't Ivan tell her?

"Vhat vas your plan for getting off The Edge once you had killed me?"

"I was supposed to call on the sat phone." There was a sharp stab to her heart. What if she had actually succeeded in killing him?

Sergei flipped open his handy switchblade and surrendered it to her, handle first.

She paused in taking his weapon. How could he trust her like this after all she'd tried to do and what he was accusing her of now?

Or was he accusing her?

He held her gaze for a long time. She slowly accepted the blade, and a satisfied smile curved his lips.

She cut into the bottom of the backpack, freeing the tracking device. It was small but effective, though the tracker wouldn't find her unless they were within a twenty mile radius. Who was monitoring her besides Ivan? Had he planted this on her without telling her as a backup? But why wouldn't her tell her?

"Why didn't you destroy this when you found it?" She had no clue where this had come from, but didn't try to defend herself. There was no way to prove her innocence.

"I vant whoever is tracking your movements not to suspect things have changed between us." He paused as though waiting for her to object. His nostrils flared when she didn't.

She handed the knife and the device to Sergei. He took them, stashing away the knife and the disk in his pocket. He then seized her face between his large hands and kissed her.

Something monumental passed between them without a word being said. Trust had been formed, reinforced and then sealed with a hard exchanging of lips and coffee-scented breath.

"*Ya lublu tebya*, Katja." He released her, his eyes boring into hers.

She wished she was more up on her Russian, because whatever he'd just uttered sounded important.

Wait a damn minute. Had he just told her he *loved* her?

Before she could ask for the translation, he'd fished the satellite phone out of her pack and held it out to her. "Call and say job is finished."

"No." She slapped the phone out of her way.

"Katja," he warned.

"In English. Translate what you just said." Her lungs refused to inflate as she waited him out.

"You know vhat I said."

Oh God. Her heart launched into hyper drive. "You love me?"

"*Dah*. Now make call. Ve'll discuss feelings for each other once job is finished."

"Oh, no we won't. We'll discuss it now."

"Are you ready to tell me your feelings?"

She froze. What did she really feel for him? She'd hated him for so long, or was there more to it? Was the hate covering up how much he'd hurt her by leaving her to flounder like he had because she cared for him too? She didn't know if she could use the word love, yet, or ever.

Sergei's face hardened into an unreadable mask. "First vork and then ve'll talk." He gave her a hard kiss. "Make call."

CHAPTER SIXTEEN

Sergei loaded his 12-gauge sawn-off Remington 870 pump-action shotgun, liking the feel of the weapon in his hands.

"Think that's big enough?" Kate asked, securing the kerambit to her belt.

"Is back-up."

"If that is your secondary weapon, what's your first?"

"You." He'd returned Kate her 9mm.

She reclaimed her weapon with one hand, and then traced her other hand down his chest as though she couldn't help herself.

Damn this woman. He knew she cared for him. Telling her he loved her had been a slip. He hadn't meant to reveal so much when they needed to focus on the job ahead. So he shouldn't feel hurt that she hadn't gushed out her feelings to him. She'd come a long way from wanting him dead to loving him like she had last night. He needed to be patient just a little longer.

Her fingers hooked into the waistband of his jeans and drew him in. Her lips took his and desire clouded his focus.

"*Katja.*" He growled.

"Right. Battle first." She nipped at his lower lip before stepping back. "Don't get hurt. I have plans for you later."

He uttered an animalistic promise, yanked her in for another kiss, and lingered longer than he should have. Now he was hard and hungry with the need to kill. A dangerous combination.

The afternoon had been spent fortifying The Edge since he'd demanded Kate call her contact. She was lethally outfitted in knives, Glock, and sheathed all in black, her deep red hair restrained in a tight bun. The woman was a stunning femme fatale, and he was completely ensnared.

Whoever thought he was dead would be arriving on the iced beach in full view of the lodge. The waters were still choppy from the blizzard stirring up the winds the night before. Since they had access to a helicopter, from dropping Kate in behind, he kept his ear attuned to the skies. He wanted this business over with. He'd waited too long already. Kate was within his grasp. This business needed to be finished. He just had to tie up these loose ends in order to secure a life for them. One where they wouldn't constantly need to watch over their shoulders.

"Do the owners of the lodge know who you really are?" Kate asked.

"*Nyet*. They think I'm lonely Russian vithout country. Since there is Russian village outside of Homer, vhich I make time to visit vhen in town, it helps with the pretense."

"Are you content here?"

Not without you, was on the tip of his tongue. "*Dah*, I have been content." By the evening he'd have a better idea where she stood. He heard the repetitive whoop, whoop of chopper blades. "Time," he said. "Ready?"

She nodded, her face expressionless.

Now the real test.

Would they be allies or enemies? Would she lead with her heart?

Kate took up a stance next to the glass French doors, her back to the log wall. No bullets were getting through those thick walls. He was loath to leave her, but knew from experience she could handle herself. She'd been in dangerous situations before, though none of them with him or because of him.

She glanced over her shoulder and frowned, finding him still rooted in the middle of the great room. "Hide," she hissed, motioning her hand low by her thigh.

It grated on him to secret away in the deep shadows of the stairs. He never hid. But in order to ferret out the players, he didn't have much choice. Not since he was supposed to be dead.

Kate glanced out through the glass, her shoulders relaxing. She shared another look with him and then stood in front of the glass and opened the door. There was a hollered "Kate" and then she was scooped up in a burly man's arms.

Sergei saw red. He wanted to tear the man to shreds. It took everything he had to stay put.

Ivan entered the lodge. His arm casually looped over Kate's shoulders.

"So where's the body?" Ivan asked.

Sergei waited for Kate to move away from him, but she didn't.

"I do my best work in the kitchen." She pointed that direction, but Ivan stopped her. "I don't think so." His hand tightened on her shoulder. "Come out, Sergei."

"I told you, he's dead," Kate said, her voice monotone as though she didn't give a damn.

"Don't get me wrong, Kate, you're good, but Sergei wouldn't have let that happen," Ivan said.

Sergei stepped out of the shadows. "Ivan."

"Comrade." Ivan let go of Kate and grabbed Sergei in a bear hug. "I was getting worried that she'd actually killed you. You said she wouldn't, but you don't know how much she's wanted your head."

Sergei glanced at Kate. Her expression confused, the kerambit already palmed. Light slowly dawned.

"Wait a fucking minute." She turned to Ivan. "You two have been playing me?"

"For reasons you vill understand soon," Sergei said. "There isn't time. Are they coming?"

"Yes, brought them myself."

"Brought who?" Kate asked. "What the hell are you talking about?" She glared at Sergei. "Talk fast."

"I needed to know, Katja."

"Needed to know what?" Her voice continued to harden, become deadlier.

"If I was still alive or not," Perry said, entering the room from the kitchen, a gun pointed at Kate's head.

Chapter Seventeen

Kate stood perfectly still, the barrel of Perry's Sig pointed at her forehead.

Perry was alive.

He stood before her, a cocky sneer on his modestly attractive face. She used to see that look as confidence, wishing she could be more like him. Average height, and average build, hid his muscled-physique and wrestler-prowess well, making him a formidable weapon. Part of her wanted to hug him. The other wanted to run a knife through him. Before she could decide anything, she had to know what the hell was going on, and why everyone seemed to know everything but her.

"You're dead," she said to Perry. "I indentified your body."

A sick smile played over Perry's mouth. How had she not noticed its cruel bent before?

"The morgue didn't have the best lighting," Perry said. "I did enjoy your tears, my dear. Heart wrenching really, but I was a tad disappointed you didn't stay around long enough to feel for a pulse."

She'd been so overcome with grief and guilt, she'd lit out of that two-bit hospital like the shameful, sullied woman she'd been.

"You knew he was alive?" she demanded of both Sergei and Ivan. Why had she been left in the dark? Manipulated.

"I'd begun to suspect," Sergei said.

"I wasn't sure until these brutes jumped me in Homer outside the Salty Dawg," Ivan said, stretching his neck. "I've been their 'guest' until your call this afternoon."

Kate looked closer and could see bruises darkening Ivan's skin around his jaw. Her hands itched to slice.

"Drop the knife, Kate," Perry ordered. "Knives," he added after summing her up. She tossed the knives at his feet, coming close to stabbing his booted-foot. "Still as brazen as ever. I always did like that about you." Still holding the gun on her, Perry reached around to her back, seizing the Glock where she'd stashed it in the waistband of her pants, and stuffed it into the pocket of his Columbia jacket. "I'll put a bullet through her head. Toss over your weapon." He waited for Sergei to lay down the Remington. "Kick it over here."

Sergei's sharpened stare centered on Perry as he did as instructed. "There are three of us. Do you really think this is ending vell for you?"

"I'm not alone," Perry scoffed. Two big thugs stepped into the room from behind Perry. "I think I've more than leveled the playing field," he added, smug as hell. He looked at Kate. "Besides, one of you is a woman."

"You should know better than to underestimate me, you son of a bitch," Kate said.

"You've always been so droll, Kate. Content to be told what to do. A government lackey."

"Are you going to let him talk to you like that, Katja?" Sergei asked, his tone dry as dust.

"*Katja?* Oh, isn't that sweet," Perry sneered. "Twenty-four hours and you're back to being his whore."

"Don't call her names just because you couldn't satisfy her," Sergei said.

"Shut up." Perry aimed his weapon at Sergei.

Kate used it as her opening to kick the gun free of Perry's hand. Much like a flare going off at the races, they charged. Thug One and Thug Two went for Sergei and Ivan leaving her to face off with Perry.

Gladly.

Perry made a tsk-tsk sound as he advanced. "You really shouldn't have been so straight-laced, sweetheart. You and I could've had something promising together."

She'd thought they had. The feeling must have been conveyed in her expression, for Perry laughed. "You were such a delight at first. Willing to learn, to please."

She lashed out at him, and he deflected. Each kick, fist, series of volleys, he easily dodged. He'd been her teacher and therefore knew all her moves. They'd worked together, covered each other's backs for six years. She'd thought the world of him. How could he have done this to her? He'd set her up. Played her. And she'd let it happen, never suspecting Perry of being a traitor. He'd been her mentor, and she'd followed everything he'd told her like some devoted dog. No longer. This ended.

Tonight would be his last Christmas Eve.

Letting him get in a few good swings, she lured him back toward the fireplace. One blow had stars blinking in her vision and slammed her into the hearth, the force of the punch knocking her into the beautifully glazed pottery vase. It tumbled to the floor, breaking, and she followed after it.

Sergei roared her name as she went down. She struggled to her feet, slicing upward, the Ulu she'd stashed inside the vase gripped in her hand.

Perry's look of shock was comical as the wound registered. She'd cut close to his balls, slicing through his femoral artery.

The Remington recoiled, and glass shattered, deafening as it echoed in the tall ceiling. The Arctic wind raged in, and the room froze.

Perry hit his knees.

Sergei cocked the shotgun and aimed at Thug One. "Move," he dared. "Give me reason."

Not strong in the brains department, Thug One charged, and Sergei pulled the trigger.

Ivan broke Thug Two's neck, and he crumpled to the floor.

"You bitch," Perry hissed, blood soaked through his pants, bubbling through his fingers as he tried to stanch the wound. The man was dead, and he knew it. Kate had a hard time feeling bad about it. She'd already grieved for him once.

"I've got to know," Perry gasped, color draining out of his face. "Where's the money?" He pitched forward.

CHAPTER EIGHTEEN

"I'm tired of being your clean-up man," Ivan said, shaking his head over the body count.

"Let's hope this is last time." Sergei laid down the shotgun and confronted Kate. "Vhy did you let him vail on you like that?"

"Easiest way to take a man down is with his ego." She dropped the Ulu on top of Perry's body. "What did he mean by, 'where's the money'?"

"The arms deal in Afghanistan. I couldn't let Perry keep the money."

"This has all been about *money*?"

"*Nyet.* This is about love, Katja."

"How much money?"

There was a look exchanged between Ivan and Sergei.

"Thirty million."

Thirty million. Again, she was nothing but a pawn to be played with between two dangerous men. Pain pounded in her chest, making it hard to breathe. "Where's the money?" she repeated Perry's dying question.

"In an off shore Cayman account."

"And you're living here as a handyman?"

"I don't need the money, and I like to fish. I told you it vasn't about the money."

She turned on Ivan not able to look at Sergei. "What has the last two years been about? You egging me on to go after Sergei?"

"You didn't need any egging, Kate," Ivan scoffed.

"What is your role in this?" She hadn't even met Ivan until after Afghanistan. The twisted trails started to make a map that she could now see from a different angle. "I can't believe I ever fell for that bullshit. You weren't sent from some government outreach program to help traumatized agents readjust to society."

Ivan shrugged. "Sounded plausible at the time."

"If you're his *comrade* why don't you have an accent?"

Ivan smiled. "I assimilate better into your American society as I'm not as untamed as this guy. More cultured."

"I sent him," Sergei said. "To vatch over you. Keep you safe since ve suspected Perry vas still alive. Katja, you must understand, Perry knew you vere falling for me and that I cared for you more than I should. The order to kill each other vas test. One that I am glad ve both failed. He liked the hero vorship, and vanted more from you, but knew you vere beginning to see the rust in his armor."

"You've been spying on me? Sending babysitters?" She gestured to Ivan. "Why didn't you come yourself?"

"I couldn't contact you. Keeping avay from you kept you alive. Besides, you veren't ready to see me again. Not vith how you blamed me. You needed time, Katja."

"Fuck time. Who the hell are you to manipulate me, decide what's best for me, and use me as bait to lure out Perry, leaving me in the dark?"

"Okay, I'm out of here," Ivan said. "I don't want to get between the two of you and your domestic dispute. Besides, it's Christmas Eve. I wouldn't mind being home with my kids and wife by morning to open presents."

"I'm going with you," Kate said, turning for the stairs.

"*Nyet*, Katja." Sergei grabbed her arm, pulling her into the side of his body. "*Pozhaluista*." It was a whispered plea in her ear from deep within him that caused emotion to choke off her throat.

"Perry vas vatching you," he added. "Ve couldn't prove it, or fish him out. Leaving you in the dark kept you safe. Kept you alive."

She'd been sent to kill him. Ordered by her government, or so she'd believed. "Why take the risk that I would have killed you?"

"I couldn't vait any longer. I love you. The only thing I had to build on vas your vengeance. I had to know if you could love me in return."

"You son of a bitch." Her voice broke on the last word, taking the heat out of it. She hurried up the stairs to gather up her belongings.

CHAPTER NINETEEN

Kate entered the bedroom, and regarded the broken pieces of the bed.

How could you build a relationship based on vengeance?

She gathered up her backpack, realizing that besides the clothes she wore, there wasn't anything of hers here to take. Sergei had taken everything else, her bra, her winter gear, her heart.

Oh God. She loved him.

That line between love and hate was so damn thin and razor sharp, cutting until she bled. How was she going to live without him? He'd been her whole focus since she'd met him two years ago. He'd been everything, and she'd been so blind to the reasons why.

She wiped at her eyes, realizing that tears were trailing silently down her cheeks, and saw the blood on her hands. She glanced down at her clothes. There was blood on them too.

She headed to the bathroom and ran the water in the sink, catching her reflection in the mirror.

Who was this woman?

Spy?

She no longer felt like one nor felt the desire to continue being one. As it turned out, she'd been rogue for a while if Ivan was her contact and he worked for Sergei.

Lover?

Pain expanded in her chest at the thought of not lying with Sergei again. Not sparring with him. He kept her on her toes while sweeping her off her feet at the same time, and she loved that about him. Loved the woman she was when with him.

She turned off the faucet and stared at her reflection. She could leave with Ivan or stay with Sergei.

Slowly she stripped off her clothes and unpinned her hair.

She stepped into the shower, turning on the water, catching her breath as the iciness stabbed her. She forced herself to stand under the needling spray until it warmed up, then she took the pulsating water as hot as she could handle, washing away all the blood, all the pain, all the indecision.

There was only one decision to make, and she'd made it when she'd stripped off her clothes.

The shower door opened. Sergei stood there, naked, his heart bare for her to see. Love and fear warred in eyes greedily taking her in. He waited a heartbeat for her to object. When she didn't, he stepped into the shower, crowding her back against the wall.

"Ivan?" she asked, though getting words past her swollen throat was difficult.

"Gone." He braced himself for her reaction.

"The garbage?"

"With him."

She didn't ask any more questions. A good clean up man was hard to find. Besides, Alaska was a big state with the deep, bottomless seas surrounding three sides of her.

Kate offered the soap to Sergei. "Wash my back?"

He took the soap.

She turned, offering him her back, a thrill shooting up her spine at the strangled sound escaping his throat.

He slowly worked a lather over her skin, and then reached around her to set the bar down in the dish, his body rubbing up against hers with the action. She had his full attention. He massaged her back, kneading sore, battle-weary muscles until she moaned.

"Katja, forgive me, but I had to know." He buried his nose in her hair. "You'd come to me once on orders. I needed you to come to me for love, not duty." He turned her in his arms. "Duty kills. Love does not." His eyes intent, his mouth a mere breath from hers, he murmured, "And you could not kill me."

"That is a dumbass reason. You've read too much Dostoevsky—"

"Actually, I prefer Tolstoy."

"Do you have any idea what it would have done to me if I had killed you?" It would have destroyed her. "I love you, you barbaric Russian."

"I know." A pleased smile spread over his face.

She growled and pushed him up against the tiled wall. Her hands dove into his hair and pulled, bringing his lips down to hers. She kissed him, her mouth desperate, her heart full of love for this infuriating man.

His arms tightened around her, and he switched their positions, grabbing her bottom and hitching her into his arms, positioning himself between her thighs. Her legs automatically locked around his waist and he surged inside her.

Grunting with satisfaction, he held her bound within his embrace. He didn't move as though he needed a moment to get himself under control. "Is after midnight, vhich means tis Christmas. I have not had many Christmases that I could celebrate. I'd like that to change. I vant family, Katja. I vant you for my family."

Pleasure lanced through her at his words, and her heart tumbled further.

He'd stripped her bare. Not just physically but emotionally as well. Tears filled her eyes as he asked her to take everything she'd ever wanted.

"You have unwrapped me, Sergei. I have no other gift to give you today but me."

"You are the greatest gift I've ever received, Katja." He took her mouth, and took her body, giving everything he had of himself. Their release was fast and shattering, promising a new life, a new beginning.

He turned off the shower, dried them both off, and then bundled her up in a towel. As though she were something precious, he carried her to bed.

The night was silent, snow drifting on the air in fluffy flakes outside the window. Before joining her in the shower, he'd lit a fire in the fireplace. The flames had warmed the room and gave it a comforting glow.

For a Christmas scene it was pretty perfect.

"Do you think you could learn to like it here?" Sergei snuggled her into his arms. "Vill you consent to stay until you've experienced vhat I can show you about living on The Edge?"

"I don't want to go anywhere, right now." She burrowed against him, loving the heat of his body, the warmth of the bed, the promise of a treasured tomorrow.

A prickle of worry intruded. "What about the occupants of the lodge?" she asked. What would they think of her when they returned? Would she be welcomed?

His arms tightened around her as if to ward off her unnecessary worries. "Ve are a family of misfits, here on The Edge. You vill fit in beautifully. They vill love you as I do, Katja."

A family of misfits. They sounded like her kind of people.

"And vhile I do love a brisk vinter, I'm not averse to visiting the tropics and little scraps of clothing decorating your luscious body." He kissed her shoulder. "I have a bit of cash to spend." He glanced around the room, eyeing what she'd done to the bed. "Shopping to do." He lifted her left hand and kissed her ring finger. "A ring to buy."

Her breath caught as her heart expanded in her chest.

"Katja, let me buy you the world."

"I don't want the world, Sergei. I just want you." She proceeded to show him how much.

THE END

Prologue

Twenty Years Earlier

The knife reflected the setting sun on its upward arc, resembling a torch as well as the instrument that would end her life of twelve years. She struggled against the ropes tying her down until her skin tore and bled, slickening the rough stones on the altar she lay on.

All the while Jedidiah Dawson, leader of the Ascension, quoted bible verses.

Methodically, he sliced a length of her long, golden hair, and turned toward one of the nine homemade beeswax candles placed at strategic points around her body. Like a sick nursery rhyme the candles marked head, shoulders, knees, and toes, with her hips added in. The solstice sun highlighted his handsome, strong features, his smooth shaven face, adding shots of fire to his groomed maple-colored hair. Tonight he had donned a coal-black robe, embroidered with white and blue threads, over his simple cotton, button-down shirt and jeans.

Praying for her deliverance, he brushed the burning locks of hair over her nude body. Sparks flared from the blaze, burning her skin where they fell.

Her hoarse screams went unanswered.

"Don't," she cried. "Please, don't do this." She'd done what they wanted. Stopped fighting them months ago, resigned to her fate from being a kidnapped victim to the prophesied daughter and wife to Jedidiah.

The knife trembled in his hand, and he tightened his grip. "You failed to conceive and therefore must be cleansed." He brushed tears from her face with gentle fingers. "Now, hush. It's time." The knife rose above her and he closed his eyes, his voice ringing throughout the verdant forest. *'Kill every woman that hath known man by lying with him.'* *Numbers 31:17.*

Like that had been her choice.

He bestowed a look of caring patience upon her. "My child, I will make you sacred in order that you may ascend into the Kingdom of our Lord."

"I don't want to ascend. Let me go home. Please. I just want to g-go h-home." Sobs shook her emaciated frame.

"I am sending you home, my daughter, my wife. Soon you will be with our Lord." Tears filled his dark eyes. *"'O daughter of Babylon, who art to be destroyed; happy shall he be, that rewardeth thee as thou hast served us.' PSALMS 137:8."*

He kept repeating chapter and verse as though still teaching her. He brushed his lips across her forehead. "Know that I will miss and pray for you often as you prepare a place for me and our brothers and sisters in our Lord's Kingdom." The hand holding the knife rose above her again. The blade didn't tremble as it sliced downward.

The thick forest embraced her screams and the rich earth swallowed her blood.

CHAPTER ONE

"For we are but of yesterday, and know nothing, because our days upon earth are a shadow."
~ JOB 8:9

Present Day

"Cache, I know you're in there. Open up!"

Cache Calder hobbled to his front door, a crutch under his left arm. He was going to kill the son of a bitch on the other side. Why was it so much to ask to be left the hell alone?

He yanked open the door to find his poodle of an editor, Tom Passey. "What do you want?"

Tom pushed his way into the apartment. "If you'd answer your blasted phone, I wouldn't have had to trek all the way across Manhattan to tell you." Tom looked around the dim and dirty apartment. "Wow. I'd heard you'd gone into cave-mode, but this...is disturbing." He kicked an empty pizza box out of his way and continued toward the drape-shrouded windows.

"Get the hell out of here, Tom." Cache held the door open, using the doorknob to keep himself upright.

Tom flung the curtains wide and turned. Cache averted his head as the sun sliced like fire through his brain.

"Fell off the wagon, huh?" Tom surveyed the sea of Chinese takeout containers rivaling the discarded pizza boxes. He wrinkled his nose and fingered the edge of a Styrofoam box containing leftover petrified chili cheese fries. "What happened to your health nut regime?"

"Can't find a health food store that delivers," Cache grumbled. Obviously Tom wasn't going to leave until he had his say. Cache pushed the door shut. Pain radiated up his leg, and he shook with the effort it took to stay on his feet. He limped to the recliner, sank into the cushions, and tossed the crutch to the floor, feeling every tense and aching muscle in his forty-two year old body sigh with relief.

"Cache, I know that the last few months have been tough, but it's time you got back to work. *World Events* needs you."

Cache glared at Tom standing there without any effort, dressed in a navy Versace pinstriped suit, his dark hair slicked back, the top buttons of his paisley silk shirt left purposely undone. What did this pompous piece of leftover runway model know about how tough the last few months had been? Tom hadn't been in the Middle East when the insurgent's bomb had exploded. He hadn't watched helplessly as his friends had been blown to bits.

He hadn't been cursed with surviving.

"I don't give a rat's ass about the magazine." Cache gestured to his leg wrapped in a brace. "I can't work with this." His leg was a raw jigsaw puzzle stitched back together. He had more steel pins and screws holding it together than a Frank Lloyd Wright house. He was lucky to still have it. Though there had been times, when the pain was so intense, he'd wished it gone. Guilt drowned him. What right did he have to bitch and moan over a little thing like pain, when Hank and Sarah were dead?

"I have the perfect assignment for you. One that will give you time to recuperate and help you rediscover your 'edge'." Tom's face lit as the passion for the sell stole over him. The man would have made a killer used car salesman. As it was, he was making a fine name for himself as an editor for *World Events.*

"What possible assignment would allow me time to heal?" He was a photojournalist. His job required that he be ready at any moment to chase down the story. Capture the soul of his subject that portrayed a story with a single snapshot. How was he going to accomplish that with a bum leg? Besides, scary as the thought was, he didn't think he had it in him anymore. The spark which usually fired his "shutter bug muse" was snuffed out, extinguished with the force of the blast that wiped out the lives of so many people in the Middle East.

"Remember Amelia Bennett? The magazine wants to do an exposé." Tom held his hands up wide, his fingers simulating quotes. "Twenty years later. 'Where Is She Now'?" He lowered his arms, his eyes glowing with excitement. "What do you think?"

Amelia Bennett.

His breath caught in his throat. He swiveled in his chair and studied the award-winning photograph, framed and hanging on the wall in the prized spot. His walls were covered—a gallery of his work—with pictures depicting people and places. All told their own story of life, and death, and hope.

But Amelia...

Amelia was special. The image of her he'd captured just following her rescue—after being kidnapped and held for nine months by the cult leader of the Ascension—had jump-started his career.

Made him who he was today.

Tom moved into his line of vision, breaking Cache's journey into the past. "I knew you would remember." He shrugged. "I mean, how could you not." He pointed to the little girl the media had labeled *Shattered Innocence*. "Don't you want to know how she's doing now? The rest of the world does. *You're* the one who captured the essence of her broken soul. Aren't you curious to know what kind of life she's made for herself?" Tom's voice picked up speed, moving in for the kill. "You have to be the one who does this story, Cache. I know how much she got to you. Her story affected the world.

The world needs to know the little girl we all looked for and hoped would be returned to her grieving family was not only found, but survived—and let's be optimistic here—triumphed over her ordeal."

Cache's gaze returned to Amelia's picture. Long, white-golden hair framed a too thin face of smooth alabaster skin. She'd been twelve. Just a kid. Her wide blue eyes, as pure in color as forget-me-nots, spoke of the horrors she'd suffered. They filled her face. Drew you in and refused to let you go.

Damn. Why now? Why now, when he was so broken?

Could he let someone else tell Amelia's story in his place? He studied her photograph again. *She was his story.* Always had been. What would his camera lens tell him now?

Ah, hell. Cache raked fingers through his uncombed hair and sighed. "Give me the details."

Tom smiled, rubbed his hands together and shoved aside a stack of unopened mail, taking a seat on the couch. "It turns out Amelia Bennett is part owner of a lodge in Alaska. So—" Tom reached into his breast pocket and produced two airplane tickets "—we're leaving for a two-week Alaskan adventure."

"We?"

"I'm going with you." He reached into his other pocket and whipped out a brochure. "They offer salmon and halibut fishing, hiking, kayaking, whale and bear watching. The list is endless."

Cache narrowed his eyes. "*We?*" he repeated.

Tom gestured at Cache's injuries. "Come on. You can't very well go alone. Think of me as your companion or co-worker...no, no forget that. Boss? Yeah, I like that. Think of me as your boss."

"Think again."

"Okay, then...what about buddy?"

Cache stared at him for a minute. "What's really going on here?"

Tom sighed and crossed his legs, his leather wing-tips shining in the late afternoon light pouring through the windows. "The starched shirts are worried about you. They know you've been to hell and back and want me to make sure nothing more happens to you."

"In other words, they're sending you to make sure I don't fuck it up."

"Well—" he shrugged "—basically. Come on, Cache, its Alaska, and we get to go with the magazine footing the bill."

Cache reached for the brochure. Massive mountain ranges. Glaciers. Steel-blue Pacific Ocean. Not a forgiving place. How would he navigate this kind of territory in his present condition?

"Turn the page to see pictures of the lodge. I know it looks imposing, but I've been assured that they've taken handicapped patrons before."

Cache narrowed his gaze.

"N-not that you're handicapped in the sense of wheelchair bound. Be comfortable in knowing that you'll be able to navigate the lodge. Plus, they offer sauna and hot tub facilities and have a masseuse on staff."

Cache reviewed the pictures of the lodge. Rustic sophistication described the nest of three large log structures connected by a mammoth deck across the front and supported on pilings. Cobalt waters licked at a black sand beach. Wildflowers bloomed in a riot of rainbow colors surrounded by dense forests and rocky cliffs. A sapphire sky topped it off.

The Garden of Eden, sourdough style.

"Think of it as a paid vacation where you can recuperate, and in the process see some great stuff. Besides, we don't leave until the end of the week, which will give you time to get this place—" he gave the apartment a disgusted look "—fumigated or something." Tom lifted his shaped eyebrows. "What do you say?"

There wasn't anything to say. The subject was Amelia Bennett.

Of course he was going.

About the Author

Photo by: Kelli Ann Morgan

Tiffinie Helmer is an award-winning author who is always up for a gripping adventure. Raised in Alaska, she was dragged "Outside" by her husband, but escapes the lower forty-eight to spend her summers commercial fishing on the Bering Sea.

A wife and mother of four, Tiffinie divides her time between enjoying her family, throwing her acclaimed pottery, and writing of flawed characters in unique and severe situations.

To learn more about Tiffinie and her books, please visit www.TiffinieHelmer.com

FUN FACTS
about the author

- Tiffinie spends most of her summers working as a commercial salmon fisherman (er, woman), in Bristol Bay on the Bering Sea of Alaska.

- She has a Green Tea Frappuccino addiction. And no, she does not require a 12 step program because she is perfectly happy with her addiction.

- Goes weak in the knees for "muscle cars." Mustangs, Camaros, and Chargers are right at the top of her list to own, race, or just sit in.

- She is an accomplished potter with her own studio. When she's not writing, fishing or traveling, you can usually find her throwing clay on her wheel.

- Is a gypsy at heart, with a wandering spirit and restless feet.

- Has a secret crush on Daniel Craig, which her husband quietly tolerates.

- Enjoys flying in airplanes or being on the ocean, yet she suffers from motion sickness. When deep sea fishing, she's always the first one to chum the waters. That's usually when the fishing really gets started. Coincidence? I think not.

Made in the USA
Lexington, KY
18 May 2013